THE SCANDINAVIAN AGGRESSORS

Praise for The Scandinavian Aggressors

"Rowdy Geirsson reaches out like a *draugr* from a barrow to pull your leg down a rabbit hole full of plausible but preposterous lunatics and doomed sailors in this very funny neo-faux saga. If you're the type of armchair traveler who would rather carry a drinking horn than the *Hitchhiker's Guide*-recommended towel, read *The Scandinavian Aggressors* and follow Geirsson to the land of the midnight sun, troll snot liquor, decapitated mermaids, and doofus viking warriors."
—Corwin Ericson, author of Swell and Checked Out OK

"An outrageously Norse-sensical shaggy dog story. Rowdy Geirsson is a cross between Loki and the Venerable Bede."
—Tony Williams, author of Nutcase and Hawthorn City

"Funny as hell! Kind of like *Rolling Stone* for the Álfablót crowd."
—Scott Oden, author of A Gathering of Ravens
and Twilight of the Gods

"I had a very good, and by good I mean weird but in a good way, time reading Rowdy's travel guide to parallel Scandinavia. It's as if early Louis Theroux was making a documentary about almost, but not quite, somewhat entirely successful modern vikings while the authors of *Illuminatus!* nodded in approval and now I need to lie down. Also, beer."
—Bjørn Larssen, author of Children and Why Odin Drinks

"Not only is Rowdy's writing superb, but the book delivers on its promise, providing a colorful and entertaining look into the life of a man searching for something more and finding it—maybe—in the cold north of modern day Scandinavia. This book was a stand out for me. I loved its creativity, its storytelling, its stick-in-your-craw characters, and its ability to make me laugh...if you love vikings and offbeat humor, and aren't afraid to stretch your imagination, you should give it a try."
—Eric Schumacher, author of the Hakon's Saga
and Olaf's Saga trilogies

"*The Scandinavian Aggressors* is the visionary account of a silenced movement that shocked the Nine Worlds. A thoroughly Scandifuturistic chronicle of Neo-Norse extravaganza, so burlesque and Baudrillardian that you will thoroughly doubt your own sanity by the end of it. Rowdy's most shocking exposition of Boreal apocrypha yet."
—Eirik Storesund, errant Old Norse philologist and host of the *Brute Norse* podcast

"As a big fan of Norse mythology and viking history, I found Rowdy's book as comfortable as an old Bathory t-shirt and as surprising as a perverted troll. Mermaid beheadings, enslaved leprechauns, and other unstable tales of mead-soaked adventure await! I had a grin from ear to ear reading this whole damn thing."
—Matt Smith, creator of *Barbarian Lord* and illustrator of *Hellboy: The Bones of Giants*

"In the satirical tradition of More's *Utopia* and Swift's *Gulliver's Travels*, with a healthy dash of gonzo journalism, Rowdy Geirsson's *The Scandinavian Aggressors* is a hilarious read. Fans of the Icelandic sagas will be pleased by the modern spin on their favorite scenes and stories from the sagas."
—Andy Pfrenger, professor of medieval studies and co-host of the *Saga Thing* podcast

"This is one of the most entertaining books I've read in a long time. Geirsson's journey through the Modern Viking Movement is a feat of exploration worthy of Leif Eriksson himself. Witty, informative, thought provoking, and at times laugh-out-loud funny, there is something here for everyone from scholars of medieval Icelandic sagas to fans of Bill Bryson, and particularly for those who are both."
—Tim Hodkinson, author of *The Whale Road Chronicles*

THE
SCANDINAVIAN AGGRESSORS

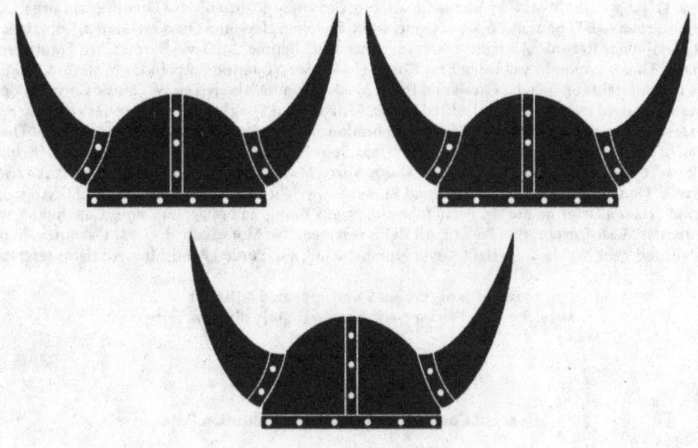

ROWDY GEIRSSON

PUFFIN CARCASS

An Imprint of Scandinavian Aggression
www.scandinavianaggression.com

Portions of this book first appeared online at
Metal Sucks and *Jersey Devil Press* in slightly different forms.

Manufacturing by IngramSpark
Book design by Rowdy Geirsson

Library of Congress Cataloging-in-Publication Data

Names: Geirsson, Rowdy
Title: The Scandinavian Aggressors
Description: First Edition | Norumbega: Scandinavian Aggression
Subjects: Scandinavia, Vikings, Modern Viking Movement, Neo-Norsemen

ISBN: 978-0-578-34856-8

Puffin Carcass
An Imprint of
Scandinavian Aggression
Norumbega, Vinland
www.scandinavianaggression.com

"After a thousand years of oppression
Let the berserks rise again
Let the world hear these words once more
'Save us, Oh Lord, from the wrath of the Norsemen'"

—Johan Hegg / Amon Amarth,
Thousand Years of Oppression

"How many truths can you hold on to?
How many lies have you been told?
How many times have you been under
Another system of control?

Trusting everything you read
Lost in your conspiracies
I want to believe
Cover ups and blacked out lines
Everything is classified
Follow me down the rabbit hole
You want the facts, now listen to me
Only the truth can set you free

Meet me at the edge of the world
To watch it all burn
Forget what you've learned
Meet me at the edge of the world
To watch it all burn"

—Eric Bloom / Blue Öyster Cult,
Edge of the World

Till Familjen

CONTENTS

CONTENTS CONTINUED

THE
MODERN
NORTHLANDS

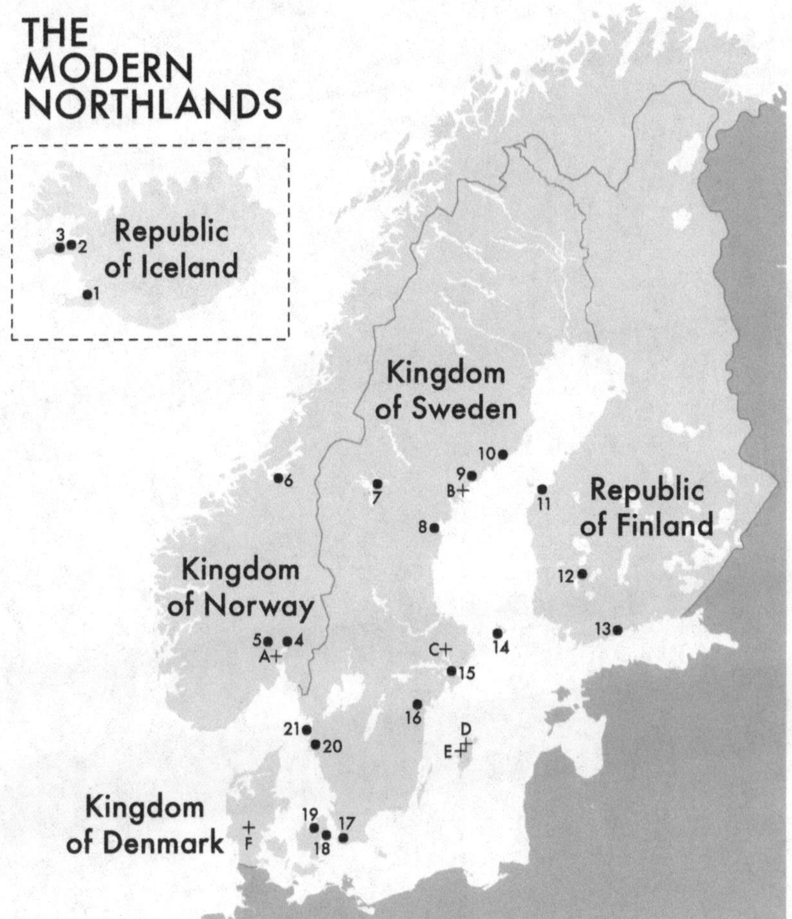

● **THE JOURNEY**	10 Umeå	20 Gothenburg
1 Reykjavík	11 Vaasa	21 Klädesholmen
2 Stykkishólmur	12 Tampere	
3 Bjarnarhöfn	13 Helsinki	**+ PLACES OF INTEREST**
4 Oslo	14 Mariehamn	A Drammen
5 Geithus	15 Stockholm	B Skuleskogen National Park
6 Trondheim	16 Norrköping	C Uppsala
7 Östersund	17 Malmö	D Lickershamn
8 Sundsvall	18 Copenhagen	E Visby
9 Örnsköldsvik	19 Skuldelev	F Billund

INTRO

Roger Hodgson, the great vocalist of the famed English musical troupe, Supertramp, once sang these words:

> "When I was young, it seemed that life was so wonderful,
> A miracle, oh it was beautiful, magical.
> And all the birds in the trees, they'd be singing so happily,
> So joyfully, oh playfully, watching me.
>
> But then they sent me away to teach me how to be sensible,
> Logical, oh responsible, practical.
> And they showed me a world where I could be so dependable,
> So clinical, oh intellectual, cynical.
>
> There are times when all the world's asleep,
> The questions run too deep
> For such a simple man.
> Won't you please, please tell me what we've learned
> I know it sounds absurd,
> But please tell me who I am."

These verses of "The Logical Song" not only describe Hodgson's own personal disappointment and disgust with the experience of coming of age in our modern era, but also perfectly capture the prevailing sentiments that instigated the underground Nordic phenomenon that has come to be known as the Modern Viking Movement. The confusion, disillusion, frustration, and general erosion of individual selfhood that Hodgson alludes to, and that remain in such strong evidence throughout the world today, are precisely the same qualities that fueled the individuals who ushered in this new era of 21st century Scandinavian aggression.

---

* "The Logical Song" by Supertramp, 1979

The phenomenon's leading men and women were people who, like so many of us, had spent their childhoods bright-eyed and bushy-tailed, dreaming wistfully about the future and the promises that they had been assured that it held, only to be spiritually crushed by the relentless and pointless drudgery of adulthood in modern society. While such emotions and experiences are rather commonplace throughout developed nations today, these particular men and women reacted in a very atypical manner. Rather than simply succumbing to their own rampant, internal despondency by silently sliding down a spiral of suicidal depression or by suddenly snapping and going on a psychotic, murderous rampage as is so often the tragic and terrible case, these individuals instead took to their ships and blazed a new path full of adventure and daring-do towards a more satisfying and meaningful way of life. In short, they rejected the reigning constraints of society and in doing so reinvented themselves with a newfound sense of pride and purpose.

The Modern Viking Movement began with a bang in the early 21st century when a crew of renegade Norwegian whalers unexpectedly sacked the Holy Island of Lindisfarne off the coast of Northumbria in England, looting a historic monastery's gift shop before accidentally almost razing it to the ground and returning to their ship. Thanks to this single, unanticipated act, the whalers unwittingly kicked off a remarkable Neo-Norse renaissance that would persist until a series of monumental defeats eventually obliterated the phenomenon, utterly stopping it in its tracks. This epoch, epic in spirit but short-lived in duration, witnessed numerous Scandinavians from all walks of life follow the whalers' example as they plundered unsuspecting coastal settlements, fought brave battles, and drank lots and lots of mead.

As the phenomenon expanded and gained momentum, it also began to attract individuals who did not simply seek to break free from their own lives' meaningless existence, but instead were primarily motivated by the more traditional incentives related to personal revenge, the demands of divine dreams, or simply the timeless quest for fame and glory. The phenomenon began to encompass a certain life of its own, expanding beyond the standard viking purview of seaborne raiding to include the ancient thrill of the hunt, the fearless exploration of unknown territories, and the honor-bound slaying of fearsome foes and monsters. The spirit of the Modern Viking Movement seeped into all crevices of society, including schools and unsuspecting family households where it began to influence the behavior of minors.

Yet, despite these significant advances, the Modern Viking Movement remained a completely underground phenomenon known only to the rare few. It was never an organized entity; those who fell under its sway did so independently of one another without any conscientious acknowledgement of their shared, obscure Nordic zeitgeist. In general, the movement failed to register on the radars of, quite literally, just about everyone who wasn't directly involved in it. This is certainly attributable to its own short-lived life span, but also to our instant-gratification-obsessed, media-sensationalized, and morally bankrupt modern times. The Modern Viking Movement did not go viral and the traditional media largely neglected it in favor of more profitable stories involving celebrity sex scandals, the conniving of various political parties, unfounded speculation regarding both natural and man-made disasters, and recurring non-news clickbait lists. Even the international academic community turned the other cheek in favor of its own preferred special interests.

The Modern Viking Movement quite simply never broached the mainstream in any notable way, even in its homelands. Outside of a small handful of immediately-forgotten Scandinavian-language social media posts and obscure chatroom threads, the only other references suggesting the Movement's existence are to be found in the archived pages of a single, small-town Norwegian newspaper's website and a tiny handful of Swedish news articles. While provided by legitimate sources of news, the Swedish reports in particular focused solely on a single event and the disruption caused by it; the modern viking cultural aspect was fully disregarded. The result is that all knowledge of the Movement's actual history remains incredibly murky and shrouded in mystery.

And that's where my own personal involvement enters the story.

The purpose of this book is not just to shed new light on this heretofore obscure phenomenon, but to shine the first, and perhaps only, substantial light on it. The story of the Modern Viking Movement is educational on many levels, revealing unique insights about the human condition and the world in which we live, particularly in its most highly-developed regions where the acquisition of food and shelter often tend to be taken for granted. It also provides a glimmer of hope in our current era of darkness; a testament to the indomitability of the human spirit to rise above the mire of overwhelming defeat and hopelessness that defines modern life, particularly in the wealthy western states of Europe and North America.

It is, of course, fair to ask how I came to be aware of the Modern Viking Movement myself. If it was such a small, secretive, and short-lived phenomenon confined primarily to the edges of Northern Europe, then how did some guy living in Massachusetts even discover its existence in the first place? And the short answer to that is: with the help of my own increased state of pointless futility in the wake of the 2008 financial meltdown.

At the height of the Great Recession, I had found myself freshly unemployed, recently dumped by a long-time girlfriend, and, quite frankly, with a ton of time on my hands to devote towards going down my own preferred rabbit holes of the internet. It's not something that I'm proud of, but those hours spent in the nether regions of the world wide web nonetheless provided me with an introduction to the phenomenon, and because of that, I like to think that perhaps it wasn't an entirely vapid coping mechanism.

I have always been interested in all things viking-related. Ever since I was a little kid, vikings have fascinated me, and they still do. And I'm not unique in that. The history, sagas, legends, myths, and general exploits of the Viking Age (usually considered to have ranged from the years 793-1066) have fascinated people for generations, directly inspiring and influencing the imaginations of such luminaries as Richard Wagner, J.R.R. Tolkien, and Quorthon, who basically created the entire viking metal musical sub-genre singlehandedly in the 1990s. But for all the inspiration that their epic escapades have provided over the centuries, the vikings, of course, weren't always heroic—there is no denying that the rape and pillage that comprises part of their legacy also tarnishes their collective reputation. The word "viking" itself is actually a bit of a garbled moniker because it originally denoted the Norsemen who specifically took to the seas to raid innocent victims. It eventually expanded to include men and women who left Scandinavia for trading or colonizing reasons as well, but their compatriots who stayed home throughout the Viking Age simply remained Norse. Further argument could be made about additional delineations and nuances inherent to these terms, but the distinction provided here should suffice for the purpose of this book. Bad things certainly happened at the hands of the vikings, but they also accomplished many impressive feats and embodied a spirit of adventure seldom seen in the present day. In short, for me, the vikings and their fascinating Norse culture provided the ultimate source of escapism for our 21st century shit-show.

So, I geeked out on all things Norse, even going so far as to create a personal blog about vikings where I would post bad jokes that I thought were funny in a futile effort to be productive in some ambiguous manner. Some of these jokes proved to be mildly popular and as a result I eventually became a columnist for the *McSweeney's Internet Tendency* website. But most frequently during this era, I found myself browsing the web, searching for strange and fascinating facts about the ancient Norsemen. In doing so, I discovered such forgotten and overlooked cultural relics as Boston's own misguided 19th century Leif Eriksson monuments, a handful of contemporary breweries thematically based on Norse culture, and recurring Norse-inspired festivals such as Up Helly Aa, which is celebrated in an awe-inspiring conflagration of fire and mead every January in the Shetland Islands. And through that in-depth internet browsing experience, I also eventually became aware of a number of rumors circulating about a series of strange incidents involving seafaring Scandinavians shortly after the turn of the new millennium.

These rumors initially came to my attention through MySpace, which still dominated the stupid social media scene in those days. They were perpetuated by people whose real names I've never known but who claimed to live in the Northlands themselves and who communicated exclusively in their native tongues.

I had completed a study abroad program in Sweden while in college and had lived in the nation afterwards to conduct a post-graduate research project. That experience had absolutely nothing to do with anything Norse-related, but it had allowed me to develop a decent degree of proficiency in the Swedish language. And proficiency in one of the core Scandinavian languages (Swedish, Danish, and Norwegian) means that the others are also generally comprehensible, at least in written form (Icelandic and especially Finnish, however, remain a separate matter).

So, for me, the door was blown wide open and the stories were wild. The threads themselves remained few and far between, but the ones that I could find on platforms such as MySpace and Reddit described a murky shadow world unlike anything I'd ever heard of before. I read about the aforementioned group of Norwegian whalers who had raided a little gift shop in northern England. I read about a Swedish warrior-poet who had beheaded the statue of the *Little Mermaid* in central Copenhagen. I read about a series of raids on the abandoned medieval market town of Dorestad in the Netherlands. And I read about an epic showdown between Swedes and Spear-Danes at an otherwise wholesome, family-friendly amusement park.

Naturally, I was intrigued, and as I dug deeper, I came up with ...well, nothing, aside from the few aforementioned articles from a very small newspaper in the rural western fjords of Norway and the heavily-censored Swedish news reports. I was baffled. Was everything else a lie, one mistruth fabricated on top of another as so often happens in the cesspool of cyberspace? Contact information was at least provided for the Norwegian reporter, so I emailed him to inquire if he could provide me with any further information. He was kind enough to respond, but the additional details that he provided were very sparse; he simply did not know much more himself, either.

But between his feedback and my own research, including a heavy reliance on the Nordic nations' online telephone directories, I gradually compiled a list of purportedly real people and places that correlated to a good proportion of the rumors propagated by the trolls of the digital dump known as the internet.

And that's when the epiphany hit me. Why not seek out these so-called modern vikings myself and try to convince them to tell me their stories in their own words?

My personal future wasn't looking so bright at the moment, so what did I have to lose? In a way, the notion presented an opportunity to break free from the dejection and pointlessness that I'd been experiencing my entire adulthood and that had only increased with a special, new burst of vigor since the recession had hit. I wouldn't be doing anything as glorious as going a-viking, as the modern vikings had done themselves in an effort to break free of their own shackles and find some semblance of meaning, but I would be making some sense of this muddle called life on my own terms, even if just briefly. Most people, conventional to the core, would have scoffed at the entire idea, thinking it to be a completely foolhardy waste of time, but once it had penetrated my cranium, it burrowed deep down inside and would not vacate its mushy, gray abode.

So, putting great faith in my modest savings account and the Commonwealth of Massachusetts' ongoing unemployment benefits program, I bought a ticket to Oslo via Reykjavík and began to map out my journey. I attempted to establish contact with the individuals whose whereabouts I had already traced online. Not all replied to my inquiries, but most did, and they responded favorably; they would be happy to meet me and tell me about their involvement in some of the Modern Viking Movement's most celebrated incidents. And so it was on. I knew I was naive and that I was in over my head, that I had no idea of how to properly investigate the events or conduct effective interviews, and that I was going to be forced to wing the whole thing, but I was going to give it a shot.

The result of that expedition is this book. I will never claim that it is the world's finest work of investigative journalism—far from it, in fact—but I do claim that it is the only one that unveils at least some of the secret history of the Modern Viking Movement. Because my efforts involved directly interviewing a selection of key individuals and recording those conversations, I had initially considered compiling the manuscript simply as an oral history. Unfortunately, I was less rigorous with my methodology than I had hoped to be. I was, and still am, an amateur at the investigative journalism game and failed to properly record a few instances of my firsthand conversations with the modern vikings with my digital recording device. But I kept a detailed journal throughout my travels and I have reconstructed every conversation to the best degree possible, relying primarily on the actual recordings themselves and filling in the gaps as necessary based on my extensive notes. I have also provided the pertinent background information relating to general Scandinavian history and geography as I deemed appropriate for the reader's benefit. The final manuscript therefore bears more resemblance to a travelogue than to an actual history book or some other standard work of nonfiction.

Of course, I did not know exactly what form this manuscript would take at the time I departed Boston. Those specifics were very far from my mind as I boarded the IcelandAir Boeing 757 to Reykjavík one frigid January evening. At that time, I was simply excited and, admittedly, a bit nervous. A highly reserved individual myself, I knew I was heading towards one of the most culturally reserved populations in the world—in the darkest, bleakest time of year—to meet and interact with total strangers. But the die had been cast, and as the plane began to taxi away from the terminal at Logan International Airport, the words of "The Logical Song" entered my head uninvited, but appropriately so, since that's how fate works.

STORIES OF BLOOD FEUD AND KIN-SLAYING

DESECRATION OF THE
SNÆFELLSNES SHIT-SKERRY

"I just couldn't stop shitting," Olafur Gunnlaugsson said as he stared me in the eye from across the table. He was an elderly man who looked sweet, so I was surprised to hear the filth that was coming out of his withered, old mouth. "I was shitting my brains out and I just couldn't stop. Holy Auðumbla's salt lick, it burned. It burned like Mt. Hekla itself was erupting from my fiery rectum."

And such was the glorious start to my first ever interview with a modern viking. His choice of rhetoric lent a hyperbolic, albeit crude, element to his narration, which diverged drastically from the usual understatement that had been considered most poetically appropriate for Icelandic oratory a thousand years ago.

I just sat there, looking at the old man and feeling awkward. We were seated at the kitchen table of his modest house in the small, remote village of Bjarnarhöfn on Iceland's Snæfellsnes peninsula, and night was already descending despite the time of day being only 3:30 in the afternoon. The room was dimly illuminated by a single lamp that cast long shadows across Olafur's bearded face, making it difficult to read his expressions. The pastel color scheme that dominated his kitchen complemented his soft, woolen snowflake sweater, both of which contrasted starkly with his harrowing tale of doomed seamanship and, apparently, digestive plight.

"Low did the lava-flow lay me that fateful day," Olafur continued, veering into more traditional word-play territory that mildly echoed the skaldic tone of his ancient forefathers. When performed properly, a kenning—a poetic device popular among the ancient Norse to identify one subject in terms of a completely different subject, such as the sea's famous kenning of "whale-road"—has the power to render any topic both epic and great, including the eternally relevant anguish associated with irrepressible diarrhea.

"Well...that sucks." I sympathized.

"The shepherd's pie that I ate that night was the work of Loki, the deceiver, no doubt. Bad lamb for sure. Usually, Icelandic lamb is the best that money can buy, but Loki has his ways. Had it not been for his interference with that shepherd's pie, I would have sailed off to Greenland with the others. But they left me behind, and now here I sit, while the *hákarl* ferments out back, wasting my days making the sorts of wooden trinkets that you idiot tourists like to buy."

The *hákarl* that Olafur mentioned is a notorious type of Icelandic culinary delicacy consisting of rotten shark meat. It stinks to high heaven and has gained a newfound status as a semi-famous food item in recent years as its reputation has spread across the globe in conjunction with Iceland's meteoric rise as a travel destination following the nation's economic collapse during the height of the recession. Tourists now enjoy speculating about *hákarl* and sometimes even go so far as to attempt eating it themselves, not out of any genuine interest or enjoyment of the taste, but rather for the typical and timeless reason of simply wanting to be able to say that they did it, as well as to acquire photos of the occasion to then share on social media in the hopes of gaining positive attention.

Olafur held up the figurine that he'd been busily whittling during this initial round of conversation.

"Thor," he stated matter-of-factly. Sure enough, the piece of wood resembled a muscular humanoid holding a massive upside-down hammer.

"Impressive. So, you're going to sell it?" I nodded in feigned admiration.

"Of course I am! Normally I sell these to a gift shop in Reykjavík that then marks them up for a sizable profit. 'Genuine Icelandic Handicraft' it will say on the price tag." He paused before adding,

"Would you like to buy it directly from me? I'm nearly done. Save me the hassle of haggling with that prick of a store owner in the city, and I'll give it to you at a discount. We both win."

The figurine possessed an extremely menacing aura. The workmanship was fairly crude and its face bore a scowl of severe discontent. In all honestly, this was probably the crappiest depiction of Thor that I'd ever seen, and I did not want to take it home with me.

"Sure," I said. "I'd love to buy it from you. How much?"

"I'll let you have it for 2500 *krónur*, which is a bargain."

I did a quick calculation in my head and came to the conclusion that he was asking me to spend slightly less than twenty dollars on a crudely hand-crafted wooden statue that's only unique features appeared to be a hammer and an exaggerated frown. Nonetheless, this was still cheaper than the object would likely cost in any of the shops back in Reykjavík. Assuming Olafur could make a couple of these per hour, his wooden figurine gig wasn't too shabby from a business point of view, especially for a retired gentleman such as himself.

I withdrew the bills from my wallet and proffered them across the table. Olafur immediately snatched them up and began counting. He had no reason to trust me at face value, after all. I had only just arrived on his doorstep a few minutes earlier and remained a complete stranger for all intents and purposes.

When I first knocked on his door, I had assumed that he would greet me somewhat warmly. We had, after all, already spoken on the phone, if only briefly to arrange this particular meeting. So, I was a bit confused when he opened the door, swore at me harshly, and then pleasantly invited me inside for a cup of coffee.

My meeting with him was actually one of the biggest uncertainties of my entire itinerary because I had been unable to establish contact with him before I arrived in Iceland. I found his name and telephone number in the nation's largest online public people-finder directory back in Boston, so I gave the number a call from my hotel room in Reykjavík upon arriving, and praised be the norns—the three fates who sit beside the Well of Urðr beneath the great world tree and weave the threads of our lives—he answered and agreed to an in-person discussion. To both my surprise and great relief, he spoke English incredibly well; his primary education clearly pre-dated the advent of compulsory English language courses in the Icelandic school system, so I had been concerned about possible communication difficulties. I commented on his impressive fluency when I first entered his kitchen and his hostile reply of "I spent many of my younger years in the States dealing with complete jackasses and total bullshit" convinced me to drop the topic.

I had decided to hit the hot-spots of modern viking activity in a geographical rather than chronological sequence; it was just logistically simpler that way. Iceland, sitting halfway between Europe and North America, thus became the location of my first attempted interview. It would certainly have been much simpler to just change planes at Keflavík Airport and continue directly on towards Oslo rather than rolling the dice with Olafur's ability and willingness to meet me and thereby potentially finding myself in Iceland without a purpose. But I knew that I'd enjoy my brief sojourn in any event.

After disembarking from the plane the previous morning, I took the bus into downtown Reykjavík and proceeded to spend the rest of the day wandering the city in a sleep-deprived haze that was punctuated by stops at various coffee shops to fuel up on the lifeblood of caffeine. After a jet-lagged night of pseudo-rest, I emerged from my hotel and walked to the nearest car rental business, just a few blocks away on the busy thoroughfare of Lækjargata, and acquired a junky little Peugeot for the drive up the island nation's western coast. I would have preferred to take a bus, and that would have been doable most of the way, but there were no public transportation options that accessed Olafur's remote outpost. Renting a car in Reykjavík became the easiest option.

And what a drive it was. The snow and ice on the roads didn't faze me, but the resplendent beauty and wide-open vistas of the country nearly became a distraction in their own right. The visual experience of driving through the frozen Icelandic landscape is a far cry different from doing the same thing in New England, where the constant shadows and encroaching snow-dusted woods always seem like they're about to swallow entire roads outside of the cities. Signs indicating the turn-offs for historic sites and museums related to the Icelandic sagas, such the the Settlement Centre in Borgarnes and Snorri Sturluson's house in Reykholt, provided strong temptations for detours, but I was here to learn about the recent viking past, not the distant viking past, and so I stayed my course.

The Icelanders in general maintain a certain reputation for being the most "viking" of the collective citizens of the Nordic nations in present times. Their language is the most similar to Old Norse, their cultural heritage has provided us with the majority of our primary sources of Norse mythology, and their land is the literal one of fire and ice. So, it is somewhat surprising that the Icelanders made a notably smaller splash during the Modern Viking Movement than did their brethren in the other Nordic nations. Of course, some of that disparity may be entirely due to the pronounced lack of knowledge about the Modern Viking Movement as a whole, but whatever the case may be, Olafur Gunnlaugsson had emerged as the most talked-about Icelander to have been involved with the nation's most significant incident associated with the 21st century Neo-Norse outbreak: a failed attempt to establish Icelandic sovereignty over Greenland, which is a semi-autonomous territory of Denmark. As with each of the other Nordic nations, smaller modern viking incidents had also occurred in Iceland, such as the plundering of the Icelandic Phallological Museum's souvenir shop in Reykjavík and the temporary take-over of the historic site of Thingvellir by a group of irate sheep farmers, but the attempted invasion of Greenland remains the nation's most renowned modern viking event by leaps and bounds. According to the online forums, the gist of the matter was that one summer day, a group of Icelanders had set sail for Greenland in a wooden, dragon-headed longship and were never seen nor heard from again.

And so here I was now, staring out a kitchen window at the clean, cool waters of the Breiðafjörður bay as they glistened in the fading glow of the low winter sun while a cranky old man counted the money that he had basically extorted from me.

"Well, it looks like you're not a complete piece of shit." Olafur's matter-of-fact tone of voice broke the silence and I turned back to face him, shrugging.

He shoved the money down into his pocket and resumed whittling Thor's frown.

"So, as I said," he began, "I did not join in the voyage to Greenland because of my uncontrollable shitting. Do you have any idea how hard it is to row a longship when your bowels are under the sway of the dark *seiðr*?"

Naturally, I wanted to ask: "Of the force?" but I refrained, stifled a smile, and solemnly shook my head instead. *Seiðr* is the term for a type of ancient Norse magic involving shamanism, and while I knew what Olafur was talking about, that didn't prevent visions of Darth Vader using his arcane abilities to wreak havoc on Luke Skywalker's digestive tract from popping into my jet-lagged mind.

"Well, I'll tell you—it's hard, very hard. What happens is you shit your pants and then everyone else on the boat hates you once they've noticed that you've shit yourself. Because it smells like shit. Because it is shit. Because you've shit yourself. It's a shitty situation and there's shit everywhere."

"Oh, for sure..." I felt compelled to agree. "But whatever happened to those other guys who sailed off while you were stuck with the...uh, the uncontrollable shitting?"

"Oh, them? They all drowned on the voyage to reclaim Eystribyggð from the *skraelings*."

Eystribyggð, or the Eastern Settlement, was the Norse settlement situated around present-day Narsaq in Greenland. Erik the Red, the discoverer of Greenland and father of Leif the Lucky who later went on to explore North America, had himself settled in the vicinity at Brattahlíð, where the tiny farming town Qassiarsuk is now located. Qassiarsuk itself has become one of Greenland's most popular tourist destinations, thanks specifically to the presence of Brattahlíð and its reconstruction. The town now even hosts a Leif Eriksson statue and a Leif Eriksson hostel for good measure.

The majority of present-day Greenlanders, however, are the Inuit descendants of a people whom the Norse called *skraelings*, hence Olafur's usage of that word. The term isn't specifically exclusive to the Inuit or their ancestors; it is more of a catch-all phrase that the Norse used for anyone that they encountered in their explorations beyond the parts of the world known to Europeans at the time. *Skraeling* is not a particularly friendly term because it contains connotations denoting barbarism and weakness, and Olafur's use of it reinforced my general sentiment that he was neither a kind-hearted nor sensitive individual.

I repeated his last statement as a question because I didn't know what else to say.

He gave me a disapproving frown. "Yes, they were going to retake Erik's farmstead from the *skraelings*, but they never made it there."

"But why would they even bother?" I asked. "Eystribyggδ was abandoned by the Norse five hundred years ago."

An uncomfortable silence settled over us and Olafur went stiff. He stopped working his wood and pointed the sharp end of his knife at me when he spoke.

"A common myth and you're a fool to believe it!" he declared with clear agitation. "Yes, it was long ago, but it was nothing as innocent as abandonment, as everyone likes to say. It was the *skraelings*! They came in from the icy wastes further to the north, and they just slaughtered everyone."

I looked at him, speechless.

"History is a continuum. We've been at war with the *skraelings* for hundreds of years. The battles may not be as frequent as they used to be, but this isn't a new war, and it's far from over."

I finally took my first sip of the coffee that he had poured for me; it was strong and very good. Several canvas bags of local Icelandic Kaffitár brand roasted coffee beans leaned against the wall near a stainless steal grinder and some top-of-the-line brewing equipment, all of which struck me as out of place in this dingy house on the edge of subarctic nowhere. I had incorrectly assumed that the old man would be more of a low-quality, instant coffee drinker. It seemed that Olafur embodied the age-old lesson that appearances can be deceiving and he was proving it in every aspect of his life.

I set the mug down on the rustic wooden table and asked, "So, who started the war?"

"Are you kidding me!?" Olafur slammed the butt of his knife on the table and started to rise from his rickety chair. "They started it, of course!"

He was fuming. I had inadvertently managed to piss off a delusional, elderly so-called ex-viking who wielded a sharp knife and suffered from a known history of irritable bowel syndrome.

"Sorry! I'm sorry—it's just, well…I'm ignorant about all of this. Could you, you know, enlighten me a bit? I don't know much about this war, but I'd like to know more."

His tension appeared to dissipate and, as he resumed his whittling, he began to tell me his version of events. Thus for the next thirty-some minutes I was subjected to a grand performance in the time-honored and fanciful tradition of Icelandic oral storytelling.

If one chooses to believe Olafur's story—as so many of the world wide web trolls apparently do—one would believe that an intense feud that had initially been sparked between the ancient Norse and the ancient Inuit was still being waged today in a sort of perverse twist on the unending violence of the Middle East. I didn't doubt that hostilities between modern Inuits and whites existed; such unfortunate circumstances are the case with race relations everywhere. But I doubted that the two groups had been engaging in actual naval warfare, burning down one another's farms, and basically conducting massacres at every possible opportunity in an unbroken string of violent confrontations for the past thousand years.

According to Olafur, the Inuit had gained a great victory when they killed off the last Norse inhabitants of Greenland roughly five hundred years ago. There is some substance to the notion that the Norse Greenlanders may have succumbed to the encroaching Inuit at that time, in conjunction with other factors such as a worsening climate, dwindling contact with Iceland and Norway, and a general failure to adapt, but there has never been any historical or archaeological substance to the notion that the collapse of Norse Greenland was part of prolonged and focused Inuit military campaign fully intended to oust the Norse from a land of ice and infertile soil. A series of failed Icelandic attempts to reconquer Greenland supposedly comprised the majority of the past five hundred years in Olafur's version of unfounded revisionist history. At one point, I considered asking him about Denmark's involvement, since Denmark had acquired Greenland in 1814 from Norway, but decided that interrupting him would probably just upset him, and I had no desire to provoke any further hostility than I had already encountered.

As Olafur explained it, the particular incident in this ongoing and ancient conflict that had gained so much attention and reverence online—the rumored loss of a longship and its crew—had been the unfortunate outcome of a great deal of planning by Olafur's good friend, a man supposedly by the name of Sigurður Atlason. He also claimed that Sigurður's motivation in organizing the voyage to Greenland in an attempt to reclaim Eystribyggð had been initially suggested by the elves.

"The elves?" I asked.

"Right, the elves. The elves. The fucking elves!"

His gaze was serious, menacing, and crazed, which actually complemented the tufts of white hair protruding wildly from his otherwise nearly bald scalp. If my goal in coming here had been to interview someone who looked like a mad scientist, my objective would have been achieved with flying colors. As it was, my disappointment in the reality of the situation, both in the here and now of the present interview and the there and then of Olafur's story, propelled my already dying optimism to sink further and further to new, irrevocable depths.

"So, what kind of boat did Sigurður and the others sail off in?" I asked, trying to lighten the mood and divert the conversation away from the subject of war-mongering elves as well as my own increasingly grim thoughts about what I was even doing here in the first place.

Olafur cleared his throat and set the figurine of Thor down once more.

"The ship was built in the style of the old ones, not too far from here, over in Stykkishólmur." He nodded with his head in the direction of the town, which was also where I had booked a hotel room for the night. "It was a sturdy little Snekke vessel and we added a ferocious-looking figurehead to the prow. Sigurður said that a grand wooden boat with a fearsome fucking serpent would scare the enemy of lot more than a boring black and red fishing boat. And I think he was probably right, but then again, like I said, I can't be totally sure because the boat sank while I was suffering from the uncontrollable shitting. The uncontrollable shitting was both powerful and explosive."

He held the Thor figurine up to his eye, examining the details of his handiwork.

"Looks good," I said. "So, what kind of wood are you making it out of?"

"Oh, this is native Icelandic birch," he answered. "Or, more specifically, downy birch or hairy birch. One of the few species that forms the rare forested areas in this country. Horticulturally known as *Betula pubescens*, if you like. The word *pubescens* is Latin, and is related to your English word 'puberty.' Thor never experienced puberty, because he was born fully grown. His balls are so massive and so hairy."

He then thrust the figurine towards me, clearly expecting me to give it a close examination of my own in the dim light. I leaned forward to oblige and found that, sure enough, Olafur had taken the time and care to carve spools of pubic hair upon the surface of a finely detailed scrotum directly behind the hammer that this particular likeness of Thor wielded.

"Elegant craftsmanship," I said, leaning back.

"You're damn right it is." Olafur beamed with pride.

I wanted to leave.

"The boat was elegant craftsmanship, too," Olafur continued. "But it was not made of birch, of course. We used oak for the hull and fir for the mast. Imported from the tyrannical nation of Norway, naturally. We needed stronger wood from larger trees, so there was no choice."

Norway had been considered tyrannical by the original Icelanders during the colonization of the island during the 800s and 900s. I doubt many people still feel this way today, but I kept quiet and let the old man continue talking without interruption.

"But swallowing our pride on that matter was a small price to pay to get revenge on those Greenlandic cowards," he grumbled. "So, we built the ship of Norwegian wood, and then on the eve of the ship's completion, those of us who followed the old ways headed over to

Helgafell and held a mighty *blót* at the site of Thor's former temple, ceremoniously pledging ourselves to the old gods and offering them the greatest of sacrifices." Olafur made the sign of the hammer as he said this, which is a motion similar to the Christian sign of the cross. "But we neglected to honor Ægir and Rán."

He then proceeded to explain how their negligence had upset Ægir and Rán—the husband and wife Norse god and goddess duo of the sea—and how the two deities had responded by drowning the ship en route to Greenland. Rán in particular has always revelled in her reputation for taking a certain amount of glee in the drowning of sailors. Her husband, on the other hand, generally seems to be more content to brew lots of beer and drink heavily at his hall under the sea. At any rate, it was a very fateful *blót* even if—as I was quite sure at this point—it had only transpired in Olafur's mind. According to him, all of his friends had died, and he had gotten a terrible case of the runs.

"It was during that celebration that I ate the accursed shepherd's pie," he said. "And once the shit-storm struck my stomach with its severity and strength, I was doomed. I barely made it to Dritsker in time. My muscles were so weak from battling the beast within by then."

Dritsker is a small skerry near Helgafell, where Olafur claimed the *blót* had been held. Both sites receive special attention early on in *Eyrbyggja Saga*, which chronicles the initial settlement of northeastern Snæfellsnes as well as the feuds and battles that eventually took place among the region's medieval inhabitants. The saga is especially renowned for its numerous instances in which dead men and women wake up from their graves and proceed to frighten and annoy the local living population.

Dritsker's role in the saga is, admittedly, rather small and inglorious in comparison to that of Helgafell, the mountain where Thorulf Mostur-Beard had founded a temple of Thor. The first settler of the area, Thorulf initially chose the location because it was where his pillars of Thor had washed ashore when he cast them into the sea while searching for land to claim as his own. As a very religious and domineering man, Thorulf then decreed that since Thor himself had selected this location, it could never be desecrated with human waste. Consequently, Dritsker, or "Dirt-Skerry" as it translates in English, became designated as the literal dumping ground for visitors to Thor's temple or any of the local assembly meetings held in its vicinity. Thorulf's rules of etiquette, however, ceased to apply long ago when Thorgrim Kjallaksson and Asgeir of Eyr decided to disregard this bathroom embargo and instead relieved themselves wherever they wished. And in typical Icelandic saga fashion, this act of unruliness resulted in a subsequent series of killings and an escalating blood feud.

At any rate, while it was completely unnecessary for Olafur to abide by Thorulf's ancient law, he still chose to do so anyway. And in that sense I commended his integrity for making the trek to Dritsker when the turd-turbulence hit his bowels. His decision to splatter Dritsker with his own filth had allowed him to establish and experience a connection with the ancient past as well as the spirit of the place that was both deep and exceedingly rare in our modern times.

Olafur grimaced in retrospect of those painful, diarrhea-besieged hours.

"The shit burned," he complained. "It burned like liquid fire."

"Ass lava," I chimed in.

"Yes, ass lava." His eyes met mine and then he smiled. "Good kenning. Very good kenning. There may still be hope for you yet."

He then explained that due to his extreme digestive plight, he had been unable to partake in the voyage when the would-be vikings set sail the next day. They left him with some food and water while he lay prostrate on Dritsker and bid him farewell as they headed back to Stykkishólmur to board the ship. He spent the next two days convulsing and fading in and out of consciousness on Dritsker's rocky surface as the food poisoning held him in its throes. By then, it had mostly run its course, but someone had already spotted him while driving past the skerry and phoned the authorities out of concern that he was actually a corpse that had washed up from the sea. Considering the high number of murders that occur in Nordic noir novels and television series each year, it is not entirely unfathomable that an unsuspecting passerby might entertain such a concern.

So, in the end, Olafur was taken to a hospital, examined, treated, and released the following day in good health, if somewhat weakened.

"Did you ever try to go look for your friends?" I asked despite my belief that they were only imaginary ones.

"Of course I did!" Olafur snapped back. "What sort of an asshole do you think I am? Made several trips all around Breiðafjörður, but never found a single goddamn trace of them. And each time the sea was stormy. Perfect, clear day, and then, soon as I was in the little skiff setting out, in came the storm clouds. I was almost overturned twice. That's when I started to suspect that Ægir and Rán and maybe even their vicious little daughters all had it out for me. I had been a part of the *blót* that had disgraced them, after all, even if I was the only one who ate the shepherd's pie. I shouldn't have been so selfish, helping myself to the entire thing before anyone else got a chance, but if I hadn't been, I wouldn't be alive today. Either way, I had also disrespected Ægir and Rán. Why wouldn't they want to claim me as well?"

"Well, why didn't they succeed then? Shouldn't it have been easier to drown you in a small skiff all alone than an entire crew in a longship?"

"You don't fuck with the gods of the sea."

"But—"

"YOU DON'T FUCK WITH THE GODS OF THE SEA!!!"

Olafur glowered at me. Neither of us said anything for a moment.

"I think it's about time for you to go." He broke the silence as he handed me the Thor figurine. "Get the hell out."

I accepted the figurine and stood up without saying another word. Olafur remained seated, glaring at me as I made my way through his kitchen to the front door. I took one last look back. He continued to frown at me. Then I opened the door and slipped out.

I walked back to the rental car and started it up. As I pulled the vehicle out onto the road, I felt simultaneously perplexed and frustrated but also mildly uplifted. I had just completed my first interview with one of the 21st century's supposed modern vikings. It was nowhere near the smash-hit, home-run, out-of-the-ballpark success that I had hopelessly hoped for, but it was a start. The reality behind the rumors about Olafur's modern viking escapades remained disappointing, but my overall goal was to get to the bottom of these rumors, whatever that may be. In that sense, the interview had been successful. I considered it to be a decent warm-up at the very least. Good practice for the upcoming conversations I would have, but if they all proved to be similarly grounded in internet lies and delusions of insanity, then this entire expedition was going to deteriorate into something much less interesting and meaningful than I hoped.

The glowing aurora danced across the night sky when I finally pulled up to the Foss Hotel in Stykkishólmur where I had already checked in earlier that day. I entered the lobby and exchanged a smile and nod with the receptionist as I walked past her desk to the corridor with the elevators. When I finally entered my room, I collapsed on the bed under the all-too-familiar feeling of befuddlement and defeat.

Norway was next.

BURNING DOWN
THE DOLL'S HOUSE

The train hugged the harbor as it headed west out of Oslo and gradually passed through less and less densely populated neighborhoods that in turn gave way to a snow-covered landscape full of rolling hills and coniferous woods dotted with lakes and farms and the occasional cluster of quaint buildings. An hour later, we entered the village of Geithus. Despite being my actual destination, Norway's national rail operator does not include stops in Geithus itself, so I disembarked at the station in the next town over and called the number of the taxi company that the manager of the youth behavioral institute had provided over the course of our recent email correspondence.

The institute at Geithus reputedly housed four of Norway's most troublesome youths. Even if you measured such things by the highly temperamental nature of medieval Scandinavian standards, these young ladies and gentlemen would still have been considered juvenile menaces to society during the Viking Age. That's because, while it was certainly a more common practice to trap your enemies in their home and then burn the whole place to the ground one thousand years ago, such actions were nonetheless still generally frowned upon.

Luckily for the emotionally distraught children of the Helmer and Linde-Krogstad families, contemporary Norwegian juvenile law stipulated that, rather than exile or outlawry, therapy and behavioral rehabilitation should be the sentence for their hostile acts of vandalism and arson instead. Consequently, they were confined to the institute and held under close watch. And they were slated to be the subjects of my next interview.

The online accounts had made it apparent that four culprits were involved: two boys and two girls from two different families. The fathers of both families had supposedly been actively engaged with and frequently away on official modern viking business themselves (whatever that meant—the rumors didn't divulge those details) and in their absence the children had waged a campaign of remarkable cruelty against one another. Each new action had instigated an opposite and significantly harsher reaction, and the situation quickly spiraled out of control.

The story, as relayed online, went something like this: prior to the sudden disintegration of their valued friendship, two young ladies (both preteens at the time of the incident), had often played together growing up and continued to enjoy one another's company as their bodies surged towards the horrors of puberty. As next-door neighbors, meetings were easily arranged and they could often be found at one another's house, conversing about boys, reading magazines, or listening to music, among other favorite past-times. On less frequent occasions, a third and sometimes even a fourth companion would be shown hospitality, as was the case one fateful afternoon when a third girl received preferential treatment. A conflict arose and the trouble began.

The details circulating in the forums and chat-rooms about this particular incident were among the most detailed of any associated with the Modern Viking Movement. The names of the children were mentioned, as was the name of the institute in which they were supposedly being sequestered. A simple series of email exchanges with the institute had confirmed the truth of the matter and I had decided to make Geithus the first stop of my formal itinerary on the Fennoscandian mainland, the landmass that comprises the nations of Norway, Sweden, Finland, and part of Russia.

The journey from Iceland itself had passed uneventfully. I had made my way back to Reykjavík and flown out to Norway the day after my encounter with Olafur Shitty-Pants. As with my first day in Reykjavík, I had spent my first day in Oslo trolling around the center of the city, consuming enough coffee to give a whale a heart palpitation. I had visited here once before, during my undergraduate years, and the city had clearly changed. The Norwegians were building like crazy, apparently unaffected by the raging global economic crisis that had halted construction in most places around the world during the Recession. Boston itself featured a massive crater in the center of downtown where the demolition for a new skyscraper had been completed but the new construction had never actually started before the financial collapse struck. The Norwegians possessed some serious black gold in the North Sea and it was on clear display in the capital city.

In my highly-caffeinated state, I had strolled up and down Karl Johans Gate, the Norwegian equivalent to New York's 5th Avenue or Boston's Newbury Street, took a swing around the Royal Palace, gawked at the sixteen massive, wooden reliefs of Norse mythological iconography adorning the outer facade of the city hall, and ambled up the exterior ramps to the roof of the recently completed Oslo Opera House, an icon of contemporary architectural design that evokes the likeness of an iceberg sliding into the sea. So, it was an enjoyable day and I had topped it off with a beer at an English-style pub named after Winston Churchill before heading back to the hotel for the night.

The taxi driver dropped me off on the side of the road and sped away. The youth center, or *barnevernsinstitusjon* as it's called in Norwegian, looked warm and inviting, if somewhat simple, from where I stood observing it on the quiet street. The house was constructed of wood with vinyl siding painted in a cheery, off-white color and finished with red roofing tiles. The frozen water of the Snarumselva shimmered just a stone's throw away behind the surrounding trees.

I walked to the front door and rang the bell.

A plump, elderly woman opened it. She was dressed unusually, wearing a short, blue cloak that partially concealed a delicate necklace of glass beads that lay upon her breast. White leather gloves covered her hands and a cumbersome-looking pouch was slung from a felt-like belt wrapped around her waist. Oddest of all was her headpiece: a black leather cap with white trim covered in runes from under which her long, gray hair spilled out.

"Ah, so you must be Rowdy." She smiled, holding open the door. "I am Agneta. It is good to meet you at last. Please, come in; we've been expecting you. The children are in the kitchen. They have made some cookies and hot chocolate in anticipation of your visit."

I thanked her and expressed equivalent sentiments as I stepped inside and looked around.

If the exterior of the place had appeared inviting, then the interior was downright cozy; not in a plush-leather-sofa-beside-a-wood-stove-in-the-winter sort of way, but in the simple, modern, and elegant sort of way that is characteristic of modern Scandinavian design sensibilities. The walls were painted white and remained mostly undecorated while the floor consisted of a light-hued hardwood. The furniture and fixtures featured simple forms that nonetheless provided a cheery, soothing effect.

Agneta closed the door and turned to face me. "Well, Mr. Geirsson, this is our facility. We try to keep it orderly and calm for the benefit of the children."

"It looks like a very pleasant place, and I really appreciate you inviting me in like this," I replied.

"Of course! We are happy to help and answer any questions you may have, but before you meet the children, I must first give you a little background information about our institute and go over the rules of the house."

She proceeded to explain that Norway's national policy has been to enact a restorative and rehabilitative approach to punitive measures for both juveniles and adults, as opposed to the more traditional approach that fosters gang violence and shower rape as found in most other nations. The idea is to psychologically heal the transgressors before releasing them back into mainstream society with the presumption that they will be less likely to become repeat offenders if their time in the big house has emphasized emotional therapy rather than primal survival instincts. Statistics show that Norway's approach is effective, but statistics can also be manipulated. Although his crimes had not yet been committed at the time of my visit to Geithus, I personally tend to doubt that someone like Anders Breivik, who massacred seventy-seven people in the summer of 2011 in a psychotic Neo-Nazi rampage, would really be effectively rehabilitated by living out the rest of his days in a place like this, but then again, his is also a rather exceptional case.

"Here at Geithus, we have twelve staff members who tend to the needs of the four children who live on the premises," Agneta declared with a measure of pride. "We respect their need for space and privacy and provide support and regular therapy sessions. This helps them mend emotionally so that they will become productive members of society when they leave."

"So, there's three of you for each of them?" I asked, unsure if I had heard the ratio of staff to patient correctly.

"Well, in numbers yes, but we work collaboratively rather than exclusively with each of the children, and we are not all always here at the same time. Today, it is just myself and two others; however, they are taking care of other duties right now. We'll go see the children now, but you must understand that I need to ask you not to say or do anything that might stir up the children's negative emotions. They have come a long way in their healing, but we must continue to take precautions to avoid inciting any hostile behavior."

I wasn't sure what she meant by this so I reminded her that my sole purpose of visiting the children was to talk to them about the very events that had landed them in this living arrangement in the first place.

"Oh, that's quite all right," Agneta calmly answered. "Discussion of past behavior and why it was harmful is a regular part of the process and it is therapeutic for them to speak about it with an occasional outsider. I simply mean for you not to say anything that might cause one of them to become agitated. They are not as temperamental as they once were, but we must still tread lightly. Now, shall we go see them?"

She grabbed an ornate-looking cane that leaned against the wall and started towards the kitchen where the children were seated quietly around a rectangular wooden table. Two blond boys sat facing two blond girls, and in the center of the table rested a large plate full of warm, chocolate chip cookies. All four children appeared to be physically suffering from the awkward, hormonal ravages of adolescence.

The closest of the girls stood up as we entered the room and said, "*Hallo. Vil du ha en kopp varm sjokolade?*"

"*Javisst, det låtar jättebra,*" I answered in Swedish because that's all I can muster Nordicly, but it didn't really matter because Swedish and Norwegian are very similar overall.

She walked over to the stove and ladled some steaming, home-made hot chocolate into a ceramic mug that she then handed to me before sitting down again. I thanked her as I pulled out the chair at the head of the table where Agneta gestured for me to sit. Agneta then went to the corner of the room and sat on the most outlandish bar stool that I've ever seen. It was completely bedecked in animal furs, including its legs, and reindeer antlers protruded from the sides of its seat. The walls behind the stool were decorated with ancient tapestries sporting colorful runic inscriptions and a depiction of Odin astride his eight-legged steed, Sleipnir. If any blood splatters had been present, the whole scene would have looked like the set for some twisted, child-oriented folk metal music video.

I tried to put Agneta and the bizarre decor out of my mind as I turned to face the children. I started by thanking them for taking the time to see me and explaining that I wished to talk to them about their past destructive behavior before asking whether they minded if I proceeded in English.

"Totally, dude." This came from the boy sitting diagonally opposite the girl who had given me the hot chocolate. "Your Swedish accent sucks."

I shrugged and before I could respond, some movement at the corner of the room distracted me. Agneta had started to sway on her stool slightly as she stared blankly into space, completely expressionless. Her irises seemed to have vanished and her eyes appeared completely white with a glossy sheen. One of her hands fumbled around in the pouch that hung from her belt.

Startled, I turned back towards the children and asked, "Is she okay?"

The girl who had given me the hot chocolate answered, "Oh yes, she does this all the time. She's from the far north, so this kind of thing is normal for her."

"Really?"

"Yes, don't worry. She's weird but cool."

"Okay then…" I decided to ignore Agneta as best I could and concentrated on the children. "Well, why don't you all tell me who is who?"

They took turns introducing themselves. The girl who had given me the hot chocolate and sat nearest to me was Nora Helmer. Beside her was Kristine Linde and directly across from Kristine sat her stepbrother, Nils Krogstad, who had already proclaimed his disaffection for my terrible Swedish accent. Next to Nils and across from Nora sat Torvald Helmer, Nora's brother, in silent observation.

Nils bid me take a cookie after pronouncing his name. "We baked them just for you."

I reached for one and took a bite. "Very good."

Each of the adolescents uttered a quiet "thanks" as I took another bite.

I decided to jump right into the thick of things. "So, I heard you all started a fire a while back."

"That was Nils who did that," Nora muttered, then looked over at Agneta, whose swaying was quickly becoming faster and more articulated, and quickly added, "but I realize that I shouldn't have given him any reason to do it."

"And I shouldn't have given him the idea," Kristine jumped in. "I was angry at Nora. I thought it would be a good way to get back at her."

Nils and Torvald just sat there staring at the table in mutual silence while their sisters espoused their self-blame.

"So, what exactly happened?" I asked. I still didn't really know; the internet runs rampant with sensationalized rumors that claimed half of Drammen had been burned down. Drammen is the nearest urban center to Geithus and the city where both families had lived at the time of the incident.

"I set Nora's dollhouse on fire," Nils answered casually, "with all of her dolls trapped inside it."

A wild tale of escalating adolescent fury, manipulation, and revenge then began to unfold. Confirming the online chatter, the juveniles seated before me related the entire sequence of events that had started with a slight to Nora's preteen dignity when Kristine forbid her from sitting in one of the two cushioned, high-top kitchen chairs during snack time at the Linde-Krogstad residence. Kristine had relegated Nora to an inferior barstool instead and bestowed the special, favored-chair distinction upon a third friend, Anne-Marie, who aside from playing an unwitting yet pivotal role in the instigation of hostilities, remained incidental to the whole affair and continues to live a normal life with her family to this day.

"Before then I had thought that I was your best friend." Nora looked accusingly at Kristine as she said this.

In the corner of the room, Agneta suddenly became still and sank into what appeared to be a deep, trance-like state. In a low, raspy voice, she began to speak:

"The bold best friend's honor
  Brazenly besmirched and belittled
  Denied the high seat of the hall
  Hurries to her hallowed stead.

  Downtrodden daughter of Drammen
  Declares to her daunting brother
  The precariousness of her plight
  And the dire of her dishonor.

  His ears an unwilling audience
  To the ignoble affront's audacity
  She duly prolongs her protestations
  He ponders apathy's abandonment."

"What is going on with Agneta now?" I asked.
Nils answered, "She's communing with the Vanir."

The Vanir are one of the two main tribes of Norse gods and goddesses and are known primarily for their advanced skills in growing crops and making babies. Their most famous members include Freyja, the goddess of love; her twin brother Frey, the god of the harvest and penises; and their father Njord, the god of the sea. The Æsir constitute the other tribe, whose members tend to be more grim and war-mongering and include the likes of Odin and Thor. The myths tell us that long ago, during the world's earliest days, an extremely devastating war erupted between the Vanir and the Æsir when Odin murdered a witch who had been aligned with the Vanir. The war eventually reached a stalemate and a truce was settled between the two tribes. I harbored certain doubts about Agneta's psychic link with the Vanir, but if one existed, I was glad that she chose to interact with the gods of love rather than the gods of war.

"She does this whenever she thinks we need positive reinforcement," Nora added. "It keeps us alert and helps prevent us from getting angry at one another whenever we have to talk about our difficult past."

"Is she okay though?" I wondered. "Her breathing doesn't sound good."

Nora answered, "It does sound horrible, doesn't it? But she is okay. She does this all the time. She'll probably do some more poetry-talk before she gets back to normal."

The lady had initially seemed like a typical, grandmotherly-type, so I was genuinely surprised to see her pagan seeress side, especially given the fact that she worked for the modern Norwegian state in a capacity that involved the well-being of minors. Mystical soothsaying just didn't strike me as the type of thing that the authorities in a highly secular society would permit, or that the general public would condone. But inquiring about the validity of Agneta's state-sponsored *seiðr* as performed on delinquent juveniles was not the purpose of my being here, so I instead inquired about what had happened after Nora returned home and complained to high heaven to her brother, Torvald, about Kristine's unfairness.

"So, the next time I was over at Nils and Kristine's house, Nils and I played *Call of Duty: Norman Conquest*." Torvald, who had been quiet so far spoke up. "Nils paused the game to go pee and while he was gone, I went into Kristine's room and ripped off the head of one of her dolls."

"Yeah, I had no idea he had even done it," Nils chimed in, "but then, like an hour later, when my stepmom and Kristine got back from wherever they were, Kristine went into her room and she freaked out."

Agneta stirred once again from the corner of the room and began speaking in the same raspy tone she had used just moments earlier:

> "Bear-shirt's battle-rage rises
> Death-doom starts to spin
> Threatened threshold of Freyja's friend
> Lady of the house lashes out.
>
> Hurt and harm must be avenged
> Deliver judgement and justice
> Free the swords from their sheaths
> No soul can forsake the fate of norns."

The four youths and I all exchanged glances and shrugged.

Nils then continued, "Well, anyway, so Kristine's mom burst into my room a few minutes later and told Torvald he should go home because she needed to talk to me."

"Yeah..." Torvald fidgeted and looked at the floor. "You know, I didn't mean for you to get in trouble..."

"Yeah, I know." Nils remained calm. "It's all right. But my stepmom, though, she was so pissed off. As soon as Torvald was gone, she completely chewed me out. She wanted to know why I had ripped the head off of Kristine's doll, and I was like, 'I don't even know what you're talking about; I didn't do anything like that.' I mean, I didn't think Kristine even still played with those dolls, so if I had wanted to mess with her, I wouldn't have gone for a doll."

"It was my favorite one since I was little!" Kristine declared with exasperation. It was almost a shout, but not quite. In the corner of the room, Agneta began to sway again on her stool and we all turned to look at her.

"So, anyway, Kristine's mom yanked the cord for my game from out of the wall and told me that I could just sit in my room and think about what I had done," Nils continued. "But I hadn't done anything and didn't know what was going on, so I went over to Kristine's room and told her I didn't do it and she actually believed me."

"I did believe him," Kristine said, "and I hadn't even blamed him in the first place. My mom just jumped to that conclusion. I was already thinking Nora was behind it all. It's just so like her to hold a grudge and then manipulate her brother into doing something like this."

Agneta's swaying suddenly stopped and she spoke another one of her verses:

"When wrongs must be righted
　Noble-hearted warriors rise up
　Wielding swords and spears
　Honor's sordid stain cannot be stood.

　The warrior wave will wash upon
　Helmer's hearth bringing bloodshed
　Body-feast for bold-winged brethren
　Ever watchful Thought and Memory.

　Heroes hasten and heed the battle call!"

Agneta's voice rose dramatically for the final line of her latest incantation. Once it was spoken, she slipped back into silence with a blank look upon her face and resumed her swaying.

"And this is normal?" I once again asked the four former, juvenile delinquents.

They assured me it was and that only when Agneta started reciting verses about sacrificial rites in pre-Christian northern Norway should I be concerned.

The story of the sequence of events that led to their present incarceration resumed. Shortly after the doll decapitation incident, Nils had gone to the Helmer residence to join Torvald for an afternoon of *Grand Theft Auto: Medieval Wheeled Wagon Madness*. While in the midst of a particularly bloody rampage of trampling pedestrians with a horse-powered cart in the busy streets of virtual Kaupang, Norway's historic medieval market town, Torvald paused the game to take a dump. It was just the opportunity that Nils needed. Motivated by having unjustly taken the blame for Torvald's prior doll-slaying and encouraged by Kristine herself, Nils rushed into Nora's room and ripped off as many heads of her cherished childhood dolls as he could possibly manage before he heard Torvald flush the toilet. Nora had been at a ballet lesson at this time and therefore could not defend her dolls from the carnage inflicted upon them. When she returned home she became immediately incensed and called Torvald into her room to plot revenge.

And the next time Torvald was at the Linde-Krogstad house, he carried it out.

"I ran into Kristine's room and not only decapitated but fully dismembered as many of her dolls as I could," Torvald explained. "Of course, it was while Nils was in the bathroom as usual. Even though we never really talked about it specifically, it's like we had this mutual understanding that we could vandalize each others' sisters' dolls during bathroom breaks, which was kind of fun, actually. And Kristine was off at some swimming lesson or something, so it was easy to get away with."

"There was no way I was going to let Nora get away with it!" Kristine's voice started to crack. "I had used to think she was my best friend..."

Agneta stiffened again and we all stopped talking to listen to the redes of knowledge that she would bestow upon us.

> "The wielder of war wisdom
> Sets the strategy of strife
> Storm of sword and shield
> Cast the breaker of oaths aside
> Render no pleas for peace
> Weregild is for the weak and woebegone.

When burdensome grievances breach
The bonds of brotherly love
Seek council from the all-wise
Pay the price of pleasure and pain
Receive the rewarding wisdom
Revenge is the way for the rightful.

None shall escape the schemings
Wrath woven by the weary wronged
Found in the flickering fire's flame
Solace awaits the strong-hearted
Deemed fit to forfeit their fortunes
The ever-after awaits assailants of the ill-treated."

Staring at the table, Kristine sighed and uttered morosely, "Uh...so, I basically convinced Nils to set fire to Nora's dollhouse with all of her dolls trapped inside it."

"I thought it sounded like good advice," Nils confirmed.

"So, how did you do it? And where was Nora while this happened?" I asked.

"I was home this time," Nora explained, her voice completely emotionless, "but I was downstairs watching a movie...so I wasn't in my room."

"Yeah..." Nils' voice trailed off. His eyes wandered around the table at each of us. The story now neared the climax of the events that had landed these four minors in a special detention facility and it was impossible to determine whether he reveled in the glory of his past actions or was ashamed to have to repeat the telling of them yet again.

He took a deep breath and continued, "So, I had brought a box of matches over with me and did pretty much the same thing as before. Torvald paused the game and went into the bathroom, and while he was in there, I went into Nora's room and put all of the dolls that I could find in her dollhouse, and then I lit a few matches and set them on the roof. The fire spread fast. But then I heard the toilet flush. I didn't get back to Torvald's room before he came out of the bathroom."

"Yeah, so I had just come out of the bathroom," Torvald said, "and I saw Nils walking down the hallway from Nora's room and I was like, 'What are you doing?' And then I smelled the smoke and went over to her room and saw that her dollhouse was on fire."

Before long, everyone stood outside the Helmer residence, watching the blaze burn while waiting for the fire department to arrive and extinguish it.

"So, how bad was the damage?" I asked. "I read online that the entire house burned to the ground and that several neighbors' houses were also destroyed."

"Oh, it wasn't nearly as bad as that," Nils answered. "Nora's room was pretty much ruined and the hallway had some smoke damage, but that was about it. They put the fire out before it got worse than that."

In the corner, Agneta shifted her weight and signs of normal lucidity seemed to return to her eyes. She directed her gaze towards us, now watchful rather than distant.

Kristine gulped and quickly stated, "Things could have been a lot worse, but no one was physically hurt and the damage was repairable. The more serious problem was our destructive behavior, which we now realize."

"How much longer do you have to stay here?" I asked. "Do you think you're improving?"

Nora answered this time, "I think we've made improvements but we also suffer relapses."

I asked what sort of relapses those might be.

"Well, there was the time that Kristine convinced Nils to challenge Torvald to a *holmgång*," she replied.

A *holmgång* is a form of hand-to-hand, one-on-one combat, somewhat similar to a duel. During the Viking Age, *holmgångs* were generally fought over personal conflicts or matters of principle and honor. The weapons used and the specific rules of conduct varied over time and from place to place, but they were typically performed within a specified space that utilized a prescribed boundary of some sort. As with most medieval conflict resolution strategies, *holmgångs* usually resulted in someone dying a very painful and gruesome death.

"Why do you girls keep encouraging your brothers to violence?" I wondered. "And why do you boys keep letting them push you around?"

At first no one said anything, but then from her special spot in the corner, Agneta began to once again speak in her raspy voice, albeit with a starkly renewed clarity in her eyes.

"Their *wyrd* is not their own," she said, referencing the ancient pan-Germanic concept of destiny.

"Then why bother trying to rehabilitate them?" I said it without thinking and all four juveniles gasped. Agneta said nothing, but stared at me in silent judgement.

"You DID NOT just say that!" Nora exclaimed after the pause.

"What?" I knew my comment had been crass, but I also felt that it had been a valid question. If these minors really had no chance, if their *wyrd*—their fate—was really out of their own hands as Agneta claimed, then that essentially implied that they were puppets of some higher force. And if that was the case, then what was the point of all the rehabilitation efforts? Wouldn't it make more sense to just let them live their lives with regular check-ins and take proper action whenever they showed signs that they might start behaving destructively again? The treatment seemed inconsistent with Agneta's stance on the diagnosis.

Agneta's fingers began to move and then so did her lips, though they made no comprehensible sound.

"She is going to put the worst curse on you," Nora said.

Agneta began murmuring in an archaic tongue, and when I asked whether she could hear me or not, she only began to move her fingers faster. I looked questioningly at the children and they all shrugged, saying nothing. Nora mouthed "I told you so" at me.

Officially weirded out in every sense of the term, I thanked them and decided that it was time to leave.

I stared out the train's window on my way back to Oslo, watching the shadows creep across the ground, slowly overtaking the remaining patches of reflected afternoon sunlight. I didn't feel cursed, not any more than usual anyway. Luck had pretty much abandoned me during puberty and has always turned and run the other way each time I have caught a glimpse of it ever since. So, what was the worst that an unfounded curse cast by a kooky social worker could do? I didn't believe it. I felt more like the butt of a strange but elaborate prank conducted by Bufdir, the Norwegian Directorate for Children, Youth, and Family Affairs, than anything else. But my journey was far from over, and there would be upcoming opportunities for me to be proven wrong. I hadn't yet been reported to the Swedish police for suspicious behavior or experienced my strange night of hallucinatory damnation on the cold, hard ground of a pagan grave site in Denmark. In retrospect, maybe there was something to Agneta's curse after all, and I just didn't recognize it at the time.

At any rate, my short visit with the troubled youths in Geithus had at least convinced me that some of the rumors about the Modern Viking Movement were rooted in truth, which constituted a major improvement upon my previous meeting with Olafur Shitty-Pants. It gave me hope for the remainder of my itinerary, and I was content to ruminate on that while I rode the train back to Oslo. The next day I would be heading farther north, to the Trøndelag, to meet the man who had inadvertently begun the whole damn thing.

TROND TROLL-BREATH'S SAGA

WELCOME TO THE MEAD HALL

The Neo-Norseman's voice echoed across the vast mead hall and suddenly all eyes were on me. I froze where I stood and observed the unwelcoming stares with a less than admirable dose of trepidation.

I stammered, "Huh?"

"*Jeg sa, 'Hvem faen er du?!'* " Trond Trondsen was screaming at me in Norwegian from the comfort of his massive wooden throne.

Even if my own verbal Swedish language abilities didn't suck harder than an Electrolux vacuum cleaner, there's still no way in hell I would have been able to understand his thick *norsk* accent through all the chunky bits of reindeer steak caught in his jowls. It didn't matter, though, because he recognized the expression on my face as one of universally unmistakable stupidity and switched to English.

"Who the fuck are you?!"

Discombobulated from the twelve-odd hours of travel required to reach this remote Norwegian outpost from Oslo, I attempted to remind him that he had agreed several weeks ago to let me interview him. He just stared at me at first, but then a smile broke across his blond-bearded face, which was followed by the most sincerely jovial sound that I have ever heard. Drunken viking laughter is truly a wonder to behold and apparently highly contagious, because everyone else joined in.

Still standing in the doorway with the cold winter wind gusting at my back, I finally slouched inwards and pulled the heavy door closed behind me. It was covered in ornate Neo-Jelling style carvings of long, twisted animal figures and as I bent closer to admire the artistry in the dim torchlight, my mind drifted towards what little I actually knew about the man whom I had arrived here to interview.

Nicknamed "Troll-Breath" since his youth as the boy with the worst breath in his home city of Trondheim, Trond is a complete throwback to the robust gusto of the original viking glory days of the medieval era. It was his fateful decision, made single-handedly during a fit of drunken rage, that guided his ship and crew of whaling buddies to sail off course towards northern England. The whalers' subsequent and highly renowned sacking of the Holy Island of Lind-isfarne provided both the impetus and inspiration for so many other despondent Scandinavians to follow suit, and as a result the Modern Viking Movement was born. But as is the case with, quite literally, every online report pertaining to the Movement, the rumors about Trond, including his later looting of the Ardbeg Distillery in Scot-land and his highly public ritual involving beached whale sacrifice, remained completely unsubstantiated. During our prior email correspondence, he had promised that I could stay with him for a week, and I hoped that length of time would allow me to do a more comprehensive job of uncovering the truth than I had already done in my journey so far.

My thoughts were soon interrupted by the unholy stench of ass mingled together with that of fermentation. The perpetrator, a vicious, little devil dressed all in green, was scampering around on the ground down near my feet. I jumped backwards when he began to grope for my bags and hoisted them out of his reach. He stretched for them in vain, spitting out a harsh string of Irish-tinged profanity. "Give 'em here, ye muzzy bastard! No feckin' malarkey, ye hear? I'll give ye a feckin' mighty wallop with me shillelagh, I will!"

An unusually lanky modern viking then stepped forward. "Shit's all right, Rowdy. You can give them bags to that there little fucker. He'll take 'em on over to yonder guest quarters for ya."

I awkwardly relinquished my bags to the little bugger as the lanky viking bent down closer to him.

"Ya git now, ya here?" he admonished. "You git now n' don't ya be messin' nothin' up! I'll be a-comin' right after ya n' there'll be hell to pay if I catch ya causin' any trouble. Now, git!" And with a swift kick to the rear, the diminutive porter scampered away with my luggage.

The viking turned back to face me. "Name's Henrik. I handle the leprechaun wranglin' 'round here. That little bastard ya just met's been assigned to some household chorin' duty for some no good recent mischief. Ya see, we caught his yeller ass makin' some moonshine out in the barn not so long ago. Somehow he'd done managed to smuggle in all them raw materials n' I'll be damned if he didn't set himself up right quick a miniature distillery underneath our very noses. We don't generally keep too close an eye on them bastards once they's been all locked up at night. Hell, he probably coulda even gotten away with all that there hootenanny, too, if he hadn't gone n' started blabberin' all 'bout it soon as he done got himself hammered. So, now's it's all these here chores till he's got himself cleaned up enough to get back on the assembly line 'gain."

"Assembly line?" I was beyond confused.

The enslavement of numerous leprechauns had been another of Trond's many purported accomplishments, but not one that I had ever suspected of having any foundation in reality, because, well, it had to do with leprechauns for fuck's sake. But as the story goes, the whalers-turned-vikings had been chased out of Dublin after a brazen attempt to lure ordinary Irish citizens into shackles on their vessel for an ensuing life of slavery. Leaving the city ingloriously behind them, they scoured the countryside for pillaging opportunities and coincidentally stumbled upon a pot of gold. A vast leprechaun colony thrived nearby, and the Norwegians subsequently conducted a large-scale enslavement operation.

Henrik didn't seem too surprised by my bafflement.

"Why, a'course." He smiled. "We got them there little bastards makin' shoes for us on a big ole assembly line down in one of the buildings right here on the property. Sure is lots of booty to be made in the shoe-manufacturin' business, I tell ya what. But I best be gittin' now myself; you have yourself a fine evenin', Rowdy."

And with that, he abruptly nodded farewell and headed after the short miscreant.

I remained standing there, too dazed to move, when an incredibly attractive woman appeared beside me. Her clothing constituted a modern spin on traditional Norse garb—a colorful apron dress supported by two glinting brooches, only much more form-fitting and low cut than would have been the case in the ancient past. It was as if the outfit's designer couldn't decide to prioritize genuine historic authenticity or ludicrous video game sex appeal and consequently decided to split the difference instead. The result effectively detracted all further thoughts on my part away from folkloric Irish imps, though.

"Would you please follow me?" She smiled.

I just nodded the affirmative and speechlessly trailed after her.

I noticed plenty of other attractive women circulating the length of the great table, attentively satiating the modern vikings' needs so that no mead horn need run dry. Surprisingly many women, actually, considering that Norway is a nation famed for its supposed progressiveness, but I wasn't about to complain; the abundant cleavage felt soothing to my tired eyes. My guide motioned towards a seat near the foot of Trond's throne.

"Would you like a drink?" she inquired. I couldn't tell if she was saying it flirtatiously or if it just seemed that way because of the particulars of her trade and the generally mysterious nature of Neo-Norse Hooters girls.

"I guess," I answered.

My lack of expressive enthusiasm derived from sensory overload and chronic jet-lag. This functioning mead hall, full of life and activity, on the Edge of Nowhere, Norway provided a stark contrast to both Olafur Shitty-Pants' solemn cottage in Iceland and the juvenile behavioral institute in Geithus. It almost seemed more like the type of immersive experience that tourists would pay top dollar to visit rather than a genuine, authentic thing. It looked and felt like a retreat for medieval enthusiasts to get away from it all and take their minds off of the relentless, downward spiral of human progress.

Personally, I was both frazzled and exhausted. The past few days had been spent traveling solo, wandering the streets of Scandinavian cities alone and occasionally engaging in very limited interaction with baristas, bartenders, and, of course, my previous interview subjects. I had just completed another grueling leg of travel, combining train, bus, and taxi, to reach Trond's remote home in Norway's central Trøndelag region. I had just encountered a supposed leprechaun and a leprechaun wrangler. And I had just given my drink order to a beautiful modern day shield-maiden. I was both simultaneously overstimulated and in the process of shutting down both mentally and physically. If now wasn't the time to throw caution to the wind and go all-in with a gigantic horn full of sweet, sweet mead, then when would be?

The centerfold-worthy lady returned and set my frothy beverage down on the table with a delightful, "*Varsågod.*" I looked from her to it, then back to her, and felt my loins quiver as she walked briskly away.

I stole a glance at Trond on his throne beside me. A large man with long, blond hair and a prominent amulet of Thor's hammer hanging from his neck, he sat unmoving, looking down at me, his face unreadable. Intimidated, I gave a quick grin and turned back to my mead, but before I even had a chance to sample the brew, he suddenly cleared his throat and stood up.

"Be still, my friends. I have a few words I'd like to say," he announced, his voice booming across the entire hall.

The silence was immediate. He surveyed the hushed crowd and began: "A few years back, we endeavored to perform some noble deeds—and perform them, we did! We wrought much honor and glory, not only for ourselves, but for our forefathers as well, who watch over us now from their seats at Odin's hall up high." He paused for dramatic effect. "Most of you know the story of how this all began, but not all of you." His eyes shifted downward to glower at me as he said this. "So, let me tell it from the beginning once again!"

There was a low hum of approval as the men all murmured their agreement.

"I fell into a dark and mournful era," Trond continued. "Prior to that sorrowful stretch, life had been bountiful as it was wont to be in those early days, but the fates rarely allow such high fortune to persist unbroken. First came the untimely demise of my sturdy Saab-steed. 'Arise!' I commanded it, but my words were powerless. It lay stricken where it was, and I had no choice but to call upon the car healers for mending. That cost me a great fortune.

"Not long after that, I received word from one of my closest companions, Rune the Deep-Minded, that he had decided to heed the call of post-graduate study in the realm of the Danes. He soon departed to pursue his degree in maritime law. I lamented the loss of his companionship and felt no small sense of betrayal because maritime law and commercial whaling only seldom make for good allegiances. I counseled him otherwise, but his mind was set. So, we parted as best of friends, but I knew I would sorely miss his quick wit and sharp tongue at our late night feastings.

"And shortly thereafter, the time once again came for us to conduct our whale-raids, and so we set sail. First we plowed the Norwegian Sea, and then we plowed the North Sea, searching for the seed of the minke in all its fertile soil. And as we neared the island of the Anglo-Saxons, I received a most unwelcome electronic communication from my former flame. 'We are no longer together,' the wretched one wrote. 'And when you return from your voyage, I will be gone.'

"Later, when I emerged from my cabin freshly fortified by a bottle of aquavit, I ordered the ship to head to the nearest coast."

His tone was utterly somber and a heavy silence permeated the room.

"We made landfall at Lindisfarne," he continued with a slight smirk. "And we sacked the souvenir shop!"

A cacophony of cheers erupted from the gathered vikings as they uniformly raised their horns to the man speaking.

"The norns wove us an unusual thread," Trond resumed as the noise subsided. "The raid on Lindisfarne was simply the first of many. Our destiny took us far and wide over the whale-road to places of wondrous beauty and unimaginable wealth. And, my friends, we shared some excellent adventures together, too. I, for one, will never forget the time that old Ture over there nearly got himself smothered to death by a damned walrus in heat when we were up near Baffin Island hunting for ivory!"

Chuckles resounded throughout the hall while a grizzled, old viking seated about midway down the length of the table nodded and grunted. The women nearest to him oohed and ahhed in admiration.

"Then there was that time when we were camped out near the banks of the River Shannon in Ireland and ran out of mead," continued Trond. "Knut, being the accomplished drinker and man of quick action that he is, decided to march all the way to Bunratty Castle by himself to acquire more. A good plan, perhaps, except that he forgot his sword, failed to plunder the meadery, and was forced to return empty handed!" Everyone laughed heartily, including a viking who beamed beet red. "There's no doubt about it, we had a good run, a really good run...till that disaster at Stamford Bridge when the wily Lord of Battle decided to favor our Anglo-Saxon enemies...but our fate had been fortuitous before that woesome day.

"And yet, the story of our deeds has gone almost completely unnoticed in the outside world. But that is all about to change. As you all saw earlier, our new guest today, this here Rowdy Geirsson as he calls himself, don't know Norwegian." A murmur of disapproval at this. "But we will forgive him that transgression. You know why he is here. It is the same reason I called for this little reunion to be held in the first place. The weavers of fate have chosen him for the mighty task of recording the glory of our deeds and making them known to the rest of the world!"

Waves of cheering erupted, effectively raising my already heightened sense of self-consciousness. Personally, I liked to think that I had arrived at the mead hall of my own volition, that it was my own impetus that drove me to seek what truth, if any, could be divulged from the rumors of reincarnated viking activity.

With the cheering still shaking the rafters, Trond looked over at me and said, "Drink up, *fremmed*."

I rose to my feet, doing my best not to spill my mead, and looked around. Not knowing what else to say, and desperately hoping to avoid being coerced into giving some dumb speech that I would surely ruin, I said the first thing that came to mind, and it was probably the best thing that I could have possibly said: "Skål." The all-purpose Scandinavian word for "let's cut the shit and start drinking." I looked at everyone in the room and they all looked at me and then at one another, and in unison, we all lifted our horns and drank deeply.

Or at least I thought we drank deeply. When I lowered the horn, I noticed that my effort was, in fact, completely pathetic. Now, to my defense, I'd like to make it clear that this was a very large horn. It had to have held at least two and a half pints when full, and this was no chugging mead. This wasn't watered-down, frat-boy horse piss; this was a carefully crafted nectar of the gods. Nonetheless, embarrassment and disappointment, which are never really ever very far away in the game of life, quickly reentered mine with a crushing victory and reaffirmed the fact that I am no viking.

Trond put his arm around my shoulder as I stood gaping at my sorry performance. "Not bad for a *nithing*," he said curtly.

The crowd hushed and I could feel the color drain from my face. This word, *nithing*, is not a compliment, and a thousand years ago it certainly wasn't a joking matter to call somebody one. But this wasn't a thousand years ago and things were obviously done differently now. A thousand years ago, the host wouldn't have forgotten or disregarded that a guest of honor was even on the way. But then maybe I'm not considered an honorable guest. I don't really have a whole lot of honor. Maybe he thought of me as more of a glorified, talking pet than anything else.

I just looked up at him, my mouth agape.

His face twitched and then he burst out laughing. "Ah, I'm just messing with you!" Even the gorgeous mead maidens thought that this was hilarious, so I pretended to share their sentiment. "Skål!" he shouted, and all around the drinking began anew.

Trond introduced me to a few of his closest companions and we chatted about the unique advantages of viking diplomacy in international relations, the future challenges presented by locally proposed legislation concerning the heretofore legally undefined, folkloric shoe-manufacturing industry, and the recent, interesting developments occurring within the viking metal musical sub-genre's unique Sápmi-focused variant. But as the night wore on, the men's attention gradually drifted away from conversation and towards the various mead maidens hovering in ever-increasing proximity.

They tended our mead needs with excellent service and several even exchanged a few polite words with me during those in-opportune moments when competition for the attention of Trond and company was at its fiercest. Despite this, my initial thoughts of cavorting gave way to total apathy. The endless deluge of alcohol had dulled my senses and I no longer cared. Besides, unlike the men surrounding me, I didn't flaunt any impressive arm rings or any other blatant symbols of status and wealth. And so there, under the pro-tection of the wooden serpents adorning the mead hall's pitched roof, finally in the company of some real-life modern vikings, and with only the vague ponderings of what the next day might bring, I slipped into the firm grip of drunken darkness.

WRATH OF THE NEO-NORSEMEN

When I woke up the next morning, it was to the soft caress of a wolfhound gently lapping up dried mead droplets from my face. Although the animal's tongue was warm and inviting, his breath was nauseating and decay-ridden, so I flinched and sat upright. I had been lying on a pad of straw in the corner of the mead hall, which I vaguely remembered collapsing upon after puking into my drinking horn late the night before.

The fire in the center of the space had died down to embers, and the snoozing bodies of Trond's retinue could be seen scattered around the large room. A dazzling mead maiden lay beside each man, except for several of the more muscular and loquacious men, who each enjoyed the warm embrace of two or three female companions instead. I took a closer look at my own immediate vicinity and saw that the wolfhound who had awoken me was just one of several. I had apparently spent the night sleeping with the dogs. I stood up, grabbed my coat from where it hung beside the door, and walked outside.

Because I had arrived during the darkest depths of a winter's night, I hadn't previously noticed just how truly spectacular Trond's piece of real estate was. It might have been a freezing January morning in the Trøndelag, but the view was nonetheless breathtaking. The mead hall itself sat perched atop a western-facing cliff with expansive views in all directions while dense coniferous forests crowded the surrounding hilltops. The glow of the distant sun wavered along the horizon, casting long shadows across the frozen fjord below.

But as beautiful as the view was, I didn't linger. Instead, I trudged through the crusty snow to a clump of pines off to the side of the hall where numerous yellow splatters disrupted the uniformity of the icy white surface surrounding them. I fumbled around with the zipper beneath my long-hanging winter coat and set about my business.

I scanned my surroundings, wondering if there really was no privy out here, but saw nothing of the sort. The apparent size of the mead hall itself, however, surprised me. The walls extended much further on each side of the main entry than I had realized.

I also noticed a well-worn path that had been trodden through the snow behind the pines. Zipping up, I decided to see where it might lead. I didn't exactly cherish the notion of returning to the mead hall simply so that I could idle in a lousy bed buried beneath a pile of dogs while everyone else slept in.

After a few minutes, I came to a desolate clearing with a dilapidated old barn at the far end. Rather than the somewhat romanticized appearance one typically associates with the Norwegian countryside, this looked more like a decrepit and forbidding farmstead from rural Soviet-era Russia. The structure was slightly slanted, its windows were broken, and its wooden cladding was worn and weathered with substantial gaps pock-marking its surface. A chainlink fence topped with barbed wire encircled the entire perimeter.

I walked across the field and stopped in front of the fence. I hadn't noticed it initially, but the fence was oddly short—the barbed wire only reached to chest height. And the ground on the opposite side appeared trampled in stark contrast to the surrounding field, where the fallen snow remained pristine. The animals probably huddled together for warmth inside the ramshackle barn.

The cold was starting to seep its way into my bones, and I was about to turn back and return to the hall when I noticed a small trail of smoke wafting into the brisk air from a small wooden structure set off to the side of the barn. Freezing but intrigued, I followed the fence in that direction. Unlike the barn, this little structure was solidly built of square logs without any visible gaps, which meant that I couldn't see the source of the smoke inside of it. And strangely, the wooden logs were topped with barbed wire of their own.

My feet crunched on the snow as I stepped closer and caught a scent of the smoke; it was pipe tobacco.

"Who goes there?" an irate-sounding voice with a distinctly Irish brogue asked from inside the wooden box.

"What?" I asked.

"I said, 'Who goes there?'" the irate voice repeated.

"Uh...me," I answered. "Who are you? Where are you?"

"I'm down here, ye bollocksed tosser!" the voice cried angrily. It clearly came from within the enclosure.

I stepped closer to the chainlink fence and carefully leaned forward over the barbed wire. The top of the wooden box was open to the sky and the whole contraption was close enough to the fence that I could just barely peek in from where I stood in that awkward posture. A wee little man adorned in green attire and an old-fashioned top hat was standing there, smoking a pipe and glaring at me.

"Well, what have ye got to say for yeself, ye feckin' tosser?" he asked.

Nothing apparently, as I stood speechless and just stared at him.

"Blimey, I've got a nasty hangover wailin' in me head this mornin'." He looked forlorn and a tear slid down his cheek. "Be a good lad n' go n' fetch me a feckin' whiskey, will ye?"

I disregarded his request and instead asked, "What? No. Why are you in this strange wooden...container?"

"Just doin' a stint in solitary," he sighed. "That's how them tyrannical fellers up in the feastin' hall react whenever they catch me dispersin' me pamphlets among the workers down here. 'Propaganda' they calls it."

"Propaganda?"

"Aye, the lords up the hill don't like me pamphlets, ye know. They say I be stirrin' up trouble. And well, I am, but rightly so. Ye see, they just want to keep us down here, stripped of our individual liberties, divided amongst ourselves, doin' hard labor in poor conditions and for no feckin' pay!"

"There's more of you?"

"Ye daft, man?" He sounded more defeated than annoyed. "Ye think it's just me down here? Those *norsky* bastards would lock me right up all by my lonesomes in the barn bein' if that was the case. No, no, my comrades all be in there right this minute, keepin' one another warm n' sleepin' off the whiskey from last night. Them tyrants, though, they locked me up out here in this feckin' box in the cold last night so as to punish me misgivin's as they call them...but say, I sure could use a whiskey right about now. Ye right sure ye can't help a feller out?"

I looked down at his pleading eyes and felt an inkling of remorse. Last night had so overwhelmed my senses as well as my capacity for rational thought that I'd completely forgotten about the brief encounter I'd had with the miscreant so-called leprechaun who had portered my luggage away to an undisclosed location. Was this the same guy? I had no idea and likewise had no idea where my luggage had ended up, unless it was lying somewhere in a puddle of alcohol and canine slobber that I just hadn't noticed yet. And I wasn't sure that I believed my eyes now, either. I had woken up without the slightest hint of a hangover and I wondered whether there was something strange about Trond's special honey brew.

Baffled, I turned around without saying another word and trudged back up the hill as a string of colorful Irish curses followed in my wake.

"The wee folk are an accursed race," Trond stated rather matter-of-factly between spoonfuls of organic muesli coated in strawberry-flavored yogurt, a staple of modern Scandinavian breakfast food, and one that I was pleased to see available at the mead hall. I hadn't really been in the mood for roast pork loin or rack of lamb at this early hour.

"They are driven by hate," he continued, "an insatiable lust for whiskey, and unhealthy pot-of-gold mongering. And, yet, they make a damn fine shoe."

By the time I had returned to the hall after my little outdoor excursion, people had started to wake up and several of the mead maidens had taken on the adapted role of muesli maidens. They moved about the space, filling the men's bowls with their sweet sustenance. One of them had noticed me standing beside the doorway, gawking in confusion at the whole scene, and gestured that I should take some as well. I retrieved the bowl that a heaping portion of meat stew had been served to me in the night before from beneath a slumbering dog and exchanged it for one full of muesli and yogurt. It was then that I had noticed Trond sitting at the long table, waving me over.

He had forgone taking a seat on his throne for one of the mead hall's otherwise nondescript wooden benches and I sat down opposite him. He seemed to be in a cheerful mood despite his stoic manner of speaking because he smiled non-stop.

A muesli maiden approached to give us each of a cup of coffee. I simply thanked her as she leaned over the table to set the cups down and averted my eyes from the tantalizing cleavage revealed by her form-fitting and low-cut bodice. Trond, on the other hand, stared unabashedly at her breasts and squeezed her ass, causing her to feign shock and then giggle as she walked away. I was still confounded about the regressive roles that these women seemed to have so willingly slipped into, particularly in this nation at this particular point in human history, but that was just one, individual item in a long litany of grievances that my brain was presently struggling to process.

"So, you want to know what happened in Lindisfarne?" Trond asked directly. His amulet of Mjölnir—as Thor's hammer is officially called—glistened in the morning light that shone in through windows set high in the mead hall's walls.

"Of course," I answered, eager to finally hear first-hand the tale of the iconic watershed event of the entire Modern Viking Movement.

"As I mentioned last night, I was going through a tough time," he began. "My car croaked, my best friend moved to Danish territory to study law, and then my girlfriend broke up with me while the men and I were at sea. I read her email on the *Hvalavlinger*—that was our ship's name—where she claimed to no longer have feelings for me. No other explanation, no previous hints or discussions that indicated she was unhappy or that this was the direction her thought-wheels were moving in. Just a sudden, unanticipated communication."

"How cruel," I commented. I could actually relate, because I had experienced a similar personal downfall. Perhaps I had more in common with the founder of the Modern Viking Movement than I had originally assumed.

"Indeed, it was cold-hearted," he agreed. "So, I was fed up. It was the last straw. I lost my temper and determined that we should attack the nearest coastal settlement. I knew that would make me feel better."

And the illusion of my overlap in personal qualities with Trond abruptly ended.

"I knew not our destination." He swallowed some coffee. "Only that I ordered the *Hvalavlinger* to make for land. We put our trust in Thor to guide us safely to the nearest shore and the norns decreed that we should hit landfall at the Holy Island of Lindisfarne, just off the Northumbrian coast."

Lindisfarne is renowned as the site generally considered to have experienced the opening performance of the Viking Age. In the year 793, the "ravaging of wretched heathen men destroyed God's church at Lindisfarne" as the *Anglo-Saxon Chronicle* describes the incident. Basically, after a warm-up show at the Isle of Portland off the coast of Dorset in 789, the original vikings achieved their big international break-through at Lindisfarne, sacking the monastery and slaughtering and enslaving the monks. Trond, without planning it, had simply followed in his ancestors' ancient footsteps as his fate decreed he must. Only he hadn't hurt anyone, and his actions only caused a mild commotion that the news media hadn't even bothered to cover.

At this point of our conversation, the few remaining warriors who had continued to sleep through the morning din began to stir. Several headed outside while others joined us at the table to groggily slurp up the muesli that the maidens had bestowed upon them. A scruffy man with a less muscular build than his compatriots came over and sat down beside Trond with his own mug of coffee and bowl of muesli. I recognized him immediately as Henrik, the guy who had berated the imp who had taken my luggage the previous night and claimed to be in charge of leprechaun wrangling on the premises.

"No doubt wealth and glory awaited us on English soil," Trond resumed his tale with a heartfelt laugh. "We cut the rope and shot our harpoon at the monastery's foundations. It was a valiant effort, but missed its target and instead struck the ground near a group of gawking photo-takers. Then it detonated."

"That's on account of them there whalin' harpoons havin' explosives inside 'em nowadays," Henrik added in his rough voice. His dental hygiene was so bad that it almost entirely detracted from what he was saying. "None of them onlookers was hurt, but they sure was scared n' went off runnin' n' screamin' in all directions."

"Then we stormed the beach, whaling knives and hooks in hand, and sought our adversaries to earn glory, fame, and riches. But none were to be found. The place had been abandoned long ago. All the gold was gone. All the silver was gone. All the monks were gone. So, we turned our attention to the humble house of souvenir-wares that stood nearby. Returning to the ship empty-handed was entirely out of the question."

The hall had grown quiet as Trond spoke. The men who sat nearest us nodded in agreement and the muesli maidens had slowed their movements and were careful not to speak or giggle too loudly while Trond recited his story.

"But praise be to the Lord of Spears. That humble homestead was stocked with great provisions." He smirked devilishly then took a sip of coffee and spoke these words:

> "Keepers of kitsch were no match
> For fiery flames of fleece-arms
> Cowering in closet's corner
> As fierce men plundered freely."

Which was simply his own eloquent way of saying that the Lindisfarne gift shop's few staff members had happily stepped aside when the store was suddenly swarmed by a group of swarthy Norwegian whalers wielding blubber-flensing utensils intent on stealing the various mugs, magnets, t-shirts, stuffed animals, and other souvenir items that were stocked on the shelves. While I certainly understood how the hostile liberation of an entire box full of canvas bags manufactured in China and emblazoned with the text "My people went to Lindisfarne and all they got me was this lousy bag" or a package of plastic, monk-shaped keychains might have been cathartic for whatever issues Trond had been experiencing at the time, I failed to see the point of actually keeping any of it aside from an item or two.

"It sold well on eBay for substantial profit" was all that he said in response, which seemed believable enough; every penny of such a sale is profit when you paid nothing to acquire the items that you're selling in the first place.

"So, you just loaded it all up on the ship and then came back to Norway and started selling the stuff online?" I asked. "And no one tried stopping you the whole time?"

"One Anglo-Saxon complained to us," he answered. "But no blood was drawn. The enemy attempted to strike Thorolf over there, who sprained his ankle when he stepped on the edge of the curb to dodge the blow. And dodge it he did, earning the nickname Thorolf Twist-Ankle in the process."

The man I presumed to be Thorolf laughed at the far end of the table. Everyone in the hall had crowded around us by this point to listen to Trond tell the tale of their heroic exploits. It was becoming clear to me that he had that effect on people, or at least the sort of people who would choose to inhabit a mead hall, anyway. He didn't possess the typical charisma or charm I tend to associate with the usual snakes of the human race who are always so adept at attracting attention and asserting their will in boardroom meetings, establishing cults, or influencing others on Instagram, but he nonetheless commanded a forceful presence in his own unique way.

"The norns decreed that we should begin our sales aboard ship," he continued. "The *Hvalavlinger* was equipped with satellite internet and had been for sometime—that's how I was able to read that fateful email from my ex-girlfriend, after all. And it provided for good trading opportunities. We set our prices low, and others were eager to buy. Clearly, we learned that the lands to the west offered much bounty, and the men and I took council to discuss future voyages before we arrived back in Trondheim. We talked of many possibilities. The riches of the British Isles lay wide open for our taking."

He leaned back and declared more loudly to all the listeners, "But now, as I see that you all have woken up and gathered for this rumination, what say you all to some winter games today?"

Everyone around the table shouted their agreement and the hall was swept into a flurry of motion as the muesli maidens began whisking away empty bowls and mugs from the table. The men who hadn't finished theirs began to slurp it up rapidly.

The story that Trond had woven constituted a valiant attempt to explain the vicious rumors circulating about himself, his Norwegian buddies, and their purported slaughter in England, which wasn't a slaughter at all but rather a very strange disturbance of the peace combined with petty theft. I wasn't sure what I had been expecting, but trying to make a quick buck with pilfered souvenirs wasn't it. There was more to the story, of course. You don't go from operating a shitty eBay store on a whaling boat one day to running an opulent mead hall the next.

But that matter would have to wait till later because now it was time to go participate in something called "berserkockey."

ENSLAVEMENT OF THE WEE FOLK

The thick leather swim trunks felt awkward and resisted all motion as I slowly lowered myself into the steaming hot tub. The heat shocked my nerves after having spent such a great portion of the day skating around in utterly frigid temperatures with a shield in one hand and a hockey stick in the other. Finally submerged up to my chest from where I sat on the bench beneath the water's surface, I leaned back against the wall and surveyed the setting.

Seen from above, the hot tub resembled a large Thor's hammer, which meant that there were some strange nooks and crannies in its layout that, in a practical sense, served to compartmentalize its users into several smaller groups, enabling more private and intimate conversations to take place should the crowd become large. There was no need for that now, though, as only a few of us were here. I sat beside Henrik in the hammer's shaft of the tub and opposite us sat Trond himself. The tip of his long, manly beard dangled below the surface of the hot water, which he didn't seem to mind.

The hot tub was located outdoors on the patio of Trond's mead hall, overlooking the fjord and snow-capped mountains beyond. The sun was setting now, even though it wasn't yet evening, and the orange glow added an element of warmth to a color palette that otherwise consisted entirely of blues, grays, and whites. Several fires cast light along the hot tub's periphery and the speakers that hung from the nearest walls of the mead hall gently streamed Trond's ambient Neo-Norse playlist, which consisted of excellent musical artists such as Wardruna, Fejd, and Eivør.

A beautiful beer maiden wearing only a skimpy leather bikini emerged from the hall, gave each of us a bottle of Dahls Fatøl, and then slipped into the water beside Trond, who immediately put his arm around her. We clinked our bottles, skåled to one another's health, and drank. It was a light, easy drinking beer, and a mainstay of Norway dating back to the mid-1850s. And boy, did it hit the spot.

"So, Rowdy." Trond broke the ice. "Your deeds upon the ice this day were neither great nor sorely lacking in skill. Your conduct was admirable in its integrity considering your status as an interloper. You almost brought pride to your forefathers."

I still hadn't become completely accustomed to being addressed as Rowdy, but I knew I'd better start getting used to it. This was simply one of the side effects of selecting a fake name for oneself while trolling around online and then making the dumb decision of sticking with it in real life, too.

"Uh...thanks..." I replied and took another sip of beer.

Berserkockey had actually proven to be both simultaneously a lot of fun and absolutely terrifying. The premise is relatively simple and clearly inspired by the sport of ice hockey, hence its name. The game consists of two teams comprised of five players each who attempt to score points by sending the puck into the opponent's goal. Like ice hockey, it is played on ice with skates and the players use sticks to handle and shoot the puck. Unlike ice hockey, there are no boards or set boundaries, the players are covered from head to foot in animal pelts rather than typical protective equipment, and the sticks are trimmed down in size to allow them to be easily handled with a single hand since the other hand is fully occupied with holding a wooden shield. Opposing players are allowed to openly pummel one another with both sticks and shields without fear of penalty, and rather than the presence of a goaltender, players scramble to form a defensive shield-wall in front of their net when the opposing team attempts to take a shot on goal. Two points are awarded rather than the traditional one point if a player manages to successfully score a goal while biting down on his shield at the same time.

I had spent most of the game skating away from men much larger than myself in an attempt to prevent my ass from getting kicked, and occasionally swooping in toward the goal when my team had clear possession of the puck. I succeeded in scoring a single goal in this manner, thanks to a great pass from Trond himself who, beyond his blatant and cutthroat obsession with winning, might have also just wanted to give me a chance to prove myself.

After the game's conclusion, he told everyone that he was going to take a couple of hours to rest before the big feast later in the evening. They could go back to their rooms, go skiing or snow-shoeing, get an early start on drinking—whatever they felt like. As the group started to disperse, he came over to me and put his arm around my shoulder.

"You, Rowdy, should come join me in the hot tub," he said. "We shall share good counsel and wisdom in private. You will find a bathing suit on the bed in your room."

This was the first that I'd heard anything about having an actual bed to sleep on, much less my own room, and he must have seen the confused look on my face because he then explained that every guest had a room of his or her own. It was simply a fun tradition that the first night everyone gathered for one of these reunions that they should all feast and drink in the main hall and sleep on the benches and floor, in accordance with the old ways. But no one actually wanted to spend a whole week in such uncomfortable accommo-dations, and his mead hall housed many guest rooms that were accessible via a hallway from the corner of the main room that I had obviously overlooked. So, while the interior of the main room had been designed and constructed with authentic, historic detail, the rest of Trond's property was basically a sprawling mansion with all the modern accoutrements one would expect of a boutique bed and breakfast. My initial guess as to the nature of his establishment therefore proved to be quite apt, because in addition to the income that he makes from his leprechaun slave-labored shoe enterprise, he also makes a killing in the tourism industry renting out his rooms and providing an authentic and rousing modern viking experience for travelers interested in getting a taste of the Neo-Norse lifestyle.

Henrik showed me to my room on the second floor. It was spacious and light in the modern Scandinavian style, but with trimmings and decor strongly influenced by medieval aesthetics, such as the wooden serpent-head bed posts and the strange upholstered thing in the corner of the room that looked like a miniature longship and that I surmised was some sort of ottoman chair. Wide windows provided a majestic view of the surrounding landscape, and a simple but stylish bathroom replete with shower, sink, and toilet could be seen through a doorway to the right. The luggage that the diminutive porter had taken when I first arrived sat on the floor beside the foot of the bed.

"Now, you just make yerself at home here, Rowdy," Henrik said. "Them swimmin' trousers on the bed there's what ya gots for to wear down to the hot tub, which is right down the stairs at the end of this here hall to the left."

"Thank you," I told him, surprised but also relieved to see that I wouldn't be sleeping with the dogs every single night that I was here.

"Ain't no thing. I'll see you down there in a few," he said and went out, closing the door behind himself.

"I understand that ice hockey is a popular past-time among the Anglo-Saxon settlers of Vinland the Good," Trond stated as his beard dipped beneath the surface of the warm water in accordance with the movement of his jaw.

"It is, though the part of Vinland that I believe we're talking about tends to be more heavily Irish and Italian than English these days," I responded.

"The language of both the Celts and the Romans is much more difficult to understand than that of the Anglo-Saxons. It must make trade wearisome."

And so we bantered back and forth about the dialects of the various tribes who inhabit the northeastern territories of North America, or Vinland as Trond preferred to call it. The conversation meandered aimlessly for a while, covering many irrelevant topics in good spirits, except for a brief interlude during which Trond became visibly irritated when I attempted to imitate the accent of French

Canadians. The beer maiden within his embrace laughed and I would have been tempted to continue talking about poutine and Celine Dion if Henrik hadn't shot me a dark glance that clearly indicated that I should give it a rest. It seemed that Trond might harbor some unspoken and unresolved issues with the Quebecois, though he never actually acknowledged what those may be.

Our conversation continued to amble its way along about nothing in particular until Trond segued rather abruptly from an elucidation regarding his own personal frustrations with the tweezing of troublesome nostril hairs to the advantages offered by raiding Ireland over other places. He and his fellow Neo-Norsemen, just like their medieval forebears, had found Ireland to be a paradise for plundering—especially for the acquisition of slaves.

According to Trond, Ireland has always been a pragmatic option for finding victims to enslave. He also claimed that not everyone fully appreciates the subtle differences that exist among the varieties of slaves available for the taking. Apparently, Irish slaves have always been a very sensible choice for Scandinavians because they hail from a dreary North Atlantic island, making them much better suited for toiling in the Nordic climate than the peoples of the Middle East, Africa, and Southern Europe, for example. Ireland, furthermore, lies a much shorter distance from Scandinavia than do these other lands, which also makes the Irish a more economical choice.

I suspected that Trond was bullshitting me with all this talk about present-day Norwegian slave-taking, but having so recently upset both Olafur Shitty-Pants and Agneta of Geithus, I decided to tread lightly and play along. So, I simply asked him why Ireland was so much better than England, Scotland, France, Poland, or the Baltic states, to name just a few. Those locations all seemed likely to fit the bill for slave-taking just as well as Ireland for the reasons he had provided.

"As Norwegians, we have always sailed west in pursuit of plunder and conquest," he answered. "It is the natural order of things as well as of geography. Sailing east to the Baltic would bring us past the mark of the Danes and the realm of the Swedes. Not a risk worth taking."

"Sure, but that still leaves England, Scotland, France...?"

"We also wished to reestablish the traditional Norwegian base in Dublin," he replied. "Certainly, we could have chosen the Orkneys or Northumbria instead, but the lure of Guinness and Jameson proved too great to resist. We sailed across the western seas to the Emerald Isle and moored our ship in Dublin's Grand Canal. The paperwork was fearsome, but that victory was ours, and soon we went ashore in search of silver, slaves, and stout. It was late in the day when we stepped off the boat, but the sun had not yet set, so we continued inland, taking stock of our surroundings. We came upon a cheerful tavern and decided to stop in and discuss our next steps. The Guinness flowed freely...well, not freely, as we did pay for it since we had no wish to arouse the suspicions of the natives of the land so soon, but we drank deeply as the Irish minstrel played his music and the lasses eyed us curiously for we smelt of herring and sea salt and spoke in a tongue that they did not understand. Do you know who the belle of Belfast city is?"

I looked at him questioningly as I took a sip of beer.

"The minstrel sang that she is handsome and that she is pretty," he continued. "And that she is also the belle of Belfast city. She sounded like she would make a splendid wife, so on a later voyage, we sailed to Belfast and looked for her. But she was nowhere to be found."

"Well, I think she died a long time ago, when the song was written," I replied. "And maybe she never even existed...it's just lyrics, you know. There are probably many belles of Belfast city, or have been over the years."

"Hmm..." he seemed to ponder this for a moment before quickly diverting his attention back to the raid on Dublin. "Well, be that as it may, we drank our fill at that tavern and then emerged back into the soft light of the waning Irish evening—for it was summertime—and began to scout the streets for slaves to take. It was a challenging feat, for while the folk there were very unsuspecting, they also fought back with bitter enmity. The first woman I approached laughed when I stepped in front of her and spoke this verse:

> 'The fertile necklace soil of foreign shores
> Meets the *Norsk* knower of strength
> Let your ship-bow of words stay silent
> Submit to the strong-minded lord now.'

She slapped my face and ran away while I tended my injury. The same happened with most of my men."

Henrik sighed loudly beside me while Trond's beer maiden made a pouty face. Trond's eloquence with words made even his failed pick-up attempt sound rather epic, after all, and I found myself becoming gradually accustomed to his unique manner of speaking.

"But through those early setbacks, we persevered," he continued. "A group of Irish hooligans approached us from the south. Eager for a fight, they flung insults and threats our way. More words were exchanged, hostilities grew, and we knew that these were good fighting men and would make even better slaves. Our numbers even, the fight began. But neither side could gain a clear upper-hand as the battle raged. Men fell on both sides, wounded but none dead.

"And then the wailing of the sirens began. Not the sweet songs of those mysterious women who lure men to their doom off the isles of Greekland, but rather the glaring screeches of the four-wheeled steeds of the enforcers of the law. The battle ended as quickly as it began, with our foes fleeing in the direction from whence they came, and us back towards our ship. We reached the *Hvalavlinger* before the Irish Guards could apprehend us and we sailed swiftly from Dublin's harbor, back into the open sea.

"It was not honorable to leave Dublin that way. The battle may have been a draw, but the mission was a defeat, and to confront the Guards would have been nothing short of foolhardy. Things were different back in my great-great granddaddy's day. In those days, the Irish were disorganized, warring amongst themselves, and as a result the slave-taking was like taking candy from a baby.

But our fates are as the norns decree, and idle lamentations achieve nothing. So, we sailed onward, south towards Wexford with the idea to try our luck there, and it was on that voyage that Henrik spotted the rainbow bridge descending over the land to the west. Isn't that right, Henrik?"

"Yessirree!" Henrik straightened up as he spoke. It was a motion that I sensed more than saw because the steam that wafted off the surface of the water had thickened since we had first entered the hot tub. Now, rather than merely wrapping around us, providing a sense of seclusion, it was obscuring our vision so that we all appeared as slightly amorphous shapes in the mist to one another.

"That there yonder rainbow," Henrik continued, "gots me to thinkin' that maybe Asgård lie at the end of it. I seen it in a vision onboard bright as day. A city all sparklin' with shiny gold n' whatnot, I tell ya."

Henrik was alluding to Bifrost, the mythological rainbow bridge that connects Midgård, the land of humans popularized as Middle-Earth by Tolkien, with Asgård, the realm of the gods. Asgård is not typically reputed to be a city of gold, but rather a naturalized landscape located in an otherworldly dimension that hosts the homes and abodes of the gods and goddesses, such as Valhalla, Odin's hall of the slain, and Bilskirnir, Thor's homestead. Asgård is said to be encircled by a forbidding fortress wall that was constructed by an evil giant intent on fornicating with the beautiful goddess, Freyja, as part of a bet with the gods. The bet hinged on the giant completing the wall in an allotted period of time and when it began to appear that the giant might actually succeed, Loki, the trickster god who had brokered the terms of the deal, transformed himself into a mare in heat. He then allowed the giant's horny horse, who had been critical in the wall's speedy construction, to desecrate his divine body. But the slow-down in work that resulted from Loki's carnal sacrifice allowed the gods to win the bet.

"Anyways, so we set anchor n' good ole Trond here sends me n' some of the other guys to go n' check it out," Henrik continued. "N' so we goes n' we gets to the end of that there rainbow n' what we finds is instead of some sort of inter-dimensional portal type thing, there's a genuine pot o' gold lyin' there right smack out in the open. Really cheered me up too, I gotta say, 'cause I was feelin' pretty dejected the closer we was gettin' to the rainbow's end. I was gettin' to thinkin' that this wasn't no Bifrost n' that I'd done made the ship stop n' called the guys out 'ere fer nuttin' when we stumbled ontahs it. It was only about yea big"—he carved out an invisible sphere roughly a foot and a half in diameter in the swirling steam—"but, you know, that ain't bad, I tell you what. So, me n' the guys picked it on up n' we hauled it on back to the ship where the rest of the men were waitin' for us."

"The treasure was bountiful," Trond cut in. "We praised Thor and then sent several additional search parties ashore. I had decided that it would be unwise to leave that quarter of Wexford before seeking further discoveries of gold."

"Yup, that there's how it was done," Henrik added. "I reckon we had, what, four search parties out there, snoopin' round?"

"Your account is both well-spoken and well-remembered," Trond confirmed.

"Yeah, so's you see, we was now out there, scurryin' 'round, lookin' for more of them there rainbows n' any other signs that might lead us to some more of that there hidden gold, you know, things like entrances to caves as maybe there was some dwarves in the area or a dragon even. N' so I'm out there with a few men n' we sees a cave on a hillside, so we goes up there to check it out, but it's got no gold, just some rodents, but as we come back outtah it, there's this new rainbow shinin' clear across the field in front of us since as you pry well know, Ireland's a rainy place n' the sun had started to shine again, n' so anyways we starts followin' that rainbow when alls a sudden we stumbles upon the biggest goddamn leprechaun colony this side of a bowl of Lucky Charms."

"They're magically delicious," Trond reminded us in a very serious voice.

I nodded in agreement and let Henrik continue talking.

"So, we walks up to them there leprechauns real quiet-like, yah know," he said. "N' it appears that they had been sleepin' all through the day. They're all just lyin' out there on top of this little fairy mound, which I reckon was their home. By this time the clouds had all gone n' it was turnin' into a real beautiful day. It smelled real fresh with all them plants soakin' up the rain n' the flowers burstin' into bloom, till we got closer to that fairy mound. And boy, I tell you what, the smell comin' off of that lump of dirt sure was somethin' foul."

"We have since learned that leprechauns loathe bathing," Trond elaborated.

"Oh, they hate it to high heaven, but we didn't know that at the time. So anyways, I sends one feller on back to the ship to let Trond know we got some slaves here ripe for the pickin' if they can come real quick before the snoozin' devils all wake up."

"We set out immediately," Trond said. "I left a few men to guard the ship from whatever ruffians and vagabonds might have been lurking in those waters, and took the rest of the men straight to the site."

"Yup, n' all the while them leprechauns slept sweet n' sound. Now, I don't know what you alls been told, but I for one never once suspected the leprechaun of being a nocturnal-type creature, but them buggers all started wakin' up soon as the sun was goin' down, one by one, but by then we'd done already surrounded that entire fairy mound upon which they was out there lyin'. N' thanks to Harald Hole-Plug who went n' snuck past their lines without 'em ever even noticin', we got the openin' in their mound sealed up tight as a package o' *lutefisk* since he jumped intah it n' blocked it with his own body right up to his belly."

Fairy mounds—the type of earthen structure about which Henrik spoke—are found all over Ireland; in fact, some estimates suggest that over thirty thousand exist in the country. They typically consist of a mound of earth constructed in ancient times and all sorts of folklore have sprouted up over the centuries about them, their archaic purposes, and the mystical creatures who inhabit them. In particular, fairy mounds have historically been viewed as gateways to the Otherworld of Irish mythology, as well as possibly being the homes of various supernatural entities such as the leprechauns that Henrik found snoozing atop the one presently under discussion. Fairy mounds are also known to have commonly incorporated subterranean passages in their construction, though the discovery of such a passage with an extant opening that is neither blocked nor fully grown over is incredibly rare. But the Neo-Norsemen nonetheless reacted as required by the uniqueness of the situation and successfully blocked the leprechauns' one and only escape route back to the Realm of Fairy.

"So, rounds 'bout now most of 'em are comin' to, but they don't quite realize what's going on yet." Henrik took a gulp of beer as he continued telling the story. "But then one of 'em figures it out when he sees their whole colony's done been encircled by armed warriors n' he raises the alarm. So, now they're all panickin' n' prancin' about but Harald's barred the way back into their home so a fews of 'em try chargin' our line but we force 'em back n' then they all starts to calm down a bit till one of 'em started whoopin' n' hollerin' all sorts n' he dropped his trousers n' shat in his hand, n' I'll be damned if he didn't fling that fecal matter right at us."

"He's the one you met in solitary confinement down by the barn," Trond interjected. "If he weren't already a slave, I'd sentence him to outlawry and put a ransom on his head."

"He told me his crime was distributing propaganda," I countered.

"Oh, that son'a bitch does that, too," replied Henrik. "He's a right real trouble-maker he is, n' when he shat in his hand n' threw it our way, well then all the others all started joinin' in, too."

Trond cleared his throat, and we all remained silent, because this signaled that poetry was in the process of being composed. He then spoke this verse:

> "Sewage-stench wafted unruly
> Shield-wall repelled shit-storm
> Sky-swallower set over sword-reddeners
> Spear-assembly slowly softened.
>
> Harsh helmet-trial of wee-folk
> Heralds victory's high hopes
> Hardy men of Harald's Hawk-Isle
> Held hostage fettered fairy fellows."

There was silence as Trond finished, then Henrik and the beer maiden give him a round of applause and I likewise joined in.

The long and the short of it was that the Norwegians rounded up the leprechauns and put them in chains after the fecal-flinging had subsided. Many of the leprechauns tried to sweet-talk their way out of the ensuing slave-taking operation, promising more gold if only their shackles were severed and they were set free. Some even offered to grant the vikings three wishes in exchange for their freedom, but it was all to no avail. In the end, the Norwegians just wanted slaves more than anything else.

"Truth should be told where honest words are due," confided Trond. "I really wanted to start a shoe factory with these new slaves."

"Yup, that's how it was!" Henrik beamed with excitement. "So, we just kept our eyes on 'em, n' when one of 'em tried to make a run for it, I sliced the top off his hat, n' I tell you what, I never would have guessed it, but they treasure them top hats like you wouldn't believe n' so none of 'em tried nothin' funny again after that. They sure swore up a storm in old Irish Gaelic, though, believe you me, on the march back to the ship."

"We boarded the *Hvalavlinger* in high spirits." Trond leaned forward. "We had found some great loot that we divided up equally among ourselves per the ancient custom; that was a mighty pot of gold, so we all became rich men. We chained up the little slaves down below deck where their stench could not reach us as readily and set sail for home. It was fair weather the whole journey."

"Boy howdy!" Henrik clapped. "Ain't that right!"

At that precise moment, a red-bearded, impish figure wearing nothing but a bright green top hat streaked past us and into the snow. Before I even had a chance to react, Henrik was out of the water, bellowing fierce, old-fashioined Norwegian obscenities in pursuit of the enigmatic streaker. The two disappeared into the shadows and the sounds of Henrik's threats faded into the distance.

I remained seated, half shocked and half too confused to care. Trond just shrugged his shoulders and explained that sometimes one of the leprechauns will get loose and do something like this. The beer maiden beside him grinned and nodded in a manner that indicated that this wasn't the first time that she'd seen such leprechaun antics herself. Trond then related a few stories about past incidents, such as the time when one of the leprechauns had scaled the outer wall of the mead hall, dropped his trousers, and started urinating off the roof above the main door whenever anyone entered or exited.

"But the absolute worst was when one of them snuck inside the hall and defecated into our vat of mead as it was brewing," he said. "We had to discard that entire batch."

Henrik returned a few moments later, shivering and with a look of stern disapproval stamped across his face. In addition to his leather swim trunks, he now wore snow boots that he must have managed to slip on at some point during the chase or perhaps even after the capture of the culprit. He quickly removed the boots and slid back into the water, taking a massive gulp of beer.

"Catch him?" Trond asked.

"Yup," Henrik answered. "That there little bastard's gonna be doin' solitary 'gain tonight."

"Good."

"How do they even get loose?" I asked. I had seen the barn and the solitary confinement cell. The entire perimeter was fenced in with barbed wire, and while it was a low fence, it was also certainly tall enough to give any adult-sized human hesitation before attempting to clamber over it, much less someone as short as one of these supposed leprechauns.

"Magic," Trond answered curtly. He took a sip of beer and tilted his head toward Henrik.

"You see, Rowdy, them leprechauns, they don't always be abidin' by the usual laws of the natural world." Henrik took up the conversational reins once again. "Bein' as them's fairy-folk, they can sometimes bend the curvature of that there space-time continuum to move between planes of existence. But everything's gotta be in the right alignment for 'em to do that. They can't be doin' it all willy-nilly-like whenever they wants, but only when the moon's full and at a certain distance from this here Earth n' Earth itself is aligned in a particular celestial configuration n' whatnot. It's times like those when the Otherworld damn near merges with our own n' allows them leprechauns to get free. Well, the ones that be payin' attention anyway, that is, as most'ah 'em are usually drunk as a skunk n' miss that there window of opportunity, if you get what I mean."

"I see." I nodded, deciding to let the whole matter rest for now.

"It's usually worst 'round the end of October so you's best be glad you ain't visitin' us at Halloween."

Puzzled but unwilling to object to any of the comments that Trond and Henrik had made, I silently reflected on the multitude of scientific principles that the men so openly flouted. Our conversation gradually turned towards the timeless topic of music, particularly that of the Neo-Norse artists whose songs played over the speakers, while we finished our beers. Before long, we climbed out of the water and a perky towel maiden emerged from the hall to hand us each a fluffy, dry one with which to wipe ourselves down and wrap around our goose-bumped bodies. It was time to go inside and prepare for another evening of feasting.

LAST SASQUATCH OF JOTUNHEIM

Henrik reclined in his loose-fitting denim overalls, thread-bare stained white t-shirt, and straw hat while puffing on his pipe, giving off the impression that he was the embodiment of an accidental love-child between Tolkien's Gandalf and the Scarecrow from *The Wizard of Oz*.

"So, you see," he said as a trail of pipe smoke twirled up into the darkling sky, "we'd done let them leprechauns out to graze for 'while since the sun had finally started to shine when all'ah sudden out popped that damned sasquatch n' he went n' he ate 'em all up right good n' fast, he did."

We were seated at the edge of the icy fjord, reclining on pastel-colored Adirondack chairs and watching the sky turn a bright pinkish orange hue as the sun descended behind the cliffs overlooking the frozen water in front of us. Trond's men had shoveled the two-foot deep snow away from this spot earlier in the day to create the clearing in which we now found ourselves so that we could converse once again in private, which also gave his men the chance to enjoy his massive Mjölnir-shaped hot tub while we drank cheap alcohol and pretended it was summer at the frigid beach.

Despite the luxurious warmth that several portable space heaters provided, I was still wrapped up tightly in my L.L. Bean winter gear. Initially, my puffy winter coat, thick boots, and woolen cap had drawn admiration from my two Norwegian companions for their quality and stylishness. But after we had completed our trek down the slope and they realized that I had no intention of removing any of my outer garments, they had taunted me for it.

Trond sat between Henrik and myself and had forsaken his usual attire of leather pants and medieval tunic for black jeans and a Bathory *Hammerheart* t-shirt. His winter coat and cap, like Henrik's, lay in a lump by the base of one of the space heaters. I watched him take a sip of Ålesund's Best—the shittiest canned mead available in the entirety of the Trøndelag and the bordering counties—and nod reminiscently while Henrik spoke.

"That son'ah bitch sasquatch," Henrik continued. "He done ate them leprechauns all up n' he didn't even leave no bones either."

I looked from one man to the other and nodded silently because I didn't really have anything to contribute to the conversation nor did I want to directly engage specifically with the topic of bone consumption and open myself up to the potential for further ridicule, which was all too likely considering how last night had gone.

After returning to my room from the hot tub, I had changed into the medieval garb that Trond was kind enough to let me borrow for the night's festivities. It consisted of a traditional Norse tunic and pants made of wool, complete with a belt to tighten around my waist. The outfit was not comfortable. Normally, it would have been rented out to the guests vacationing at his establishment for an additional fee, but I luckily remained exempt from all charges thanks to my special role in attempting to record and eventually promote the story of his deeds.

I sat in the same spot as I had the previous night when I returned to the hall and watched the carousing unfold around me. Initially, it seemed no different than the night before. The men all sat at the large wooden table in the middle of the room and the women floated around the periphery, delivering drinks and openly flirting. A few women sat on the benches as well, and I assumed these were the higher-ranking wives of some of the men in attendance. Trond sat on his throne at the head of the table surveying the crowd as everyone made merry and swapped stories of past glories involving bravery and courage. His beer maiden from the hot tub had nestled up beside him and seemed to enjoy the status that he had clearly bequeathed upon her.

I chatted a bit with the men nearest me, but for the most part, I simply listened to their conversations about defensive berserkockey shield-wall formation strategies and the advantages of wearing bear-pelts over wolf-pelts while playing the game. They commanded a much better understanding of English than I did of Norwegian, but it remained very evidently only a second language to them and most eschewed it in favor of their native tongue. The men weren't all natives of the Trøndelag and, consequently, a number of different dialects flew about the hall, which made it all the more difficult for me. Adding to the complexity on a level that I couldn't even begin to comprehend is the fact that there are actually two official versions of the Norwegian language: Bokmål and Nynorsk. Bokmål is the more common of the two, but both, fortunately, sound more similar to Swedish than does Danish. I could therefore at least decipher some of the dialogue here, whereas if I had visited a Neo-Norse mead hall in Denmark, it would have been a hopelessly lost cause. So, I followed along as best as I could but certainly missed many juicy tidbits.

Eventually, the mead maidens began to bring out the food for the feast. Trays filled with roast chicken, pork loin, beef shank, and pickled herring soon covered the table and everyone dug in, including the mead maidens, who each found an empty spot on a bench or an open lap to sit upon for the feasting. My own lap naturally remained vacant, but as soon as I reached for my first drumstick, the wolfhounds rushed to my side. Surrounded by these large, furry, and somewhat aggressive animals, I attempted to eat without being nipped or licked.

While I ate slowly compared to my companions, I nonetheless enjoyed the thrill of discarding everything that I had ever been taught about proper table manners. But then a few minutes later, as I was about to take a bite of roast pork, a spare rib struck me in the face, causing me to drop my food, which the closest wolfhound snapped up without a moment's hesitation.

Laughter immediately echoed throughout the room and before I could even attempt to recover from this debacle of public embarrassment, a great number of partially eaten projectiles were suddenly being hurled in my general direction. Whether they were intended for the wolfhounds or were simply meant to pelt me for humor's sake, I didn't know, but the rain rapidly amplified with relentless tenacity. Fearing that I had unwittingly bought a one-way ticket on the express train to suffering the age-old shame of being buried alive beneath a pile of gnawed upon bones, I jumped to my feet and ran as fast as I could back to my room with the missiles following in my wake and the wolfhounds nipping at my heels. I remained there for the duration of the night.

The following morning at the muesli-table, the smirks and knowing glances had been everywhere. No one had said anything, and for that I was grateful, but the awkwardness that hung in the air could have been cut with a dull butter knife. It didn't improve much during the day's round of berserkockey, either, as the players on the opposing team seemed to be more focused on chasing me around the fjord, trying to clobber me with their short sticks, than they were on scoring goals, which at least permitted my team to easily win the match.

I remembered the curse that Agneta of Geithus had supposedly cast upon me. Could this deterioration of relations be related to that? The idea entered my mind but I doubted it; if that were the case, I probably wouldn't have escaped the bone-throwing incident relatively unscathed. Plus, this ongoing sort of petty, social behavior was all too typical to be the consequence of a real curse. The dynamic at present was frustratingly similar to that of high school, wherein the cool/aggressive/popular/outspoken kids totally dominate the social scene and everyone else just gets ignored at best or bullied to the point of committing suicide in the extreme worst. But, of course, high school really is just a toxic microcosm of the actual bullshit social dynamics that generally rule all ages and segments of society anyway, so why was I so surprised here? I was starting to fear that I was going to have to do something incredibly stupid just to have a chance at earning anyone's respect.

Fortunately, it didn't really matter at this particular moment because we were busy talking about the carnivorous consumption of leprechauns by a deviant Norwegian sasquatch.

Trond himself broke the silence that had settled over us. "Nobody fucks with my livestock." He looked both fierce and lazy where he slouched in his wooden chair.

"No sirreee!" Henrik exclaimed. "You sure done showed that sasquatch a thing or two he ain't never gonna forget!"

I took a sip from my can of Ålesund's Best and swished some of the fizzy honey piss around in my mouth. "You guys talk about these leprechauns as though they are some sort of domesticated animal," I said. "Like, as if you could go out to the barn to try and milk them or shear them or something."

"We do not milk the leprechauns," Trond stated very matter-of-factly with a thunderous belch fueled by too much weak mead.

Henrik explained further, "Sometimes we let them little bastards out to graze 'cause every now n' then one'ah 'em will dig up a pot of gold we didn't even know was buried out there. Happens most often after big rain storms. N' yah know, it ain't their treasure that they're findin', but some'ah that there buried gold that our forefathers brought back from their raids hundreds of years ago. Had to bury it tah hide it from the Danes or that tyrant, Harald Fairhair, you know. Someone's always tryin' to take it. But one'ah the great things 'bout leprechauns is that they function sort of like a livin', breathin' metal detector for gold, so they's real good at homin' in on any treasure buried beneath the ground, no matter whose gold it is."

"But sometimes all they find are sewage pipes and septic tanks," Trond uttered. "You never know what those gold-digging fecalphiliacs are going to dredge up."

"N' then in those cases I gots to give 'em a good wallopin'!" Henrik slapped his knee with enthusiasm.

"Either way, letting the leprechauns out to graze at strategic intervals just makes good financial sense. And it rejuvenates them for when they return to their shoe-toil."

"Speaking of the shoe-toil," I interjected, "how is the cobbling business going? You guys haven't told me much about it. I saw the barn my first morning here, but it was all fenced off and the only leprechaun I saw there was the one doing a stint in solitary confinement."

"It is profitable," Trond replied in his usual stoic manner.

I wasn't sure whether I should continue down this line of inquiry or not. It almost felt like poking the bear, so to speak, but I decided to risk it with a rather benign effort. "So, are the leprechauns making shoes right now?"

"Yes," Trond answered. "Henrik will check on their production before tonight's feast."

"Yup," echoed Henrik. "That's when I always check on 'em. That, n' first thing in the mornin'. They knows they got to meet certain quotas each day if they want to get their whiskey for the evening."

"Sounds like you know how to motivate them," I said. "What's the name of your company anyway? Could I buy some shoes?"

"The company is called Trondsko," Trond answered with a proud smile. "And while we are still only a very small operation and it is rare to find our wares beyond the borders of the Trøndelag, those who have benefitted from our premium footwear have sung its praises high to the heavens. Guests to our hall are always offered a generous discount should they desire to obtain a pair, but we will gladly bestow a pair upon you free of charge because your runic skald-craft will bring us great renown."

Free shoes for free publicity—a fair trade, I supposed. I eagerly wanted to see these shoes because I wasn't convinced that the Neo-Norsemen hadn't just set up some Norwegian equivalent of a Chinese knock-off shop in the barn and that all the men and women who feasted with me nightly weren't actually occupying themselves with that enterprise while I enjoyed these private conversations with Trond and Henrik. I also worried that, despite my best efforts, my runic skald-craft, as he called it, would never actually see the light of day and that he would feel that I had failed to live up to my end of the bargain and might subsequently hunt me down with his whaling weaponry and enslave me as a result.

Another thought occurred to me, and now seemed like as good a time as any to bring it up. "That miscreant leprechaun that I saw in solitary confinement said he was being punished for pamph-leteering. What's the deal with that?"

"That guy..." Trond sighed and then crushed his empty mead can against his chest. He tossed it into the cooler and took another. The cooler looked forlorn and, honestly, quite useless with all the snow packed around it, but it had helped facilitate the transportation of a multitude of cans from the mead hall to the frozen water's edge.

Trond cracked his latest victim open and resumed speaking. "He's the most troublesome of them all. Always trying to unionize for fair wages and whatnot. What he doesn't get is he's a slave. They're all slaves. Now slavery isn't permitted in Norway—but that only applies to human slavery. Leprechauns aren't human."

"It's one hell of a legal entanglement, it sure is," Henrik added.

Trond shot him a menacing glance. "I don't want to discuss this much, but that leprechaun you saw managed to escape one night last year and hire a lawyer. We tracked him down and brought him back, but not before his lawyer had managed to file a motion to revise Norwegian law to recognize leprechauns as people. It's a messy case, and it will be held up in the courts for years, decades even, maybe. But in the meantime, it's just business as usual."

"Well, that's good," I said, not knowing whether it really was good or not. I don't support slavery, but I also don't believe in lep-rechauns. I'd seen several so far but remained unconvinced that they weren't just part of some big ploy in which Trond had hired a number of short people to dress in green and play the part as a form of amusement for the tourists who visit his establishment. I had to admit, they did liven the place up a bit and provided a unique fantasy element that none of the other recreated mead halls in the Northlands could match.

There was a momentary pause as all three of us sipped our canned meads. I broke it by asking about the sasquatch that Trond and Henrik had been discussing before I had sidetracked the conver-sation with my comment about the milking of leprechauns.

"Well, yah see, we'd always done known 'bout him." Henrik was the first to speak. "News'ah his presence wasn't ain't no news, but he'd been a-hidin' out so long ain't no one gave him no heed no more. He lived up there in them glaciers in that there Jotunheim National Park these last several thousand years n' he'd hardly ever even show his face no more, but when he did, I tell yah, it was somethin' ugly. That ole boy sure was a mean'un."

Trond had apparently already finished his latest can of mead because he crumpled it in his fist and cut to the chase. "I ripped his fucking arm off and hung it on the mantle above the fireplace inside. Then he ran off and died."

"Oh..." I had seen the dismembered appendage mounted on the wall inside the mead hall but had also figured that it was probably just some trophy from hunting bears. I grabbed another can of crappy mead from the cooler for myself.

Henrik continued, "So, yah see, that there sasquatch, he'd done been pickin' off some of our leprechauns on a nightly basis. We'd hear all this commotion goin' on down at the barn n' bys the time we got down there, he was gone. Now, thing 'bout sasquatch was he's a big guy, so he just steps right over that low fence we keep them leprechauns penned in with n' then he goes n' he rips off the door to the barn n' he grabs one or two of them leprechauns n' then he makes off for the hills like there ain't no tomorrow. N' well, as you can pry figure, this is right terrible news as we ain't got no female leprechauns to reproduce the male one's with. All we gots is all we gots n' there ain't gonna be no more baby leprechauns bred, at least not around heres anyway."

"Goddamned sasquatch," Trond muttered.

"N' this is all happenin' during a normal time, too, meanin' we didn't have no big gatherin' at the hall to help scour the land to look for him. It was just Trond, me, n' the few other regular staffers. Nothin' like the crowd of good fightin' men we got here right now. So's I gets to thinkin' n' I goes n' I talks to Trond n' I says, 'You know, ain't nothing that sasquatch hates more than people havin' a good time, so let's throw a real big shindig n' invite all our friends over as that's sure to be one guaranteed sasquatch pisser-offer. N' then when he comes down from outta them there hills, we kill him.' "

Trond inhaled deeply and Henrik stopped speaking. We waited quietly as Trond formed the obviously forthcoming poetry from his word-hoard:

> "Foul-faced feaster of foreign feces-flingers
> Flies forth from far-away fells
> Down dales of dusky darkness
> Enters the abode of eager arrow-assemblers
> Ambushed, assaulted, arm-riven slinks away
> Drops at death's doorstep on distant shore."

Essentially, Trond was saying that the sasquatch had heard the merry-making of the party, as predicted. And if the raucous cheering, shouting, and laughter at the mead hall hadn't been loud enough, Henrik had ensured that their noise would carry far and wide by strumming his guitar and growling his heart out to some of the most expertly-rendered acoustic death metal covers of classic country hits like "Norseman of Constant Sorrow" and "Mammas Don't Let Your Babies Grow Up to Be Berserkers" ever performed.

Without fail, the music and other sounds of joy drew the sasquatch out of his far away hiding place. He came lurking down out of the frozen mountains, bypassed the leprechaun barn, and entered the mead hall to wreak havoc once everyone had gone silent and the lights were out for the night. Except the warriors were wide awake and waiting for him. Trond engaged the sasquatch in single, hand-to-hand combat the moment the creature crossed the threshold, though his men stood ready at his side should the tide of battle turn against him. But it didn't, and Trond ripped the sasquatch's arm off with his own bare hands. The wounded sasquatch ran off, crying for his mother, and supposedly died alone next to some glacial lake or pond up in Jotunheim National Park to the south.

"Did you ever find the body?" I asked.

Trond answered, "No."

"Did you ever even try to, though? I mean, how do you even know if he's really dead? What if he's still alive somewhere up there in the national park? How do you know he doesn't have any family or friends who are plotting against you right now as we speak?"

"They are free to try, and if they do, the battle-rage will take me again, and I will slaughter any sasquatch that comes down from those hills and threatens my homestead or my livestock. Isn't that right, Henrik?"

"Yessirreee, ain't no sasquatch ever gonna get outtah here alive."

And with that, our conversation began to rapidly dissipate as we watched the shadows grow ever longer across the landscape. It would soon be time to head back up the steep slope to the hall for the next feast. And thanks to my ignoble exit the night before, I was not looking forward to it.

RETURN TO STAMFORD BRIDGE

It had been a dreary September morning during the early part of the 21st century in the East Riding of Yorkshire, England. The steady drizzle of rain from the previous night had snapped into a stinging spray as a strong easterly wind moved inland, prompting the populace to avoid the wet chill as much as possible. Only Trond Troll-Breath Trondsen and his crew of renegade former whalers willingly ventured forth in the great outdoors on such an unpleasant day. Eager for glory, but mostly for the promise of wealth and power (as had become their habit ever since the incident at Lindisfarne), the Norwegians followed the landscape's path of least resistance, which in this particular case had proven to be the A166 motorway heading east out of the city of York. The men, all dressed in a strange blend of medieval garb and ocean-going whaling attire, had spread across the road as they slowly trudged towards Stamford Bridge, providing a road-rage-inducing cocktail for the volatile and angry drivers who honked their horns at the traffic impediment.

"We saw many, many birds of the human hand variety that morning," Trond sighed. "I did not know it at the time, but such avian insults were only a premonition of things to come. Our mood was good despite the rain and the angry Anglo-Saxons, but the norns did not smile upon us that day."

I had joined him for a walk along one of the trails that criss-cross his property. The snow was hard-packed from having been trodden upon by Trond and the members of his retinue in recent days, so snowshoes or skis weren't necessary to make our way through the woods. It was early in the afternoon, and we ambled along side by side beneath the frosty coniferous branches that rose high above us, beyond which the pale blue sky could be glimpsed. Everyone else, including Henrik who usually accompanied Trond, had gathered at the other end of the vast property to enjoy another round of berserkockey. Trond had elected to tell me his final story out here, far beyond the earshot of others while they kept themselves preoccupied with their favorite sport's fast-paced action and nonstop, senseless violence.

The end of my designated week-long stay at his mead hall rapidly approached. The latter half of my stay had passed much the same as the first, with muesli in the morning, followed by berserkockey and a slew of other outdoor activities for the remainder of the day, and feasting in the evening. My berserkockey skills hadn't improved much, mainly because I hadn't altered my primary tactic of striving my utmost to avoid the opposing players, but I had become better acquainted with the Neo-Norsemen in a general sense, thanks to my reliance on some jester-like tactics.

Recognizing that I needed to do something to at least attempt to mitigate the social damage that had been done when I was pelted with an onslaught of half-eaten meat bones, and knowing that I would never best any of the Neo-Norsemen at anything worthwhile, I had opted to perform a skill that I'd practiced and honed since my early teenage days with the family dog. So, that first evening after the ill-fated bone-throwing incident when I emerged from my room, rather than taking a seat on the bench and immediately burying my concerns in a massive horn of mead as might have been the most obvious course of action, I instead walked to the nearest wolfhound, scooped him up in my arms before he even had a chance to react, and began carrying him around the room.

I approached the nearest mead maiden, making gibberish noises to encourage the furry animal to sniff and lick her face in a wild display of friendly curiosity before moving on to the next mead maiden. The sight of a large dog dangling in my arms as I walked around the room and approached giggly women had brought laughter to the seated whaler-warriors. They soon wanted in on the fun themselves and approached me of their own accord to greet the starstruck wolfhound face-to-face, who despite his initial squirming, loved the attention. This feat had earned me the rather doldrum but appropriate epithet: Rowdy Dog-Carrier. While being likened to the sort of plastic crate that one buys for the transportation of pets isn't exactly the sort of achievement I'd ever aspired to, it did help ease the tensions immensely. The only downside was that now everyone expected me to perform the stunt each night, but considering the myriad of possible antagonistic alternatives that could have transpired, I was only ever too happy to oblige.

Since that major breakthrough in socializing with these modern vikings, I had heard additional tales of their adventures, ranging from the plundering of the gift shop at Iona Abbey in the Inner Hebrides of Scotland to the "liberation" of several crates of Bushmills Irish Whiskey from their "prison" at the distillery in Northern Ireland to an unsuccessful raid up the River Thames, which had been immediately aborted when the Port of London Authority refused to allow the *Hvalavlinger* to dock at Canary Wharf Pier. But I had yet to hear about the cataclysmic event in Yorkshire that had put an end to Trond's viking expeditions as well as the final nail in the overall Modern Viking Movement's coffin, at least symbolically. The entire phenomenon had supposedly already been waning by the time that it had occurred; an earlier battle between Swedish and Spear-Danish armies had ended in disaster for both sides (and received special attention among the world-wide-web trolls), but Trond's crushing defeat in Yorkshire had definitively marked the end of an era.

It had become increasingly obvious over the course of the past few days that he harbored no desire to discuss his last hurrah. I suspected that each time he relived this moment it wounded his pride and that he did not wish to show such weakness and vulnerability in front of his men, though they of course already knew the history, having experienced it together with him first-hand. He would, no doubt, have preferred to leave the tale untold altogether, but I think that deep down inside he recognized that it was a crucial component of his own personal saga. Not all vikings end their tales with a victorious bang. Some get thrown into a snake pit to die, like Ragnar Lodbrok, or get betrayed and assassinated as part of a secret Danish conspiracy, like Harald Greycloak. Trond's fate wasn't nearly as grim as either of those; he just simply got arrested by the United Kingdom's regional Humberside Police force.

"The place was ominous," Trond muttered in reference to Yorkshire as we continued winding our way through the trees. "Praise be to Odin, we had infiltrated deep into the territory of the Anglo-Saxons without any serious resistance and we felt confident in our plans. Jorvik had fallen out of Norwegian rule long ago, and we sought to reestablish it."

Jorvik is the Old Norse name for the city of York, which was once a hotbed of warring and conflict. The city changed hands many times between English and Norse overlords during the medieval period as the two factions sought dominance over Northumbria, the kingdom to which York had belonged prior to the unification of the larger Kingdom of England as a whole. Perhaps the most famous of its Norse rulers during this period of time was Erik Bloodaxe, who had killed his own brothers and became the life-long nemesis of Egill Skallagrímsson, Iceland's greatest as well as most deranged Viking Age poet and star of his own eponymous saga.

Despite the inclement weather, Trond and his men had marched across the dreary English countryside in admirably high spirits because they had just successfully reclaimed sovereignty over Northumbria and a promise that hostages would soon be delivered to them at Stamford Bridge. To achieve this accomplishment, they had sailed into the mouth of the Humber, past the city of Hull, up the River Ouse, and anchored the *Hvalavlinger* at the small town of Riccall where the Ouse grows too shallow for both longships and whaling vessels to continue further upriver. From there, they marched northwards to York. After a minor run-in at a convenience store in Fulford regarding a certain lack of payment for a number of stolen bottles of iced tea and packages of peppered beef jerky, the vikings entered the ancient city and immediately seized control of the Jorvik Viking Centre.

It was a highly ironic act of fate that allowed them to progress directly to the center of York without any confrontations or other delays. This is because the Jorvik Viking Centre is one of the foremost museums in the world dedicated to the history of the original Viking Age; it has become one of the United Kingdom's top tourist attractions and has been visited by more than nineteen million people since it first opened in 1984. The museum is built around the site of the Coppergate Dig (conducted between 1976 and 1981), which greatly advanced our collective knowledge of the daily lives of the people who lived at the site during the Viking Age. Visitors to the museum are not only given the chance to view its rare collection of unearthed artifacts as well as the foundations of the ancient city, but to also experience its interpretive exhibits and multimedia extravaganza showpieces. Because of the site's archaeological significance and the museum's own renown, Viking Age reenactors have become a rather commonplace commodity in the vicinity of the Jorvik Viking Centre. The sight of a group of swarthy Norwegians bedecked in Old Norse garb and oilskin sou'wester hats wandering the streets of modern York therefore hardly went noticed. Upon arrival, Trond and his entourage casually entered the museum and demanded its immediate surrender.

"Originally, they tried to charge us an admission fee," he recalled. "That's when we unsheathed our swords and flensing knives and declared that the premises were under our control."

They were met with very little resistance, and a few of the museum goers apparently even clapped, thinking that Trond and his cohorts were putting on some sort of historical reenactment performance for their benefit. Shortly afterwards, when the Norwegians refused to depart and the situation rapidly grew awkward, the manager (or "ruler of the house" as Trond preferred to call him) emerged from his "throne room" to "conduct peace talks." In short, the entire museum capitulated to Neo-Norse demands within minutes, agreeing to submit to Norwegian rule and to relinquish all of the gold and silver that had been stored in the ticket booth cash registers. Furthermore, the manager promised to give Trond hostages.

The exchange of hostages was standard procedure in medieval peace negotiations; the transfer of loved ones and/or high status individuals to the victorious party generally ensured that the defeated party would comply with the terms of the agreement, since hostages could very easily be killed by those who held them captive. Arrangements were thus made for Trond to receive the English hostages later that day at the village of Stamford Bridge. Leaving several of his most trusted men behind to guard the museum, he and the rest of his gang set out for the journey to the agreed upon location nine miles east of York. They say that history repeats itself and appropriately so, because Trond marched into a trap just as Harald Hardrada had done nearly a thousand years before him.

Stamford Bridge was the site of a decisive battle that had been fought in 1066 between the English forces of King Harold Godwinson and the Norwegian forces of King Harald Hardrada and Earl Tostig Godwinson, Harold's brother. Harold Godwinson had assumed the crown at the start of the year after the death of his predecessor, King Edward the Confessor, which had resulted in a highly contested matter of succession. Multiple claimants vied for the throne, including Harald Hardrada and Tostig Godwinson. The English army won the Battle of Stamford Bridge, killing both Harald and Tostig and effectively ending Norway's meddling in medieval British affairs. The battle, however, took such a toll on the English army that when it next marched south to face the invading Normans three weeks later at Hastings, it was easily routed and William the Bastard claimed the crown. The rest, as the saying goes, is history.

But whereas Harald Hardrada had been able to enjoy some nice weather when he marched his troops to Stamford Bridge, Trond Troll-Breath was not so lucky. Plus, he and his men, all of whom were well aware of Hardrada's resounding defeat, experienced a strange and unsettling sense of déjà vu that only grew increasingly pervasive as they neared their destination.

"A sudden stillness fell over the men as we crossed the bridge and entered the village." Trond stroked his woolly beard as we walked the trail. "Echoes of the distant past wailed on the wind, and the cries of our fallen brothers who perished so long ago came alive on the stages of our memory-theaters. All was eerie, and all was foreboding."

The Norwegians continued eastward through the small village center until they encountered a monument dedicated to the battle that had taken place there nearly one thousand years before. The monument itself consists of an erect stone mounted atop a boulder set within a small paved space overgrown with weeds and surrounded by freestanding brick walls on three sides. Two of these walls are very low and simply serve as back-rests to the wooden benches mounted to their faces. Adjacent to the monument is a parking lot and the village's main road.

Having reached the agreed-upon location before the English retinue that was designated to bring the hostages, the Norwegians spent the intervening time paying their respects to their forefathers who had perished somewhere near here so long ago. Some bent their knees in quiet contemplation while others simply took a seat and reminisced aloud about the historic significance of the location. And it was precisely in the midst of these individual reflections on the past that the Humberside Police careened into sight with sirens blaring and surrounded the vikings.

"One minute we were silently respecting the dead while we waited for the hostages to arrive," said Trond of the sudden turn of events, shaking his head. "And the next we were surrounded by the Anglo-Saxon infantry."

He paused and sighed, giving away his little tell-tale sign that he was conjuring up some majestic word-play.

> "Bright-eyed warriors of bobby-sticks battled
> Fierce wielders of flense-hooks fell
> Broken in Britain's brooding gloom
> Forever defeated in deafening doom."

It was apparent that the weight of the defeat still clung to his spirits like a damp sack of rotten potatoes and he elaborated further as we walked.

Basically, the Norwegians didn't even stand a chance. Caught by surprise, the police rounded up the men who were too slow to react and then chased down everyone else who had attempted to flee; their baggy woolen garments and thick furs slowed their movement and they were easily apprehended. Trond claimed that he did not know how the police, or "Anglo-Saxon infantry" as he insisted on calling them, had come to know of their presence, but I suspected that a well-timed phone call from the Jorvik Viking Centre's manager combined with those of various residents who, perhaps upon peering out their windows to witness a large group of scowling men carrying an alarming assortment of medieval weaponry and nasty-looking whaling utensils, had probably notified the authorities of the trouble brewing.

"What happened next?" I asked, wondering whether the Norwegians had spent any time in an English jail cell. Though I said nothing of the sort aloud, it also occurred to me that this incident probably presented the English legal system with its most bizarre case since 1975, when a group of marauding Knights of the Round Table were arrested for a series of hostile and violent altercations.

"The Anglo-Saxons confiscated our ship and all the loot we had stowed on board," Trond answered. "We were held prisoner for several days, at which point we were quickly arraigned and deported back to Norway. The *Hvalavlinger* was returned to us and we were given leave to sail it home. Our voyage was accompanied by three Anglo-Saxon vessels until we arrived in Oslo, where we awaited an audience with the king. He levied a steep were-geld on behalf of the prime minister as payment for our actions, which he slandered as criminal. In the old days I would have sought freedom in Iceland, away from such tyranny, but all the good land has already been claimed in that country. The world is not what it once was, and I was forced to sell the *Hvalavlinger* to pay the fine. But the king and his retinue never learned about the leprechauns and I had already established the shoe-manufacturing business here, which has only prospered ever since.

"The Anglo-Saxon victory was decisive," he stated. "And I have learned to accept that. Fate goes ever as fate must."

I nodded in agreement at his blatant rip-off of Seamus Heaney's translation of *Beowulf* and neither of us said anything more. Silently, we changed direction and began the trek back towards the mead hall. One more evening of revelry remained.

The next morning was a typical one at the mead hall with breakfast served by the muesli maidens as sleepy men sporadically drifted in and out of the main room from their private quarters. Trond called a water-taxi to come fetch me and then presented me with two fine gifts: a pair of top-quality, Mjölnir-embossed Trondsko hiking boots that I intended to keep in my suitcase, safely protected from the grime and muck of my present travels so that they'd be fresh and ready to tackle the mountains of New England in the coming spring, and the massive mead horn that I'd been drinking from every night during my stay. I still didn't know what kind of animal had been used to make it and I feared that U.S. Customs would probably attempt to confiscate it when I eventually returned home, but it was a glorious and meaningful gift, engraved with exquisitely detailed snakes and serpents along its outer circumference. Fortunately, I had come prepared myself, and so I presented him with a can of B&M Boston's Best Baked Beans and a box of Maine-made maple leaf-shaped sugar candy. He seemed uninterested in the beans, but immediately opened the box of maple candy and began devouring the pieces ravenously.

I shook hands with the rest of the men and hugged the maidens good-bye, which constituted the only physical contact I encountered with any of those glorious valkyries. The wolfhounds sensed something was amiss and collectively wandered towards me, nuzzling my leg, and I knelt down and gave each one a good ear scratch and belly rub.

"Well, Rowdy, sure's been good havin' ya here with us." Henrik approached to say good-bye. He had been out checking on the leprechauns while most of this had been happening, and I was glad to see him. While I admired Trond for his impressive leadership abilities, his tendency towards overwrought and poetic oratory, and his just general resolute vikingness, he always seemed to be a bit aloof. Henrik, on the other hand, was the one individual among the entire lot who I felt I was able to connect with somewhat on a more personal level.

"Thanks, Henrik," I said, standing up. "It's been a blast and I appreciate all that you've done for me."

We chatted a bit, covering the usual pleasantries that one does during good-byes, when Trond shouted from across the room, "Rowdy, your vessel awaits!" He was staring at a smart phone—the first instance that I had seen him use one—and I realized that he must have received some sort of text or in-app status update about the boat's arrival. I grabbed my bags and hurried out the door to the sounds of raucous cheering and the salutes of raised coffee cups.

I saw the small boat at the bottom of the hill and scuttled down the path towards it as quickly as I could. I crossed the trail that led to the leprechaun barn and momentarily considered making a detour. This was the first time that I'd been outside the facility on my own since my first morning here. The nagging sensation of a bad conscience crept up my spine and I considered whether I should throw caution to the wind and rush to the barn in an attempt to set the leprechauns loose. They were clearly being mistreated and kept in horrid conditions.

But then again, that's only if they even actually existed. Nothing I had seen in the past week could actually confirm that I wasn't being played for a fool; the enormous ass of an elaborate prank involving a group of modern-day Norwegian medieval enthusiasts who simply run a top-notch tourist facility and whose members perhaps conveniently include several men afflicted with a standard case of human dwarfism.

But the boat waited, and like so many times before in my life, I gave apathy the victory and continued down towards the dock. I consoled my guilty conscience by telling myself that as improbable as the existence of leprechauns might be, I had better get used to encountering such fabulous contradictions to my generally science-driven world view. The notion of folkloric beings actually existing, even if only in the minds of the individuals whom I sought out, was at least very real.

I would next be heading east, to the Kingdom of the Swedes, to meet two men who had supposedly not only encountered a most peculiar dragon, but had also slain it.

THREE TALES OF
NORTHERN HEROIC ROMANTICISM

DUMB DRAGON'S DOOM

It had happened that a dragon awoke from his slumber and began to ravage the countryside along Sweden's High Coast, an eighty-mile stretch of rugged landscape facing the Baltic Sea roughly midway between Stockholm and the Arctic Circle. The dragon was malevolent, as dragons are wont to be, but this particular specimen's behavior was uniquely characterized by some atypical peculiarities. Rather than bringing widespread despair and destruction to the people by scorching their fields, livestock, and farmhouses, or stealing away maidens and loot, as is the habit of most dragons, this creature only haphazardly attempted to accomplish these deeds, failing more often than succeeding, with the result being that he became more of a destructive nuisance than a serious threat to the population. Potential victims observed that he bobbed up and down and sagged to one side as he struggled to fly and, when diving towards the ground in an assault born of some sort of enfeebled fury, he would frequently crash into his target rather than engulf it in flames. Furthermore, he made a deafening roar that sounded garbled and confused as he flew above the otherwise not-so-fear-stricken Swedes. Nonetheless, it was all too much to bear and his otherwise ineffective harassment affected the contentment of the people. It became clear that this dragon, like so many others before him, needed vanquishing.

That's what the unsubstantiated reports about this legendary creature boiled down to, anyway. I reviewed them as the train sped through the densely forested mountains of Swedish Jämtland, an interior county that borders Norway about 2/3 of the way up along the axis of the Scandinavian peninsula. The luggage bins were now cluttered with the skis and ski poles of Stockholmers and other Svealand and Götaland urbanites who were returning south from Åre, a town known primarily for its downhill ski resorts, to resume their office jobs after a brief respite from the godforsaken daily grind.

The Scandinavian nations, excluding Denmark, are rather large in land area in comparison to most Western European countries. The terrain is rugged and the population is sparse, and as a result, the transportation networks are less extensive than one might assume, particularly the farther north one goes. So, despite having begun my journey in central Trondheim at the start of the morning, I would be spending this entire day on trains and at train stations. I wouldn't arrive at my destination in Örnsköldsvik till nighttime.

The sun was already sinking in the west over the big lake that bears the name Storsjön as the train rolled into Östersund, the capital of Jämtland. I watched as the uniformity of the lake's frozen, white surface slid past just beyond the windows. The island of Frösön—literally and appropriately meaning "Frozen Island" in Swedish—could be seen across the sheet of ice.

Storsjön is rumored to harbor a monster of its own beneath its frigid and crusty surface. Storsjöodjuret, as the beastie is called by locals, was first sighted in 1635 and is said to still inhabit its aquatic lair. Resembling a serpentine-reptile-thing with a dog-like head, Storsjöodjuret was put on the endangered species list in 1986 by the local county administrative board. This special designation has since been revoked, so the creature can now be legally slain if ever found, but fewer and fewer sightings have occurred in recent years. Nonetheless, its notoriety lives on at Jämtli, a museum in Östersund dedicated to local history and culture, including that of the monster.

I read about all of this from actual, legitimate online sources as the train once again began to move. I would certainly have enjoyed stopping in Östersund for a few days to explore the city and the lake and learn more about Sweden's own little twist on the Loch Ness Monster, but there had been no unsubstantiated online rumors about modern-day Norsemen infiltrating its lair or interfering with its livelihood, so I had not designated any time in Östersund. Instead, I had a hotel reservation waiting for me at the First Hotel in Örnsköldsvik later that night and an itinerary that I needed to keep.

I was surrounded by everything Boston. Victory-banners that displayed the years of every professional sports championship that the big four Boston teams have ever won were on prominent display. Bill Belichick glared at me from the far wall, Larry Bird smiled at me from his nook in the opposite corner, and the music of The Dropkick Murphys reverberated throughout the establishment, reminding everyone present that it was, in fact, time to ship up to Boston to find our wooden legs. I had just entered the O'Leary's Sports Bar and Restaurant in Örnsköldsvik.

O'Leary's is a Swedish chain that has basically out-Bostoned Boston at being Boston ever since it first opened the doors of its original restaurant in Gothenburg in 1988. It is now a hugely successful franchise located in every moderately-sized or larger Swedish city, as well as Singapore, oddly enough. The chain was founded by Jonas Reinholdsson and Anne O'Leary in the wake of a romance that had sparked between them one summer when their paths crossed on Nantucket. Anne eventually followed Jonas back to his home in Sweden where they subsequently launched their business.

All of which makes sense because, aside from summer vacationers and the seasonal service-sector workers hired to cater to them, Nantucket is a place that most people would choose to flee. I know this because I have lived across the sound in Buzzards Bay on Cape Cod; Massachusetts' entire Cape and Islands region seesaws dramatically between the one extremity of insanity-inducing hoards of summer tourists and the other extremity of complete and utter winter desolation with no happy middle-ground to be found.

Örnsköldsvik's O'Leary's establishment was at least conveniently located close to my hotel and occupied prime real estate in the heart of the city, right on Stora Torget (a generic term for "the big square" found in many Swedish cities). The square itself, while pleasant enough with its open space, cobbled pavement, and trees at its opposite end where it transitioned into a park, was mostly bounded by brutalist, modern buildings.

The square's pavement was covered in a two-inch-thick slab of ice upon which bucketloads of gravel had been dumped in an effort to help with pedestrian traction. The north-facing shadows cast by the adjacent concrete behemoths further contributed to the scene's pervasive feeling of frozen forlornness. O'Leary's itself was housed in one of the exceptions to the dominant architectural brutality, occupying the ground floor of a more ornate, historic building instead.

After my initial BOSTON BOSTON BOSTON sensory overload dissipated, I began to notice some distinctions between O'Leary's and actual sports bars in Boston, namely that the television screens here were all tuned to European soccer matches and that the bartender, waiters, and waitresses all wore matching white and green uniforms that, perhaps without coincidence, made them look like they were all part of an Irish soccer squad. Additionally, a mannequin decked out in full hockey gear and a Modo jersey lurked near the bathrooms in deference to a major source of local pride for the city. The great Peter Forsberg had played for Örnsköldsvik's Modo hockey club before making his NHL debut with the Nordiques during their final season in Quebec in the mid-1990s. They had moved to Denver the following season, becoming the Colorado Avalanche and winning two Stanley Cups with Foppa (as he's locally known), Joe Sakic, Patrick Roy, and for the latter of the two, Boston's own Ray Bourque.

I arrived early for my forthcoming meeting with the self-proclaimed dragon-slayers, so I walked to the bar and took a seat by myself. The burly and heavily tattooed bartender with a shaved head saw me and idled his way closer.

"*Tjena. Något att dricka?*" he asked.

I surveyed the tap line, which included several staple Swedish lagers, a few local microbrews, a Czech beer, Guinness, and two different beers by Brooklyn Brewery. I personally feel that it is a roundabout insult to Boston's pride that O'Leary's has established some sort of agreement with Brooklyn Brewery rather than Samuel Adams; it is actually easier to find Brooklyn Brewery beer on tap in Sweden than it is in the U.S. outside of the Tri-State area. I'll openly admit that I like Brooklyn Brewery's beer, but I felt the ancient rivalry rising up within me, and so I resolved myself to refrain from imbibing a New York beer in a Boston bar in Sweden and instead went for the Stora Oredan, a strong English-style bitter ale meaning "The Big Mess" brewed by Bryggeriet Stenhammaren in Sundsvall, another small city about two hours south of Örnsköldsvik where I had changed trains for the final stint of my extended rail travel the day before.

The bartender nodded, fetched a pint glass, and began pouring the frothy ale. We watched the liquid cascade into the glass in mutual silence. When it was full, he wiped it down with his rag and set it on the wooden bar in front of me.

"*Ska du äta?*" He looked at me blankly.

"*Nej...eller inte just nu in varje fall, men får jag ta lite popcorn?*"

He nodded his head affirmatively, scooped some popcorn into a straw basket from the popping-machine behind him, and left me to nibble the buttery morsels and nurse my beer undisturbed.

I had finished all of the popcorn and was about halfway through my beer, contemplating the meaning of life while listening to Steve Tyler croon about dudes who look like ladies over the speakers, when someone sat down beside me and asked, "*Är det du som är Rowdy?*"

I answered that, yes, I am Rowdy, and he introduced himself as Stieg Blomkvist, the individual whom I had arranged to meet here to discuss the supposed dragon-slaying incident. He looked to be in his mid-to-late 20s, with bright blue eyes, a clean-shaven face, and short, blond hair.

"Your Bruins hat gave you away." He switched to English as most Swedes do when they hear my awful accent. "Everything in here is about Boston, but you are the only person who is actually wearing something with Boston on it."

Accompanying him was another guy, much shorter and completely bald except for the long strands of dyed black hair that flowed down from the follicles ringing the rim of his shiny scalp. His face remained entirely devoid of expression and his stare was distant and gone. He drooled a little as Stieg helped him onto his seat.

"Is this Åke?" I asked and Stieg confirmed that it was.

Åke Nordansjö had supposedly been Stieg's brother-in-arms in their quest to slay the dragon. All of my correspondence had been with Stieg over Facebook; finding him on that omnipotent nightmare of digital interconnectivity had been rather easy, especially since his name had been specifically mentioned in the various chat boards that I had been perusing about the incident. I had looked for Åke as well, because he too had been named by the digital trolls, but I hadn't found him, and at some point during our online exchange Stieg had mentioned that Åke was not technologically adept and essentially lived his life entirely offline. More power to him, I had thought at the time.

Åke settled into his seat and the bartender came over to take the newcomers' drink orders. Stieg ordered a *stor stark*—a common Swedish term for whatever "big strong" basic beer the bar has on tap and chooses to pour for anyone who requests their drink in such generic terms. The importance here is not the brand or style of beer itself, but the fact that it is a full pint and full strength. Sweden maintains several categories of beer strength ranging from the weak/inferior kind that only contains about 2% alcohol and that can be bought at regular grocery stores and convenience stores to the highly cherished and infinitely superior *stor stark*, which is really just normal strength beer that wouldn't be considered anything special anywhere else. Its status is revered in Sweden because the government has highly regulated the product in an effort to stem widespread drunkenness and alcoholism since the 1800s. Stieg would probably be given a pint of Åbro or Falcon Lager.

The bartender looked at Åke inquisitively and Åke, seemingly startled by this attention, twitched and declared, "Doom!" The bartender raised an eyebrow and looked from Åke to Stieg, who ordered a second *stor stark* for his demented little companion.

"Yeah...so, uh...the thing with Åke is, he has problems with his brain," Stieg explained.

"Has he always had these problems?" I asked.

"Well, no, and I'll explain that more a bit later. You will see."

The bartender brought the two *stor starks* and the three of us attempted a toast. Stieg and I raised our glasses—mine mostly empty at this point—while Åke simply grabbed his with both hands and appeared to strangle the thing. Stieg reached over, grasped the top of the glass, and tried to lift it, telling Åke in Swedish that we were toasting now. A minor struggle ensued after which Stieg gave up, turned back to me, and shrugged his shoulders. We clinked a joyous if somewhat subdued "skål!" to one another. Åke meanwhile had already begun to chug his beer.

Stieg and I chatted a bit about my trip from Trondheim and what I thought of Örnsköldsvik so far. It was a pleasant little place, to be sure, as most Swedish cities are. I'd had the day free to explore but most of the attractions for visitors in this part of the country are related to the natural wonders associated with the High Coast, which is noteworthy for its unusually rapid land uplift, a geological phenomenon that has been occurring since the last Ice Age. As a result, the region is a great place for outdoor exploration, with many trails, open-air museums, and boating excursions available in the summer. So, instead, I had basically wandered the city and then camped out with my laptop at the local Espresso House, a Swedish chain inspired by but better than Starbucks, which was located near the O'Leary's in which I was now ordering a fresh round of *stor starks* for myself and my two dragon-slaying drinking buddies.

Stieg explained that he and Åke had been students at the Umeå School of Architecture when the dragon first appeared. Umeå is the largest city in Sweden's historical province of Norrland, which comprises approximately the northern 2/3 of the country. The city itself lies about an hour to the north of Örnsköldsvik and I would be heading there when I left Örnsköldsvik the following day, not because I had found anyone to interview there, but because I needed to catch a ferry at its harbor to my next destination.

Eventually, the conversation turned to the topic that had brought us together in the first place: the new millennium's only purported dragon-slaying. Word of the dragon's reign of bother had spread far and wide by the time Stieg and Åke caught wind of it, but as with all of the other events associated with the Modern Viking Movement, reports of the dragon's disturbances were limited to social media gossip, obscure chat-rooms, and fake news outlets that catered to the unhinged and fringe elements of society. But once the first student at the Umeå School of Architecture learned of the ongoing disturbances, rumors about the misfit creature took off and spread like wildfire through the student studio space.

"You know, most of the other students were actually concerned with the dragon's well-being," Stieg said. "They wanted to protect it and were working on a petition that they were going to try to show to the municipal government or something. But me and Åke, we just looked at each other and I think we had the same thought at the same time. We thought that if we could find this dragon first, maybe we could kill it and then take all of its gold."

"Doom doom doom..." Åke babbled with mild excitement from his stool.

"Because, you know," Stieg continued, "having a big treasure like that would really make a big difference in our lives."

This was practical wisdom, I admitted. While Sweden doesn't suffer from the same insultingly high sky-rocketing costs of education that the U.S. does, the career prospects for many of its higher education students remain disappointing in comparison to those that graduates from previous generations encountered, to say the least. There may not be any tuition expenses for students in Sweden, but the cost of living isn't free, so loans are still often necessary. And like anywhere else, graduates enter a deeply entrenched job market that is only a ghastly fraction of what it once was. So, even in Sweden, education just doesn't go as far as it used to, and consequently, Stieg and Åke grew increasingly disgruntled with the knowledge that they were most likely going to plunge headlong into extremely depressing, entry-level jobs with very limited potential when they graduated. The notion of spending 50-60 hours per week mindlessly manipulating the latest bug-infested architectural software programs to update window sash details is enough to bring anyone to the brink of despair.

"We had a big decision to make," Stieg said between sips of beer. "We had a big crit coming up—you know when the students present their design ideas for feedback in an informal sort of way. Usually, you get torn apart during these crits. Not like how a dragon would tear you apart physically with its teeth and claws and all that; it's more like a verbal abuse thing. Most architects are very angry people. They wanted to be the next 'starchitect,' as you say in English, when they were younger, but their biggest accomplishment ended up being to help design a ho-hum apartment building or something like that, so they became very bitter and then they got a part-time job lecturing at a university to channel their rage onto the next generation of architects. It is a vicious cycle."

"Doom!" Åke exclaimed, slamming his pint glass on the bar and causing a handful of bewildered stares to look our way.

"Even Åke still has strong feelings about this, as you can see," Stieg added. "I don't know why he always expresses them in English instead of Swedish, but that is besides the point. Anyway, we were considering our options. We could either stay up all night and try to finish making our models for the crit the next day, or we could stay up all night and try to go slay a dragon and take all of its treasure. In the end, it was a very easy decision to make."

It was a lovely early autumn day when the two would-be dragon slayers abandoned their architectural designs and set out upon their quest. Umeå's numerous birch trees had begun to turn bright yellow as they walked along Umeälven, the river that courses through the city and runs alongside the design school, till they reached the esplanade in the center of town and began following it to the train station. Armed with only their wits and a strange assortment of utility knives and sharp architectural drafting tools, they boarded the first train to Örnsköldsvik.

Örnsköldsvik is generally considered to be the northern terminus of the High Coast, and while several dragon sightings had been reported from the city's outlook point at Varvsberget—an outdoor recreational area very close to the center of town that includes a ski jump, shops and restaurants, as well as a golf course founded by

Peter Forsberg himself—most of the creature's activity had been reported from communities farther to the south.

"Once we had arrived, we decided that taking the High Coast Trail would be the best thing for us to do," Stieg said. "The trail, you know, starts in Örnsköldsvik and goes all the way down to Hornön where the famous High Coast Bridge is."

I had seen photos of this bridge, but famous is a relative word. Well-renowned in Sweden, and perhaps Finland, but few from any other nation would likely know of it. But the point was well-taken because it is one of Sweden's most impressive bridges; it is, in fact, the longest suspension bridge in the country. It looks somewhat similar to California's Bay Bridge, except that instead of a backdrop of sky-scrapers, automobiles, ferries, and the sprawling filth and urbanity of twenty million people, the High Coast Bridge anchors a serene scene of sparsely-populated and heavily-forested hills with water spreading in every direction.

Upon disembarking at Örnsköldsvik, Stieg and Åke began their hike south. They passed through suburban neighborhoods and wooded parkland and then crossed over the river, Moälven, as they moved farther and farther away from modern civilization.

"We were searching everywhere." Stieg finished his beer. "In our search for the dragon."

"Ready for another?" I asked.

It was basically a rhetorical question and I made eye contact with the bartender. He came over and I ordered us all another round. O'Leary's playlist was now blasting the classic rock hit "More Than a Feeling" and the establishment had filled up in the time since Stieg and Åke had joined me. A middle-aged man who appeared to be alone had sat down beside me at the bar, but most people who had entered the premises were couples, friends, or families, and most were here to partake in the chain's hugely popular "After Work" all-you-can-eat dinner buffet. Sweden has always been a very family-friendly nation, even at its drinking establishments.

Stieg attempted to pay for the latest round of *stor starks*. I, of course, objected, feeling that I should cover all of our drinks for the evening since he and Åke were doing me a favor by joining me and recounting their exploits for my personal benefit. He backed off but insisted that he get the next round, which offered a clear indication of how he envisioned the rest of the evening going. When Swedes drink, they drink to win, and so we weren't likely to reach the end of standard regulation time for this match anytime soon.

We clinked glasses with Åke actually attempting to join the toast this time. His spastic motion sloshed beer onto Stieg's shirt and while Stieg and I each declared "skål!" in unison, Åke quite literally shouted "doom!" which in turn caused other patrons to once again stare at us disapprovingly.

Stieg immediately reprimanded Åke. He spoke quickly and harshly in Swedish, telling Åke to use his big boy voice.

"So, what signs were you looking for in your search of the dragon?" I asked once the chastising had ended. "How would you know if you were getting close or not?"

"Ah, yes, so you see, there were reports that the dragon had burned many trees in the area," Stieg answered. "I don't know why he was burning trees. I think he attempted to burn a few farms as well, but the farmers had chased him off with their remote-controlled drones. For some reason, he was very scared of those small things. Maybe it was the buzzing noise they make, I don't know. But he was very bad at breathing fire onto buildings, so I think he vented his frustrations on helpless, defenseless trees instead."

"So, in a way, he was kind of like the dragon equivalent of one of your professors," I quipped.

"Yes, yes, he was!" Stieg lit up at this comment. "He could not succeed where he wanted to, so he just caused mindless destruction. But because of that, we expected that we would start seeing dead trees. So, we thought maybe if we followed the most burned-out parts of the woods, we would eventually find his lair."

The two adventurers continued their journey south along winding roads and pedestrian-only trails that wove through the High Coast's glacially carved landscape. Dense woods made way for tranquil lakes and the small villages and pasture lands that had originally cropped up beside them in a bygone era. Away from these settlements and the eternal life-giving force of fresh water, the woods closed in again, leading down dark, shady valleys before ascending up to the crest of rocky ridges that offered spectacular views of the slate gray sea on the eastern horizon. On several occasions, a forlorn logging truck ambled past the two trekkers towards some unknown, distant destination.

After nearly six hours of walking, and as civilization gradually faded farther and farther away while the countless birch and pine trees crowded in closer and closer, Stieg and Åke found themselves at the northern entrance to Skuleskogen National Park. Here, the road for vehicular traffic came to a complete and final end, and only those on foot could continue along established trails.

"That was when we first knew we were on the right track," Stieg noted. "It had been a long walk already, for sure, and we had not seen any signs of dragon destruction. So, you can understand that we might have been feeling, oh…a little uncertain about our choice to follow this particular path. But then when we got to the little rest area at the park's entrance, we saw so many burned up trees. The building with the toilets was, of course, untouched. But the trees around it were all dead, black and burned with dragon fire."

"Doom!" Åke sloshed his beer excitedly.

"So, we took a quick break because, you know, the rest area was nice and clean, and then we went into the park. We followed the trail and enjoyed the nature. It really is a spectacular place, and I was afraid that the dragon would have destroyed many of its natural wonders. For example, the long-bearded old-man lichens hanging from the tree branches. Do you know about these?"

I answered that I did not.

"Oh, well, they are quite rare, and we were quite pleased to get to see them on our way to kill the dragon. They are very spooky-looking and Skuleskogen is one of the few places that has many of them. The dragon had left the trees they were on alone, though, thankfully. But as we walked farther into the park, we could see that he had been busy. There were more and more dead trees the farther we went."

Stieg and Åke continued following the High Coast Trail as it wound its way deeper and deeper into the park and closer to

Slåttdalsberget, the main focal point of the landscape. This massive granite outcropping rises two hundred and eighty-two meters above sea level and the extensive views offered from its crown are often the primary goal of visitors to the park. It is dramatic terrain, rarely level, with many damp and shady gorges and crevices hidden from the light.

"It was when we were passing by Tärnättvatnen—a little lake at the base of the mountain—that we noticed the first dragon droppings," Stieg said. "They were very large and appeared to have bird and rodent bones in them. I suppose because the dragon was ineffective at eating people or their pets or animals like cows and chickens, he had to resort to small wildlife."

Something about this seemed symbolically appropriate to me. In the worldview of Norse mythology, a mean-spirited dragon known as Níðhöggr gnaws upon the roots of Yggdrasil, the celestial world tree, while a smart-ass eagle perches atop its leafy limbs and the two creatures trade vicious insults with one another via a squirrel-messenger known as Ratatoskr who runs up and down the tree's trunk to deliver these defamatory remarks. So, Skuleskogen's dragon was simply enacting Níðhöggr's ultimate revenge by killing, eating, and defecating both its enemy and the messenger.

"Shortly after we spotted those droppings, we found its lair," Stieg continued. "Actually, it was Åke who found it—"

"Dddooooommmmmmm...." Åke interrupted with a long, drawnout rumination on his favorite word.

"Yes, so anyway, Åke found its lair not far from there. The droppings led straight to it, actually. It was in the base of this big gorge with rock walls on both sides. It was late in the day, and so the sun was low in the sky and the gorge itself was very dark, but you could clearly see the droppings leading into it. So, Åke just took off without saying a word and I had to hurry to catch up. We didn't have to go very far. There was a small ledge a short ways into the gorge, and beneath it the dragon was sleeping. He was smaller than we thought he would be. Maybe about the size of a big horse, not counting his tail, which he seemed to have in his mouth while he slept, like an infant sucking its thumb or something."

"Or the Midgård Serpent," I added. The Midgård Serpent is the monstrous snake-thing that lies at the bottom of the ocean. The mortal enemy of the thunder god, Thor, he is so large that he fully encircles the world, biting on his own tail in his aquatic abode beneath the waves.

Stieg nodded in agreement and took another sip of beer. All three of us were nearing the bottoms of our pint glasses again and another round would soon be in order. Åke appeared to have lost what little interest he had maintained in our conversation so far for the moment. His head was turned away from us and he appeared to be mindlessly gawking at two very attractive blond women who had just recently seated themselves beside him at the bar.

"*Hej du, Åke—Åke, lyssna nu!*" Stieg tapped Åke on the shoulder and began to lecture him about proper public behavior. It seemed to work because Åke turned away from the women and looked up at Stieg with big, puppy-dog eyes, then guzzled the rest of his beer, set his glass back down, and stared off into space once again.

"Right, so...yes, we saw the dragon sleeping and so we crept up to it," Stieg resumed his story. "And then we got out our utility knives and our T-squares."

A T-square is an architectural drafting tool used to accurately draw perpendicular lines, usually made of metal or a combination of metal and plastic, that consists of a longer piece attached to the midpoint of a shorter piece, thus resembling the letter T in shape. Held at the base of the long piece, a T-square could potentially function as a dorky, make-shift axe.

"At this point, Åke stepped on a twig," Stieg continued. "Which of course made a loud sound, and the dragon woke up. I think we startled him because he bit the tip of his tail, and then he roared with the fire going right past us but not touching us, and then he turned and looked at us and you could see that he was angry. Very, very angry. Fortunately, we were standing next to a boulder, so we jumped behind it when he tried to burn us alive. But his tail was still fluttering around by his head when this happened, so he accidentally set his own tail on fire and began to freak out. We just stood behind the boulder and watched as he burned himself to death."

"I always thought that dragon's were immune to their own fire." I was surprised.

"So did I, but it was very dark in that gorge, and it was a close-quarters situation, and this dragon seemed very clumsy."

"Doom!" Åke rejoined our conversation with his loudest outburst yet. Stieg shot him a stern, disapproving glance, to which he of course seemed utterly oblivious. Thankfully, Ric Ocasek of The Cars was now singing rather loudly about his best friend's girl over O'Leary's sound system, so the patrons farthest from us did not seem to notice Åke's disruptive behavior. The women sitting beside him, however, jumped in their seats, and the bartender told us to keep it down. Stieg apologized on behalf of his friend and ordered another round of *stor starks*.

Not wishing to plunge through the fire and flame to inspect the bedding beneath the dead dragon for signs of treasure, the two architecture students had simply watched the dragon's corpse burn until it slowly began to smolder. Using their T-squares, they then poked around at the belly of the beast, hoping to discover whatever gold coins may have lain hidden beneath the animal's scaly gut.

"There was no treasure," Stieg sighed. The melancholy of his voice was as thick as the pile of chicken wings and rice on the plate of the middle-aged loner sitting beside me. "That had been the whole reason we were there, you know? We wanted the treasure, but this dragon, he had some sort of mental impairment. He couldn't terrorize farmers properly; all he did was set trees on fire, and now we found out he had never bothered to steal any gold to use to make his bed, either."

"But you were witness to the first death of a dragon in...well, maybe you witnessed the first death of a dragon ever." I tried to be supportive without being too blatantly incredulous.

"This is true, and we made sure we weren't going to return home empty-handed. We had our phones with us, so we took many photos of the carcass. And then we decided, hey, maybe somebody would be willing to pay us for the dragon's skull, so we cut it off. It took quite some time, as we only had our utility knives to use and dragon spines are awfully thick and boney."

"Doom," Åke stated matter-of-factly.

"Could I see the photos?" I asked.

"Sure," Stieg answered, pulling his phone out of his pocket. His fingers swiped across the glossy screen till he found the images of interest and handed the device to me. I scrolled through them slowly, digesting them as best I could. The quality was very poor. Even though a fire smoldered in each image, providing some source of light, it wasn't enough to capture much detail. For all I knew, I was looking at photographs of a trash heap burning in the woods. I thanked Stieg and returned the phone.

"Anyway, as you can probably imagine, we were becoming quite hungry by this point," he continued. "We had only eaten granola on our entire journey, and now we had worked up a sweat sawing the dragon's head off. And, well, the dragon was already cooked since he had barbecued himself in front of us. The roast meat smelled so good."

"Doom," Åke stated again.

"So, we finished with the head, and set it aside, and then we began to carve off pieces of dragon meat for dinner."

"Doom."

"You know, dragon actually tastes very much like chicken. But the wings are much meatier."

"Doom."

"We had quite a feast that night. There was no sauce, though. I would have liked some sauce, but the dragon had cooked himself perfectly, so we were happy."

"Doom."

"I was getting full, but Åke kept going back for more meat. He has always had an insatiable appetite, even though he is so short. Eventually, I noticed that he had started to cut through the dragon's rib cage."

"Doom."

"So, he finished cutting through the ribcage, and then he stuck his hand into the dragon's chest cavity, and he pulled out the dragon's heart."

"Doom."

"And he held it there in his bare hands and he looked at me with this strange smile on his face, and then he took a bite out of it."

"DOOM! DOOM! DOOM! DOOM! DOOM! DOOM!..." Åke erupted into a blaring cacophony of chanting and, with The Pixies' "Where is My Mind?" playing in the background, we were immediately instructed to leave the O'Leary's premises.

I took a bite out of my cheeseburger and wiped the grease from my lips. We were seated at one of the spartan white tables of Örnsköldsvik's local Max, one of Sweden's largest, home-grown fast-food chains. The restaurant was housed in a little, stand-alone building beside a traffic circle on the edge of the central part of the city near the train station. We had walked a half mile to get here after our ignominious departure from O'Leary's. Åke had continued to mumble his thoughts and opinions about the concept of "doom" with various intonations, and the few people that we had encountered en route simply assumed that we were the drunken hooligans that we only appeared to be and steered clear.

Stieg had explained while we walked that prior to Åke's attempt to make a final dinner course of the dragon's heart, he had been a fully functioning human being of normal intelligence. The Norse myths are riddled with stories of heroes who slay dragons, eat their hearts, and gain arcane knowledge, like the ability to understand the language of birds. But none of them have ever broached the subject of what might happen if one attempted to eat the heart of a mentally-impaired dragon, and Åke had unfortunately found out the hard way.

"But that skull, you know, it fetched a good price," Stieg said while dipping some fries in an accompanying honey curry sauce. As with most home-grown Swedish restaurant chains, Max offers more interesting and extensive menu options than we are generally accustomed to in the U.S. "Of course, it was the state that paid for it, but we have a decent finder's fee here. We tried to sell our photos to some of the local newspapers, too, but none of them were interested."

Having seen the photos, I could understand why, but I was surprised that there weren't any reports about the transaction with the government. It seemed like the sort of thing that journalists would have eaten up, especially if doing so could make the local authorities look bad for potentially having been duped by a couple of students. Maybe Åke genuinely suffered an injury that caused brain damage in Skuleskogen National Park, perhaps from eating a dumb dragon's heart, or perhaps from falling down a ravine. Or maybe he was just damn good at playing his role. I didn't know, but as with each of my previous experiences so far in this mission, I had yet to see any truly conclusive evidence that supported the story I was being told.

"Well, it sounds like in some ways it all worked out, at least," I acknowledged. "Except for Åke's issues, anyway."

"I suppose you could say so."

"So, what do you do now? You had to fall back on architecture, right, since there was no dragon treasure?"

"Yes." Stieg dumped the remaining fries out of his carton onto the paper sheet adorning his plastic tray and began to pick at them. "I got hired by one of the big Swedish companies after graduating, though I had to repeat a year of school because chasing down that dragon and then dealing with the various government officials and journalists caused me to fall behind and fail that semester. But it's okay, you know. Some of the projects are interesting, but it depends on your role on the team. There can be a lot of unnecessary stress sometimes."

"That just kind of comes with the territory of working in a private-sector office environment, I think," I responded. It is actually something that I know a great deal about. And although I have no personal experience with public-sector office environments myself, my understanding is that they are basically more meaningless but less demanding, at least in the American context, anyway. The common denominator is, of course, the abominable, interpersonal dynamics of office environments. "So, what does Åke do now? He couldn't have finished his degree, right? I mean, with his condition..."

"He wanders around town and collects recyclables from other peoples' trash and redeems them for a little extra money, but mostly he gets state assistance, since you know, he can't really function on his own."

"I see."

We finished our meals and the conversation turned towards routine, everyday things, like music and women. Stieg was by far the most relatable member of the Modern Viking Movement I had yet met, and though I didn't know it at the time, he would maintain that status by the end of my journey as well. Åke sat silently as we talked, staring out the window at the cold darkness and occasional set of car headlights that passed by.

We said our goodbyes when we decided that it was finally time to leave. Åke looked at his feet and uttered a barely intelligible "doom" when he shook my hand. Stieg and I promised to stay in touch with one another—easier said than done, but godless entities like Facebook and WeChat have made the impossible possible in our present era.

I headed back to the hotel, took a hot shower, and went to sleep. Tomorrow would start with an early rise in order to catch the train north to Umeå, where I would then continue by ferry across the Gulf of Bothnia to one of the most culturally isolated outposts of Europe known alternately as the Land of a Thousand Lakes, the home of the language that intoxicated Tolkien and helped inspire his Elvish language, the modern territory of ancient Kalevala and Pohjola, the birthplace of the sauna and ice-cold skinny-dipping, the one and only unofficial suicide capital of the world, and the promised land of heavy metal. I was going to the Republic of Finland.

REKINDLING THE VARANGIAN FLAME

The ferry connecting Umeå, Sweden to Vaasa, Finland takes three and a half hours to cross the Kvarken, the narrowest stretch of the Gulf of Bothnia that separates the two Nordic nations. They share a land border as well, but most of it lies north of the Arctic Circle and far out of the way of the main population centers. Sápmi—or Lapland, as the Arctic region was once called—is vast, covering the northernmost territories of Norway, Sweden, Finland, and an adjacent parcel of Russia combined. It is the ancestral home of the Sámi people, an uncommon European ethnic group that, like that of the Finns, is neither Germanic nor Slavic in origin. Sápmi is a harsh, unforgiving, and sparsely populated place, swampy in the summers, desolate in the winters, and in most tracts the reindeer outnumber the people. It is the land of the true midnight sun because it never sets at the height of summer, and it does not rise in the dead of winter. But as unique and exotic as Sápmi may be, taking the ferry to Finland saves a lot of time and is more economical than traveling over land through the Arctic, and so I found myself staring out the window of the M/S *Wasa Express* at the aquatic horizon rather than chugging along the rails into the farthest reaches of the frozen tundra.

I sipped a mediocre coffee and watched the ice-encrusted islands of the Kvarken Archipelago drift by under a dim gray sky as we approached the Finnish mainland. The Finnish city of Vaasa, known in Swedish as Vasa, was given its charter by King Charles IX of Sweden in 1606, who named it after his own royal family of Vasa in a grand gesture that lacked any sense of humility as properly befit an early modern European monarch. The historical, cultural, and administrative connections between the two countries had been strong for several centuries already at that time—since the 1100s in fact, when Sweden first set about conquering Finland and making it a colony.

Most of Finland's history resembles that of Ireland's, but perhaps with fewer recurring and blatant atrocities and tragedies. While the Swedes certainly harassed, dominated, and subjugated the Finns, they weren't nearly as effective at total displacement or cultural annihilation as the English. Fittingly enough, Sweden was allied with England during much of this time, which upset the French, who then conspired with the Russians to weaken Sweden as a means to further antagonize England. Russia was, of course, delighted to oblige and invaded Swedish territory, delivering a series of astounding military defeats. The upshot is that Sweden lost all rule over Finland in 1809 and essentially began its famed policy of military neutrality, with the notable exception that occurred between 1812 and 1814 when the country embroiled itself in the Napoleonic Wars primarily for the purpose of conquering Norway as a sort of misguided recompense for its loss of Finland. Finland itself emerged as a semi-autonomous Grand Duchy of Russia and didn't achieve true independence until 1917 when it cast off the tethers of its tsarist overlords amidst the chaos and upheaval of the Bolshevik Revolution.

Although Finland's Russian domination has been more recent, the Swedish domination lasted much longer and, as a result, Swedish influence remains more visible to this day. The irony now is that a nation that was once subservient to the Swedes for six hundred years presently beats Sweden at virtually every measure that data collectors bother to tally and record, such as happiness, equality, and quality of education. But the lingering effects of centuries' worth of colonization are difficult to erase completely and there are still pockets within Finland where Swedish is widely spoken, if not the outright majority language. And the city of Vaasa anchors one of these heavily Swedish regions.

The ferry eventually docked at Vaasa's industrial port district of Vaskiluoto, an island in the harbor on the outskirts of the city.

A transfer bus waited for those of us that hadn't brought a vehicle on board to take us across the causeway that connects the island to the city center. The bus motored its way down a tree-lined boulevard rimmed with a typically Nordic blend of pastel-colored historic buildings and brutalist 20th century glass and concrete blocks. It was a pleasant-looking city for the most part, clean and well-kept but without any strong, distinctive features, at least which could be observed from a simple fifteen minute bus ride in the dead of winter.

The bus pulled up outside the train station and everyone disembarked. The building was a small, single-story structure clad in wood painted a light shade of yellow with pale green trim and a dark gray, heavily gabled metal roof. Dirty snow was piled up around it and the warm light coming from within looked especially welcoming.

Once inside, everyone stood apart from one another to avoid feeling potentially obligated to engage in conversation, for which I was grateful. I suspected that most of these people would be my companions on the high-speed train to Helsinki, and that once we had boarded, we would continue to do our utmost to avoid any interaction.

The signage at the station favored Swedish over English, and I was eternally grateful that I could actually read it so that there was no need for me to ask a question of any Finn. The Finnish language itself is utterly alien to anyone who isn't Finnish, Sámi, or Estonian. Unlike the citizens of Iceland, Norway, Sweden, and Denmark, the Finns speak a Uralic language rather than a Germanic one. It's a part of their unique cultural identity that has long been subjected to both Swedish and Russian antagonism. The Finns also possess a unique mythology, encapsulated in the great national epic, *The Kalevala*, and they gave the world the sauna. More recently, they gave the world another unique cultural icon: the first metal band to ever attempt to literally go a-viking.

"Never have I seen a more complete denouncement of the meaning of human life than that murky, yellow obscenity that hovers above the rooftops of Miklagård like a celestial plague raining its poison down upon the feeble souls below during the darkest depths of the eternal night," Alexi Laihiala sighed heavily, his face serene despite the grimness of his statement. "It made me want to kill myself."

Sitting beside him with an appropriately dangerous-looking acoustic axe resting on his lap was Ville Mäenpää, who played a few strings and quietly hissed,

> "Kiss of the death-cloud!
> Burning in your lungs.
> Kiss of the death-cloud!
> Now your life is done."

Alexi twisted his neck to avoid the strands of long, dyed-black hair that the wind insisted on blowing in his face as though he were currently filming a melancholic music video and continued speaking once the short musical interlude had ended. "The infinite pointlessness of the travesty known as human life overwhelmed me, as did the vastness of all the blasphemous airborne particulate matter. I could barely breathe and thought only of slipping away into the quiet embrace of the final, black void."

And thus began my formal introduction to Varjagikaarti, the most influential and innovative band to emerge from the underground extreme metal scene that has since come to be known as the New Wave of Finnish Varangian Metal (NWFVM). Essentially a spin-off of its viking and folk metal brethren, NWFVM altered the course of music history forever when its adherents abandoned their mock longships and medieval war gear on stage and actually went a-viking, thereby living out the content of their lyrics rather than just growling about them into a microphone.

While Varjagikaarti's music brings new meaning to the phrase "obscure Scandinavian metal," it has nonetheless made a profound impact on the underground extreme metal world, and its influence continues to spread. The band has secured record deals with small but increasingly reputable labels and inspired a new generation of Nordic musicians. Reviews of Varjagikaarti's albums now sometimes even grace the pages of such illustrious magazines as *Decibel* and *Metal Hammer* and websites such as *Metal Sucks* and *Loudwire*, but very little has ever been discussed about the band's formative early days, much less committed to the historical record.

The noxious chatroom discussions that I had discovered suggested that Varjagikaarti's founding was turbulent, regressive, and glory-seeking as befit the spirit of the Modern Viking Movement, but as usual, no legitimate sources confirmed any of the rumors. So, here I was, seated with the four members of the band atop an icy eighteenth century stone wall on the island fortress of Suomenlinna watching the sun fade over Helsinki's harbor.

Alexi, the band's enduringly pessimistic front man, sat beside me, an intense expression of forlorn hopelessness on his face as he stared at the rippling white and blue cross of the Finnish flag flying atop the nearest stone tower. Next to him sat Tuomas Laiho, the stereotypically bald drummer, and beyond him sat the guitarist, Ville Mäenpää, a pale, skinny guy with long, blond hair and a morbid northern disposition, and Jari Holopainen, the mostly silent bassist, hardcore drunkard, and creator of the bands' epic and fantastical album cover art.

I had arrived in Helsinki the previous night after my four hour journey through the heart of Nokia country. The train, in fact, had passed through the city of Tampere, a brick-factory dominated northern Manchester of sorts that neighbors the smaller town of Nokia, birthplace of the telecommunications giant and from whence its name is derived. A little less than two hours after leaving Tampere, the train rolled into Helsinki central station, a massive and imposing art nouveau structure built in 1919 and clad in granite infused with a distinctively Finnish sense of national romanticism. The building was designed by Eliel Saarinen, a renowned architect in his own right who is yet perhaps best known for having been the father of the more famous Eero Saarinen, who designed the Gateway Arch in St. Louis, JFK International Airport in New York, and Dulles International Airport in Washington, D.C., as well as a smattering of iconic modernist pieces of furniture.

In our earlier communications, the members of Varjagikaarti had graciously granted me an exclusive interview and we had decided to meet at Helsinki's open-air, waterfront Kauppatori, known as

"Market Square" in English, and take the ferry out to Suomenlinna because a decommissioned Baltic island fortress just seemed like an appropriate place to discuss their pioneering role in NWFVM. The fortress, originally known as Sveaborg—or "Swede Fortress" in the Swedish language—had unsurprisingly been constructed by the Swedes in the 18th century as a defense against their timeless enemy of Russia. Little difference its presence made in the end, though, because the Russians overran the place barely fifty years after its completion. Now it is an impressive historical site, full of earthen ramparts, stone walls, and enormous relics of naval artillery.

We had fortunately chosen to visit the island fortress on a clear day. The snow-covered landscape glistened against the gray stonework and slate blue of the harbor. Being wintertime, the island was rather desolate and devoid of people, but the museum facilities and other tourist-oriented amenities nonetheless remained open. The ferry runs year-round, partly because the island remains accessible to the public year-round, but also because eight hundred people actually live here while another four hundred work here.

Though we were bundled up in some of the heaviest coats money can buy, we nonetheless chose to combat the biting cold in the most Finnish of ways: by passing around a bottle of raspberry-flavored Finlandia Vodka like candy among school boys. Jari, the bassist, was currently inhaling its contents like a newborn baby going at his mother's ripened red nipple. I leaned forward to watch this public display of adult suckling with an expression on my face that must have belied my inner thoughts because he uttered a barely intelligible "fuck you" after swallowing and passed the bottle over to his guitar-wielding neighbor.

The liquor simultaneously accentuated and alleviated our shared silence and generally depressed mood. I easily suppressed my American urge to say something simply for the sake of saying something and instead contented myself with being thrust deep into the throes of another lengthy bout of traditional Finnish silence. It seemed that none of us wished to comment on Alexi's latest proclamation about the sub-par air quality of Miklagård—otherwise known as Istanbul to non-Old Norse speakers—and thoughts of suicide.

After a few more minutes of silence and vodka-suckling, Alexi finally chose to expound further on his personal evaluation of Istanbul's air quality. "The ephemeral mucus lining the tender passages of my nasal cavity turned black with the stench of diesel-death and man-made toxicity," he sighed. "Life has no meaning."

As much I had really gotten into the swing of not saying anything at all, my primary motivation for meeting these metalheads had not wavered; I still wanted to extract print-worthy interview material from them. Staring at the cobblestones on the path at our feet, I tried to think of something constructive to say.

"So...uh, why was it that you even bothered to go there then?" I asked.

I thought it seemed like a reasonable question, plus it was about all that I could muster. On the one hand, I've come to recognize that I'm a pretty shitty journalist. On the other hand, I'm not good at dealing with people, especially people who express emotion of any sort, be it of the positive variety that we generally goad on to the point of irresponsible and reckless phoniness in the United States, or the negative variety which is much more endemic to the Nordic condition.

"To die," Alexi answered after a moment's silence. "We went to Miklagård to die."

And then silence engulfed us once again, only to be broken by the squawk of a seagull in the distance and some harsh guttural noises being made by a small group of obnoxious German tourists walking nearby. Suomenlinna seemed mostly desolate on this day, so I was surprised to overhear a language other than Finnish or the English that I was forcing the band members to speak.

When it became apparent that Alexi had no intention of elaborating on his last remark of his own accord, I took the bait and asked the obvious follow-up question: why?

"Because life has no meaning," he answered. "The pointlessness of life is as vast and deep as the murky oceans that engulf this waste of a planet. We are nothing more than tiny specks of self-consumed insignificance cowering under the might of the infinite cosmos."

"But, hey, you know, the thing is, dying on an adventure in Miklagård would have been just so much more epic and brutal than, like, jumping off a bridge or drinking bleach or something like that,"

Tuomas, the bald drummer, chimed in. He spoke with a light-pitched, quirky accent that reminded me of Canada and Canadians. "Most of the suicides that happen here in Helsinki, they aren't very creative, you know?"

"Yeah, but, I mean, why did you guys all want to die in the first place?" I didn't get it. "Were you all depressed or something?"

"Yes," stated Alexi matter-of-factly over Tuomas, who had also begun to voice his own response at precisely the same moment.

The two eyed one another disapprovingly as Tuomas began to speak once more. "Well, it was really only Alexi here who was depressed or whatever. The rest of us just thought going a-viking would be really cool and informative since we had been taking the band in a viking metal direction anyway. What other metal band has actually ever gone a-viking before?"

I just sat there and looked at him.

"Okay, so the thing is," Tuomas continued, "we were having a lot of disagreements as a band at that time, you know? And most bands break up when that happens, just creative differences or whatever that guys can't get over and so they just want to go in their own separate directions. And we came close to breaking up, too, but then we had this idea to go a-viking together first as sort of like a last-ditch effort to resolve our differences, so we thought, hey, it's at least worth giving it a shot, right?"

"And just how would going a-viking resolve your guys' differences?" It still didn't make any sense to me.

"Well, we thought it would at least kind of get us all on the same page with a common vision for the band's direction," Tuomas answered. "Ville, Jari, and me, we wanted to go a-viking because it'd give us some creative insights for our music and just be cool, like I said. I mean, no other band had ever actually gone a-viking before, so we would be the first. We didn't really want to die, except for Alexi here who kept saying he did, if you can believe him. But either way, you can get yourself killed pretty easily when you go a-viking, so this idea, it offered something for all of us to be happy with."

"Death by going a-viking..." Alexi muttered with a hint of approval in his voice "...is truly a man's way out."

While I fully understood that going a-viking has always offered an abundance of means and methods by which one could get oneself killed, I remained baffled about the band's decision to actually engage in the pursuit of vikings themselves. I figured the decision probably tied into the Finnish concept of *sisu*, which lacks a direct translation to English, but essentially equates to a sort of grim determination. It's an element of the national character that Finns often tend to be proud of, particularly the men, who enjoy proving how tough they are while remaining relatively silent about it, which inherently makes the entire concept a completely foreign and incomprehensible one for most Americans.

The bald drummer, Tuomas, seemed to be much more willing to share useful insights than Alexi, so I looked at him and asked, "So, how bad were the band's differences that you guys actually had to go a-viking just to fix them? I mean, they had to have been pretty bad, right?"

"Oh, totally," Tuomas agreed. "We were in really bad shape as a band at that point. So, the three of us"—he pointed to himself, Ville, and Jari—"we were all basically on the same page about being a viking metal band with everything that goes along with that, you know? But then, for some reason, Alexi had gotten into being all about the most darkest blackened blackest black metal of eternal blackness of all time. I mean, we'd go do a gig and the audience, they'd see the three of us wearing our medieval tunics and leather pants and runic necklaces and whatnot as we took up our positions on stage and then Alexi would come out wearing all black with an inverted cross around his neck and have white corpse paint all over his face and pig blood spattered and dripping around his mouth. I mean, sometimes, he even took it so far that he refused to stand in the spotlight because he was philosophically opposed to it and preferred to stand back in the shadows."

"The false illumination of the unnatural stage spotlighting is for the weak of heart and even weaker of mind," Alexi pontificated. "How few of us realize that we're all just sitting idly by, trapped on a one-way express train rushing headlong towards a final destination six feet below ground. Our bags are packed, the doors are sealed, and the tickets are non-refundable."

"You see what I mean?" Tuomas looked directly at me as he said this. "So, like, he'd just stand there in the back corner of the stage where it was all very dark and no one could see him, and then he'd start screeching about bathing in the blood of newborn infants in the Winter Palace during the October Revolution or whatever and we'd all be like, 'Okay, so what the fuck ever happened to the lyrics about Thor's goats?' "

"That's pretty fucked up." It just sort of slipped out, but I recovered quickly, albeit without grace: "But, uh, why were you guys even together as a band in the first place? I mean, isn't it usually pretty important for band members to all pretty much be on the same page about this type of thing?"

"Well, we started out as a Motörhead cover band, so back at the very beginning we were all on the same page," Tuomas answered.

"Lemmy rules!" Jari, the alcoholic bassist, blurted out between gulps of raspberry vodka.

"But, you know, with time, our tastes and interests evolved," Tuomas continued, undeterred by his bandmate's slurred outburst. "So yeah, we all started out really into Motörhead, obviously, but also all the old standbys like Maiden and Ozzy and the Big Four, of course, but then we all started getting more and more into the harder, heavier, more extreme stuff and pretty soon we were listening to bands like Bathory and At the Gates and Entombed, that type of thing. So really, all four of us still had similar tastes and interests in those days, but then Ville and Jari and me all started getting more and more into the viking/folk metal thing. We were listening to tons of Enslaved and Thyrfing and of course the stuff put out by our Finnish brothers in Moonsorrow and Ensiferum, too, along with all the others. But then Alexi was going in another direction entirely and started listening to nothing but Norwegian bands from the second wave of black metal, and then he joined a Satanic study group. That's when the problems really started."

"So, why didn't the rest of you just kick him out and get a new frontman?" I asked. "I mean, this is Finland, right? Don't metal frontmen just kind of fall from trees around here?"

"Eh...maybe," Tuomas replied, "but thing is, back in those days, we all still lived with our parents and Alexi's dad had a really nice cabin out in the woods where we could practice and get drunk together. None of the rest of us had anything like that. So, if we had gotten rid of Alexi, not only would we have had to go searching for a new frontman, but we'd also lose such an awesome place to practice and drink. We could have always rented out a rehearsal practice room or whatever, but who wants to do that when you have a nice cabin in the woods surrounded by dark forests and lakes?"

Alexi looked from Tuomas to me and back to Tuomas, a displeased frown stamped across his face. I suspected that this topic of conversation had been a sore spot for him ever since the trouble in the band had first reared its ugly, corpse-painted head.

"Eh, so you know, we were trying to make it work," Tuomas continued. "But it just kept getting more and more difficult to keep it all together. It eventually reached the point where our cover art didn't make any sense for the song titles and lyrics that we had on the album. And Jari here"—he pointed at the silent bassist who was still suckling the raspberry vodka bottle like his life depended on it— "he's always been a really, really good artist and so he always does our cover art but then we ended up with this one album that he did cover art for and it showed the forging of the Sampo—"

"Sampo?"

"Yes! The Sampo. The all-powerful magical artifact of ancient Finnish mythology. That was on the cover, and we had all agreed that it would be a concept album, all about the Sampo of course. But then Alexi showed up with his lyrics and all the songs were named things like 'Embracing the Long Silent Desire for the Rotting Blackness of the Eternal Grave' or 'Murder Death Suicide Satan' and about things like murdering everyone you care about and then slitting your own wrists as you float out into the middle of a huge Finnish lake in a sinking rowboat to drown and no songs that were actually about the Sampo or viking voyages or anything."

"We had 'Blood-Eagle Suicide' on the Sampo album," Alexi said flatly, a small measure of self-defense apparent in his tone.

"Yeah, but Alexi, that has nothing to do with the Sampo!" Tuomas retorted. "That song doesn't even make sense. You can't cut the blood-eagle on yourself."

The blood-eagle was among the most gruesome of reputed medieval viking torture-murder methods. Its performance involved the victorious viking violently slashing open the back of his defeated enemy, breaking through his victim's rib cage, and finally pulling the lungs out and letting them flop on the ground to look like wings. The demented beauty of all of this was that the victim was still alive while it happened.

"That's because no one has ever had the courage to actually try it before. If only I weren't such a feeble coward..."

"But Alexi, it wouldn't work! How many times have I told you, it is not possible to cut the blood-eagle on yourself!"

"So, you guys just went ahead and recorded the Sampo concept album with Alexi's evil black metal lyrics anyway?" I didn't want the conversation to devolve into a bunch of bickering about the logistics and physical limitations of medieval torture methods between bandmates, so I did the stereotypical American thing and verbally interjected when not asked to do so. I also wondered whether any record company had ever actually released any of these early albums that they were talking about, but I didn't want to provoke the guys any further, plus I didn't really care. The early releases were probably just a bunch of poorly produced, self-published EPs.

Neither Tuomas nor Alexi said anything at first, so I attempted to dig a little deeper. "Didn't you even practice the songs first?"

Fortunately, Tuomas took the bait and started to explain why the band had used Alexi's black metal vocals and lyrics about things like the grandeur of genocide, eternal misanthropy, and Russian roulette on their otherwise epic viking metal early albums.

"Oh yeah, we practiced the songs before we recorded them," he explained. "But we never had that much lead-up time once we'd finished writing before we were scheduled for our slot at the recording studio, and we always did the writing independently of Alexi since he refused to participate. And we had already reserved and paid for our time in the studio in advance, you know? So, then Alexi wasn't ever willing to budge on the lyrics, and the rest of us weren't willing to budge on the instrumentals or album concept, so we just powered through it and made the best of it. Tensions were really starting to rise but we got through it, but things only continued to get worse after that. At this one show in Espoo, Alexi not only went into the dark, back corner of the stage to perform but instead of growling lyrics about death and being evil and worshipping the Antichrist or whatever while the rest of us marched around on stage dressed as vikings, as we totally expected him to do at this point, he instead just sort of launched into this really weird stream-of-consciousness spoken word thing about his philosophical beliefs on the meaning-lessness of life and the need for chaos to overthrow order in the world."

"It was later released as a solo sound-art album on my own label," Alexi explained in a pitch even lower than his usual tone. "You can download it and listen to it while you kill yourself. It's called *Soundtrack to Your Suicide: Standing at the Edge of Oblivion with Satan's Hand on Your Shoulder*. It's a bit of a long title but really captures the essence of what the album is all about."

"Anyway, that finally pushed us to the point where we were on the verge of breaking up," Tuomas elaborated. "We didn't want to have to go looking for a new frontman and place to practice but we were like, 'Fuck Alexi, that guy's a jerk and he's ruining the band.' "

I couldn't help but smirk just a little as he said this right in front of Alexi, whose face continued to remain completely expressionless.

Tuomas continued, "But then Ville there had the brilliant idea to combine vikings with suicide, death, and evilness."

As if on cue Ville Mäenpää chose this moment to launch into a no-holds-barred acoustic solo. He brought his hands out of his coat pockets, where they had been cocooned with enough heat to keep them responsive, and let his fingers now blaze along the fretboard in the frigid conditions for a short while. The German tourists had migrated closer, stopping on the path in front of us to watch this display of majestic virtuosity. Ville faced downwards for the better part of a minute, long locks of hair obscuring his face, before tilting his head up towards to the heavens, eyes closed and hair now fluttering in the wind as he let the final, ear-melting note ring out through the calm afternoon air. One of the tourists mumbled something in their guttural language before they continued on their way.

I assumed I shouldn't clap and instead glanced back at Tuomas.

He continued, "And so, you know, of course we were drinking pretty heavily when Ville came up with this idea and I think Jari had maybe already even blacked out on the couch by then since he's such a lush, but we thought, hey you know, most metal bands choose to focus on just one thing—whether it be on vikings or evilness or dragons or scantily-clad muscular body builders or something else entirely—but none of those things are ever usually combined. And the viking metal bands, none of them ever actually act out the lyrics of their songs. I mean just look at Amon Amarth for example, or even Quorthon himself—even though those guys are or were all really into vikings, none of them have ever actually attempted to go a-viking, but then at the same time they aren't really completely fixated on death either; even if everyone dies during Ragnarök, that's just sort of incidental to the whole viking thing. But then on the flip side, just look at Mayhem. Here's a classic band that had all these violent incidents, so they kind of lived up to the content of their lyrics, you know? I mean, maybe not in a super literal sense but all that stuff with the church burnings and Pelle Ohlin's suicide and Øystein Aarseth's murder and all. They did put their money where their mouths were, but none of it ever had anything at all to do with vikings. It was just death and evilness and chaos that they were about. So, we thought, you know, maybe we could be some real innovators with this idea and do something completely new that no other metal guys had ever done before. And it resolved our problems too, you know? Alexi would get the chance to die in a gruesome way, possibly even while attempting to do something really, really evil, depending on how badly things went on our journey, and the rest of us would get the chance to live out our own fantasies as modern-day vikings. Maybe we would die too, or maybe not, but it would be so epic. But of course, in order to go a-viking, we had to leave Helsinki. That's the whole premise of going a-viking. You have to leave your home, otherwise you're just a plain Norseman or maybe a good fighting man or something but not a true fucking viking. So, our master plan was to join the Varangian Guard and fight for the emperor in the east, unless we died along the way first, which all of us actually condoned at the time since we were drunk."

One thousand years ago, the Varangian Guard had been the elite warrior corps comprised of Scandinavians who had traveled the old Varangian routes to reach the Byzantine Empire and serve as the emperor's personal body guard in the city known by the various names of Miklagård, Constantinople, and Istanbul. To this day, the term Varangian itself has retained an implication of specificity: only those medieval vikings who traveled eastwards through Russia to Greece and the orient were considered Varangians. At the time, the Finns were not considered Scandinavians even in the loosest sense of the word because they had (and still have) a completely different language, customs, and mythology, but after hundreds of years of Swedish colonization and domination, it only seemed natural that these viking-obsessed Finnish metalheads would choose to follow in the same footsteps as the ancient Varangians.

And despite the incredulity of the situation, it was all finally starting to make some sense.

"So, what happened?" I asked. "Did you all at least make it to Miklagård? You're obviously not dead."

"We are the essence of mediocrity," Alexi answered with a deep and somber sigh.

By this point, the vodka bottle had made its way back down the line to Tuomas, who took a heavy gulp and handed it over to Alexi. Alexi sat staring at the reindeer emblem embossed on its surface, deep in thought, before hoisting it to his lips and tossing back its contents in a steady, undisturbed stream of raspberry-tinted, redemption-granting alcoholic lucidity.

He swallowed and handed the bottle to me, saying, "We are utter failures in all that we endeavor. Had we won favor with Lucifer, perhaps we wouldn't be here now. But wishful dreams are the laughing-stock of the cosmos."

I took a quick swig, tried to forget about the germs that might have been lurking on the rim after having already swallowed, and then passed the bottle on as Tuomas resumed the story. "Well, you see, we actually had many chances to die on our journey—so many chances, in fact. And we thought, eh you know, maybe we'll make some great metal as our ship sinks in a frightening gale or something, but no, nothing like that ever happened."

"So, you got a ship?" I asked.

"Oh yes, we got a ship, and it really was quite a nice ship," Tuomas answered. "It used to be a viking-themed tour boat that sailed around Stockholm's harbor before someone set it on fire, so we got it for almost nothing. Making it seaworthy again took some time and money, but we never bothered to fix the way it looked, which made it all the more brutal. A viking longship sailing out of the mist with horrible burn marks all over it will strike fear into the heart of anyone who sees it."

"Do you still have this ship? Can I see it?"

"Oh no, it never made it back from Miklagård. We got a Volvo, though, if you want to see that."

I didn't, but neither was I surprised by the revelation. "So, you guys got this ship ready and then you just sailed off?"

"Indeed. But first I prayed to his infernal majesty that he would deliver us unto evil and a slow and agonizing death," Alexi added. "I performed a proper Satanic ritual with candles and a pentagram and the blood of the innocent that I ordered off the internet. But he did not answer, that goat-fucking whore of a devil. Or maybe I should blame the online store; maybe they deceived me in an even more divine form of service to the twisted one. But it was a very legitimate-looking site. I'll never know if that blood of the innocent was authentic or not."

"And while Alexi was off praying to the devil for death or whatever, the rest of us were praying to our gods, too, in proper modern folk metal fashion," Tuomas said. "And even though we accepted the notion that we might die, we didn't want to; we just wanted glory, so we prayed for fair winds, safe waters, and super lax border patrols in the countries we would be going through. And for this, we prayed to Rán, the Norse goddess of the sea, and to Ukko, since we like him. But we also figured it might be a good idea to have the White Christ on our side, too, so we prayed to him as well."

"Ukko blows!" Jari decided to make himself heard again after Tuomas mentioned the ancient god. Ukko is the old Finnish god of thunder, akin to Thor but with a more serious personality. I have no idea if he blows or not, metaphorically or literally, but assumed that Jari must have some reason for not being overly fond of the deity.

"So, you guys mixed and matched the gods you prayed to?" I asked.

"No. Only Satan. All hail." Alexi's comment was counter-productive and not really directed to anyone but himself.

Ignoring him, Tuomas answered, "Yes, of course. With gods, the more the merrier, right? We wanted whoever we could get to be on our side."

Although he was often violently forced upon the native Scandinavian population by missionaries a thousand years ago, Jesus was also sometimes initially adopted as just another new member of the Norse pantheon. Tuomas wasn't speaking specifically of the Norse pantheon, as his self-proclaimed worship involved at least one Finnish pagan god, but his strategy of appealing to multiple deities from multiple cultures and religions nonetheless maintained a certain consistency and logic from a historical perspective. Furthermore, the Nordic population as a whole is not a particularly devout bunch, so new interpretations of and deviations from traditional religious teachings are nothing new for the region. The Nordic nations have experienced a general decline among their common Lutheran faith in recent decades and in the year 2000, Sweden, being the progressive nation that it is, even went so far as to finally institute an official separation of church and state. But even by then many of the native metal musicians had already chosen to deviate from the state-approved doctrine and follow various alternate, left-hand paths of their own. In this light, it is not especially surprising that a bizarrely blasphemous and highly unorthodox, modern-day blending of the old heathen ways with selective, medieval elements of Christianity might develop among band members on the outermost fringe of the Finnish metal scene.

"And our gods were mightier than Alexi's devil on that day," Tuomas continued. "Nothing happened when our hate-crew death-rolled on out all the way across the Gulf of Finland. There were no incidents other than the time when Jari accidentally dropped the vodka bottle overboard and then jumped in after it and we had to fish him out."

"So, what if the norns had, you know, determined that one of you other than Alexi should die in some sort of non-viking type of way while you were on this journey?" I asked. "Like, maybe that could have happened with Jari if you guys had just let him drown?"

"Well, you know, our fates were woven long ago, so it's not something we ever really had any control over one way or the other." The last rays of the day's light had started to glisten off the silky smooth surface of Tuomas' scalp. I couldn't believe that he wasn't wearing a hat in this frigid weather, but then again, drummers are very tough individuals, and he was performing quite the feat of *sisu*. "But if some magnificent storm conjured up by Rán or some other god or goddess sank all of us together in one fell swoop out in the open water but left Alexi alive, then I guess that would have been kind of ironic, right? But nothing like that happened and we're all still here."

"Regretfully alive," Alexi lamented. "And thus, I have truly become one with sorrow."

"Eh, yeah, but Alexi, you've always been one for sorrow."

"Our four pitiful souls were destined to failure, right from the start. And now here I sit, devoid of faith and bereft of hope."

Tuomas shook his head and looked at me. "Now he's just quoting another band's lyrics. He starts doing this whenever he's really depressed and runs out of ideas of his own."

"I am but a shell of a man, condemned to a world of resentment."

"Eh, whatever." Tuomas made no effort to hide his apathy towards Alexi's melodramatic moanings. "So, we survived the Baltic and it was on the crossing of the Gulf of Finland that we wrote our song, 'Baltic Seabed Bottom Blues,' which turned out pretty good, right? I mean, we put it as the opener on our *Buried in a Cold Miklagårdian Grave* album, which as you know was our big breakthrough. But eventually, we arrived and docked in St. Petersburg, and that first night we got super drunk on cheap Russian vodka and nearly burned our entire ship to ashes which, as I said, was already pretty badly fire-damaged in appearance as it was."

"Lucifer must truly hate me," Alexi uttered his frustration with the errant enemy of Christ. "He passed his judgement, on me—on all of us—and it was not favorable. The only thing worse than being sentenced to death is being sentenced to life."

"So, we continued onwards, you know?" Tuomas resumed. "We headed down the Neva River along the eastern trail, following the wind in our sails and the rhythm of our oars until we reached Lake Ladoga, which lies deep in the land of the Rus, and from there we steered towards Aldeigjuborg."

"There was no shelter in that hostile land." Alexi's comment sounded eerily familiar.

"Yes, quite so. We were constantly on guard and needed to appeal to the gods to safeguard us—"

"Or kill us," Alexi interjected.

"—since we were in foreign territory now and all. And naturally, we figured maybe we should include one of the local gods in our prayers in this frightful, new land. So, we decided to pray to Perun in addition to Ukko and the White Christ this time around. Perun is the Slavic god of lightning, fire, and war, and we thought, eh you know, maybe he could help us out. We also thought the time was right to— how do you say? Up the ante? Yes?"

He looked at me and I just shrugged. I didn't know where he was going with this.

"So, anyway, we made depictions of Perun in his honor," the drummer continued. "'Cause you know, we thought maybe it'd be a good idea to take it a step further than we did before, to really show this guy how much we honored him. He didn't know us from before, so a little extra effort made sense, you know? Like maybe he'd pay more attention to us that way. So, we had these pictures we made; they were mostly really bad because we're all pretty terrible artists, except for Jari there."

Jari burped confusedly at the mention of his name.

"But it's the idea that counts, right?" Tuomas resumed. "And just to be on the safe side, we wrote 'Perun' next to the pictures just so he'd know it was him we'd tried to draw since our drawings were such shit. And then we offered them up as ritualistic effigies. We were like, 'Hey Perun! How's it going, buddy? You see these nice pictures we made of you? We tried really hard even though we aren't so good as artists and we really want to ask you, would you please protect us on our journey? Maybe give us a glorious defeat over the Magyars if we come across any? That would be nice.' "

"Or send the Magyars to slaughter us all in our sleep," expounded Alexi. "Slit our throats, trample our bodies, and string us up to dangle, windblown and decaying from the nearest tree."

"Yeah, so Alexi didn't participate in our ritual," Tuomas continued. "He just went off and performed another one of his own Satanic rituals by himself instead."

"Little good it did," Alexi muttered.

"I like to think that Perun listened to us, just like the other gods we had prayed to before, because we never even came close to dying. We made it all the way down the Varangian way with no injuries or mishaps at the different countries' borders. We just sailed to Holmgård and beyond, to Kiev and then the Black Sea."

Alexi sighed again, "Not even the murderous rapids of the Dnieper slowed down our progress to that sprawling cesspool of humanity and air pollution, Miklagård."

"Yeah, you know, honestly, you'd think those rapids would've gotten at least one of us, right?" Tuomas added. "Not that any of us besides Alexi actually wanted that, but those rapids, they've killed all sorts of people over the years. All you got to do is fall overboard and hit your head on a rock and then—BAM! You're dead, you know, and then your body floats away to wherever it goes and then it washes up on some shore and then some bear probably comes along and eats it and you make that bear happy even though you're dead, but at least the bear, you know, he gets something out of it 'cause now he's got a full belly and he can go and take a nap before he gets hungry again if no hunter comes along and kills him first, which would be sad since he's a nice bear and he never hurt anyone, right? But, you know, we got through the rapids all fine; we had to portage the boat in a few places, but no one even got hurt."

"And not only were we cursed to continue living our hollow shells of lives," Alexi said, "but now the bear's going to go hungry."

Just then Ville launched into an impromptu riff. We all turned to watch while his fingers throttled the bejesus out of his instrument as he snarled, "Fodder for the bear!"

Following his guitarist's lead, Alexi immediately changed the countenance of his somber disposition, straightening his back where he sat on the frigid stone wall, and pumped his fist into the air, singing cleanly and clearly in his deep baritone:

> "Awash in agony,
>   Injuries aggravated beyond repair—"

"Fodder for the bear!" Ville growled his refrain.

> "Skimming the surface,
>   Floating like flotsam towards the lair—"

"Fodder for the bear!"

> "Dreaming of drowning,
>   Claws cleave and carve, your deepest despair—"

"Fodder for the bear!"

Ville struck his final chord and we all leaned back, nodding at one another with approval, except for Jari who remained too deeply enraptured by the vodka bottle glued to his face to have even noticed.

"Well, hey, that sounded pretty good, guys," I said. "It was brutal, but catchy. I think you guys might be onto something with this one."

Alexi responded, "Words of encouragement only highlight the infinite futility of our trite and feeble existence."

"Shit."

"But hey, you know, we did finally make it to Miklagård." Tuomas took up the conversational reins once more. "It is a beautiful city, and the view from the water as you approach is quite stunning. But as you get closer, you begin to notice more and more, the city, it doesn't have very good air quality."

Alexi suddenly leaned back and roared straight upwards into the cold, darkening sky. Startled, the birds on the nearest trees immediately flew away and I heard a small child in the distance start crying.

"Alexi, what the fuck, man?" Tuomas stared in disbelief. Apparently, he was just as surprised as both myself and the unseen child at Alexi's sudden outburst.

"Shit..." Alexi actually looked slightly embarrassed. "I apologize for the worthlessness of my being. If I had the nerve, I'd kill myself here and now."

"So, anyway, we docked the boat and we were all like, 'Hey guys, we made it! We can join up with the Varangian Guard now,' " Tuomas continued. "So, we get off the boat and we're walking around but it's very hard to find your way, like where was the emperor's palace? We didn't know. I thought there would be guys out there to greet us or something, you know, but there weren't, and it was kind of dirty. Up here in Finland, you know, everything's so clean."

Alexi, composed once again, elaborated, "Miklagård's fumes were thick with factory filth and the exhaust of countless combustion engines. The overwhelming density of infernal airborne particulate matter filtered through my inadequate nasal hairs, brutally wrecking chaos on my olfactory sensory neurons. The stench tightened its death-grip deep within the innermost reaches of my sinus, choking me, permeating my frail cellular membranes, and draining my soul of its meager essence as it slid deeper into a dark and squalid pit of despair from which there could never be any hope of return. I could barely walk and I wanted only to kill myself before I had even reached the emperor's court."

"But even though the air wasn't clean, we of course didn't kill ourselves and instead we thought, 'Hey, maybe we should just take a taxi,' " Tuomas stated. He looked particularly chipper at the moment, a quality that was artificially heightened by Alexi's sulking, silent presence beside him. "So, we got in this taxi and we said, 'Hey guy, can you take us to the emperor's palace?' We had to use English, of course, but he understood us and he just gave us this weird look and said there is no emperor's palace. So, we said, 'Hey, what?' Because really, that's our final destination, you know. So, we explained how we really, really needed to get there so we could enlist in the Varangian Guard and he just kind of nodded and started driving and then a while later he let us out in front of this amazing religious building. I swear, this was the most amazing temple I had ever seen. It was so ornate with this huge dome and these six giant, pointy towers all around it. It makes our big cathedral here look like a clumsy Lego building in comparison and it even puts the old temple in Uppsala to shame for sure, big time."

I assumed Tuomas was talking about the Blue Mosque of Istanbul, the city's iconic 17th century house of worship that stands near the famous Hagia Sophia and on the former grounds of the Great Palace of Constantinople. The palace had been plundered and abandoned during the Crusades before eventually being demolished a couple of centuries later by the conquering Ottomans, but I chose not to relate this to the members of Varjagikaarti. As obvious die-hard historical revisionists, any debate on the legitimacy of their version of the historical record would be like trying to convince a cock-rocking 80's glam metal musician that the emergence of grunge was a positive step in the evolution of heavy music. I did believe that Tuomas had a point about the Helsinki Cathedral and the old Uppsala pagan temple, though. While impressive in its own right, I seriously doubted anyone would ever be more architecturally impressed by the Finnish Lutheran church than the Ottoman mosque. The old Uppsala temple, on the other hand, was known to have served as a significant pagan sacrificial center of great importance throughout Scandinavia during the original viking era, but no one really knows what it looked like.

"Every present-day architect should kill him or herself," Alexi spoke again, with clear resolution stamped across his face. "When one gazes upon a temple of such magnificence, the temple gazes back into you, and the artistry of earlier civilizations overwhelms you—even the unrelenting air pollution that suffocates your ever-shriveling esophagus is forgotten in that brief, fleeting moment. There was a meaning and a grandeur that was imbued in those designs that no longer exists in the constructions that are built today. It has all deteriorated into a relentless onslaught of vapid and pointless glass and concrete boxes, and it makes me want to kill myself."

"So, we're standing there, looking at this thing right," Tuomas resumed, "and we're thinking, 'Hey, maybe this isn't the imperial palace after all and so then why'd the driver let us out here?' But we'd never seen anything like this before so we thought that maybe we can put off enlisting in the Varangian Guard for a few minutes to go inside and check this thing out."

"Perhaps spiritual salvation could be found within its hallowed walls," Alexi added. "Perhaps we could find a cleaner, quicker route to death and redemption through eternal damnation on a mission of the Varangian Guard if we offered up our prayers to the reigning Lord of Hell in this opulent house of worship."

"Oh, yeah, we were like, 'Whoever the god is that looks over this place, we need him on our side for sure.' " Tuomas took over again. "So, we go up to the door to go in, and once we got up there, they made us take our boots off."

While he said this, Alexi lifted his leg and pointed at his steel-tipped, ultra-masculine, black leather boot.

Tuomas simply nodded and continued, "And then also, we had to wear these little hats on our heads too." He gesticulated awkwardly around his shiny domed skull. "But then we got in and we were blown away. The inside of that place was so fucking metal, man, I mean, it was crazy how metal is was."

I'd never heard a mosque described as "metal" before. Normally, when I think of mosques or other religious buildings, the adjectives that tend to come to mind are words such as "divine," "peaceful," and "sacred" if contemplating the higher powers at work, or "magnificent," "imposing," and "ornate" if contemplating the architecture.

But a word that conjures up mental images of warm bat's blood dripping from Ozzy Osbourne's mouth or black-leather clad, face-painted, guitar-wielding sons of northern darkness is not one that I typically associate with the houses of the holy. But then again, the members of Varjagikaarti did not become innovators of viking-inspired Fennoscandian melodic blackened folk death metal by doing things as everyone else does them, and thus I stood corrected as I sat unspeaking and staring at my feet while Tuomas rambled on about the architectural virtues of the Blue Mosque.

"So, there we were, in this amazing place," Tuomas continued. "And it's like, hey you know, we definitely can't leave without getting the blessings from the local god for the continuation of our journey."

"Or Satan," Alexi added. "I stayed aligned with him and found a nice spot in the corner and began to draw a pentagram on the floor."

Tuomas then proceeded to explain how Alexi's desecration of the mosque's floor caused a minor uproar within the walls of the house of worship. As Miklagård's devout faithful rushed towards Alexi to make him stop his profane act of vandalism, the other band members lost track of the drunkard Jari, who simply wandered off unnoticed during the commotion.

"So, we got the situation with Alexi defused, you know?" Tuomas explained. "I smacked him hard on the back of the head and told him not to embarrass us again as clearly these people don't like having Satanic symbols drawn in their fancy temple. So, like maybe the rest of us should just offer up verbal prayers this time around, you know? The locals had clued us in to who the local god and his prophet are, so we could make our prayers to them in a more proper way now and Alexi could just keep his devil worship to himself till we left. We didn't need to go pissing off the locals before we even found the place where you sign up to be in the Varangian Guard. It was right around then that Alexi and Ville and me all were like, 'Hey, where's Jari?' "

He stopped speaking, and we all turned to look at Jari who was completely hammered and just staring out into space, oblivious to the discussion taking place about him.

"So, we're looking around and we don't see Jari, so we're just kind of like, 'Eh, fuck it.' You know?" Tuomas said. "We figured that drunk moron could find his way back out to the main room eventually from wherever he had gone off to. So, we started looking more at the nice details on the walls and tiles and saying quiet, little prayers to ourselves and all, and then Ville decided to go check out the other rooms and then a few minutes later he comes back and he's like, 'Hey guys, I found Jari. He's drawing on a wall.' "

Ville rolled his eyes but didn't say anything.

"So, we rushed over to where Jari was, and by this point, he's drawn pretty much all of the gods on the wall in this quiet side room," Tuomas sounded a bit exasperated. "I mean, it was good artwork and all since Jari can really draw well, but it's like, I don't know, maybe he shouldn't have drawn Jesus, Ukko, Perun, Rán, and Muhammad altogether on this wall in the foreign temple, and now he's doing decorative vines and dragons and shit winding around between all their faces. So, we're just looking at it and thinking, 'Hey you know, maybe this is a good time to leave.' So, we try and get Jari to stop drawing and come outside with us, but he just kind of pushes us away and starts being loud since, of course, he's drunk and that only gets other people to come over and check out what's going on, and they clearly do not think this is cool, and so they're getting all angry and cursing at us and whatnot, and we're trying to get Jari to stop, but we can't, and so the locals are now getting even more angry and we're trying to say that Jari's just a drunk fool and he means no harm. He thinks what he is doing is an honor to their prophet and doesn't mean to hurt anyone's feelings, but they don't care, and then tempers start to flare up and these people start to get downright hostile."

"I collapsed out of despair," Alexi said. "And then I began to pray to Satan once again. For death."

Tuomas paid him no heed and continued, "I mean, I think people have never really liked Varangian graffiti, so that hasn't changed much over the years, but I'm not sure it ever pissed them off quite so much in the past, you know?"

Tuomas referred to the graffiti left behind by the original Varangians during stints of boredom in the emperor's service a thousand years ago. Istanbul's most iconic building, the Hagia Sophia, contains two well known examples of runes that had been carved into its walls when it was still a Christian cathedral five hundred years before the conquering Ottomans converted it to a mosque. These runes provide exhilarating commentary on the lives and times of Scandinavian Varangians in Emperor Constantine's court: "Halfdan carved these runes" and "Ari made these runes." The most famous piece of Varangian graffiti, however, was carved onto the statue of a lion in Greece which was then pillaged by the Venetians at a much later date.

"So now, all these guys have surrounded us and they're getting real agitated and then they start pushing us," Tuomas resumed. "And then one of them punched Jari in the face, which was pretty effective at getting him to stop drawing, but by then it was already too late to tame the crowd, and before we knew what was going on, they were dragging all of us through the temple and back to the main door and then they shoved us outside onto the street, but they didn't go back inside themselves. Instead, they just kept being angry and shouting loud stuff to the other people outside who then started coming over and getting riled up themselves, and pretty soon they started spitting on us and more and more people were coming over and this mob was getting really hostile now and even starting to throw rocks at us!"

"It was the essence of pure, unbridled human rage that could only be quenched with death," said Alexi. "And it was truly a beautiful thing...but it was all too much to bear, and with the complete and utter inability to breath clean air, I was heaving and coughing and growing weaker by the second. My strength and perseverance was waning. All of ours was. I thought only of the sweet and silent embrace that death would finally bring us and then I fell to my knees, waiting to embrace the inevitable."

"I was the next to fall," admitted Tuomas. "Even though I didn't want to die like Alexi, it's just like, you know, we don't realize sometimes how clean our air is here in Finland till we go to some other part of the world where the air isn't as clean, and then someone throws a rock that hits you in the head."

While inherently misguided through his own ignorance of cultures and belief systems other than his own, Jari's sketching of the image of Muhammad on a holy wall in Istanbul constituted only one of the many colorful episodes that comprise a surprisingly rich tapestry of the collective Nordic nations' provocations aimed at the religion of peace. In 2007 Swedish artist Lars Vilks' depiction of Muhammad as a dog sparked outrage, eventual assassination attempts on his life, and a $150,000 reward for his murder by ISIS. More famously, the cartoons of the prophet published in the *Jyllands-Posten* newspaper in 2005 incited violent protests and caused large swaths of the Islamic world to essentially boycott the right of Denmark to exist as a sovereign nation. Varjagikaarti's transgression never received a similar level of attention, partly due to its relatively low-key nature and partly due to the fact that news of its occurrence never really spread beyond short-lived word-of-mouth near its epicenter. So, the band got off lucky, or unlucky as Alexi would say, since they're all still alive today with no standing death threats on their heads.

"So, there we stood on the precipice of fate, nearing the end of our journey and falling one by one under the hail of stones in the soupy thickness of the infernal smog." Alexi displayed a mildly more upbeat emotion than he had throughout the entire duration of our conversation up to this moment. "My sad desperation to enlist in the Varangian Guard vanished into the thickly polluted air and a new sensation took its place: joy, in all its boundless colors, leapt into my heart. For we understood then that the ferocity of battle would soon lead us to death's eternal embrace in the streets of Miklagård. The battle-rage fell from the hazy skies above upon the ordinary people surrounding us as the assault accelerated."

Jari mumbled something and drooled a bit. I didn't understand a word of what he said, and none of the other band members paid it any attention.

"So, what happened?" I asked. "Clearly, you guys didn't die."

"The battle-rage had grown to epic proportions among our adversaries," Alexi answered. "We were staring death in the face. Ville had already been knocked unconscious by a stone that struck him in the face. Soon, we would all be dead."

Tuomas provided a more informative answer: "So, you know, basically the authorities showed up and dispersed the mob. And then they gathered us up and took us away to some solitary holding cell since they didn't trust the general prison population to be mixed with blasphemers like us. And then pretty soon after that, the Finnish consulate found out about all this and so they came and got us, and next thing we know, we're on a flight back to Helsinki like it never even happened. And we never did find the emperor's palace."

"So many opportunities to end it all, to go beyond the point of no return, to whither away into nothingness," Alexi muttered. "How worthless are we that we can't even succeed at death? Not even the plane went down in a flaming ball of carnage and destruction."

Internally, I was glad for that, and the comment brought another thought to mind: "Well, what happened to your boat?"

"The mob torched it," Tuomas answered. "There's lots of videos of it happening on YouTube if you ever want to check it out sometime."

"And I take it you don't plan to ever voyage through the lands of the Rus towards Miklagård again?"

"Yeah, you know, honestly, we just kind of gave up at that point," Tuomas answered. "We failed to find and enlist in the Varangian Guard, and Alexi failed to get himself killed. But we did something that no other metal band had done before us, and we wrote some great songs in the process."

"Nothing is great, nothing has meaning." Alexi swallowed hard. "Everything has crumbled, all hope has long been lost, and now we are left with no choice but to continue on, plotting a long course to nowhere, our despair-ridden hearts beating slower and slower as the rain comes falling down."

"And also, we've been banned from ever entering certain countries again, so going a-viking has become a whole lot harder. Maybe we could try again sometime and pretend to be like a bunch of Norwegians and go west towards Scotland or Iceland or something. I don't know. I guess we still discuss that option from time to time, but for now, we're just focusing on our music, and our first viking voyage still has lots of inspiration left in it."

"Yeah, I bet." I figured this was true. "I mean, you guys haven't even touched on the fate of your boat in any of your songs yet."

"Exactly, and hey, that's a good point, maybe we should write a song about that poor boat." Tuomas nodded his head and smiled a little. "But anyway, for now we thought we'd at least perform one of our songs for you while you're here. Well, Ville and Alexi will perform it since I don't have my drums here, and even if Jari had his acoustic bass, he's too wasted at this point."

Just as Tuomas said this, Jari leaned forward and projectile vomited with extreme vigor to confirm his inebriation, the foremost specks of barf landing a good ten feet away on a patch of otherwise clean snow.

"Ugh, Jari, man." Tuomas grimaced and shook his head.

As he said this, Alexi chuckled mildly in his deep tone while Ville remained completely expressionless.

"Anyway." Tuomas turned away from Jari and looked back at me. "So, this song, it's one that was inspired by our misfortunes in Miklagård. It's called 'Stoned to Death Under a Smog-Ridden Sky' from our *Ice Cold Varangian Penetration* album."

Of course, I knew the song. I knew all their songs, at least all of the ones released since their Varangian expedition, and I was thrilled that they were going to give me an individual live performance, even if I didn't show it.

Ville began to play a high-speed riff, and as he did, I looked up into the clear, starry afternoon sky, glad to be alive and glad that all four members of Varjagikaarti had survived their maiden viking voyage. The bottle of vodka made its way back to me and I took a quick swig as Alexi began the opening verse:

> "Sweltering smog
> Hail of stones
> You fall to your knees
> Unable to breathe..."

Later that evening, I sat at a corner table in the back of the Roasberg coffee house, sipping a steaming hot latte and scanning through the day's photos on my laptop while waiting for the Finlandia buzz to wear off. It was a truly pleasant spot with cushioned seats, brick walls, and elegant lighting emanating from decorative globules hanging from the ceiling. As a nation, Finland consumes more coffee per capita than any other and I consequently harbored high expectations of any local cafe. Roasberg rose to the unspoken challenge, and the milky caffeine warmed my weary bones and sharpened my senses.

Spending a full afternoon of depressive wintertime vodka day-drinking in public was something I'd never done before and probably would never do again. I've always gravitated more towards beer and mead than hard liquor and while I hadn't imbibed nearly as much as the band members had—Jari was looking especially bad and had to be propped up by Ville and Tuomas when we said our farewells—I was still feeling it. But that said, I appreciated my chance to partake in what had seemed like a quintessential Finnish cultural experience. The only way it could have been even more stereotypical was if we had collectively stripped off our clothing and alternated between sweating it out in a sauna and chasing each other around with birch twigs in the snow.

Most of my photos were utterly mediocre, but a few good ones were included in the mix. Several had captured the leafless shadows of tree branches dancing across Suomenlinna's palette of snow and stone rather evocatively. I'd also captured a few candid moments of the members of Varjagikaarti themselves. There was a shot of Alexi growling intensely at nothingness, the veins bulging in his neck as he grimaced in theatrical anger. There was Tuomas smiling, looking more like a jolly gnome than a brutal metal drummer. And there was Ville head-banging to his own acoustic guitar playing while Jari coddled the vodka bottle beside him.

We had taken the ferry back to central Helsinki in silence and I thanked the guys for their time once we were back on solid ground. I had offered to buy them each a coffee as an expression of my gratitude, but they had apparently reached their limit of social interaction for the day and were a bit too hammered to really want to do anything other than slink off to their respective homes, scrounge around for some leftovers, and pass out. Tuomas had received the duty of seeing Jari home because they lived nearest one another, and together, the four drunks slowly made their way towards the nearby Kauppatori transit shelter to wait for the next tram to siphon them off to their respective abodes.

I had waved them goodbye and began the short trek towards my hotel near the train station. This part of the city is paved predominately with cobble stones, filled with overhead catenary wires that power the trams, and populated with pastel-colored neoclassical buildings, all of which combines to create a genuinely pleasing Old World effect. I had passed through the large, uniformly empty space of Senate Square, which is devoid of any architectural adornments except for a large statue in its center of Alexander II, Emperor of Russia from 1855 to 1881. Behind his lofty silhouette looms the Helsinki Cathedral, the largest Lutheran house of worship in the world. Lights cast a brilliant sheen upon its imposing white surface and massive green dome, illuminating it against the encroaching darkness of the northern night in a manner both symbolic of its purpose and befitting a major tourist attraction.

I had briefly returned to my room in the Sokos Hotel to chug some water. It was a modest room, minimal and modern but clean and airy in the typical Nordic fashion. I had then wandered the two blocks to Roasberg, where I presently found myself, to reflect upon the day's revelations and review my next travel steps while sobering up. I would be taking an overnight voyage on the Silja Line's cruise ship to Stockholm the next day. The boat wouldn't be leaving till early evening, so I had the day to take in some additional sights and sounds of the Finnish capital.

I contemplated the notion of visiting Lake Bodom in the nearby town of Espoo. The lake is famous in the metal world for having inspired the name of one of Finland's most successful bands, Children of Bodom. The reason is properly grim: in 1960, three teenagers were found brutally murdered on the shore of Lake Bodom. A fourth teenager was severely injured, but survived, and the culprit has never been found. So, this was an option, but one that required a certain degree of effort and probable letdown upon arrival. Most likely, I would wander the city aimlessly, looking for unique statues inspired by Finnish, Scandinavian, or Russian mythology and history before eventually boarding the boat back to Sweden and continuing my quest in Stockholm and Norrköping.

TROLL EXPOSURE IN EASTERN GEATLAND

The MS *Silja Serenade* calmly motored its way through the inner archipelago of Stockholm. A towering behemoth of a ship, it rose higher than any of the snow-capped hills adorning the islands that surrounded it. Cute summer cottages with shuttered windows dotted the shores. Although people live year-round in the archipelago, the present scenery was entirely devoid of human life and would remain so for the duration of winter. In the summer, the contrast would be stark, with pleasure boats covering the sea as the resorts and vacation homes swelled with many merry-makers and leisure-seekers.

Stockholm itself is built on an archipelago where the fresh water of Lake Mälaren empties into the brackish water of the Baltic. The city center covers fourteen islands, but the greater archipelago consists of thirty thousand additional islands, skerries, and shoals and extends over fifty miles towards Finland in the east. Once the Stockholm archipelago ends, it's only another twenty-some odd miles before the archipelago of the Åland Islands begins, which lies approximately midway between the Swedish and Finnish mainlands.

The ship had stopped at Mariehamn, the capital of Åland, in the wee hours of the morning. Culturally and linguistically Swedish, the Åland Islands are now an autonomous part of Finland because they were conquered by Russia in the same war that resulted in Sweden's total capitulation and loss of the colony. As an autonomous territory,

Åland establishes many of its own rules and laws, the most renowned of which is its tax-free sale of alcohol (a quality that also serves as the primary driver of the islands' tourism-based economy). The states of Sweden and Finland both tax the bejesus out of all forms of adult beverages, so Baltic crossings have developed a general reputation for being booze cruises. This is particularly true of the Silja Line's main competitor, appropriately named the Viking Line, but both shipping lines host tax-free liquor superstores onboard their vessels just for good measure.

I had foregone the opportunity to watch the ship dock in Mariehamn, instead attempting to sleep through the night in my cramped, nondescript cabin. I had been given the choice of staying in a more lively, Moomin-themed room but had declined. For those who don't know, the Moomins are Finland's grand contribution to children's literature: naked, androgynous, bipedal hippopotamus-looking things that go on adventures in the woods. Created by the Swedish Finn, Tove Jansson, originally as an illustrated children's book in the 1940s, the great Moomin empire has since grown to include animated television shows, films, theatrical productions, and even the Moomin World amusement park in Naantali in the southwestern corner of Finland. And apparently, the Moomins have now even entered the realm of Baltic ferry cruise ships as well, not only in the form of cabin accommodations that offer the unique opportunity to withdraw to private quarters featuring Moomintroll lamps and curtains, but also in the presence of costumed Moomins who patrol the deck and other public spaces on certain summer voyages. But I was on a winter crossing and I had settled for the most economical choice of a tiny and lackluster C-Class cabin: windowless, Moomin-less, and below the water line.

I stood now on the *Serenade*'s foredeck, watching the spires of Stockholm come into view in the murky morning light while we glided past well-maintained suburban waterfront homes. The white mass of Globen, the world's largest spherical building and host to Sweden's most popular hockey matches and musical concerts, could be seen silhouetted on the horizon to the southwest. The boat redirected itself away from the city's charming center and instead made its way towards the industrial port area of Värtahamn two miles to the north. After disembarking, I walked the short distance to the Gärdet Tunnelbana station and caught the Red Line train south to T-Centralen in the heart of the city.

I have always been amused that Boston's notorious Massachusetts Bay Transportation Authority modeled its graphic representation after that of Stockholm's Tunnelbana. Oslo's metro did as well and now all three systems utilize a sans-serif, bold capital letter "T" set within a smooth circle against a white background as the official logo to denote their stations. Furthermore, the lines that comprise the Boston and Stockholm systems are similarly distinguished by an iconic use of color, such as the Red Line, the Green Line, or the Blue Line. But while Boston's system is the oldest in the U.S. and lackadaisically displays all the decrepitude one would expect of a poorly maintained, outdated, and ancient urban transportation system, those in Oslo and Stockholm are clean, modern, and smoothly-operated. The Stockholm system has been called the world's longest art gallery for the site-specific decor and displays of public art that adorn most of its stations. Gärdet station is one of the less impressive specimens in the system, but it nonetheless remains clean, well-maintained, and free of the ungodly screeching of metal against metal that anyone who has ever ridden Boston's Green Line should be able to appreciate.

I emerged from the underground labyrinth at T-Centralen into the dim, gray light of day and walked the few remaining blocks to the Sheraton, where I had reserved a room for the duration of my stay in the Swedish capital. Its proximity to the train hub and short walking distance to Gamla Stan, the old town, gives it one of the best locations of any hotel in the city. Thanks to the fact that most travelers who possess the means to visit Scandinavia detest the notion of doing so in the cold, dark winter months, the hotel had reduced its rates for this time of year, and that proved impossible for me to pass up.

The room was ready when I checked in, so I dropped off my bags and spent the rest of the day wandering the cobblestone streets of Gamla Stan, taking breaks to peruse the Norse wares of the viking souvenir shop known as Handfaste, the records of renowned heavy metal store, Sound Pollution, and the books and board games of Science Fiction Bokhandeln. I finished the day off with a couple of pints of Swedish craft beer at the Ardbeg Embassy, a sophisticated pub with a rustic feel, complete with dark, wooden paneling and taxidermied stag heads adorning the walls. I gorged myself on a generous heaping of traditional Swedish meatballs, lusciously coated in creamy gravy and lingonberries, and reviewed the arrangements for my upcoming day-trip to Östergötland.

Upon first walking out of the train station in Norrköping, it is hard to believe that this was once one of the slummiest cities in all of Northern Europe. As late as the 1980s, the city was known for being a place of ruin and despair: a polluted industrial city that had fallen on the typical hard-times of the late 20th century's rampant relocation of all manner of manufacturing from North America and Europe to Asia. But now, blue skies dominate rather than the smoke-ridden ones of the past, and trolley cars idle by in front of the train station along a tree-lined boulevard that, in the summertime, features verdant, green grass growing between and alongside its tracks. Gardens, the river, and a smattering of mostly historic buildings lie just beyond the wide boulevard before the dense core of the city's downtown and mill district truly begins.

This is the part of Sweden with which I am actually most familiar because it is where I spent a year after college conducting my own little post-graduate research project. This was, of course, before I was thrust into the harsh and never-ending monotony of the office world. I had attempted to pursue a relatively practical path as a student, so my studies involved city planning rather than ancient and medieval history, which quite honestly would have been of greater interest to me. But be that as it may, I nonetheless learned a great deal about Swedish urban redevelopment policies, which, in turn, interested absolutely zero employers back in the U.S.

Norrköping together with its sister city of Linköping, twenty-five miles to the southwest, forms the fourth largest population center in Sweden after Stockholm, Gothenburg, and Malmö. The sister cities have long been rivals. Linköping, representing the well-to-do upper-classes, is the capital of the county of Östergötland and has long been a diocese in the Church of Sweden, administering a territory larger than that of just Östergötland itself. Additionally, it hosts a major university and has become a hotspot of tech businesses. Norrköping, on the other hand, has historically been a very working-class sort of place, full of factories, poor quality tenement housing, and a life expectancy lower than the national average. It's no coincidence that it is known as the Manchester of Sweden.

Östergötland is Swedish for "Eastern Geat Land," and anyone who paid attention in high school English class will recall that Beowulf himself was a Geat. There is also a "Western Geat Land," known as Västra Götaland (why Östergötland is one word but Västra Götaland is two and contains an extra "a" remains an unfathomable mystery), which comprises the part of Sweden that surrounds Gothenburg, or Göteborg as it's known within Sweden—the Fortress of the Geats. In the Middle Ages, Svealand—the area anchoring Stockholm and Uppsala and the ancestral home of the tribe that eventually came to be known as the Swedes—emerged as the dominant player in the region and assimilated the two lands of the Geats into its fold. Though lacking any semblance of certainty, it is this trifecta—the two Geatlands and the one Svealand—that may have inspired the national emblem of the Tre Kronor, or the Three Crowns. Various theories of the symbol's origins abound, but the Tre Kronor is found throughout the country with more frequency than the bald eagle is in the U.S.

I walked away from the train station down Drottninggatan, the main thoroughfare leading across the river, the Motala Ström, and into the center of town. Now the tenth largest city in Sweden, Norrköping was once the fourth largest, but that was prior to its decline when the textile and paper mills began to permanently close their doors in the middle of the 20th century. The northern end of the city center still maintains the luster of its bygone heyday—the city hall in particular looms large with its towering brick facade. The streets are paved with cobblestones and several open squares provide relief from the long shadows cast by the surrounding historic buildings. Not far from here is the city's Industrilandskap—a remarkably well-preserved collection of former mills and pedestrian pathways that crowd the river and its impressive manmade waterfalls.

I turned down the street of Knäppingsborgsgatan and headed towards Norrköping's industrial heart. My meeting for the day was located in an old flour mill, which appropriately had been converted to a modern-day bakery that now operates under the name of Bagarstugan.

Helena Bringholm was already inside and waiting for me when I arrived. She wore a thick, white outer coat and light blue winter hat replete with a fluffy ball on top, a fashion style that seems to be particularly popular in Sweden. We said our hellos and joined the line to order coffee and a pastry at the counter. We each ordered a steaming hot latte and Helena asked for a cinnamon bun whereas I went for a cardamon bun, a delicacy that I'll never grow tired of. I'll also never understand why this particular spiced gift from heaven suffers such a lack of popularity in the U.S. I've only ever encountered cardamon buns stateside at a tiny but great bakery in Portland, Maine. There is no denying that there are many other bakeries throughout the country that I have never visited, but I've made it a personal mission to visit as many as possible in New England. The dearth of cardamon buns is very real, and there is no satisfactory explanation for it.

Anyway, I offered to pay for us both since Helena was doing me a favor by meeting me here, but in typical Swedish fashion, she declined and paid for herself. We carried the trays bearing our pastries to the bar that ran along the window and began the seasonal ritual of unencumbering our bodies of our heavy winter gear.

Helena asked how my ride down on the train had been and we conversed about the usual basic introductory matters. She now worked for the city as a landscape architect, participating in the planning, maintenance, and design of the city's public parks and other open spaces, but she had been a student at the Swedish University of Agricultural Sciences in Uppsala when the incident that had brought me here today had occurred. It had been summer at that time, and she was in Norrköping simply to pursue an internship in her chosen field.

"And the troll just exposed himself to you?" I asked. Our lattes had been delivered piping hot and I took a sip; the injection of warm caffeine felt good. "He didn't say anything, he just jumped out on the path in front of you and exposed himself?"

"Yes, that's correct," she answered.

"Well, how does that even work with a troll? I don't get it."

"He opened up his trench coat and jiggled his willy at me."

"Well, that just sounds like a crazy person!"

Helena laughed. "I know! Believe me, I know how it sounds, but this was no man. I got too good of a look to know that."

Her observations could have proven priceless to cryptozoologists the world over if word of the incident had spread more widely. That's because troll genitalia have traditionally been overlooked by the classic artists of iconic troll illustrations, such as Theodor Kittelsen and John Bauer, as well as the toy manufacturers and movie producers who have more recently dominated the industry of troll aesthetics and established the prevailing depictions of such creatures in the name of their own commercial products. As it is, there are many different types of trolls ranging from the cute toy kind with neon hair to the sluggish moronic kind of Tolkien to the nasty, invisible kind of the internet (and vile though these latter trolls might sometimes be, they nonetheless deserve some modicum of credit for helping inspire my ongoing mission in the Northlands). But basically, there is no single type of troll, and no one really knows exactly what each of the various permutations of trolls look like, much less what their genitalia might look like, except, and unfortunately for her sake, Helena.

Apparently, this pervert had been lurking behind a clump of trees when she had innocently jogged by. The incident had occurred along the Åpromenad, a wooded trail system that runs along both sides of the Motala Ström immediately beyond the westernmost cluster of Norrköping's mill complexes. The pathways there are frequented at all times of the year but are especially popular in the warmer months when the rhododendrons are in bloom and the outdoor cafe along the river's bank is open and serving fresh coffee and warm slices of blueberry pie.

"Well, what did he look like?" I was intrigued, if a bit dubious in my belief. "And no one else saw him?"

"Oh, yes—he was very secretive," she said after taking a sip of her latte. "He clearly had waited for me, or for someone alone, anyway. There were plenty of people around that day but not always within sight of each other. I was by myself and when I came close to where he was, there was no one else around at the moment. So, he just jumped out, which startled me, and then he did...what he did. He was hairy and very ugly. He was a troll. I am sure of it. What more can I say?"

"So, what did you do? Just stand there staring at his little performance?"

"No!" She gave me a mischievous smile. "Well, I froze up at first, just from the surprise of it all, but then I turned around and hurried back the way I had come from."

"So, he didn't follow you, though, right?"

"No, but I could hear him laughing."

Helena proceeded to report the incident to the local police, who logged the complaint and then did nothing because they had their hands full processing mandatory routine paperwork and responding to reports of gang-related violence on the outskirts of the city. Violence, in a general sense, has increased dramatically in Sweden since the 1990s but has mostly been localized to the suburbs of the nation's larger cities. People generally tend to claim that this rise in violence is either entirely a result of *utanförskapet*—a Swedish word conveying a sense of outsidership and the failure of the social welfare safety net—or entirely a result of uncontrolled immigration from non-western countries. As with most divisive issues that are plagued by two completely and diametrically opposed viewpoints, the reality probably lies somewhere between the two most vocalized extremes. I'm American, so I know all about deeply entrenched, two-sided political division and an outright cultural refusal to compromise, but I've been disappointed to see a nation like Sweden, which has so long been famed for its ability to usually achieve broad consensus and compromise even on sensitive issues, fail so dramatically with this one.

At any rate, Helena's troll was allowed to walk free, and so being a mentally unhealthy pervert, he sought out another opportunity to flash her again.

"Was it the same location as the first time?" I asked.

She had just taken the final bite of her cinnamon bun and chose to politely finish chewing and swallowing before she answered. My cardamon bun, however, was already long gone because I had ravished it like a madman.

"It was on the same trail, but a little ways away from the first incident," Helena admitted. "And he used the same tactic. He was hiding behind some trees, and then he jumped out in front of me and exposed himself."

"It sounds like jogging along the Åpromenad was starting to become a bad idea," I commented.

"I was not going to let him win! I have just as much right to use those trails as anyone. They are open to the public."

I agreed with her but also knew deep down inside that if it had been me, I would have probably just altered my routine and selected a different part of the city for my run, at least for a short while, anyway.

"I turned around and went back the other way again, like I did before," Helena said. "And I reported him to the police again, and still they did nothing." She shook her head and exhaled in frustration as she said this.

Outside, it had started to snow. It was the light, flaky kind of snow and it swirled around in the wind tunnel created between Bagarstugan and the private elementary school housed in the chic, renovated Knäppingsborg mill complex opposite the large glass windows by which we were seated. Several university students hurried past en route to the campus facilities just a few blocks away across the river.

In Scandinavian mythology and folklore, all significant things tend to happen in threes, or multiples thereof, and so it was no surprise to me that Helena encountered the flasher-troll a third time. Whether due to her own obstinance or the workings of fate, she could not be deterred from her rightful claim to the responsible access and use of the jogging lands, and thus she set out upon her preferred Åpromenad trail once again. Except this time, she was prepared for the evil that lurked in the shadows.

"I found some old cat skin gloves at an antique store," she confided. "Mainly, I was looking for some cheap gloves that I would not mind throwing away. The fact that this pair was made out of cat skin was kind of gross, but they were so cheap. Only ten *kronor*."

That was slightly more than an American dollar, so I agreed, it was quite a bargain. Plus, cat skin gloves are special in the context of the Norse myths. Freyja, the goddess of fertility, is known to wear cat skin gloves as she drives her chariot pulled by two gigantic felines through the ether.

Wearing these fur-lined gloves, highly unfashionable and very conspicuous in the context of a typical running outfit in terms of 21st century standards, Helena set off along her favorite Åpromenad trail once again. And once again, the perverted troll leapt out at her from behind a tree when no one else was around. Only this time, Helena did not stop, nor did she turn around and run back in the direction from whence she had come.

"Instead, I ran straight up to him and gave him a powerful shove," she explained. "It's not like he was going to be able to move very fast, standing there in the middle of the trail like that with his arms spread out to hold up the folds of his trench coat while he gyrated his hips like Elvis. So, I just kept running at him and shoved him as hard as I could and he fell over."

I chuckled aloud; I couldn't help it. The mental image of this creep getting pushed onto his ass while doing his jiggly-dance by a woman who charged at him wearing bizarre gloves crafted of cat skin was too much for me to refrain. Helena smirked a little herself.

"But the thing is, he landed in a patch of sunlight," she continued. "And I had not thought about this before, but he had always stayed in the shade. The trails are very shady in the summer—the canopy is dense with all the trees, but there are some areas where it opens up, and I had pushed him into one of those gaps where the sunlight got through, and he immediately turned to stone."

So, now there was a troll turned to stone, lying in the middle of the path on his back with his arms in a strange flailed out position and his full, gruesome troll-hood on abhorrent, graphic display. Helena could not, in good conscious, leave him lying there for unsuspecting children or other innocents to accidentally stumble upon and be permanently scarred by, so she pushed his rocky carcass into the river.

"He was a lot lighter than I thought he would be." She took a sip of her latte. "His corpse was more like pumice than granite, which made it easy to push. And it floated, so I just watched it float away towards the mills. I suspect it got broken apart in the various waterfalls and that the pieces were eventually washed out to sea. But there were never any reports of anything strange floating down the river in the news, so it's impossible to know for sure."

But perhaps the troll's spirit lingers in the water between the vegetated banks of the Motala Ström. Maybe the life-force of this pervert was still lurking in the riparian flow, transformed into a *strömkarl* or *näck*, two variants of mischief-causing Scandinavian water sprites. I did not voice these unfounded speculations to Helena, who probably preferred to view the lout as having been vanquished forever.

She told me that she discarded the cat skin gloves, which were clearly tainted with troll germs, in a nearby rubbish bin and resumed her run, and when she returned home, did not bother to report the incident to the police. She had resolved the matter on her own and very effectively at that. I praised her courage, and gradually our conversation drifted back to normal, everyday things like the annoyances of coworkers, the drudgery of adulthood, and the evil genius of Walter White's meth-making empire, word of which had even infiltrated this relatively remote Northern European outpost.

Eventually she needed to end this little *fika*—the quintessential Swedish coffee break—and return to her job, and so we gathered our trays and carried them to the rack for used dishes, a ubiquitous feature of most Swedish dining establishments that don't offer full sit-down service.

I wished that my previous experience in Norrköping had overlapped with hers and that we had met then, but it's impossible to change the past, and the weavers of fate like to sport with us mere mortals. Helena and I promised to stay in touch with one another, said our goodbyes, and exited into the cold air, heading in opposite directions.

I intended to explore the trail system where Helena's awful encounters with the perv-troll had occurred. I had, of course, walked them before, but I also had some time to kill before I was scheduled to take the train back to Stockholm in advance of my interview the next day with one of the most formidable warriors of the Modern Viking Movement: the notorious Ingrid Törnblom.

HONVIKINGA SAGA

SELF-CONDEMNED IN THE TUNNELBANA

So, there I was, standing on a desolate Stockholm street corner in the swirling snow and wind, wondering to myself, "What the hell just happened?"

Only moments earlier I had been comfortably seated in Ingrid Törnblom's sleek, modern, and—most significantly—warm office, discussing the story of her unusual life. An entrepreneurial woman, she had been the founder of a short-lived but exclusive sisterhood of warriors that had harried settlements up and down the Baltic coast during the peak of the Modern Viking Movement. This achievement had made her one of the most prominent Neo-Norse figures, so I was certainly pleased to have conducted and completed my scheduled interview with her. Unfortunately, I could not recall most of the details that she had confided in me because, much to my own increasingly pervasive chagrin, I had not been paying much attention to what she said. Instead, I had been distracted by her amazing physique like a dog in heat.

Her hair had shone with the natural blond hue as stereotypically befit her northern nationality, and her eyes had sparkled with a shade of blue so intense that they had pierced my anxiety-ridden heart and reduced me to a lump of general imbecility at first sight. In retrospect, my immediate surrendering of social aptitude, not to mention proper brain functionality, was so complete that I now actually considered it something of a minor personal victory that I'd somehow remembered to record the conversation.

But what little contentment I did feel didn't last long because the snow was now gusting at me with all of the ferocity of a Bofors 40 millimeter anti-aircraft cannon. It thoroughly coated my thick out-erwear, and my mood grew as depressingly dark as the grim Scandinavian sky above.

Lightning flashed, ushering in the arrival of that rare weather phenomenon known as thunder-snow, and the sonic boom of an-other giant falling victim to Thor's wrath jarred me into motion. I began to run down the eerily quiet pedestrian thoroughfare of Drot-tninggatan towards Sergels Torg and the underground Tunnelbana station located beneath it. I dashed down the stairs and pulled my damned recording device out from the snow-dusted folds of my coat, hitting the rewind and play buttons in sequence.

Ingrid's subtle but perkily accented voice streamed out: "...so we took those guys as slaves. We figured they could keep the fortress clean and cook for us while we worked on improving our shield wall formations and ship maneuvering skills..."

She was referencing the booty that she and her loyal followers had infamously acquired through the threat of physical violence against a group of mid-summer male revelers on the Baltic island of Gotland. In an achievement heavily heralded by the cyber-trolls, she and her compatriots had supposedly stormed the beach like a me-dieval-weaponry-equipped version of the Swedish national bikini team and attracted the attention of a number of red-blooded male vacationers. A small handful of these men had then followed the women back to their home, where they were subsequently shackled and pressed into a life of contemporary thralldom, a degrading social status during the original Viking Age akin to slavery or indentured servitude.

But that was neither here nor there because what I wanted to know now was why Ingrid had suddenly tossed me out on the street like most employers that I've known. I'm used to dealing with rejection and being asked to leave, but I also usually operate under a heightened state of self-awareness that borders on paranoia and so when a boss tells me to get lost, I know full well why, and really, I can't blame them. With Ingrid, though, it was different. I had no idea why she had suddenly told me to leave, but I knew I hadn't hit on her with an atrocious pick-up line from a cheesy '80s movie or repeatedly fumbled a simple task such as making a stack of photocopies for her.

I reached the bottom of the stairs and made my way towards the wall where I stopped beside a map of the train system. Two Swedes approached and gave me furtive, disapproving glances while quietly determining the route of their upcoming underground journey.

I moved further away from the map, feeling highly self-conscious about drawing undue attention from the locals. In a land where conformity rules, you don't want to be the weirdo in the underground station slouched against the wall next to the system map giving off a sickening odor while listening to a bizarre audio track. Even though—and I believe this to the deepest core of my soul, despite certain plausible theories to the contrary—I didn't stink, neither did I face any nearby competition in the contest to win the title of freakiest underground loiterer of the day.

On the recording, Ingrid's voice stopped speaking and a short, awkward pause came next, followed by the sound of myself making some sort of incomprehensible gurgle indicative of positive concurrence. I began to hit the fast-forward and play buttons in the hopes of finding the section of interest by trial and error.

The Charioteer must have pitied my misfortune enough to take a break from his thunderous giant-slaying expedition in the sky to help me in my current pathetic endeavor because I succeeded in finding the relevant bit of the recording in short order.

A phone rang on the playback and Ingrid answered in her native tongue: "*Hej...nej...vad fan?! Hans kropp ligger var!?! Ursäkta, bara en minut...*I'm sorry, but I have to take this call, it's sort of an emergency. Thank you very much for coming. I look forward to reading your book. If you could show yourself out, I'd really appreciate it...*vad har hänt med kroppen?...den upptäcktes i en grovsopscontainer?...*"

And then there was the sound of a door opening and closing and the recording ended. It was yet another encounter that had come to an awkward, premature conclusion, and as usual, I had done as the lady bid, showing myself out, this time straight into the shit-show of weather that was now raging outside. But I hadn't understood everything that her voice had so rapidly proclaimed over the recording, so I cranked up the volume and replayed the section, straining my ears to better grasp the fragments of her hastily spoken comments.

I realized that she was saying "what the fuck?!" followed by something obscure about a corpse. The "what the fuck" part sounded kind of sexy, but the dead body part was off-putting. Why would she be talking about a dead body? To my knowledge, she and her cohorts had only ever enslaved their victims, not killed them.

I still hadn't fully comprehended all of Ingrid's comments, so I replayed the recording again. After a few more listens, I emerged triumphant over my previous failings and recognized the Swedish words for "authorities" and "dumpster." So, a body had been found in a dumpster?

Just then, something flashed, and it wasn't lightning from Thor's hammer. Instead, it was a smart phone possessed by a passerby who had just snapped a photo of me from a few paces away. Consumed by my own internal bewilderment, I hadn't seen him approach.

It was an awkward moment, and I lacked the mental capacity to react in any manner other than by staring straight back at him, mouth slightly agape, drool forming on my lips while he took another photo. I had increased the volume more than I probably should have during my rapture of attempted translation and had completely disregarded the potential side effects that could arise from the world outside of my own immediate preoccupation. Most likely, he had overheard all of the incriminating-sounding elements of the recording.

Then the station's lights flickered—ominously, just to add to the atmosphere of defeat—and the man backed away, dialing several numbers and raising the phone to his ear as he did so. "*Hallå, polis? Just det, jag har en sak att rapportera...*"

But it doesn't take a genius or a native speaker to recognize the word "*polis*" in the man's clearly articulated accusation, and the next thing I knew, the recorder was being stuffed back in my pocket, and I was back out in the snow, running down the bleak streets of Stockholm towards the inevitability of my fate.

KRAKI'S SEED IS SPREAD

It turned out that my fate lead me to the Espresso House located in the lobby of the Sheraton Hotel where I was staying. After a quick sojourn to my room to ditch my coat and fetch my laptop and ear buds, I settled myself onto one of the establishment's cushioned chairs with a steaming hot latte and cardamon bun and set about the task of reclaiming my memory from the mind-claws of the femme fatale that I had just so recently encountered. I prefer tinkering with my laptop to tinkering with my pocket-size recording device, so I set the recording to transfer between the two as I pondered the day's earlier events while staring out the window at the confluence of the Vasagatan, Tegelbacken, and Vasabron roadways and the medieval spires of Gamla Stan beyond.

I was only mildly concerned that I had been reported to the police because I suspected that they would do nothing. Even so, this turn of events brought the memory of Agneta's curse from the behavioral institute in Geithus storming back into the forefront of my mind. On the upside, I assumed that if the curse was going to adversely affect me in this matter, then local law enforcement would have already arrived and hauled me off to the nearest police station. At any rate, I had no desire to do anything overly stupid that might unnecessarily call negative attention to myself. Fortunately, it has always been rather easy for me to adapt to Sweden and Swedish culture. I have a natural talent for quietly melting into the shy crowd and had simply suffered an atypical moment of panic earlier when I spazzed out in the Tunnelbana station.

The recording finally finished transferring to my laptop, so I plugged in my ear buds, opened the file, and hit play.

"Chain mail is for pussies," Ingrid Törnblom's voice declared through the tiny speakers. "We wanted to prove ourselves as the toughest, roughest vikings to sail the northern seas. And that meant foregoing the more protective metal armor that other vikings of the time were using. Same thing with the use of leather armor. The amount of armor you wear is inversely proportional to the size of your balls, and we were going to show the world just how big ours were."

She had said this near the beginning of our conversation when my concentration was initially assaulted by her stunning figure. I distinctly remembered that she had worn a delightfully tight but very classy formal dress, leaning back in the chair behind her desk. She was an intimidating woman, and while her blatant physical attractiveness certainly solidified that fact in an old-as-time-itself sense, her Neo-Norse accomplishments were no less intimidating.

She had been the founder and former leader of the notorious, all-female band of modern vikings known as the Honvikings. And as with every other instance of activity relating to the Modern Viking Movement, reports of the sisterhood's activities had been confined almost entirely to the gossip and mistruth-ridden abyss of the world wide web, where they festered and spread, adopting the larger-than-life status that only the virulent toxicity of the internet can engender. The online accounts of the Honvikings ballooned from unremarkable reports of Swedish beach party/medieval re-enactment antics to eventual comparisons with the Spartans of ancient Greece, the Samurai of feudal Japan, and perhaps most flattering of all, the Jedi Knights of the Intergalactic Republic.

But nothing lasts forever, and the order of the Honvikings eventually collapsed under increased pressure from outside forces. Confronted with a harsh new reality in which she could no longer make a living as a rapacious, rogue shield-maiden, Ingrid had reinvented herself and pursued an alternate career that appropriately fit her nature as a predatory, uncompassionate, and conflict-seeking battle-axe of a beauty: she became a personal injury lawyer.

My own knowledge of the American legal system remains rudimentary at best, so grasping the nuanced details of the Swedish system was an endeavor that I had no desire to undertake. It didn't really matter, though, since the main thread of my conversation with Ingrid had involved her oration of the history of the Honvikings while I occasionally made strange grunting noises. But that did not stop her from lauding the lawsuit-obsessed culture of the U.S. with lavish praise.

"Is it true that in your country anyone can sue anyone else for pretty much anything?" she had asked eagerly, her eyes lighting up as she said the words, the dollar signs flashing a sickly green neon glow behind her pupils as if she were an avaricious cartoon character. I had been concentrating on giving her eye contact in an effort to prevent my glance from drifting downward and the sudden change in her tone to one of barely restrained enthusiasm had momentarily snapped me out my trance.

"That's basically how it goes..." was all I had been able to muster, but it was an answer that pleased her. The grin that spread across her face had been cold, hard, and calculating. I suspected that she was plotting something, like a deviant Icelandic *gothi*.

Back in medieval Iceland, a *gothi* was akin to a chieftain. Iceland at that time was a land with no formal rulers and thus operated as a rudimentary republic, which initially suited the settlers who had arrived there to escape the tyranny of the Norwegian crown during the 9th century. Initially serving as a pagan religious leader, the role of the *gothi* had gradually evolved to become a more secular position for men who had amassed substantial land holdings. Serving as arbiters in legal disputes, they were sworn to uphold the law and remain fair and impartial, but the honor system didn't prevent some *gothi* from using their status to advance their own personal agendas. As with legal matters of our own era, medieval Icelandic court decisions generally favored those who possessed the most power and money.

But Ingrid's comments about lawsuits came at a later point in the conversation, and right now I was listening to it from the very beginning.

"My old business partner, Viveca, had forced me out of our business," Ingrid's sultry, greed-driven voice explained in my ear. "We ran a small law firm together that specialized in tax and real estate law issues, and we made a killing at it. The business was young; only a couple years old when this happened, but it had gone remarkably well up to that point. We had both obtained our law degrees about ten years before that and had been hired by the same firm when we graduated, so we knew each other well and generally made a good team. I wouldn't say we were ever close friends, but destiny brought us together and we had similar goals. As we got to know each other better and advanced in our careers, we began to discuss plans of opening our own firm. And our plans grew more detailed as time passed, and eventually, we felt that we had each gained enough experience and knowledge and built up enough personal savings to split off and start our own firm. We were to be equal partners, of course, but every lawyer knows never to trust another lawyer. I had no reason to doubt Viveca's loyalties or intentions, but we drew up a proper business operating agreement to protect ourselves from one another in case our relationship might ever deteriorate. And the business really took off. What I didn't know was that Viveca had been building a case against me ever since we had first met in our first year at our previous company."

For the next eight minutes of the recording, Ingrid delved deep into the nuances of legal back-stabbing, the loopholes that allow such incidents to occur, and the masterful manipulation of highly circumstantial and occasionally completely fabricated data required to effectively remove a partner from a business venture with a severely reduced payout from that which had otherwise been established in the operating agreement. Honestly, I didn't understand most of the things that Ingrid had said because it was highly technical and boring and my mind started to wander. I found myself focusing on her hourglass figure while she discussed the nitty gritty of the unfounded violations that Viveca had used against her to take full possession of the business.

A police officer walked into the Espresso House at that moment and I felt my heart skip a beat. I sat in a corner of the establishment and shifted slightly to better hide my face. A patrol car was parked on the street outside with the driver behind the wheel, his face staring down at his lap as the obvious glow of a smart phone lit up the interior of the vehicle. I heard his partner order two black coffees and a couple of cookies and then walk back out.

I stopped paying attention to the recording while I fretted about the highly unlikely scenario of being accosted by the Swedish police for the crime of listening to a strange recording in a subway station. I told myself that I needed to stop worrying about this. I tried to convince myself that Agneta's threat was not only empty, but that it also had no bearing on my present circumstances. Plus, I'd seen on the news that a substantial proportion of the local police had bigger fish to fry today thanks to a bout of car arson that had erupted during the night in the suburbs of Husby and Rinkeby. My case was no doubt lumped in with the same heap of pointless crap as the reports about a neighbor's dog who had barked too loudly or a juvenile delinquent who had littered and crossed a street while the walk signal remained red.

"Women were highly underrepresented among most 21st century viking raiding fleets," Ingrid now said over the recording. "I needed a break from practicing law but also needed to do something that would allow me to amass a fortune. Having a fortune would make it much easier to eventually exact my revenge on Viveca. So, the notion of establishing a new, utopian all-female viking society from the ground up was fated. I wasn't happy about what had led to that moment, but this new door had opened, and if I took command of the situation properly, the new sisterhood would not only help bridge the viking gender gap but also allow me to become filthy rich and plot against Viveca with an entourage of battle-hardened berserker women backing me up. But for such a sisterhood to live up to its full potential, we couldn't have any weak links, so it was necessary to hold tryouts. And the tryouts involved an epic free-for-all battle at Fyrisvellir near Uppsala."

Lying alongside Fyrisån, the river that runs through Uppsala, Fyrisvellir was an important parcel of land that visitors to the ancient Swedish royal residence or heathen temple at Uppsala had needed to cross after disembarking from their boats at the riverbank. Due to the warlike nature of historic Scandinavian kings, who constantly vied for domination and control over one another, several legendary battles have been fought at Fyrisvellir. Most notable, perhaps, is the one that pitted Eric the Victorious against his nephew Styrbjörn the Strong, with Eric emerging victorious, hence his nickname. Fyrisvellir is also said to have been the place where the Danish King Hrolf Kraki scattered gold coins amidst a wild retreat in an effort to distract the blood-thirsty Swedes who were chasing after him and his men. Such tactics were all part of a usual day's work back then thanks to the recurring dynastic conflicts between the Swedish and Danish royal families of the era.

I wasn't really sure what Ingrid had meant, however, when she claimed that she had held the Honviking tryouts at Fyrisvellir, since it doesn't exist anymore, at least not in the same manner that it used to. Uppsala has grown to be a substantially sized modern city—the fourth largest in Sweden—and most of the land between Fyrisån and the location of the old hall and temple is now built up with housing. Fields remain in the area, though, and I assumed that she had arranged the tryouts at one of these. But rather than ask her for clarification, which would have required some modicum of effort, self-control, and assertiveness, I had just let her continue to tell her story uninterrupted.

"I advertised on all of the usual online viking forums and word of mouth spread pretty quickly," Ingrid's voice continued. "I got a lot of responses. Hundreds of potential shield-maidens turned out for the event, and the battle din rang loud and shrill that night and curious spectators crowded around to watch. After several hours, there were twenty-seven of us still left standing; I announced that the tryouts were concluded and the Honvikings were officially formed. I was immensely pleased with those who made the cut; we had quite a variety of women from all walks of life. We had a shepherd's wife from Tromsö, a professional businesswoman from Örebro, a government worker from Ribe, and a former hotel concierge who had somehow made it out to Fyrisvellir all the way from Nova Scotia in Vinland, just to mention a few. But the important thing was that we all came together and united under a common goal: plunder and pillage with the highest possible distinctions of prestige, excellence, and, most importantly, monetary gain."

She next explained how she acquired substantial seed funding from a venture capital firm to get her operation up and running. Apparently, it had been an easy task because she presented a very convincing case that the Honvikings' total revenue in unlawful plundering would vastly exceed their expenditures, and of course the investors were eager to get in on that. It also didn't hurt that she possessed a natural talent for effective public speaking and that her audience had been mostly male. The sole woman who had been present on behalf of the venture capital firm expressed some doubts about Ingrid's plans and figures, but had quickly been overruled by the firm's good ol' boys.

Ingrid herself loathed the aspect of the arrangement that required her to relinquish an equity stake in the Honviking enterprise as part of the brokered deal, but strong allies with deep pockets have always come at a high price. Personally, I appreciated the irony that Ingrid had received seed funding for a war-mongering start-up that had been founded where the "seed of Fyrisvellir" itself had been sown— which is what the ancient skalds called the gold that King Hrolf Kraki had scattered upon the field so long ago during his epic retreat to Denmark.

With Kraki's seed metaphorically in her hands, Ingrid had set about achieving two milestones critical to scaling the Honviking enterprise up to effectively enter the fiercely competitive plundering market. First was the acquisition of a proper longship, which she explained was purchased from Vikingeskibsmuseet in Roskilde, Denmark. Vikingeskibsmuseet, or The Viking Ship Museum in English, is a highly renowned museum and learning center established on the island of Zealand, where Copenhagen is also located. In the late 1000s, five viking ships had been intentionally sunk in the Roskilde Fjord near Skuldelev in order to create a barrier below the water's surface as a means to prevent other vikings from sailing further towards Roskilde itself and sacking the settlement there. The ships have since been excavated and are now on display at Vikingeskibsmuseet, which also houses the authentic Norse boat-building center from which Ingrid purchased her ship. Supposedly, they make the best replica viking ships that venture capital seed investments can buy. My own travel plans would lead me to the Roskilde region after I departed Stockholm, but I would be visiting a mystical modern viking burial ground rather than Vikingeskibsmuseet.

Ingrid's second crucial business investment was the purchase of land for the establishment of Honborg, the Honviking's glorious Baltic fortress of legend. Built on the shores of Honholm, according to hearsay as propagated by the internet, its reputation preceded itself as a shining beacon of Neo-Norse valor and camaraderie.

But as Ingrid's voice continued to whisper these sweet nothings into my ear about the ancestral seat of the Honvikings, I came to understand that Honborg's physical structure wasn't really anything all that unique or special. Neither was Honholm. She simply gave the plot of coastal land that she had purchased with the seed funding the name of Honholm, which only implies, albeit incorrectly, that her property was a small island. Likewise, Honborg wasn't really a fortress as its name suggested, but rather a regular summer cottage in the village of Lickershamn on the northwestern shore of the Swedish island of Gotland, which lies just over 100 miles southeast of Stockholm.

But despite the incongruence between reality and rumor, it was nonetheless from within the hallowed halls of Honborg that the Honvikings hatched their schemes for wealth, glory, and total domination of the Baltic Sea.

THE SACKING OF ALMEDALSVECKAN

"I made the decision to sack Visby first," Ingrid's voice explained through the miniature speaker in my ear.

The medieval walled city of Visby lies about fifteen miles south of Lickershamn, where the Honviking's base of Honborg had been established. The city is incredibly well-preserved and has consequently become a major destination for summer tourists who either arrive and choose to stay in town or pass through en route to another supremely pleasant spot elsewhere on Gotland. Massive cruise ships load up thousands of passengers and hundreds of vehicles in the port towns of Nynäshamn, Oskarshamn, and Västervik each day to ferry them the two-to-three hour journey across the whale-road to their idyllic vacation destination.

"It was a simple decision, really," Ingrid's voice continued. "We had just finished settling into Honborg earlier that week, and our longship had been delivered from Denmark. It was a beautiful ship with a fearsome dragon figurehead on the prow. I named it the *She-Serpent*, of course. Once I saw the ship, there was no doubt in my mind that this was the only name for it. And at that point, summer was already in full swing. Visby was close by, and full of loot for the taking, so it was time to launch our first raid. It was a hot day when we boarded the boat for its maiden voyage, so we just dressed in our most comfortable and airy tunics and leather pants. And armed with swords and shields, we began rowing towards the walled city.

"Our timing was perfect. No one knew that we were coming. They had to have seen us approaching in the *She-Serpent*—we were hardly inconspicuous. But Almedalsveckan was going on, and everyone probably thought that we were part of some stunt planned by one of the political parties in attendance."

Almedalsveckan is an annual week-long political rally for the major Swedish political parties that takes place at Almedalen, a city park adjacent to Visby's shoreline. This event has occurred every July since 1968 and allows politicians the chance to give speeches, hold seminars, and deploy various attention-getting devices in a casual, summertime party-like atmosphere. It also gives the media a full week of political pandering to swarm like flies on dog shit. The whole thing is essentially the inverse of the American presidential getaway. It would be as if, rather than fleeing to Martha's Vineyard to enjoy some privacy and escape the public's eye for a short while, the president and the leaders of all the other major political parties (which in the U.S. would, obviously, only actually involve one other individual) were to gather at Martha's Vineyard for a generally good-natured, non-hostile, open-air political convention expressive of most viewpoints with an added dash of the delirious insanity of Nevada's Burning Man festival thrown in for good measure.

"When we sacked Visby, none of the spectators realized what was going on," Ingrid's voice explained. "They all assumed our warship was part of the festivities for the political event, and the reality only settled in after we had started harrying the people standing around closest to the water."

As Ingrid described it, the Honvikings had beached their ship on the small, rocky stretch of beach just below Visby's seawall, then charged up the stairs to street level and began running amok in the park. The spectators transitioned quickly from stupefied to befuddled when Ingrid strode towards the nearest news crew and destroyed the camera with a blow from her sword and a deafening warcry. The clip can still be seen on YouTube and shows the shield-maiden approach, heft her sword high above her tussled blond hair, and then slice downwards directly at the camera itself. The footage, naturally, ends at this moment.

Still perplexed about the viking newcomers, the attendees of the political convention continued to simply stand in place as the situation unfolded, looking at one another with increasingly confused expressions on their faces.

"Clearly, they were expecting one of the political leaders to step forward with an explanation," Ingrid had mentioned. "It wouldn't have been the first time such a dramatic stunt was pulled at Almedalsveckan."

Such attention-craving spectacles have become increasingly commonplace at Almedalsveckan, with the 2005 declaration of the creation of a fake political party founded by artists and entertainers being one prominent example, and the burning of 100,000 *kronor* on stage by Gudrun Schyman in 2010 being another. Schyman had claimed that torching such a large pile of cash demonstrated her condemnation of the wage gap between men and women, presumably because actually donating that money to a charity that might have benefitted women would have never garnered the same degree of celebrity-style spotlight from the Swedish paparazzi. Considering the carnival-like showmanship of previous Almedalsveckans, there was nothing surprising about the attendees' expectations that some politician would soon grab a megaphone and start lecturing everyone present about some political issue that he or she cared about passionately, or at least hoped to appear to care about passionately.

"We had hoped that Gudrun would have another pile of money to burn that we could plunder, but such was not the case," Ingrid's voice sighed with a vivacious exuberance in my ear. "I suppose some stunts are only effective once and repeat incidents lose their luster. But on the upside, everyone was so baffled about what was going on that we were able to just start walking up to people and yanking purses away from the women, expensive digital cameras away from the men, and backpacks away from anyone who wore them. It wasn't until one of the Honvikings knocked another woman onto the ground and cut her purse strap with her sword that people began to realize something was wrong and started freaking out and running around in all different directions."

Of all the epic deeds committed during the Modern Viking Movement, the Honvikings' sacking of Almedalsveckan had garnered the most attention from traditional journalists. In addition to the aforementioned YouTube clip, *SVT* (short for *Sveriges Television*, the state-operated television broadcaster), *Dagens Nyheter* and *Svenska Dagbladet* (two of the major Stockholm newspapers), and *Gotlands Tidningar* (Visby's local newspaper) each covered the incident, but in a very scrubbed-down and censored manner. The commotion caused by the Honvikings was clearly reported, but nothing was stated about the identities of the perpetrators, just that a group of troubled individuals had caused a disturbance and that some property had been damaged. Coverage and the public's interest quickly blew over when only two days later a new study that compared the prevailing sexual habits found in each of the Nordic nations was unveiled and the day after that Jeff Bezos bought the small island nation of Tuvalu. Such incidents quickly overshadowed the relatively tame and insignificant harassment of Swedish politicians and their entourages that had occurred on Gotland.

But Ingrid and her loyal Honvikings acquired substantial plunder—in addition to cash, many credit cards and phones were also found in the various purses and backpacks that they forcibly confiscated. And the digital cameras they looted would resell for good value on eBay—a tactic that had already been proven lucrative by Trond Troll-Breath Trondsen and his Neo-Norse whalers. All in all, Ingrid considered it an excellent days' work and a highly successful maiden voyage, until the return trip back to Lickershamn, anyway.

I remembered that she had looked at me coldly and said, "That's when we ran into some trouble."

THE ACQUISITION OF THE MAN-SERVANTS

I leaned back in my chair and assessed the situation. My cup was now empty but my bladder was full and growing increasingly agitated with my ongoing deliberations. I didn't really want to go back to my room for the rest of the day—it was only the middle of the afternoon, after all. And I knew myself well enough to know that if I went back now with the intention of doing anything remotely productive, I'd most likely pass out on the bed instead. Being located in the lobby of a hotel, there was no public restroom in this Espresso House, and I didn't trust any of the assorted strangers sitting nearby to save my seat and watch my computer while I dashed off to the nearest water closet, anyway. So, I gathered my belongings and took the elevator up to the floor where my room was located.

A few minutes later I savored the sweet taste of relief and decided that I would head back out into the snow for the fifteen minute walk to Aifur, Stockholm's very own viking tavern. It's an excellent spot, replete with proper decor (not in a cheesy way—which is a testament to the establishment's owner and interior designer) and a menu authentically derived from the material remains found on cooking and eating utensils at Viking Age archaeological sites. Aifur also serves mead, and thus it seemed to me like an optimal place to finish listening to Ingrid's tale.

Twenty minutes later, I was seated at Aifur's bar with a goblet of black currant mead in my hand. The tavern was dimly lit with candles and lanterns and the space felt somewhat cramped—the bar is nestled into a rather insignificantly-sized platform that overlooks the main dining floor below. As with many eating and drinking venues in Stockholm's Gamla Stan, Aifur occupies an ancient cellar with vaulted ceilings and no natural light, an architectural circumstance that actually lends itself very well to the restaurant's chosen theme. A grand, wooden hall might perhaps have been even more appropriate, but such a structure would need to be built anew and would certainly not be found in such a prime location in the historic heart of the city.

It was late in the afternoon but still earlier than typical work quitting-time, so the place was mostly empty. I pulled my laptop out of my backpack and set it on the wooden bar. Turning the machine on added an unnatural glow to the otherwise fire-lit, cavernous depths of the establishment, and the bartender raised an eyebrow. He was dressed in a proper off-white medieval tunic and wore a Thor's hammer amulet around his neck, all of which contrasted starkly with my modern day clothing of plain jeans, black sweater, and Boston Bruins baseball cap.

"*Känner du till Ingrid Törnblom och Honvikingarna?*" I asked.

His response indicated that he was not only unfamiliar with Ingrid and the Honvikings but that he also had no idea why I would ask such a seemingly random question. I explained that the Honvikings had been the female sea-raiders who had sacked Almedalsveckan some years back.

"*Just det, just det...*" he uttered before adding that he remembered hearing something about the incident at the time that it had happened but that he had also completely forgotten about it since. I related how I had just interviewed the group's leader earlier that day and was listening to the recording on my laptop. He shrugged and nodded, clearly apathetic to my reasons for piddling with computer technology in a business built to resemble the aura of the 9th century. He began cleaning a glass and I put the earbuds in my ears, took a sip of mead, and resumed listening to Ingrid's story.

"We were rowing past the Novi Resort, which is just a kilometer north of Visby's city wall, when the trouble began," Ingrid's voice continued from where I had paused the recording earlier. "It's a big beach resort with bungalows, a pool, a bar and restaurant, the whole works. And it turns out there was a group of guys on the beach playing volleyball. They were basically trying to show off to any woman willing to watch, of course."

I pictured the beach volleyball scene from *Top Gun* and Kenny Loggins' song, "Playing with the Boys," began to reverberate in my mind, overshadowing Aifur's medieval-style music that had become the faint background to the playback of Ingrid's voice. It was easy to imagine the whole situation as an '80s movie scene: the ball drops to the ground as the men stop and stare at the Honvikings who row past, the oars dipping below the waves in perfect unison with the women's masterfully synchronized motion to propel their vessel across the waves. And just like Maverick, several of the men lost all interest in the present round of volleyball in favor of pursuing their lust. But rather than hopping aboard a motorcycle to rendezvous with a sexy civilian flight ops instructor, they instead climbed onto their jetskis and tore off in hot pursuit of a full crew of shield-maidens.

"There were four of them that chased us," Ingrid's voice elaborated. "By the time they had gotten to their jetskis and started them up, we had made some good headway past the resort, and it was not till we had rowed another few miles that we saw them in our wake, but some of those jetskis can go upwards of sixty miles per hour, so they gained on us fast. The men were unarmed, but they proceeded to do loops around our ship and other stunts, trying to show off and impress us. It continued like that all the way back to Honholm, at which point we enslaved them."

Apparently, the Honvikings had beached their ship first along the narrow strand of Honholm just east of the Lickershamn village harbor. The women jumped out and collectively pushed the ship far enough up the beach to firmly anchor it in the sand while the men hung back, silently watching as their now-idling watercraft steadily bobbed up and down with the motion of the surf. They soon joined the women on land and proceeded to do what dude-bros do best.

"They hit on us, of course," Ingrid's voice explained. "And they were probably used to it working in nightclubs and bars and the usual summer resorts. They weren't ugly men, and it was clear that they worked out. Under other circumstances, it might have been tempting to flirt with them. But they had invaded Honholm, and that left with me with no choice but to order that they be taken captive. Which they didn't seem to mind. I don't know what they thought we were going to do with them, probably something perverse, to tell the truth. But all I intended was for these slaves to basically just keep Honborg clean and prepare our meals for us while we practiced our skills of seamanship, combat, and poetic oratory."

And that's what happened. The men became Honborg's de facto—for lack of a better or less literal term—man-servants. And for the most part, they didn't seem to mind living their lives as modern-day thralls. The entire situation basically evolved into a Neo-Norse microcosm of the prevailing trajectory of gender relations in Sweden as a whole, which has gone further to up-end the traditional roles of men and women than most nations. The man-servants stayed home with their house-wife duties while the woman-warriors sailed to new lands to rape and pillage.

"Although we never actually raped anyone," Ingrid had clarified with a look of disgust stamped across her face. This comment had come during one of my rare moments of lucidity in her presence during which I had asked if the Honvikings ever actually conducted the atrocious act as a follow-up question to her generalized comments about the plundering voyages that they had embarked upon.

"I simply said 'rape and pillage' as a figure of speech," she had continued. "I didn't mean for you to take it literally. We were more of a stealth operation. Quick strikes in and back out with plunder, then back to Honborg."

And the voyages were effective. The Honvikings sacked many summer resorts around the Baltic. They visited Sopot, Poland, looting many of the city's best spas for high-end health and beauty products. They harried Pärnu, Estonia, and plundered its jewelry shops for gold, silver, and precious stones. And they made landfall at Binz on the German island of Rügen, where they destroyed a gazebo and filled the hold of their ship with casks of stolen wine.

All in all, the Honviking experiment was going amazingly well. The plunder exceeded Ingrid's expectations, which also pleased the seed investors. Honholm was thriving, and Honborg itself operated as a well-ordered and well-maintained establishment. The man-servants obeyed their masters and friendly relations developed between the two distinct social classes of thrall and free-woman. And, as was often historically the case with the original Norsemen and their thralls, the Honvikings' man-servants were given certain protections by law, including the opportunity to eventually purchase or earn their freedom. Original Viking Age owners of thralls were even known to sometimes set them free out of good will, and it seems plausible that such a scenario might have also eventually happened with Ingrid's man-servants, too, considering how harmonious the relations became.

But then an ominous message arrived during an otherwise typical, raucous night of traditional Honviking mead pong and set in motion a sequence of events that would upend everything.

THE MEAD PONG PROCLAMATION

Mead pong exploded in popularity during the Modern Viking Movement and nowhere was this more true than at Honborg. The tradition has left an indisputable mark on Honborg and its surrounding countryside; it is nigh on impossible to explore Honholm without encountering a modern-day rune stone that praises glory won by the paddle or that honors the memory of a pong warrior who fell in drunken combat (literally, as in lost balance and crashed to the floor beside the pong table). Furthermore, treasure hoards containing mead pong artifacts are still sometimes uncovered in the region, often to the chagrin of professional archaeologists who are then called to investigate the discoveries. Additionally, the surviving manuscripts of the Honlandic Sagas—which primarily take the form of undeleted text messages that have been uploaded to a website dedicated to their posterity—mention numerous instances wherein mead pong served as the primary means of arbitration between two quarreling Honvikings. Elaborate pong-inspired artwork etched into the walls, doors, and fixtures of Honborg is still visible and was largely responsible for the reduced asking-price when Ingrid eventually decided to sell the property after the collapse of the Honviking sisterhood. Yet, despite this rich legacy, which so clearly proves that mead pong was much more than just a casual pastime for the Honvikings, its primary role as a fun drinking game was never fully diminished, either.

The game is basically a more ferocious, Neo-Norse variation of its collegiate cousin, beer pong. The basic principle remains the same: for an individual or team to direct a ping-pong ball into one of the opponents' drinking vessels, forcing them to drink the alcohol contained within. The first person or team to empty all of their drinking vessels loses the game, but also, in a figurative sense, wins. The most notable difference introduced by Neo-Norse mead pong is that the table is made of polished oak and is not covered with plastic cups filled with cheap beer but instead with hollowed-out animal horns filled with strong, high-quality mead that are stabilized on the playing surface with special iron horn-holders. Additionally, the game is played with paddles as opposed to the more common but benign beer pong practice in which participants simply try to toss or bounce the ping-pong ball into their opponents' cups. The handles are removed from these paddles and the broad, flat surface is cupped in the palm of the hand by participants while playing. And in true Norse fashion, these paddles are often elaborately decorated and given illustrious names such as Mead Biter, Splash Giver, and Sinker.

"Mead pong is spectacular entertainment, but it also laid the groundwork for our eventual downfall, unfortunately," Ingrid Törnblom's voice stated over the audio recording as I took another sip of my own mead from where I sat in the dim light of Aifur's bar.

"We had just returned from a very successful sacking at Mariehamn," her voice continued. Mariehamn is the small city in the Åland Islands between Finland and Sweden with the lax booze laws that I had sailed past myself en route to Stockholm. "And we had liberated massive amounts of alcohol, so a mead pong tournament after the feast seemed like a no-brainer. Our tournaments were usually single elimination rounds of Thor's Hammer, but to commemorate this special occasion, I decided that it would be appropriate to play one giant round of Mighty Fjord."

As with beer pong, various permutations of mead pong also exist, in which the nuances of the specific rules, arrangement of the horns on the playing surface, and number of players varies. Thor's Hammer, Rune Stone, Cock n' Balls, Freyja's Sheela Na Gig, and

Mighty Fjord are just some of the most popular variations, with Mighty Fjord being the one that allows the most players to compete simultaneously. Players are partnered up in pairs in what is an other-wise giant, free-for-all mead pong bash.

My recording of Ingrid's voice continued: "To accommodate a match this epic, we had to push all three of our heavy oak game ta-bles together so as to form one gigantic playing surface, and then we filled the horns with mead. We partnered up and started out with a dozen balls in play, since we had so many players—we also allowed the man-servants to play, too. It was the Ragnarök of mead pong tournaments and the competition was extremely fierce."

Ingrid had explained in great detail how chaos soon reigned and the forces of darkness unleashed themselves upon the three tables, covering their surfaces in splattered honey booze. The war cries and ping-pong ball clatter echoed through the hall's rafters and drowned out everything else. But as the battle raged on and players were elim-inated, the number of balls in play was also reduced. Those who were eliminated simply gathered around and cheered on until eventually only a single ball and two paddle-warriors remained: Ingrid herself and a thrall named Stefan Hagerfors.

"He had shown himself to be a highly talented pong warrior prior to this time," Ingrid had elaborated. "So, I knew I had my work cut out for me if I was going to defeat him. And it was an even match, too; both of our partners had already been eliminated and we both had exactly two full horns of mead remaining. But before the compe-tition between us really started, the ball rolled away from the tables and while someone went and chased it down, Stefan erupted into an explosion of drunken vows. As I mentioned, he had already proven himself to be a very strong pong warrior in previous tournaments, but he had never actually won one before. We were all already very drunk, but he really went overboard with all of his boasts. He talked about how if he won this match, he'd finally purchase his freedom with the gold he'd steadily acquired as gifts from some of the Honvikings who liked him best. He said he'd sacrifice nine oxen and erect a monument in honor of Thor. The list of things he said he'd do for Thor just went on and on. And he was a thrall, remember, so this was very out of line. Then as he was blessing Meadmagnet, his paddle, someone burst into the hall. We all turned and looked at this intruder and Stefan himself stopped abruptly in the middle of casting Fehu—the rune of luck—over Meadmagnet."

A lone stranger stood silhouetted against the diffuse sunlight shining in through the outer doorway of Honborg's backyard entrance. Despite the lateness of the hour, the almost-midnight sun still shone and prevented the figure from being clearly discerned by the gathered Honvikings and their attendant man-servants. A hush settled over the crowd as the figure stepped inside, took off his hat, and approached Ingrid.

Ingrid had sighed, "He was a messenger sent by my parents. He explained that he had tried to ring the front doorbell, but no one had answered and that's why he snuck around to the back like some sort of thieving scoundrel. But I bid him welcome, and after some initial greetings, I asked him why he had come and what news he had. He explained that since I had not been answering my phone or responding to emails, my parents had become worried and hired him to look for me. Fair enough, I supposed; I had locked that stuff away since moving into Honborg. Part of our utopian experiment involved severely limiting the use of electronics. It's amazing how much you can accomplish when you're not wasting time with digital technology. But he also delivered us news from the outside world and there was one piece that really shook me up. My old business partner, Viveca, he said, was planning to sell the business to a larger firm down in Copenhagen. First she had forced me out, and now she stood to profit greatly from her traitorous behavior. I could not tolerate it; she had to be stopped. So, right then and there, I made some vows of my own. I asked Freyja for her favor, promising her great sacrifices if she would grant me victory over Viveca. And I asked for a sign of her good will—a sign that we all would see that day, if she favored me. I asked her to grant me victory over Stefan in this mead pong tournament."

The atmosphere was tense and Stefan finished casting Fehu upon Meadmagnet, but his effort had been interrupted, and because he was completely plastered, he also fumbled the rune. Ingrid, on the other hand, perfectly cast Tiwaz, the rune of victory, upon her paddle, Sinkwand. Thus prepared, the two pong-warriors faced off as everyone else resumed their cheering and jeering.

"I remember the messenger remained entirely expressionless the whole time," Ingrid's voice related. "At least I think he had been expressionless; it was hard to tell with his thick beard. He just stood off to the side and watched all of this unfold. I would have been happy to let him join the Mighty Fjord tournament if he had arrived earlier, but he hadn't. Plus, he only had one eye, so I'm not sure if he would have even wanted to play anyway with that disadvantage. In the end, I think he had a good time and drank plenty of mead from the sidelines.

"Anyway, I served the ball to Stefan once we resumed the game, and he actually gained the upper hand early on with a sink in one of my horns. I drank up and the game continued, and in all honesty, it was a sloppy mess. Battles are always sloppier near their end than when they begin, whether on an actual battlefield or beside a table covered in mead horns. I eventually managed to even the score, but the quality of the match really deteriorated; it was mainly just a stop and start competition between two drunks with deadened reflexes. I'm sure if the messenger, who wasn't nearly as drunk as anyone else, had stepped in to play, he could have dominated either one of us even with his limited range of vision. But the rules are the rules, and in Honborg we adhered to them with honor. There was a lot of suspense since it was an even match, and the fulfillment of the vows to Thor and Freyja that Stefan and I had each made hung in the balance.

"I eventually returned the ball on one of Stefan's serves and it went straight towards the messenger's face. It smacked him in the forehead and then landed in Stefan's horn. He tried to object because we didn't have any rules regarding bounces off spectator's faces one way or the other, but everyone else was already going crazy with the victory. It set a precedent. Stefan recognized the hopelessness of his situation and admitted defeat. He chugged his last horn and stood there in silence. And we all knew then that Freyja favored me. We would sail to Copenhagen to stop Viveca's treachery, and, with Freyja on our side, we would surely be victorious."

FATE OF HONVIKINGS

All this talk of mead pong had made me thirsty for a mead refill of my own, so I made an inquisitive facial expression at the bartender who ambled over and listened to me butcher his language as I asked for a glass of the native Swedish linden mead. Aifur's drink menu stated that this particular mead replicated the taste of the mead that had been consumed at the ancient Norse trading outpost of Birka.

Birka had been one of the few substantial settlements to have existed in the Norse homelands twelve hundred years ago. Located on the shore of the island called Björkö in Lake Mälaren some eighteen miles west of Stockholm's Gamla Stan, Birka essentially grew to become Sweden's first town (although depending on the specific qualifications used, the nearby town of Sigtuna alternatively qualifies for this distinction as well), providing shelter to approximately a thousand people at its height. The Swedish kings of the era kept watch and provided protection for the town's inhabitants from the royal residence of Hovgården on the neighboring island of Ädelsö.

I didn't know how the good proprietors of Aifur were able to acquire a mead from Birka when Birka hasn't existed as an inhabited settlement for over a thousand years, but I was aware that Patrick E. McGovern and other archaeologists and brewers were working to recreate ancient beverages based on the preserved traces of ingredients left behind on unearthed drinking vessels. I assumed that the brewers of this Birka mead had concocted their beverage based on such data or some other relevant historical knowledge.

The archaeological and historical records certainly allow modern brewers to make approximations of ancient beverages with an authentic selection of ingredients, but we will never know exactly how the mead from the original Viking Age actually tasted.

The bartender set my linden mead down on the bar with a silent nod and I raised the glass to take a sip. It was light and refreshing, neither too sweet nor too dry. The flavor perfectly complemented the archaic atmosphere of the establishment and the jolly voices emanating from its lower floor. The historic mood was further enhanced by the arrival of a minstrel, who replaced the stereo system's playlist and now performed live medieval music from a nook in the wall of the lower room.

It was also at this moment that I realized that most of my time spent with the modern vikings so far had taken place with the accompaniment of various varieties of fermented beverages. My actual interview with Ingrid might have been one of the exceptions, but I had nonetheless chosen to consume some alcohol while listening to the majority of the recording's playback. I supposed it made sense in a way. The vikings—both ancient Norse and Neo-Norse—were notorious drinkers who took great pride in their ability to hold their liquor, so imbibing as much as I had been doing could be seen as an effort to embed myself as deeply as possible into the culture to gain a better understanding of it. There's also the more practical, if somewhat stereotypical, aspect to drinking in the Nordic nations: that the Scandinavians, generally speaking, are more culturally reserved than most other western nationalities, and thus they rely heavily on booze to help break past their inherent inhibitions. And then of course there is the irrefutable truth that all vikings know to their very core: that even a really great story can still be made better with the inclusion of a drink.

Having successfully convinced myself that I was properly honoring the old ways with my drinking habit, I placed the earbuds back in my ears and resumed listening to Ingrid's glorious story.

"Planning the voyage to Copenhagen didn't take long, actually," her voice told me. "We had all the supplies on hand already that we needed and I learned from the messenger the important details having to do with Viveca's meeting with the Danish executives. Our plan was to intercept her before she got there. She was scheduled to meet them at the Danish firm's office at Sankt Annæ Plads, so we would sail to the Kvæsthus Pier, tie our ship up there, and then deploy lookouts surrounding the office for all possible approaches."

The area Ingrid had described is among Copenhagen's most central and heavily visited. The Kvæsthus Pier, while once a busy docking place for steam ships, is now a modernist public plaza that hosts a variety of events and pop-up style mobile businesses. The portion of the pier that is attached to land lies immediately adjacent to Sankt Annæ Plads, a broad, tree-lined boulevard where the treacherous business meeting was fated to take place. It is generally considered to be the boundary between Nyhavn, the city's iconic 17th century canal-oriented maritime neighborhood that has grown to be immensely popular with tourists, and Frederiksstaden, the luxurious, rococo neighborhood that is home to Amalienborg, the Danish royal palace.

Ingrid's plan was to basically kidnap Viveca before she entered the firm's premises and force her to sign another legal document that she—Ingrid—had prepared herself, thereby gaining sole ownership of the business that Viveca had immorally stolen. My knowledge of the legality of business transactions is admittedly limited, but I suspected that Ingrid's plan of a forceful coercion would not hold up in court should Viveca decide to contest the matter afterwards. All of which made me think that Ingrid must have had some sort of incriminating information about Viveca that Viveca did not want made public. I assumed that I was learning about a classic case of extortion and that I just didn't know all the details. I had regained some of my mental capacity by this point during the interview but, despite the unaddressed logistical problems plaguing Ingrid's scheme that I should have inquired about further, one question in particular had jumped to the immediate forefront of my mind.

On the recording, I heard myself ask, "So, what did you plan on wearing?"

An uncomfortable silence followed on the playback. The atmospheric strumming that originated from Aifur's lower floor reached my ears with more clarity as I took another sip of the linden mead.

I remembered this part of the interview, so I knew what was coming next, although I couldn't recall exactly how long the pause had lasted.

Finally, I heard my own voice once again. "Well, I'm just wondering you know, because...well, I think wearing swimsuits and carrying swords and axes, would...uhh, well, that maybe would attract a lot of attention in central Copenhagen...more so than at, like, a beach resort..."

"Do you really think we would have sailed over four hundred kilometers all the way from Honholm to Copenhagen wearing nothing but bikinis?"

"Uhh..."

She had then proceeded to reprimand me and clarify that the official Honviking wardrobe never actually included bikinis. As is to be expected of anything reported online, rumors regarding the bikini-related attire of the Honvikings had been recklessly fabricated, propogated, and amplified without rational thought or care.

The Honviking mission to Copenhagen involved a stealth incursion into to the bustling streetscape of Sankt Annæ Plads, so the women donned standard modern attire for the journey rather than some of their more medievally-optimized woolen tunics and animal pelts. It still seemed to me that a troop of twenty-some-odd women dressed in normal attire and equipped with medieval weaponry would attract undue attention in the heart of Scandinavia's second-largest city, especially if these women arrived via wooden longship. Mooring it at the Kvæsthus Pier wouldn't exactly be inconspicuous. The nature of this Honviking mission seemed to be one that needed to rely on an ability to blend in with the local scenery. Typical Honviking tactics had previously relied on shock-and-awe, and while they were extremely effective for lightning-fast in-and-out raids, they didn't seem to me like the best approach for this particular mission.

Ingrid, of course, had concocted a stratagem to circumnavigate that issue.

"A dozen of the women would remain with the ship," her voice explained with a hint of malice. "They would put on a show for the bystanders. A mock viking battle. Such things are commonplace at that pier. And while they did that, the rest of us would melt into the crowd, armed only with smaller weapons—daggers and knives—and take up our posts surrounding the entry to the law firm. We would appear to be just your average women loitering in a fashionable part of the city."

I had to admit, it made a certain kind of sense. But I had also recognized that we had discussed this entire event completely speculatively. We hadn't been talking about it as though it were an event of the past that had actually happened.

I remembered being pleased with myself for having regained enough of my wits and the capability for coherent thought when I had asked my next question: "So, what actually happened? It sounds like you had this plan all worked out, but that it never actually got off the ground."

Several seconds had elapsed before she uttered, "Björn Svensson."

"Björn Svensson?"

"Yes, Björn Svensson," she had replied.

Björn Svensson was the Modern Viking Movement's most renowned warrior-poet. Along with Ingrid herself and Trond Troll-Breath Trondsen, Björn completed the unholy trinity of the most influential figures of the recent Neo-Norse epoch. I hoped to meet him soon; he had also emerged as the most enigmatic key member of the Modern Viking Movement that I had discovered during my initial internet research, and I intended to seek him out at the end of my itinerary. I had been unable to establish any contact with him prior to setting out on this investigative adventure, but I had found evidence indicating that his home was near Gothenburg, and so I had set that city as the terminus of my pan-Scandinavian expedition. His reputation certainly preceded him and I knew of the rumors about his monster-slaying quests and epic word-craft, but this was the first that I'd ever heard that he and Ingrid had crossed paths.

"I didn't know you guys knew each other..." I had said.

"Well, we don't, not really, anyway...we exchanged a few words, that was it. He's not really a bad or evil guy, just a moron and kind of a dick. I don't hate him the way I hate Viveca. But still, he ruined everything."

Basically, Björn's fishing trawler had rammed the *She-Serpent* midship as the two vessels simultaneously approached the Danish capital city off the coast of Zealand.

"The guy's a loser and an alcoholic!" Ingrid's voice practically shouted. "I'm sure he was drunk at the helm when he steered his boat right into ours. Well, I know he was. I could see the bottle of Absolut Vodka in his hand. The crash ruptured the *She-Serpent*'s hull. She was a great ship, but she had no chance to withstand that impact. Björn's boat hadn't even slowed down. It's like he didn't even see us. It was our right of way—he was to our port—and he just maintained his original speed and direction. Plus, his trawler was powered, and we were under sail. He violated some long-held rules of the waves. I don't know how he ever got his boating license."

Björn didn't slow down upon impact, either. He just kept pushing forward, as though it were a game of bumper boats and he was the vicious, overly zealous child who had cornered an opponent and rather than relinquish his prey and rejoin the others in the main fray, instead chose to just keep pummeling the same target he'd already hit again and again and again. The *She-Serpent* quite literally broke in half as Björn's trawler plowed through it.

"We were all scrambling to the bow or stern to get out of the way of the trawler's prow. The *She-Serpent* was letting in water like a sieve and there was nothing we could do about it. Just absolutely nothing..." Ingrid's voice trailed off.

I had hoped for a tale of an epic sea battle like the one that had unfolded at Hjörungavágr off the coast of the western Norwegian district of Sunnmøre in the year 986 when a Danish force had attempted to consolidate its control over Norway. The Norwegian vassal, Håkon Jarl, had revolted when Harald Bluetooth, the Danish ruler, attempted to force Christianity upon the Norwegians. Harald Bluetooth had already been weakened due to confrontations with the Holy Roman Empire to the south, and his loss at Hjörungavágr resulted in severing the shackles of Danish overlordship in Norway— for a while, anyway. The battle has since become the stuff of legend, helped in part by its backdrop of an incredibly intense hailstorm that pelted the sea-bound warriors as they fought on the decks of more than two hundred ships all packed tight together near the mountainous coast. Ingrid's tale, however, could better be described as an infuriating and embarrassing defeat that ended before it even began.

"Björn just stared at us through the window of his trawler's bridge and waved with his bottle of vodka as his ship finally split the *She-Serpent* in two," Ingrid had uttered with exasperation. "Our ship's pieces were starting to drift away, and obviously, we were taking on water fast. I was standing on the gunwale at the stern and just let him have it. I can't remember everything I said, but I cursed him out. He got the full treatment—modern insults combined with actual Norse curses to damn his luck and his fortune. He actually went out onto his deck at that point but all he did was shout back that he was sorry and said something about having a date with Ariel, whatever that meant. I told him that this would turn out the worse for him if he didn't pull us out of the water and make a worthy recompense for the loss of our ship. He owed us that much at least. But he just shrugged, took a swig from his bottle, and then he went back in and continued on his journey. We watched his ship sail away as we went down with ours. We weren't far from Trekronerfortet, at least, so we swam to it."

Trekronerfortet, or the Three Crowns Fort, is an artificial island that was constructed at the entrance to Copenhagen's harbor in 1713. It is one of three such manmade fortifications built to protect the city from foreign invasion, all of which now host recreational activities and sight-seeing opportunities of various sorts. Situated on a landmass shaped like a narrow, hollowed-out half-octagon, Trekronerfortet sports some well-maintained maritime architecture and hosts conferences and parties in its historic stone buildings. Of Copenhagen's three sea forts, it lies the nearest to the city's urban core and is accessible by a regular ferry during the summer months, which meant that the Honvikings were in luck—if one could call it that—once they made it ashore.

Björn's trawler had struck the *She-Serpent* north of Trekronerfortet, meaning that the artificial island's long jetty was the closest point of contact for the Honvikings to reach. After clambering up the rocks, they admired what was in truth a spectacular view of the city and then began trudging towards the fort itself.

I distinctly remembered the disgust in Ingrid's voice at this point in the conversation as she made an inarticulate snorting sound. It was the type of abhorrent sentiment that comes only with the complete and utter loss of faith in humanity as a whole.

"Everything just collapsed in a few short minutes." Her detest of the situation was palpable. "And where was Freyja? I thought she was on my side, but she was nowhere to be found. She's a goddess of war, you know, and people often forget that. But maybe she had locked herself in her house and refused to come out because Odin was trying to sell her to the giants again or something. I just don't know."

I had chosen not to say anything about the mead pong tournament's outcome. It wasn't my place and I didn't want to irk her, but I had been less than convinced that she was the true winner when she had explained how the ball had bounced off the one-eyed messenger's face and into Stefan's cup. I didn't doubt that she could have or should have won, but to me the incident seemed like it should have been replayed. Maybe Odin himself had interfered and put Thor in time-out for doing something bone-headed, and perhaps Freyja had been trapped in her house just as Ingrid had surmised.

"But no one was hurt...and that was good," Ingrid's voice continued. "And we were able to catch the ferry from Trekronerfortet back to its home berth along Langeliniekaj in the city. Of course, the tourists all just gawked at us from the fort like we were space aliens from the moon as we walked towards its walls. I suppose no one is used to seeing an all-female viking crew wash up on a stone jetty attached to a decommissioned 18th century sea fort anymore."

"Did you still have your weapons with you? Or were those lost at sea?" I had asked.

"Fortunately, we had left most of our better weapons back in Honholm," she had sighed in response. "So, we didn't lose those aside from the few that were meant to be part of the distraction at Kvæsthus Pier. As I said, this was meant to be more of a stealth operation. So, we all had daggers sheathed at our belts, and those weren't lost, at least."

I could only imagine the scene, and it struck me as no surprise that the tourists had gawked. A group of dripping wet women equipped with the smaller instruments of medieval warfare who marched along a stone jetty with a small lighthouse in the background is not something anyone sees everyday. I harbored no doubt that most if not all of the tourists who witnessed this spectacle had taken photos of it with their phones. Some of them had probably even uploaded their images to Facebook or Photobucket (since the abomination of Instagram had not yet been founded at the time), but the content must never have gone viral. And given the fleeting and generally vapid nature of social media, the posts are now even more of an element of the distant past than the three-hundred-year-old stone walls that hold Trekronerfortet together.

The big kicker to this travesty was, of course, that Ingrid and her brethren were unable to reach Sankt Annæ Plads in time to intercept Viveca and prevent the devious business deal from going down. So, in the end, it didn't really matter how Ingrid had planned to enforce Viveca's compliance and silence on the matter.

During the interview, Ingrid had started seething with internal rage when she said, "We failed to stop her and Viveca sold the business. The ferry left Trekronerfortet at 3:00 that afternoon, and the meeting had been two hours earlier. There was no hope, so we just headed straight to the train station, bought tickets back to Sweden, and eventually made our way to Gotland and Honholm."

They traveled through the night, and when they finally arrived at Honholm the next day after hiring several taxis in Visby, they learned that there had been a slave uprising during their absence. The three women who had been left behind had been surprised and overpowered by the four thralls, who looted Honborg's treasure room and escaped after recovering their jetskis.

"We returned to find the Honvikings who I'd left behind tied to the anvil in the smithy," Ingrid's voice said. "Apparently, they had let down their guard and didn't realize that the thralls were planning a revolt. Given how much leeway the thralls had at Honborg, it's not too surprising that they got their hands on some weapons when no one was looking and were able to commandeer the fortress. I should have left more women behind to look after the place. Everything about the mission to Copenhagen ended in disaster."

Having lost the *She-Serpent*, the man-servants, and most of the treasure that the Honvikings had accumulated during their summer raids, Ingrid was forced to make the difficult decision of disbanding the sisterhood and selling Honholm.

"I didn't want to..." she had said despairingly. "But there was no way we could come back from this. The investors expected a return on the seed capital they'd put into this venture. Sometimes you win, sometimes you lose, and the investors knew this—it's the name of the game for them, but this time they had invested in something that wasn't strictly legal according to either contemporary Swedish or international law, and those gangsters threatened to report us to Interpol if I didn't pay up. As it was, they still lost money, but it was close enough to break-even that they let the matter rest. And the rest, as they say, is history."

"And that's it? You just gave up and started your personal injury practice? What about Viveca?"

"Funny you should ask that." She had smiled her devilish smile once more. "But yes, I moved on. I don't like what I do now nearly as much as what I did when I was the leader of the Honvikings. But it's okay. I'm good at suing people and this is the best way to forcefully take other peoples' money aside from piracy, going a-viking, or being a tax collector. Sweden isn't as good of a country to be a personal injury lawyer as yours, but I've learned my lessons from the past and rarely lose a case these days. I don't leave myself exposed like I did with that initial entanglement with Viveca. And I have a plan to get back at her. A long-term plan, and many short-term plans, too. I've never stopped plotting against Viveca. In the time since the downfall of the Honvikings, the tires on Viveca's car have been slashed, burning dog shit has been placed on her doorstep, her house has been TPed, and the trees in her backyard have been chopped down. She knows I'm behind it all, but she's never been able to prove it. And just today, I am exacting my latest revenge."

I had raised an eyebrow at this.

She had leaned forward, excited. "Oh, the Honvikings are still very alive, but we stay out of the limelight and communicate with one another only in secret. And Viveca has this cat she is very fond of—Alfred the Noble, as she calls him. He's one of those fluffy, puffy cats. Today, we are kidnapping him and we are going to give him a full body shave."

I couldn't help but laugh at the time, or now again either, for that matter, as I listened to this part of the conversation. The bartender looked at me apathetically and then went back to playing with his phone.

"And then what? Are you going to return him to Viveca's house?" I had asked.

"Of course! We do not support hurting any animals. I just want to irritate Viveca as much as possible until I can fulfill my long-term plan of revenge. It is my life's new mission. And the more people I successfully sue, the more funds I acquire to further my cause."

"And this is happening now? One of the former Honvikings is at this moment—"

And that's when Ingrid's phone had rung, cutting me off mid-sentence. She had reached into her purse, pulled the perpetrator out, and answered immediately. "*Hej...nej...vad fan?! Hans kropp ligger var!?! Ursäkta, bara en minut...*"

She had then covered the phone with her hand and said, "I'm sorry, but I have to take this call, it's sort of an emergency. Thank you very much for coming. I look forward to reading your book. If you could show yourself out, I'd really appreciate it."

She had gestured impatiently towards the door, and with a quick swivel of the chair, turned and spoke very quickly into the phone. "*Vad har hänt med kroppen?...den upptäcktes i en grovsopscontainer?...*"

And that's when I had found myself standing outside on a Stockholm street corner in the swirling snow, wondering what the hell had just happened.

THE STORY OF
JØRGEN THE BEER-GHOST

ENTER THE DRAUGR

I stood and watched as the vast array of burial mounds burned brighter and brighter with a sickly green haze. The strange luminescence had started just moments before, and one by one, each of the mounds had come to life, emanating its own unnatural radiation while the cooling embrace of the sun's descent had crept across the desolate landscape. The frigid waves of the Roskilde Fjord lapped against the shore behind me, a soothing sound that dampened the unnerving effect of the scenery.

I had come to this remote corner of Denmark for the very purpose of viewing these burial mounds, because unlike those at Borrehaugene or Lindholm Høje, these were not more than a thousand years old. Having been constructed after the turn of the millennium, these mounds were fresh meat straight off the butcher's block, still warm and dripping with blood in archaeological terms, which is why they had piqued my interest. I had no plans to actually meet or talk to anyone here because I hadn't ever established contact with anyone associated with the mounds' construction; none of the online rumors revealed any identifying information of that sort. Instead, the rumors had simply pontificated at length about the awe-inspiring magical energies associated with the mystical site and divulged its location. So, unlike all of my other destinations, I was not here to interview anyone but rather to simply observe the place with my own two eyes.

The journey to Denmark had been easy enough: an uneventful but direct five-hour ride on a smooth, high-speed train from Stockholm to Copenhagen. The train had pulled out of Stockholm's central station on time at precisely 8:21 a.m., crossed over the frozen waters surrounding Gamla Stan, and plunged into the tunnel directly beneath the rocky cliffs of the Södermalm neighborhood. It emerged on the other side and sped through the suburban hinterlands, which were in turn followed by a mix of farmlands, forests, and small cities before reaching Malmö, at the country's southern tip, and the famous bridge to Copenhagen.

While impressive in its own right as the longest rail-and-road bridge in Europe, Öresundsbron also gained a unique, new degree of notoriety in 2011 as the eponymous bridge of the highly acclaimed Swedish-Danish television crime series, *The Bridge,* which has since been adapted into five distinct remakes in other nations, including a version produced by FX that takes place on the U.S.-Mexico border. The journey over Öresundsbron itself offers splendid views of the sound between the two Scandinavian nations before diving deep into a tunnel at Peberholm, an artificial island created specifically for the purpose of facilitating the bridge-to-tunnel transition. Trains emerge again at Kastrup, the station for Copenhagen's airport, before continuing onwards to central Copenhagen.

After arriving at the central station, I had taken the quick walk past the tree-filled 19th century amusement park of Tivoli Gardens, which was closed for the winter season, to Rådhuspladsen, the large plaza in front Copenhagen's Rådhus, or city hall. Built in the National Romantic style, the city hall is an impressive brick structure topped with the oxidized green patina of copper roofing and adorned with an ornate clock tower that asymmetrically rises above its own massive bulk. In the street median that runs beside it stands a monument called *Lurblæserne,* a sixty-six-foot tall sculpture of two ancient lur (a type of horn) blowers designed by Anders Bundgaard and consigned by the Carlsberg Foundation to celebrate the one hundredth birthday of Carlsberg Brewery's founder in 1911. Across from *Lurblæserne* is the Scandic Palace Hotel, itself a resplendent and historic brick building in which Judy Garland, Audrey Hepburn, and

Errol Flynn each stayed during the golden age of filmmaking. It's somewhat ironic that Scandic has taken over ownership of the property since then, because while Scandic is certainly a fine hotel chain, it is more of an economic one rather than a grandiose and opulent one.

At any rate, it was where I had booked a room for my stay in the Danish capital, so I had checked in, dropped off my bags, and spent the rest of the day exploring the area around Strøget, the city's splendid pedestrian shopping street. It has been car-free since 1962 and consequently highly influential to city planners around the globe. After a cursory round of exploration by foot, I stepped into ROAST, a local Danish peddler of high quality coffee to warm up in the midst of my otherwise aimless wandering.

The Swedes were very clearly invading Danish territory with Espresso House's unstoppable expansion, and while I'm a fan, I also wanted to try something unique to the local scene. Happily fueled up, I continued my journey, with a little more aim and purpose, to ensure that I caught the sites around Nyhavn, Sankt Annæ Plads, and Kvæsthus Pier that Ingrid Törnblom had told me about just the previous day. A trip to Trekronerfortet was unfortunately out of the question due to a lack of wintertime ferry service, but I made the trek to the *Little Mermaid* statue to admire her in all her lonesome glory as she stared longingly out to sea. It was rumored that she'd lost her head at the hands of Björn Svensson during the height of the Modern Viking Movement, but here she was, fully restored, intact, and endlessly sad. I hoped to learn more about her decapitation at the next and final stop on my itinerary, but for now I simply enjoyed the opportunity to take a few photos of the famous fairy tale lady in the blustery weather with no other tourists obscuring the view. I returned to Strøget, grabbed a to-go kebab from one of the local shawarma establishments, and then settled in for a couple of pints at a cozy little bar near Rådhuspladsen called Taphouse that featured sixty-one wondrous beers on draft.

When I woke up the next morning, I headed back to the station to hop aboard the train towards Frederikssund where I then caught a bus the rest of the way to Skuldelev. From the bus stop it was a half-hour walk to the water's edge where I now stood alone in a bizarre 21st century graveyard purportedly full of the rotting corpses of modern-day Spear-Danes.

The sun was setting, so it was time to go. A grim, pagan burial site—even if archaeologically unvalidated—is no place for a foreigner to be in rural Scandinavia after dark, especially when an eerie green glow settles across the land, so I began retracing my steps towards the road that led to the bus stop.

As I emerged from the maze of mounds, a sudden crashing noise shattered the quiet night air and interrupted my happy thoughts about the cleanliness of Nordic public transportation systems. Looking back, I saw a cloud of dust billowing outward from the nearest mound, its tiny particulate matter rapidly spreading grave filth in every direction. I coughed and through the murky, green haze glimpsed a pile of fresh debris that blocked a previously hidden opening in the mound's surface. Then something that looked like a human arm began to reach outward from the shadows and twitched wretchedly. The sound of a muffled voice mumbled something indecipherable from its direction.

I regained some sense of composure and took a few steps towards the debris as the appendage continued to twitch. It was indeed a human arm, and the skin appeared to be bruised and bore the markings of an ornate tattoo job gone horrendously wrong. I also saw what I assumed to be skid-marks; whomever the arm belonged to had probably escaped out here to needle up in peace and quiet, away from the bustling towns or Copenhagen itself.

The voice spoke again, more coherently this time. It sounded like Danish. Danish is not a comprehensible language to anyone who isn't Danish, so I said loudly and as confidently as I could muster in Swedish, "*Vad?*" meaning: what?

The twitching appendage froze and after a short pause its owner emitted a barrage of Danish word vomit so lengthy and garbled that I just stared slack-jawed in confusion. After several seconds of further silence, two simple words were finally moaned with sufficient clarity: help please.

Rather than jumping into action as a more mature and decisive individual might have done, I instead chose to beat around the bush by timidly asking the junkie what had happened. His response fully overwhelmed my linguistic deficiencies once again, so I switched tactics and asked, "*Engelska?*"

"Yeah...English, sure," he answered. "But, dude, my home just collapsed on me. This fuckin' sucks, bro! Can you, like, help me out here?" His voice possessed a sort of colloquial bro-ish intonation that I hadn't been expecting. It sounded like the guy was unhurt, which I supposed was a good thing at least, but I was confounded because who in Folkvangr's green fields would actually choose to live in a desolate burial mound, whether it was real or a modern-day fake?

"What? This is your home?" I asked.

"Yeah, bro. There used to be more people out here; it was actually a pretty vibrant place a while back. There was a fortress and a whole garrison of Spear-Danes, but most of that has fallen into ruin now. But my home is still in pretty good shape, overall. It's such a sweet little hobbit hole but it totally blows that it just collapsed on me right now."

His comment was the first verification that I'd encountered regarding the rumor of the modern Spear-Danish army and its great earthen fortress that had been located somewhere along the Roskilde Fjord. Supposedly, it had been a measure to help ward off incursions from the Franks and Saxons to the south and the Geats and Swedes to the north. So, maybe there was some truth to this one after all. I hadn't been expecting verification to come in the form of a homeless junkie trapped beneath grave mound rubble, but as I've learned over the years, sometimes you just have to take what you can get.

"So, bro, you think you could help me out a little here?" he asked, and I realized that I had failed to respond to his previous comment. "It kind of sucks having a bunch of shit blocking the only way in and out of my home."

I didn't trust the guy, and even though he could say the same of me, he was still a stranger lurking around a creepy pseudo-cemetery in the nighttime. But that made two of us and I felt bad for him.

No one deserves to be trapped in a cold, dark barrow of dubious origins, so I agreed and began to help clear away the rubble. I could hear him doing the same from his side of the barrier and as our work progressed, the surprisingly bright green glow from his own mound began to reveal carvings on a wooden beam that framed the opening. They clearly depicted the slaying of the dragon, Fafnir, by the hero, Sigurd.

I decided to break our mutual silence. "So, Sigurd and Fafnir, huh? That's cool."

The junkie's reply was quick and hostile: a slang-ridden digression degrading Sigurd beyond anything emotionally reasonable but oddly praising Fafnir as "a righteous dude." This struck me as odd because in the original saga Fafnir was a huge asshole and everyone hated him, including his own brother. I decided to say nothing more.

Our work progressed in silence, with the exception of the junkie's own personal death-growled rendition of "Whistle While You Work," and the rustling of the wind. Soon we had doubled the size of the gap in the debris and it was large enough for the junkie to easily climb out if he wanted. I straightened up and was about to suggest he do just that when I got my first good, clear look at him.

His arms weren't covered in tattoos or skid-marks as I had first thought. Instead, all of his skin—arms, exposed torso, face, hairless scalp—shimmered with a streaky consistency like that of a rotten banana. With only a pair of old, leather breeches on, he looked seriously bloated all over, particularly in his belly region. It wasn't a pretty sight, but worst of all were his eyes. The unnatural yellow color of his eyes lent his face the sort of casual doesn't-give-a-fuck yet completely evil expression most commonly found among domesticated felines.

And that's when it hit me. These were not the eyes of an ordinary junkie. These were the eyes of a corpse risen from the grave for the sole purpose of climbing atop the roof of the nearest farmhouse to whoop and holler all through night like a goddamned lunatic, which only meant one thing: I was looking face-to-face at a *draugr*.

The Icelandic sagas are riddled with references to *draugar* (which is the plural form of *draugr*, of course). Regarded by the medieval Icelanders more as ghosts rather than some form of marauding zombie as perhaps may seem more apt, *draugar* were known to inflict a great number of nuisances upon farmers. If left unchecked, this undead Spear-Dane would likely graduate from his bored, teenage-esque antics to a full-scale rampage targeting the local livestock and any passersby who might be unlucky enough to wander into his territorial bubble.

I wasn't sure what to do. I felt like the moron in one of the thousands of recent Hollywood movies who needs to kill the zombie or the vampire or whatever in order to stay alive and eventually impress the hot girl. The plot of the day demanded that I beat this monster to death now, before he could bite me and turn me into some sort of monstrosity myself. But that was a ridiculous fantasy. There was no hot girl, or anyone else for that matter, waiting for me to come to the rescue.

He must have seen the dumb-founded look on my face because he asked me what was wrong.

I spoke the first thought that came to mind, which was an incoherent garble, yet the meaning behind it transcended all linguistic boundaries.

"Don't worry, bro, I'm not going to eat you." He smiled, revealing a mouthful of discolored rot and decay. "You know how much it sucks being trapped in here? I mean, it's like, shit man, I can only come out at night n' all, so I just wanna get out, you know? But then when these mounds all start glowing like a bitch, all that spooky green fire or radiation or whatever the fuck it is reduces the structural integrity of my home and then the damn entrance collapses on me because that's where it's weakest. Then I have to dig all night long just to get free and the repair work afterwards always sucks ass, but you being here to help out, man, that is so rad! Like, seriously. We'll get this done so much faster. I owe you big time."

"Huh?" I replied with the utmost eloquence.

"Yeah man, seriously. Hey, after we finish clearing out the entrance we can have a drink. I got some brewskies downstairs.

Seriously, bro. I'm not going to hurt you. Yeah, yeah, I know everyone always thinks the *draugr* is pure evil, going to eat you or rip your arms off when you're not looking, or whatever, but I'm just not into that kind of thing."

He sounded pretty friendly for being a member of the unholy undead but my brain was still flat-lining, so I just continued to stare blankly at him. My mind began to form a vague notion that Agneta of Geithus' curse might have finally caught up with me here, but I couldn't process the implications of that any better than I could process the *draugr*'s own words. So, I continued to stand where I was, staring at him speechlessly.

He continued, "Like, sometimes when I get drunk, I like to go torment the neighbor's goats, but that's about it, dude. For real, I don't hurt people and I never have. I'm chill. I mean, I wasn't even a warrior when I was alive, I was just the brewmaster back before the fortress got abandoned. All I ever did was brew the beer for the other Spear-Danes, 'cause us Spear-Danes, we can't function without ale and it was imperative to have an expert brewer around full-time, you know?"

I wasn't really sure what the hell he was talking about since my own knowledge about the fortress and the modern Spear-Danes was limited to farfetched online rumors, but I was starting to believe that he might actually be sincere in his proclamations of peace. Maybe it was the knowledge that if he really wanted to kill me, I'd already be dead. *Draugar* are notoriously fast and strong, and I wouldn't escape if he didn't want me to. They are creatures of rage and passion who flip out at the drop of a pin, massacring their victims instantaneously. They are not cold, calculating killers who plan their crimes in advance like serial murderers. He wasn't going to lure me into his posh pad and then torture me in a hidden room like some freak businessman in a best-selling Swedish crime novel.

Finally, I muttered, "Okay."

Still substantially mentally incapacitated from the shock of the entire situation, I stepped forward to help remove the remaining pieces of rubble.

"Yes!" The *draugr* was pleased by my movement. "Dude, thank you. Thank you so much! N' I mean for real, I got some real tasty brewskies downstairs. Wait, you do like beer, right?"

"Oh yeah, definitely..." For me, beer has always been a good tool to help overcome befuddlement, socially awkward situations, and life in general. "So...uh, what kind do you have?"

"Oh, man, I got lots. Lots! They're all my own recipes, of course. We can try 'em all. I'm going to start with my Geatish Demise Pilsner which has a light, crisp, clean finish and is brewed according to the German Reinheitsgebot, you know the old beer purity law. I also got some maltier options like Down in the Mound Oktoberfest or my Frozen Fjord-Death Black Ale, which is probably my personal favorite. You can try whichever ones you want. Oh man, this is going to be great. I haven't had a drinking buddy in years."

I was slowly coming back to my senses, and with that, really beginning to warm up to this guy. He looked all rotten on the outside, but if his statements proved to be true, then his heart was as gold as the brightest barley on a cloudless day. We continued chatting and finished clearing the rubble in short time.

With the entrance fully accessible, I hunched over and stepped inside. The *draugr* stood upright beside me. I looked at him and he smiled a big, goofy grin. His teeth were all black and blue and crooked, of course, but most of them were there.

He extended his hand and I reached out and shook it. It was cold and scaly and I hoped he didn't notice me wiping mine against my pants afterwards.

"All right bro, I hope you're thirsty!" He beamed with excitement. "Follow me."

We were standing at the top of a stone landing and he turned and proceeded to walk down a curving staircase to our right. I still harbored some lingering doubts about the wisdom of following a reanimated Neo-Norse corpse into an earthen tomb, but I felt both too committed and too timid to back out now. Provoking the undead is probably never a wise course of action, and honestly, we were getting along fabulously so far.

I looked around as I followed him and noticed that the mound's interior was much larger than its exterior appearance belied. The lighting was dim, but the space was sufficiently illuminated by the otherworldly green glow of the turf dome above to make out its character. The walls were composed of simple, exposed rock and the room itself was surprisingly cozy-looking, with a smattering of chairs, tables, couches, and of course, the massive stainless steel tanks and bar along the far wall.

"Hey, what's your name by the way?" I asked. We had reached the bottom and I was following the *draugr* across the room.

"Jørgen," he answered and asked me the same. I told him and then he stopped and turned around. "Well, Rowdy, here we are! This, as you can see, is my brew station. I'll show you how it all works but first, how about that pilsner? Unless you'd like to try another option first?"

"The pilsner sounds excellent."

"Right on, bro." Jørgen lumbered behind the bar and retrieved two pint-sized drinking horns from beneath it. The bar featured about a dozen taps and he pulled the one that depicted a speared horse violently face-planting itself into the ground with a wounded Beowulf look-alike astride it. Shimmering brew flowed forth from the spout and into the first horn.

After he filled both horns, he handed one to me and we looked each other in the eyes and nodded. We raised our horns, clinked them together, declared "skål!" in unison, and then tilted our heads back and drank.

The sweet nectar entered my mouth, euphoric and redeeming. Crisp and clean, just as Jørgen had promised. I felt my initial inhibition fully depart and in its absence came the full, genuine realization that this was only the beginning of a truly beautiful friendship.

DRINKING WITH THE DRAUGR

That beautiful friendship concluded with my inglorious awakening on the cold, hard ground outside of the burial mound the following morning with no corporeal Spear-Danish ghost in sight.

My head throbbed and my body ached and I didn't know how I had gone from the warmth of Jørgen's splendid burial mound microbrewery to the snow-encrusted grass upon which I was now sprawled out beneath the somber, gray sky. I hadn't frozen to death, so I could count that as a blessing—and no small one, either; Denmark might be the farthest south that my travels would take me, but the winter temperatures at its latitude still aren't known to nourish the health of hapless drunks who pass out in open spaces without warmth or shelter.

I struggled against my own dead weight to sit upright, and with that noble task accomplished, noticed the empty drinking horn lying beside me. I picked it up and examined the sticky residue that had crystallized across its surface and saw that the symbol of a rudimentary spear was branded across it—the same logo that Jørgen used for his brewery, if I remembered correctly. I scraped some snow together in an effort to wipe the horn down and deposited it in my backpack; it would make a good companion to the horn I'd received from Trond.

I wasn't sure what the hell had happened and began to wonder if I had dreamed the whole thing. But the notion of a dream failed to explain where the horn might have originated. Maybe someone had come out here to carouse with friends during the warmer months and lost it during a night of outlandish drunken escapades? Or maybe blacking out in a place of death was exactly the sort of mystical punishment that Agneta of Geithus had wanted me to suffer all along? My memory of Jørgen looking me in the eye and saying, "The beer tastes best when it's drunk out of pure animal bone," was as vivid as could be, but who's to say that it wasn't just the result of Agneta's dark *seiðr* having finally struck me down with a series of twisted hallucinations next to a freezing fjord?

If my memories of Jørgen were Agneta's doing, then she did a damn fine job with the curse after all. I suppose that I will never know the full truth of the matter, but for better or worse, I at least certainly felt that I had learned something. Whether that knowledge came from a beer-brewing zombie who defied the laws of nature or from a hostile, shaman-inflicted hallucination that likewise defied the laws of nature was less important.

I distinctly remembered Jørgen explaining the nuances of bone quality relevant for making drinking vessels that exist among various bovine species—including extinct ones. The details themselves were more than I could recall, and honestly, if it had even happened, I had spaced out a little when he delved into the specifics of the process used to hollow out the horns. Spacing out hadn't been my intention, but—as the memory goes—we had already had a few drinks by then and I had lost myself in the sounds of Jørgen's excellent Norse-themed playlist. The music lent a highly complementary atmosphere to his underground taproom thanks to its ethereal choruses that evoked the lyrical themes of ancient Scandinavian folklore.

And that was the thing about Jørgen's burial mound brewery, insofar as my mind remembered it: it was just so damn *hygge*. I'd never been inside a burial mound before, either in reality or in my dreams, much less one that had been converted into a modern taproom. I had expected more of a cold-dirt-and-worms-in-the-dark vibe than a subliminal blending of archaic Norse mead hall with cozy, modern Danish design principles vibe. Of course, the space was nowhere near as large as Trond Trondsen's mead hall in Norway, but it nonetheless evoked the aura of the old ways with its wooden pillars and rafters, wood-fire burning hearth, and long central table.

The modern touches complemented it nicely, too: subtly placed speakers, subdued lighting, a couple of cozy couches, and a layout featuring tables and chairs very conducive to forming smaller groups and engaging in more intimate conversations than the typical mead hall usually permits. And being a taproom, there was also a selection of games including foosball, darts, and corn-hole at the far end opposite the bar.

It was during a round of darts that I believe Jørgen had explained to me the purpose of the modern Spear-Danish fortifications. My confidence that the entire interaction had even taken place was greatly shaken for the reasons already stated, and to make matters worse, this particular encounter also proved to be the one and only during my travels that I had failed entirely to record. Between the initial creepiness of the night, the shock of meeting Jørgen, and the subsequent descent into his barrow for some beers (or, conversely, the affliction of dark *seiðr*), I had completely forgotten about my precious little recording device. So, I can't verify anything. I have photos of the mounds, and I have the drinking horn that I found lying beside me, but I don't have any further evidence to prove anything at all whatsoever about Jørgen's existence. All I truly know is that I don't really know what happened, and that the only two plausible explanations require an uncommon leap of faith.

But be that as it may, my brain nonetheless tells me that Jørgen and I had decided that it would be good counsel to work our way through each of his beers in sequence. And my brain adds an impressive degree of detail when it tells me that we had just finished the Geatish Demise Pilsner and were enjoying a horn full of frothy Jutish Farming is Awesome Amber Ale when Jørgen decided to finally get down to business and discuss Spear-Danish activity in the 21st century.

The following passage provides a thorough description of that discussion. It should be noted that, as with primary sources from the medieval period that discuss the exploits of the original vikings, the lineage of their legendary kings, or the mythology of their pantheon, my account of the origins and activities of the modern-day Spear-Danes as related by Jørgen the Draugr must be regarded for what it is: a highly illuminating repository of useful information that, while providing valuable details, cannot be fully corroborated and should not be taken completely at face value because of the numerous flights of fancy, flaws, and general prejudices present in its creation. While my own personal experience provides our only known primary source of firsthand information relating to the modern-day Spear-Danes, it is not infallible, but the dubious reliability of primary sources is, of course, nothing new.

Like the vigilante Minuteman Project that has been monitoring illegal crossings along the U.S.-Mexico border since 2005, the modern Spear-Danes had taken their name from the narrative of their nation's glorious past and deployed themselves of their own initiative for a similar purpose. Initially, I had assumed these Spear-Danish efforts were developed to thwart and intercept the entry of non-European economic refugees to Denmark. Immigration has become a hot topic in Europe with unprecedented numbers of migrants entering the continent in recent decades, predominately from countries in the Middle East and North Africa. Emotions run high on both sides of the debate and a number of anti-immigrant political parties have risen to prominence, including the Danish People's Party which entered parliament in 1998 and became the nation's third largest party in 2001. Its establishment at that point in time, and the other political parties' general willingness to cooperate with it, has resulted in a non-Danish population that constitutes about 14% of Denmark's overall population. This is considerably lower than the non-Swedish population that constitutes about 25% of the overall population in Sweden, where a similar political development only occurred two decades later.

This recent history and the high tensions that tend to accompany the topic thus collectively set the stage for my surprise when Jørgen declared, "Charlemagne Jr. was getting too big for her britches, you know what I mean?"

Admittedly, I didn't, so Jørgen explained further.

"That Chancellor down in Germany, she's full of ambition," Jørgen said while holding his beer horn in one hand and practicing his dart aim with the other. The eerie green glow from the domed earthen ceiling of the burial mound cast a strange and menacing sheen upon his skin, contrasting with the deep shadows of his creviced and decaying face. All of which gave him a properly haunting look that helped set the mood for the forthcoming discussion. "And the Fourth Reich has been the most successful German expansionist political project ever. Not even the First Reich included such a strong alliance with the Franks. They claim that power rests with the people, but it's administered from Brussels, puppeteered from Berlin with the assistance of Paris, and assimilates everything it touches."

This confirmed that Jørgen was a bit of a populist, just not in the manner that I had suspected. His references to the First and Fourth Reichs, of course, also alluded to the Third Reich, which is the most famous of all the German Reichs. There is also a reason that it was labeled as the third, which is grounded in a slice of history that remains largely neglected, at least in my own homeland.

After the fall of Charlemagne's Carolingian Empire in 888, which had encompassed most of modern day France, Germany, and a smattering of other nations in the general vicinity, the territory fractured apart and the German-speaking lands eventually coalesced into the Holy Roman Empire, or the First Reich, which lasted for a thousand years until it was finally dissolved after suffering defeat at the hands of Napoleon in 1806. Germany united once again as a single nation in 1871, thanks to the political and military maneuvering of Otto von Bismarck. The resultant German Empire, or Second Reich, introduced the Kaisers to the world and reigned until 1918 when the empire and its allies lost the First World War. Slammed with extreme punitive measures, the Second Reich was essentially dismantled by the victors and shortly thereafter the Nazis rose to power and ushered in the infamous Third Reich. The terminology of these First, Second, and Third Reichs only dates to 1923—after the fall of the German Empire—and was subsequently coopted and used for evil purposes by the Nazis as was their habit.

The Fourth Reich, however, is more of an unofficial theoretical concept than prescribed reality. Depending upon the chosen definition, the term might apply to a future version of Europe dominated by German supremacy (independent from but not necessarily mutually exclusive from the horrors of Nazism), or the present European Union dominated by German supremacy. In either case, it implies a subversive notion that through some degree of European unification, Germany has emerged or will emerge as the dominant member state with an unprecedented ability to exert its influence, either with or without the wars and casualties involved in its earlier attempts to establish a similar status.

One common thread that runs through the centuries of these so-called German Reichs has been an enduring concern among the neighboring nations, such as Denmark, for the safety and stability of their own borders. Danish concern about its southern border is an ancient one, to which the monumental Danevirke can attest. Similar in concept to Hadrian's Wall or the Antonine Wall in Britain, the Danevirke is comprised of a series of defensive, earthen walls that criss-cross the Jutish peninsula near the German-Danish border. It was built over the course of multiple phases during the first millennium to thwart invasion from the south, particularly from the armies of Charlemagne. The defenses, however, didn't stop Bismarck's campaign of Prussian expansion during the reign of the Second Reich, and as a result, the Danevirke now lies entirely in German territory rather than Danish.

"Dude, our border defenses were in ruins and not even in our own territory anymore," Jørgen explained. "So, those Germans, man, they could just waltz across the border and start conquering us if they wanted. All they needed was for Charlie Jr. there to give the order."

I decided not to question him about his inconsistent and bizarre usage of pet-names for Angela Merkel, who has since stepped down from her post anyway, and instead watched him throw his dart with the indefatigable precision of a well-practiced drunken zombie, striking the bullseye square in the middle. I felt a strong sense of foreboding that I was going to lose.

I held my dart and practiced aiming at the target. It was awkward to do while holding a nearly full horn of beer in one hand. Because of its shape, I couldn't actually set the horn down anywhere. Not that

I minded having an alcoholic beverage firmly glued to my otherwise useless left hand, but some sort of wooden contraption to hold the horns, whether built into the furnishings or completely mobile like a beer flight holder, would have been a nice feature. The absence of such a tool slightly diminished the otherwise full-out Spear-Danish *hygge* effect of the burial mound taproom's interior design.

The idea of asking Jørgen to hold the horn for me felt like a cop-out since he hadn't asked me to do the same for him, so I made the best of it and threw the dart. I hit one of the target's outer-rings but didn't spill any of my ale, which was the most important part.

"What are you doing here so close to Copenhagen—on an island—when you could have been on the mainland watching the German border instead?" I asked after taking a large gulp of amber ale. I wondered why, if the Spear-Danes were so focused on fortifying their southern border, they had established such a significant garrison at Skuldelev?

"Hey, man, it's not like we were about to let the Geats or Swedes catch us with our pants down, either," Jørgen replied while fondling a dart. "Yeah, sure, at least we got the water separating us from them if they ever cooked up some kooky, new ideas about invading, but they've got shit tons of boats and a big, fancy bridge, so it wouldn't be smart to leave our back door completely exposed like that, you know? Those Swedes, sometimes they get frisky and hostile."

While Jørgen's postulations about Denmark's present threats were grounded in a very narrow branch of revisionist alternate history, his allusions to historical Swedish-Danish relations were grounded in distant, historical reality. Prior to adopting its two-hundred-year-old policy of neutrality, Sweden had war-mongered with the best of them, acquiring substantial territory from Denmark in 1658 as agreed upon in the Treaty of Roskilde, which was conducted between King Frederick III of Denmark-Norway and King Karl X Gustav of Sweden in Roskilde, very close to where I was now playing darts and drinking beer with a corporeal Danish ghost, or hallucinating about it, ironically enough. While Sweden eventually relinquished its acquisition of the Danish island of Bornholm and the Norwegian territory of Trøndelag (one hundred and fifty years before it conquered all of Norway), it had maintained Skåne, Blekinge, Halland, and Bohuslän, which comprise an altogether much larger tract of former Danish land than any of the German Reichs had ever conquered and held; the 1940 invasion of Denmark by the Third Reich, while utterly comprehensive, thankfully did not stand the test of time.

Jørgen threw another bullseye and elaborated further, "The Spear-Danish garrison at Skuldelev was strategically positioned, actually. 'Cause, you know, we got the capital city nearby if we needed to protect it, and we could also deploy pretty quickly further north as well if any Swedes showed up there. So, yeah, this garrison wasn't the one that saw the most action, or really any action for that matter, since it all happened over in Jutland, but it was important to have our bases covered."

Apparently, the first garrison of modern Spear-Danes had been stationed in southern Jutland (the large Danish peninsula physically connected to northern Germany) near the town of Ribe, which along with Hedeby—now known as Haithabu, near the town of Schleswig—had been one of the most significant early Danish settlements. Hedeby, however, like the Danevirke, now actually lies in the lands of the Deutsch.

In addition to the expansive, modern Spear-Danish fortification established near Ribe, additional fortifications had also been established elsewhere throughout the country. The one located midway up the eastern coast of the Jutland Peninsula at Jelling had been symbolically strategic for its physical proximity to the ancient seat of Danish power and ancestral home of the aptly-named Jelling Dynasty, which included such illustrious members as Sven Forkbeard, Harald Bluetooth, Gorm the Old, and Cnut the Great, who had ruled over Denmark, Norway, and England. Another had been located outside the modern city of Ålborg for the defense of northern Jutland from potentially troublesome Norwegians. The largest modern Spear-Danish garrison, however, had been at Odense on the island of Fyn, positioned between Jutland and Zealand. It had been chosen for its central location within the realm of the Spear-Danes, and because it is a municipality named after Odin, a god of war, which the Spear-Danes thought boded well. The garrison at Skuldelev was thus simply one of a series, and while not the largest, was mainly of importance for its proximity to the capital city.

Jørgen assured me that each of the fortresses had been cozy because, like his burial mound, they were all built according to the modern principles of *hygge* despite employing predominately medieval construction materials and techniques. But none of them had survived the ravages of time and weather or the coordinated dismantling efforts of Hjemmeværnet, the Danish Home Guard.

"Brrooo..." Jørgen uttered with complete exasperation. "Thing was, the elites holed up in Christiansborg"—the Danish parliamentary building in Copenhagen—"hadn't authorized the establishment of our Spear-Danish garrisons. We sort of took matters into our own hands, you know? And no one tried to stop us. Everyone who saw us was pretty confused, actually. It took the high lords a good while to figure out what exactly we were up to, and then even longer to discuss what to do about it, by which point we were already pretty well established."

"So, did you guys actually see any action before Hjemmeværnet shut you all down?" I asked as we strode back to Jørgen's row of taps for a refill. I had lost the round of darts, just as anticipated, and had suggested that we play foosball next, to which Jørgen had eagerly agreed.

He set his empty horn on its side, took mine, and filled it with the next brew in line, a certain Spear-Danish Victory Dunkelweizen. He handed it back to me, quickly filled his own, and we clinked, declaring "skål!" once again beneath the unearthly green hue of the mound's glowing ceiling.

As we walked back to the fun-and-games section of his brewery burial mound, Jørgen explained that the Spear-Danes had engaged in several mild skirmishes with the Germans, whom he had started referring to as the Lower Saxons, and had repelled a single incursion from the Frisians, an island-dwelling folk living off the coast of the Netherlands and northwestern Germany.

"But the only really serious invasion that we dealt with came from the Swedes," he said as we assumed our positions opposite one another at the foosball table. "They were led by this crazy guy, Björn Svensson. He brought a whole Swedish army in a massive caravan of Volvos and Saabs with him and they attacked us in the heart of Jutland."

"Björn Svensson?" I wondered aloud. This was, of course, the same name that belonged to the delinquent fisherman who had sabotaged Ingrid Törnblom's plans for revenge against the corrupt Viveca and who I was hoping to meet on the next and final stop of my pan-Scandinavian travel itinerary. None of the myth-making propagated by the online rumor mills had mentioned his involvement in a large-scale invasion of Denmark. But what was the likelihood that multiple ringleaders of a fringe, underground Neo-Norse movement that never achieved the critical momentum necessary to break into the mainstream shared exactly the same name, even if it was a relatively common one for this part of the world?

"Yeah, why? You know him?" Jørgen asked while fishing the ball out from the slot in the foosball table.

"No, but I am going to try to meet him after I leave Denmark. The guy was supposedly a fisherman based out of Bohuslän before he went a-viking. Is it the same guy, do you think?"

"Could be." Jørgen shrugged. "I never met him or even saw him. All I know is he came from Sweden and that there were reports that he had been spotted in Danish waters in a fishing trawler before the big invasion."

He held up the ball to signify that he was about to drop it through the opening and initiate play. I grabbed hold of the handle for my centerline kickers with one hand and, holding the beer horn with the other, nodded that I was ready. Holding his own horn in one hand, Jørgen dropped the ball with the other and immediately grabbed the handle of his own centerline kickers. The ball sped across the flat, wooden surface and we began twisting and thrusting our respective handles wildly and awkwardly, sloshing beer as we chased the action, moving to and fro along the length of the table in pursuit of the ricocheting ball.

Unlike darts, foosball is a pointless game in which I can at least hold my own thanks to having spent many weekends as a teenager at the house of a friend who owned such a table. While most of the guys at my school seemed to either party with drugs and alcohol or with the latest multiplayer PC shooter game on the weekends, my group of friends instead found solace in the strange no man's land of spending way too much time playing foosball and ping-pong in garages when not aimlessly wandering the local shopping mall. The upshot of this is that I don't totally suck at foosball.

I scored the first point in the present match by redirecting a sharp bounce off the board beside the opening of Jørgen's goal. He roared deeply in disgust and frustration as the ball slid past his flailing and ineffective goalkeeper. He had trounced me in darts and, even though it was only the first goal of the game, it was also the first upset he'd experienced of the night so far. Although I had no direct knowledge on the matter, it occurred to me that it might not be in my own best interests to upset a *draugr* by beating him at a dumb bar game.

I asked Jørgen what had happened with the Swedish invasion as he fetched the ball from the slot and prepared to drop it into play again.

"Honestly, man, I'm not entirely sure myself." He shrugged. "I didn't march out with the others. We always kept a contingent of guys on hand at all of our forts; I mean, we couldn't just leave them completely empty and undefended, you know? And my main responsibility was brewing the beer, which was of the utmost importance, so I stayed, along with a handful of other guys. Reports started coming in that the battle was a disaster, that both sides basically just annihilated each other. Serious casualties all around. Survivors eventually showed up. Most of them seemed to have lost their sanity and were talking nonsense, just complete nonsense, about Legos and those painted wooden horse toys that the Swedes love so much."

The painted wooden horses to which Jørgen referred are called Dalahästar, or Dalecarlian horses in English. A very traditional handicraft in Sweden, Dalahästar were formerly made as toys for children but now represent one of the most iconic souvenir items targeted to tourists visiting the country. They are rather blocky in appearance and are usually painted with a colorful, floral pattern.

"I never could make any sense of those ramblings," continued Jørgen. "The survivors who straggled back to our fortress ate and rested, then collected their belongings and went home. It was like everyone just sort of gave up altogether at once."

"So, how many of them went home and how many of them died and got placed in the burial mounds here?" I asked as I throttled my defensive foosball kickers while Jørgen attempted an offensive attack on my goal.

"What do you mean? We don't have any burials mounds here."

"What?" Now I was confused. "All these mounds here...we're in yours."

"Dude!" Jørgen burst out laughing. "This isn't a burial mound. I told you, this is my home. The other mounds are homes too, for the other Spear-Danes who were stationed here. Everyone had a cozy little hobbit hole to live in, usually four people lived in each."

My jaw dropped and I just stared at him, losing my focus on the game and a point in the process.

"Yes!" Jørgen exclaimed. "Now we're all tied up!"

I just continued to stare at him. Eventually, I found some words. "So, why are you living here then? You are a *draugr*, right? You even said so earlier when you promised not to eat me. But this is not your burial mound? And none of the others here are, either? I'm missing something..."

"Dude..." He looked exasperated. "Uh, yeah, what do you think I am, if not a *draugr*? A living person? And yeah, I live here, and yeah, technically, it is a mound. I suppose you could say it's also a burial mound now that it houses my dead body. But it was built as my home back when I was still alive. Same with all the other mounds. Every Spear-Danish garrison had the same type of houses and they were all built in the Spear-Danish vernacular *hygge* hobbit-hole style."

"So, there're no other *draugar* or bodies in the other mounds?"

"Nah, they're all empty, which is why it's always so lonely here. Almost everyone else abandoned the place after that huge debacle in Jutland, if they even made it back. And then Hjemmeværnet came in and removed everyone else and dismantled the fortresses and most of the hobbit holes. But as you saw, they left some of them alone. Maybe they didn't realize they weren't just little hills."

"All right...but well, so how'd you die then? And why are you still here?"

He hesitated, then sighed, "I'm not proud of it, but I was eating some *flæskesteg*—that's a Danish style of roast pork—down by the water. It was summer and nice out and those of us that were still here decided to have a cookout to try and take our minds off of the debacle on Jutland. Then Hjemmeværnet showed up from out of nowhere and proceeded to just take over the whole place, and it startled me. So, I choked on the piece of *flæskesteg* that I'd been chewing on. The Hjemmeværnet guys tried to give me the Heimlich maneuver, but only after they secured the entire site and by then it was too late, and they never got the piece that was stuck in my throat dislodged. I woke up on a stretcher in a modern ambulance just outside where the fortress wall used to be. And well, I didn't want to go to the morgue, so I got up and hid in my hobbit hole here after I hawked the piece of *flæskesteg* out onto the ambulance's floor."

"Damn..."

"Yeah, but you know, whatever." Jørgen just shook his head nonchalantly. "So, you going to get the ball? You gave up the goal so it's your turn to do that, you know."

Mentally numb, I just nodded and did as he asked. We resumed the game, wildly whirling our foosball kickers around as the ball clacked off the wooden sides of the table. The ambient music emanating from the speakers rose and fell in tempo. Our conversation, initially lucid and on-topic, deteriorated into a series of grunts, excited shouts, and pitiful moans. I vaguely recalled scoring another goal to gain the lead, causing Jørgen to throw his hands up in the air and accidentally lose hold of his horn. It flew towards the ceiling, banging against the glowing green surface and sloshing beer all over the both of us. He picked it up when it landed, and we stumbled back to his tap line to refill our horns with the next beer on the list, whatever that was.

And at that point, my memory goes blank. I'd like to think I won the foosball game, but I truthfully have no idea if we even finished it.

Or, as I looked around from where I sat on the frozen earth, that it had even happened. Strange and powerful forces were at work alongside the shore of the Roskilde Fjord, no doubt, but as to their exact nature, I will never know.

Utterly confounded and possibly cursed, I stood up and searched around the perimeter of the mound for the entrance but couldn't find a trace of it. Not knowing what else to do, I finally began the long slog back to the bus stop, cold, tired, and sore.

THE SAGA OF PLAGIARISM-BJÖRN

DREAM HARD ON

Björn Svensson was strutting around the rocky cove naked and bellowing fierce obscenities at the waves. I observed him from a safe distance, feeling like a genuine Euro-perv as he bent over, picked up a stone, and then chucked it into the water with a thunderous, *"Må djävulen ta dig! Du onda jävla fitta!"*

I had been searching for him all afternoon, but as I watched his nude temper-tantrum unfold before my eyes, I could only deduce that my success had come at a very inopportune moment. As I've mentioned more than once already, I'm quite comfortable with failure, so I didn't harbor any reservations about accepting defeat once again now in the hope of achieving some form of meek personal victory at a later time. I turned around to leave and that's when I heard him shout in my direction, *"Du! Hej—du! Har du sett min flaska? Jag har tappat bort min mest älskade flaska!"* This was followed by a very somber-sounding *"oi…"*

I stopped and looked back at him. He squinted at me from his perch atop a granite outcropping, shoulders slouched, belly protruding, beard frayed, and ding-dong dangling in plain sight. This was not the confident appearance of the once-proud warrior-poet that I had been expecting. This was the appearance of a regular, everyday, frazzled Swede whose glory days had long since passed him by, and now to make matters worse, he had accidentally just dropped his beloved bottle of alcohol into the ocean.

"Nej!" I answered.

"Oh, you English?" he asked because, despite my best efforts, I still couldn't even pronounce the one-syllable Swedish word for "no" with enough authenticity to convince any of the locals that I actually know some of their language. But that never stops them from always incorrectly assuming that I'm English.

"No, I'm American, actually."

"Oh, you come from the U.S.? Why are you here? This place is boring. Why didn't you stay in Göteborg?"

Göteborg, or Gothenburg as it is known to non-Scandinavians, is more fun and exciting, but not just for Americans. It's more fun and exciting for everyone. The historic center of the maritime city features countless opportunities for shopping, dining, and entertainment along its wide esplanades, whereas Björn's home on the tiny island of Klädesholmen—situated off the southern shore of the larger island of Tjörn about an hour north of Göteborg—features only a small smattering of fishing shacks, some summertime cottages, and a herring museum. In other words, it's a place where nothing much ever happens.

"Well, I'm here because I've been looking for you, actually," I answered. "You are Björn Svensson, right?"

I proceeded to explain the purpose of my self-appointed mission and how I had already met a handful of his Neo-Norse compatriots prior to finding him. He bristled at the mention of Ingrid Törnblom's name, which further piqued my interest about the nature of his acquaintance with her. But that could wait till later, because right now, Björn was staring intently at me, and though completely nude, his innate reserved Swedishness masked any emotion he might have been feeling.

"Well, this is quite something," he eventually stated when I had finished giving him the basic background history. "Not many Americans know about my accomplishments. Nor many Swedes, either, for that matter. Actually, only a few people in the world even have any idea...but I'd be delighted to tell you. I'll tell you the whole story, from beginning to end."

"Hey, that's great—thank you so much." I stared past him to the glistening surface of the water. I really wasn't sure whether I should be looking at him or not given his current state of dress. "But, you know, I can come back later. I mean, I don't want to interrupt you if you're in the middle of something—"

"No, no, I'm not in the middle of anything at all." He began to walk towards me, an action that embodied the polar opposite of what I would have done had our positions been reversed and I had been the one venting nude, drunken hostilities at the ocean when some stranger from a foreign country stumbled upon me. "I have no plans for the rest of the day. You don't happen to have a bottle of vodka there in your backpack, do you?"

"No…" I trailed off because he had closed the distance rather quickly. He wrapped his arm around my shoulder and began directing me towards the water's edge.

"Now, that is quite unfortunate," he sighed as he guided me. "I dropped mine in the water, you see. Quite a frustrating setback if I may say so. And this story I have to tell you, it really is best told over a drink. But I suppose we can make do for now, and then perhaps later we can find a new bottle."

I was both shocked and nullified by how calm and natural he seemed to feel in his birthday suit as he walked beside me, his arm still slung around my shoulder. He showed not even the slightest hint of trepidation about his complete lack of clothing. Nor did he display any trepidation about physical contact with me either, and that actually caused me some concern. According to the world-renowned myth, Swedes possess a very relaxed attitude towards public nudity, and Björn was genuinely giving it 110% to prove its truth here and now. That same myth, however, usually neglects to mention that Swedish nudity is never ever sexual or that Swedes generally abhor close physical contact of any sort in public with strangers. Björn was flagrantly deviating from at least one of these two lesser-known stereotypes, and I worried whether he had any plans to increase the count to two in the immediate future.

"You know, I only sought glory in the land of the Spear-Danes because I was commanded to in a dream," Björn said as he directed me to his favorite ledge overlooking the water. He spoke with his face closer to mine than I usually prefer of a conversation partner, especially one whose breath reeks of lingonberry flavored Absolut Vodka and stale cinnamon buns. "It was quite a thing, really. You see, normally I don't dream. Or I don't remember my dreams; I'm not so sure how it works. But this one night, I had this dream, and in this dream...how do you say...ah, boner! Yes, boner. A boner, an angry boner that is, commanded me to take action."

"An angry boner?"

"Yes!" He was as solid as oak in his conviction, but thankfully not in his manhood. "It was truly an angry boner! The angriest I've ever seen. Or dreamed, I suppose. You see, it was bent out of shape. Or more accurately, it was bent into shape and the shape it was bent into was like that of a gallows pole—for hanging people, you know? Now what boner wouldn't be angry if it had to contort itself into a shape like that?"

"I suppose you have a point..." It did sound painful, if not downright impossible, but crazy shit can happen in dreams, and who am I to judge? My dreams are usually haunted by the lame apparitions of project schedule spreadsheets and an ever-increasing deluge of unanswered work emails.

"Indeed. And do you know who the Lord of the Gallows is?"

"Odin?" I did know this but I wasn't feeling very confident thanks to all the bizarre penis talk I was having with a naked stranger who was touching me and breathing acrid booze breath in my face as we walked side-by-side.

"Correct! And as you may know, Odin lost one eye to gain the knowledge of the runes, so isn't it only natural that if he wanted to communicate with me, that he'd send to me his own little one-eyed warrior as a messenger in my dreams?"

Finally, we reached the water's edge and Björn withdrew his arm and squatted down, his trouser-less trouser snake swinging freely with the motion. He sat on the ledge, which was dry thanks to the warming effects of the mid-day sun, and dangled his legs over the edge, looking back up at me with a certain expectation clearly stamped across his face.

I sat down myself and then looked off into the distance, not really sure what to say next and wishing that he'd carry the weight of the conversation for a while longer. Making small talk with strangers has never been one of my strengths, but I've found that it's easier to do when the stranger is actually wearing clothes. I couldn't believe that he wasn't, quite literally, freezing his balls off. It was a sunny day, and though the temperature had risen slightly above freezing and partially warmed the stone upon which we now rested, the season nonetheless remained winter and the air was far from warm.

I also wondered why it was that Björn had to be the one naked modern viking I encountered in all my travels. Why couldn't it have been Ingrid Törnblom instead? She had refused to remove any of her clothing at all whatsoever while I was in her presence. Not that I had dared to even think about suggesting that she should, but still, that's not the point. The point is that I would have preferred to unintentionally catch her skinny dipping, but such was not my luck. No, instead I caught a frazzled, bearded drunk dude letting it all hang out on a bleak winter's day at the edge of civilization. Sometimes I really wish the norns would just go fuck themselves.

Björn interrupted the inner turmoil of my negative thoughts.

"You know, if the angry boner had had red hair and thrown lighting bolts from its tip, then it might have been another matter entirely." He tugged at his beard. "That might have meant that it had been sent by Thor. I also thought about the possibility that Frey might have been involved, but nothing about the boner spoke of crops or the harvest season or other boners. It was all 'kill, kill, kill, battle, battle, battle, poetry, poetry, poetry.' So, there's no way it could have been from anyone but Odin."

"Did the boner tell you a poem?" I asked.

"I think so, but it was in ancient Swedish, so I didn't actually understand any of what it was saying."

"Well, then how do you know it was carrying on about killing and battle and all that other stuff?"

"I just knew...the boner was monstrous in its own way, and it wanted me to kill monsters. Its commandments transcended the barriers of human language. There were evil monsters lurking in Denmark, and I had been chosen by the Father of War to slay them. It could not have been more clear. Sort of like when a musical prodigy can just play the piano like a virtuoso as a child without any formal training. It is a calling, and there can be no doubt about the grand designs for someone with such a gift. And that's the way it is with dreams of divine importance, too. You just know what the message is; you feel it and you see it with a special clarity that no one else shares. Either that or you have to get them interpreted by a *völva*."

"A vulva?" I wasn't sure I had heard him right, but I figured that given the rather one-dimensional territory that our conversation had ventured through so far, why not expand our horizons and start talking about vaginas, too?

"No! A *völva* is a female oracle. A seeress, you know?"

Of course I did know this; I had supposedly been cursed by one back in Norway, which was presumably why I had experienced such an awful night's sleep at an abandoned 21st century Spear-Danish grave site just a couple days before. But as with so many other moments of this journey, I just wasn't thinking as clearly as I might have liked, thanks as always to the unexpected and unfamiliar dynamics of the situation in which I found myself.

We sat in silence for a few moments until I asked, "Well...why you? Did you do something special the night before to catch Odin's attention or something?"

"I got shit-faced," Björn stated matter-of-factly.

The Swedes' mastery of colloquial English never ceases to amaze me, just as my own inability to think of constructive responses never ceases to disappoint me. This guy was slated to be my final interview subject of the entire trip and here I was, still flat-lining.

"Aren't you cold?" I couldn't resist asking any longer. "Wouldn't you like to go inside someplace where it's warmer?"

He looked me sternly in the eye and then leaned backwards, propping himself up by his elbows. I suffered a sudden fear that he was about to launch into a series of aerobic pelvic thrusts.

"We will go in soon," he quipped chirpily, his pelvis remaining motionless to my great relief. "You can join me in my *bastu*, and then we can come back out here and swim and sunbathe some more. It is good to get outside this time of year."

I felt a sudden sinking feeling as he said this.

"But, you know, it really wasn't that different from most of the times when I drink too much." He changed the subject back to our original topic of conversation. "Except for maybe that it was midsummer that night. Midsummer is a big holiday here in Sweden, you know. We construct a maypole, which symbolizes a giant penis, which is probably part of the reason why Odin chose to commune with me on that specific night...but anyway, after we erect the mighty ding-dong, we then decorate it with garlands so that it looks like it has veins writhing up and down its shaft. And then we get drunk and everyone sings and dances around the maypole pretending to be little froggies, even the adults."

"Is 'froggie' some sort of Swedish slang for testicle or something?" I didn't know what the hell he was talking about.

"No. I mean, only froggies, you know, you say what, frogs in English, right? Like eh...what's the other one...toads?" He ribbited in his throat to illustrate his point.

"Yeah, that's the sound a frog makes. Or a toad. Whatever..."

"Well then, you know. We do the frog dance."

I neither knew nor cared about the frog dance, so I attempted to guide us back towards a topic of significantly higher importance, "So...Odin's dick?"

"Yes, Odin's dick," he confirmed. "What a cock."

He shifted from laying on his back to laying on his side to face me, his frank and beans flailing with the motion. I spontaneously reacted by scooting a few inches away.

Fortunately, he didn't seem to care as he just continued speaking, now with his head resting on his hand which was in turn supported by his elbow. He appeared to be very comfortable. "Odin's dick was so angry, so very angry. It was in fact so angry that not only did it haunt my dreams that night, but it also left me with a horrible hangover. I had visions of it even when I woke up."

"What do you mean?"

"I had the image of the angry boner seared into my mind, even after I opened my eyes. The pain in my head throbbed and the boner itself was pulsating, and I was not able to focus on anything else. I couldn't even stand up, I was so weak."

"The boner was pulsating?"

"Oh, yes. As I told you, it was a very angry boner. Truly, truly, an angry boner. You have never seen such an angry boner."

"Well, I've never seen a boner bent into the shape of a gallows pole, so that's probably true."

"Of course it is true! And until you see one for yourself with your own eyes, you'll never fully understand."

I have very few high hopes or dreams of grandeur remaining in my life. The ritual of growing up and being thrust into the brutality of the real world saw to it that those youthful aspirations that I had once harbored were officially demolished and replaced instead with a steady sense of defeatism and forlorn nostalgia. I had given up on ever having a grand, new hope, but here and now, in a most unexpected way and in a most unexpected place, I had found the glimmer of something new to hope for, because I never, ever want to see a pissed-off, gallows-shaped boner on a vengeful mission from a warmongering Norse god with my own two eyes. But I didn't want to admit this to the naked stranger who was lounging beside me with his own exposed cock and balls protruding uncomfortably close to my own territorial bubble of personal space. So, I tried to make light of the situation instead and said, "Well, I suppose it's no coincidence that Odin is so well hung."

Björn laughed but remained serious when he asked, "True, but how would you feel if you woke up and had such an angry boner spying on you, stalking you in your mind, cursing you and spitting at you with its slanted, little eye?"

A horrible thought occurred to me just then: what if all this talk was just a delusional cover story for an inability on Björn's part to control his own junk or impulses? What if his sleepy tally-whacker suddenly levitated itself up into a demonic, cobra-like striking position from where it slouched so dangerously close to me? I hated the thought and I immediately regretted that it had ever even entered my mind, but it gave me a second new hope to long for, and should this hope prove to be in vain, I was fully prepared to hurl myself off the ledge and into the water below.

I turned my head to look at him and caught another woeful glimpse out of the corner of my eye of his flaccid package as it drooped down alongside his groin. I quickly diverted my eyes again as I responded, "I think I would feel distraught."

"Yes! Distraught is a good word. I was myself distraught. You see, the angry boner, it wouldn't leave me alone. And its pulsation grew faster and faster and all I wanted to do was to run away but I couldn't. You can't run from your own mind. It screamed its commandments at me, full of rage. I was overwhelmed, and when everything was said and done and the unholy spirit had vanished, I just barely managed to speak these words before I passed out:

> 'Hello darkness, my old friend
> I've come to talk with you again
> Because a vision softly creeping
> Left its seeds while I was sleeping
> And the vision that was planted in my brain
> Still remains.' "*

"Good song."

"What?" He sounded genuinely confused.

"Huh?" And I was confused that he was confused.

"That was my first ever skaldic verse," he explained with a tone of pride that belied an apparent ignorance about its true origins. "Odin's little one-eyed warrior left me with a new skill with words."

While the rumors online had indeed indicated that Björn had emerged as the Modern Viking Movement's preeminent skald, they had also failed to reveal that he was really only just a cover-poet who didn't write his own material. I didn't want to belittle his self-esteem or provoke him into a bitter Neo-Norseman's rage, so I just said, "Well, I guess Odin is a god of poetry, so that's cool."

"Yes, it's really cool," he confirmed. "At the time, it was frightening and painful, but my life really changed for the better because of that angry boner. If it hadn't been for it, I never would have achieved my

---

* "The Sound of Silence" by Simon & Garfunkel, 1964

full potential as a monster slayer. Up to that point, my life had been nothing special. I was just another Björn going through the motions with no meaning or purpose in my life. But Big One-Eye's little one-eye changed all that. That penis prevented me from becoming like everyone else who just goes to school because they have to, then gets a pointless job because they have to, and then dies because they have to without ever achieving any real meaning in their life."

"Everybody's got their dues in life to pay...and sometimes you got to lose to know how to win," I responded, thinking that maybe I could eventually become a cover-skald, too. Half my life's been wasted in Microsoft's digital pages, and if I was a fool, then Björn was a sage—albeit a loony, nude one, but even so, I sure wished I could learn from him. I genuinely admired the way he had successfully subverted his own personal 21st century grind and transcended the trivial status quo of contemporary existence. And if it had taken an alcohol-induced nightmare about a divine dick for him to be able to do it, then so be it. At least he had found a way, and like Odin's little helper, had risen to the challenge.

"You know, it is true, and all these feelings, they come back to you..." He nodded his approval of my classic rock wisdom and perhaps just for today, I hoped, the good norns would slowly take my inhibitions away.

CARLSBERG BREWERY BERSERKERGÅNG

My conversation with Björn at the rocky cove came to a quick end following our spiritual Aerosmith moment when he suddenly sat upright and declared, "My willy is getting cold!"

He then graciously invited me back to his fishing trawler, which was anchored a short distance from the ledge where we had experienced our initial encounter. Against my better judgement, I followed him. He seemed somewhat deranged, but in a harmless sort of way, and I was driven by my own highly ambitious but blind journalistic motivations.

The trawler was docked at a private pier on the northwestern side of Klädesholmen that led up an escarpment to a dilapidated house that looked more like a shed. Several other houses, all larger and in better shape, dotted the heavily indented coastline of the island.

Once on board, Björn began making us some sandwiches in the vessel's little galley. He moved blithely about the small space, still completely nude, his ding-dong dangling dangerously close to the food preparation surface as he slathered some chilled shrimp mixed with mayo onto slices of plain, white bread. According to him, it was now "*smörgås* time," which meant that we needed to stop what we were doing—which hadn't been much—to enjoy some open-face seafood sandwiches. Pretty soon it would be "*bastu* time."

I was not looking forward to *bastu* time. *Bastu* time would involve stripping down naked and sweating it out in a dilapidated sauna onboard this rickety fishing trawler. *Bastu* is the Swedish word for sauna, which itself is a loan word from Finnish. The Finns are generally much more serious than the Swedes when it comes to saunas; the concept originated in Finland and there are more saunas in Finland than cars. Björn seemed to be a devoted Swedish adherent, though.

"So, we have a light shrimp snack now, and then we will hit the *bastu*." He smiled. "And I have some cold beer for that. But you will have to take off your clothes. You can't go to the *bastu* dressed like that."

He must have seen the look on my face because he quickly added, "I have a spare towel you can wrap around yourself if you want." And then his voice deteriorated into mumblings of which I could only make out the Swedish words for "Americans" and "wimpy."

"*Nu ska vi äta!*" he declared suddenly and looked up with a goofy grin. He had just finished molding the shrimp sandwiches to perfection and now drizzled the remaining juice from a crushed lemon upon them.

"It looks great," I said meekly as he handed me a plate.

"Oh, it is a wonderful Swedish delicacy," he mumbled through a mouthful of crustaceous flesh. "We make very many good kinds of food with all the little vermin of the sea."

The sandwich, surprisingly, actually hit the spot. It had been a long day of bus travel followed by the search for this devout disciple of the clothing-is-optional mantra most commonly found among toddlers. I had wandered through the streets of Klädesholmen and Rönnäng—the closest village to Klädesholmen on the neighboring island of Tjörn where I had disembarked—inquiring of his whereabouts at several local businesses. Björn was the only modern viking who I had hoped to meet but who I had also been wholly unable to contact before making the effort to seek him out. I had even managed to get a hold of Olafur Shitty-Pants before showing up at his doorstep back in Iceland.

The online chatter had made it clear that Björn had some involvement with southern Tjörn's herring industry, and that had made Rönnäng the best place to begin my search because it is home to Klädesholmen Seafood, a substantial wholesale retailer of herring and manufacturer of herring-based products (the company is named after Klädesholmen but is not based on Klädesholmen, just for the sake of creating confusion). My plan had been a weak one, admittedly: to wander around till I found Björn, and if I didn't find him, then so be it. But everyone I had spoken to in Rönnäng knew immediately about whom I was asking. Tales of the surly fisherman who had caused some sort of ruckus in Denmark had clearly entered the local lore. Consequently, the friendly townsfolk knew exactly where he lived and instructed me to cross the nearby bridge to Klädesholmen. And as it turned out, Björn's home was hardly inconspicuous since the few other vessels anchored in the area at this time of year were of the pleasure boating variety, meaning that his industrial fishing trawler stuck out like a sore thumb. All of which made it rather easy for me to stumble upon him in the midst of his vodka bottle bereavement.

My journey northwards from Copenhagen had been uneventful, and I had been relieved to collapse into the comfortable, cushioned window seat of the train after hurriedly packing my things and checking out of the hotel. I had trudged back to the bus stop from the mysterious mound at the break of dawn, cold and aching, where I had waited for the next bus, looking like a delinquent and attracting disapproving glances from the other passengers when it finally arrived.

The train trip clocked in just shy of four hours, and I had checked into the Radisson Blu hotel, just one block from Gothenburg's central station across the Fattighusån canal. I spent the rest of the day wandering the city, perusing the fresh fish market housed at the gothicly-stylized stone building of Feskekôrka, enjoying the panoramic views offered by the former 17th century military fortification of Skansen Kronan that overlooks the city, and, of course, admiring Carl Milles' magnificent statue of Poseidon holding a fish in front of the art museum at Götaplatsen, the terminus square of the city's most fashionable esplanade, Avenyn. I finished the day with a burger and beer at The Golden Days, an English-style pub that faces the canal and an imposing statue of Gustav Adolf. Usually referred to as Gustavus Adolphus in English and nicknamed

The Lion of the North, he was the Swedish king who had orchestrated the nation's rise to power in the early 17th century during the 30 Years' War. He had also founded the city of Gothenburg in 1621, hence the special commemoration to his highness at this particular location.

I retired to the hotel early, and after a very rejuvenating sleep, woke up in the morning refreshed. After grabbing an iced latte at one of the central station's several Espresso Houses, I had settled into my seat on the bus for the one and a half hour-long ride north to Tjörn to begin my quest of seeking out this unabashed nudist on whose boat I now ate cold shrimp sandwiches.

"You see, I was initially very unclear in my mission for Old One-Eye," Björn revealed between mouthfuls of shrimp and mayonnaise. "Little did I know what the norns had in store for me. The angry penis of my dreams sent me on a series of missions against Danish monsters, but it did not tell me where in Denmark I would find these monsters!"

"Well, who were these monsters?" I asked.

I had no idea whether he was being literal or allegorical, but I hoped to extract as much information from him as possible. Whether that information proved to be nonsense or not remained a much lower priority. All I knew was that the most renowned thing that he had done, according to the online rumors, had been to vandalize Copenhagen's famous statue of the *Little Mermaid*, which could hardly be considered a monster. Hans Christian Andersen's fairy tale is beloved the world over and has been for generations. And regardless of the dubious morality of Björn's actions, the impetus behind them remained shrouded in mystery. I could not see the connection between a disturbed phallic dream about monster-slaying and the eventual destruction of an iconic landmark. But as with all prominent events of the Modern Viking Movement, the reality and the rumors would certainly both converge and diverge, and new truths would be revealed. It was just a matter of getting to the bottom of it all.

"Oh, there is much to this story that you don't know." Specks of shrimp flew from Björn's mouth as he confirmed my ignorance. "There were four monsters to be exact—the twin beasts, the mother, and the serpent. All abominations, each one of them. But the story of my deeds is not one that can be told so quickly during *smörgås* time. But I will tell you! But first, you need to take your pants off so we can go get in the *bastu* together."

Ten minutes later we were both naked and sitting in the sauna. Or, more accurately, Björn was still naked, and I now had a towel wrapped around my waist. He had thankfully let me undress in his bathroom, and when I emerged wearing only the towel that he had given me, he clapped excitedly and pulled two cold Falcon beers out of the fridge.

The cold air had shocked my senses when we stepped out on deck. I wished that Björn had moved a bit faster, but he'd seemed intent on taking slow, casual strides. When we finally reached the dilapidated wooden husk of a sauna—a ramshackle wooden affair constructed on the deck of his fishing trawler—he threw the door open and steam came gushing out. He then beckoned that I should step in first. He entered after me, closed the door, and took a seat on one of the two narrow benches.

I sat opposite him as he ladled some water from a bucket onto the heated stones positioned between us. It was a small, rectangular room with a couple of windows built into the walls at our sides to let in natural light while a small chimney in the roof allowed for the steam to escape. The whole thing was constructed of a rustic, do-it-yourself poorly nature, and I didn't even want to begin to imagine how many codes it must have violated.

"So, I had to ask myself, 'What is the one thing the Spear-Danes care about more than anything else in the world?' " Björn took a long sip of his cold beer. "You know, because the monster would try to hurt the Spear-Danes where it hurts the most, of course. It would not be a very worthwhile monster to seek out and slay if it caused no harm. Odin would never have bothered sending me his angry boner in that case. So, I needed to determine what the most important thing to the Spear-Danes is, because that is what the monster would attack. And do you know what the most important thing to the Spear-Danes is?"

Recognizing that it was a rhetorical question, I simply waited for him to answer it himself.

"Exactly! I didn't know, either. So, I made an educated guess that their most important thing is beer; probably either Tuborg or Carlsberg." He gave a sharp nod of his head in strong approval of his own personal assessment and took another sip.

But I supposed it made some degree of sense; both brands are internationally renowned among beer drinkers, although Carlsberg remains a bit more famous. I chose not to mention the simple fact that Tuborg was now owned by Carlsberg.

"So, I flipped a *krona*," Björn continued. "Which is a time-honored way of making important decisions. And Odin would approve, since he is quite the gambler and enjoys a good game of chance, you know?"

I wasn't entirely sure what he was talking about, but I did recall a particularly gruesome hoax that Odin had pulled when he was traveling the world in search of the Mead of Poetry, which had been stolen from murderous dwarves by an evil giant. Odin had been out wandering and came upon a field being worked by some slaves, each equipped with a scythe. He offered to sell them a whetstone that would help sharpen their scythes, and then he tossed it up in the air. In the excitement and frenzy that ensued, the slaves all accidentally slew one another, and Odin continued on his journey. I suspected Björn's game of flip-a-coin with himself was much more innocuous if perhaps just as misguided.

"So, I take my one *krona* coin." He lifted his hand, pretending to hold a coin between his thumb and forefinger while staring at me in the eye very intently. "And I say to myself, 'If it lands with Carl Gustaf's head face up, then I go to Carlsberg Brewery, but if it lands with Carl Gustaf's face down, then I go to Tuborg Brewery.' And you know what happened?"

"No," I answered.

"It landed with Carl Gustaf's face up! And you know, Carl Gustaf is a mighty Swedish king descended from the line of Frey—the mighty penis god of the harvest—and on this coin he only has one eye, so of course Odin had smiled upon this plan."

It's undoubtedly true that Carl Gustaf has only one eye as depicted on the Swedish one *krona* piece (*kronor*, the plural of *krona*, being the system of basic monetary units in the country), but as is the case with most coins featuring a leader's face the world over, the single eye is simply the result of the individual's face being depicted in profile rather than straight-on. The Carl Gustaf shown on the current single *krona* coin is actually Carl XVI Gustaf, the present king of Sweden, who despite the myth-making of *Ynglinga Saga* that claims Swedish royalty is descended from Frey, is most definitely not descended from Frey. At a bare minimum, this is because the Swedish crown has been passed around among royal dynasties like a nymphomaniac on a Maersk cargo vessel. The most recent dynastic change occurred in 1818 when the House of Holstein-Gottorp died out with the passing of the childless King Charles XIII. Having seen the writing on the wall in advance, the Swedish Riksdag had decided to recruit a member of Napoleon's military to become the nation's new crown prince in 1810 and thus the currently reigning House of Bernadotte was born with the transformation of Jean Baptiste Jules Bernadotte, Marshal of France, to King Charles XIV John of Sweden.

I was myself unaware of any special connections that the present monarch had to the Lord of the Gallows, but Björn seemed to be convinced that there not only was one, but that it was also of extreme significance.

"And so I went to Carlsberg Brewery!" he exclaimed with a sudden squirm in his seat, his junk jiggling with the motion.

I wiped some sweat from my brow and took a swig of Falcon beer. The crappy little makeshift sauna had rapidly become incredibly hot and I was really starting to feel it. Björn, of course, seemed completely unfazed as he eyed me quizzically after his latest revelation.

"Well, how did you get there?" I asked after I chugged half of my beer. I wasn't sure about the rationale behind so quickly drinking a diuretic while I evaporated from the inside out, but I was too thirsty and hot to care.

"Oh, I took the train down." He smiled smugly, and proceeded to explain how he had arrived at the famous Elephant Gate of the

Carlsberg Brewery where he then carried out his mission from Odin. Svenska Järnverket, the Swedish train authority, doesn't screen its passengers, so he had been able to smuggle an axe onboard beneath his loose-fitting and garish fishing clothing.

"I wished to call as little attention to myself as possible, you know," he explained. "It was my first mission on behalf of the Allfather, after all. So, I got on the train in Göteborg, and I went down to Copenhagen. And I explored the city a bit, you know. It is a very nice city that the Spear-Danes have there. Those Spear-Danes, they are quite good at urban design, you know. Eventually, I made my way to the Carlsberg Brewery, which is not too far from the city center. So, I get there, and you know what I see?"

I was having trouble focusing on what he was saying, and so I think I just stared at him.

"I see these giant elephants!" He spread out his arms to indicate their hugeness. "And they are monstrous! They had all the markings of evil on them and I knew then that if they were not killed they would stir from their slumber and slay many innocent Spear-Danes. I had to slay them first; it is what Odin wanted. So, when I saw those elephant bastards, I stepped up to the first one, and I said these words:

> 'My dreams, they aren't as empty
> As my conscience seems to be
> I have hours, only lonely
> My love is vengeance
> That's never free'*

And then I sent the monster to Valhalla! And I sent his buddy to Valhalla, too. I should say, I was not able to see them actually die with my own two eyes, but the life was very clearly running out of them when I left. I had to leave because some bad troll called for trollish back-up before I could witness their last breaths. But the trolls did not catch me; I ran away! And many witnesses helped impede those trolls because they so strongly supported my cause."

____

* "Behind Blue Eyes" by The Who, 1971

While the sight of a frazzled Swedish fisherman hacking away at a tourist attraction with a medieval-style axe must have provided a certain amount of shock-and-awe entertainment value to innocent bystanders, many of them had also cheered this seemingly spontaneous display of public rage, because, incidentally, the elephant statues in question actually sported swastikas as part of their decor. The symbols in this particular context have absolutely nothing to do with Nazism since the elephants were constructed in 1901, a solid nineteen years before the establishment of the National Socialist German Workers' Party. The symbols at the brewery were only ever meant to be tokens of good fortune as their Sanskrit origins have always intended. But since most people prefer to make assumptions based on ignorance and emotions rather than knowledge and thoughtful assessment, the sight of a burly Swedish fisherman going berserk on two inanimate, swastika-adorned elephants at a significant European landmark became a huge hit. The bystanders consequently applauded his actions and blocked the security guards who eventually showed up.

I listened to all of this in a daze, since the sauna's heat had really amped up and for all I knew I was beginning to experience the early stages of a heat stroke. I was sweating profusely, the hot steam assaulting my epidermis and consciousness with unrelenting tenacity. The towel wrapped around my waist and upper legs was drenched.

Björn must have noticed something was off because he calmed down quite a bit and poked me in the shoulder.

I wasn't particularly responsive, I think, and so he said, "You look very red, my friend! Maybe it is time for a dip in the icy cold ocean?"

I think I just mumbled something, which must have been somewhat affirmative-sounding, because his eyes lit up and he grabbed my hand and led me back out onto the boat's deck. The extreme contrast provided by the cold air snapped me back to my senses, but I remained a bit bedazzled and really didn't feel good.

"This is the best part of *bastu* time!" he declared as he led me to the boat's edge. I just looked at him as I struggled to regain control of my breathing. I neither recognized nor understood what was happening to my body.

Then he yanked the towel away from my waist, snapped my bare ass with it, and pushed me overboard. And just as the sting from the towel began to register as pain, I hit the grim, gray surface of the water and sank beneath the waves.

THE BEHEADING OF ARIEL

Death comes for us all and no one can escape his or her fate. The norns wove the skein of our lives long ago, and when our time comes, there is nothing that any of us can do about it other than to perhaps smile knowingly and embrace the inevitable with a grim wisecrack or two. Or so I thought as I spasmed around beneath the water's surface. The shock of the cold meant that I had no idea whether my limbs were actually moving in accordance with my innate survival instinct to swim upwards or not, but a surprising lucidity came over my mental faculties. Drowning or freezing to death in a remote Swedish archipelago would at least be a memorable way to bring the curtain down.

But then I broke through the water's surface and inhaled deep drafts of the cold, salty air. I treaded water despite the overwhelming sensation of needles piecing every inch of my body. Gulping for more air, I realized that I was facing out to sea, so I flailed around as best I could to turn and face the boat, and that's when I heard a deranged and heavily Swedish-accented exclamation of "cowabunga!" Looking up, I saw Björn in mid-air, the dark outline of his boat silhouetted behind him as the coast beyond sank further into shadow. He pulled his legs to his chest, giving me an all too revealing glimpse of his hairy undercarriage as he plunged into the water in true human canon ball form.

I received a fresh mouthful of seawater thanks to the frenzied nature of my ongoing, erratic breathing pattern when Björn struck the surface. I had already been shaking, and now I was choking, too.

"*Oi*! What little fishies we are now!" he declared as soon as he bobbed back up beside me.

My only response was to cough between the uncontrollable chatter of my teeth.

A startled expression grew across Björn's bushy, bearded face like that of an innocent child who had just witnessed someone fart loudly in public for the very first time. He declared, "You are quite the blue little fishy right now! Let's get you out of the water!"

He grabbed my arm and began to tow me towards a ladder on the side of his boat while I clumsily attempted to dog-paddle as the shivers further advanced their campaign to utterly demobilize me. It was a short distance to the hull, and once there, Björn took my hand and slammed it onto the lowest rung.

"Now, up you go!"

I grabbed the next rung up with my free hand and began the terrible ascent, shaking and hoping I didn't slip and fall back into the godforsaken sea.

Moments later, I was slouched in the corner of the plastic shell that constituted the walls of Björn's crappy little shower with hot water raining down over me. I didn't care much for the prickling sensation that assaulted my numbed nerves, but I was glad to be experiencing it. My inhibitions had dissipated somewhat, too. I no longer cared that I was completely naked in front of Björn nor that he was peering down at me quizzically from outside the shower's basin, also entirely nude.

"You enjoy the *bastu*?" he asked with a smile and a friendly gleam in his eye. "Very refreshing, right?"

"Ugh."

"Yes, well, I suppose maybe it is an acquired taste, you know."

"Uugghhhhh." I looked up at him with a disembodied feeling of relief and despair.

"But Rán and her daughters did not claim you today. I think they wanted to catch you in their nasty nets, but we did not let them! That is an exciting thing; you can tell all your friends of your deeds so that your fame spreads far and wide."

Rán is, of course, the Norse goddess of the sea. I had learned all about her family and her homicidal antics from Olafur Shitty-Pants back in Iceland. In a sense, Björn was trying to lift up my spirits, but it didn't work since I was still annoyed that he had pushed me overboard in the first place.

He retrieved a clean, dry towel from a cupboard and draped it over an empty hanger mounted to the wall beside the shower then left the room. I continued to lean slumped against the smooth, plastic veneer as the feeling in my limbs slowly returned.

I eventually emerged from the steam-filled bathroom, which opened directly into Björn's captain's cabin. I didn't remember passing through the room itself, probably because I had been suffering from some degree of hypothermic shock. The room was a total mess with piles of clothing and empty bottles strewn all over, and I quickly walked through it to the next door and into the narrow hallway. I made my way past the galley where we had eaten the vermin-of-the-sea sandwiches to the messroom where, much to my surprise, I found the dopey skald fully dressed in jeans and a thematically appropriate blue and yellow flannel shirt. He sat at a tall, cocktail-height wooden table smoking a tobacco pipe while reading a beat-up, old paperback copy of *Moby-Dick*.

He looked up when I entered. Exhaling a twirl of sweetly scented smoke, he nodded and said, "Now, the blue fishy looks nice and red! How does the juicy, little lobster feel?"

"Better," I admitted. While I had no desire to ever repeat the experience I had just endured, it would be an outright lie to deny that I actually felt incredibly refreshed at the moment.

I was still wearing only a towel wrapped around my waist, so I stepped into the head where I had left my clothes before the entire *bastu* debacle had unfolded. When I emerged, Björn was once again bent over, absorbed in his book.

"That white whale is quite the mother-fucker," he mumbled.

I ambled up to the table and took a seat opposite him. The space was surprisingly tasteful and comfortable. Finely carved wooden paneling gave the messroom an upscale, historic ambiance, which directly contrasted with the minimalist and decrepit vibe of every other space on the boat. Nautical devices adorned the walls and a vast stash of hard liquor beamed at us from the shelves behind the bar at the opposite end of the room. I'm fully in favor of not letting alcohol go to waste, but with a collection as extensive as this, I couldn't help but wonder why Björn had been so distraught about losing a single bottle earlier that day.

"Well, perhaps if you ever visit Massachusetts, you can kill him like you did Ariel," I said. I suspected that this was not the most tactful comment, but it was my way of directing the conversation back to the topic that I most wanted to discuss.

"What?!" Björn jerked his head upwards and glared at me. "That is not possible. No way the bastard fish could have lived that long. This was recorded a hundred and fifty years ago!" He held up the book, brandishing it around wildly.

"Ah, but his spirit lives on in New Bedford. Much like how Ariel's lives on in Copenhagen, I think."

To the best of my knowledge, this was actually a valid point. It of course relied on the dubious presumption that the spirits of characters from classic works of literature not only exist, but that they also inhabit and possess inanimate objects created in their honor. There are all sorts of relevant historic artifacts and replica memorabilia that Björn could vandalize if he were to ever visit New Bedford's Whaling Museum.

"No, Ariel's sprit does not live on," he countered seriously. "I scattered her soul into the underworld beneath the sea foam."

"Yes...but why?" I asked. This was his most famous deed among the world wide web trolls and so far we had only skirted around the issue. It was time to get down to brass tacks, as the blowhards of the business world are fond of saying.

"For that..." he sighed. "We need to have a drink."

He stood up abruptly, taking his book with him, and walked to the bar. He surveyed the extensive collection of booze before picking a crab-claw-shaped bottle that I didn't recognize. He deposited the book on the counter, grabbed two *snaps* glasses, and returned to the table, setting down all three items.

"This is proper viking firewater," he said with a glint in his eye. "Endorsed by the god of the sea, Njord himself."

He popped the bottle open and filled the two small glasses to the rim. We each raised a glass, looked one another in the eye, declared "skål!" as tradition demands, and gulped the contents. It burned on the way down and didn't have much taste aside from a mildly odd and generally unpleasant seafood-like flavor.

He immediately began refilling both glasses.

"I think I'm going to nurse this one," I commented. "I don't wish to overdo it."

"Suit yourself," he replied nonchalantly before downing his portion. He once again immediately refilled it.

"So...let me see if I understand everything." I attempted to steer the conversation back to the topic of his spiritual conflict with the Danish monsters. "You had the dream from Odin commanding you to slay monsters in Denmark, so you traveled to Copenhagen to slay the Carlsberg Brewery beasts. But you still had the mother and the serpent to slay?"

"That more or less sums it up, yes," he confirmed rather lackadaisically.

"And was Ariel one of these monsters?" I asked.

"Oh, definitely. She was the mother of all the monsters and had to die..."

"And so you went back to Copenhagen to slay her?"

"Most definitely. I sent her down Hel-road. I saw her head roll in Copenhagen's waves. Well, it was more of a thud, really. The waves just kind of washed over it."

"So, you just chopped it off?" I asked.

"Yes, with my axe."

This wasn't the first time that the fairytale statue had lost her head, and it probably wouldn't be the last. She's actually lost it a good number of times over the years, but while those other beheadings had typically been acts of subversive vandalism, this instance had been unique because it involved a genuine modern viking who publicly displayed a fit of berserker rage. However, thanks to the latest techniques in bronze surgical procedures, the *Lille Havfrue* was repaired and once again gazes longingly out to sea, just as she has always done for over a century.

"Why?" I asked.

"Well, you see, I felt something sinister awaken when I left Copenhagen after slaying the first monsters," Björn revealed as he once again refilled his own *snaps* glass. "But little did I know that it was her who had awoken or that she was going to start projecting her own damnation into my dreams. The misery of the insomnia she created was unspeakable...there was no suitable alternative...and believe me, I'd much rather dream of an angry boner any day than deal with the misery that she inflicted upon my soul...she doesn't bother me anymore, but I still worry that someday her spirit might break loose from Rán's prison beneath the sea and haunt me for the rest of my days...it is times like those that make me wish I had never heeded the call of the boner in the first place...and when that happens, I inevitably start thinking about how the glory days are gone forever..."

His voice trailed off and he appeared to gaze into the empty space directly ahead of himself, presumably lost deep in thought about the horrors of Hans Christian Andersen's most famous fairytale.

"And you think that Ariel meddled with your dreams as revenge for your slaughter of the elephants?" I hoped the question would regain his attention. "Or maybe she was the mother of the sasquatch that Trond Troll-Breath had killed and she had just accidentally gotten you mixed up with him?"

"Who?"

"Trond Troll-Breath Trondsen, you know. The guy who sacked Lindisfarne and started his own leprechaun slave-labored shoe business. He also claims to have killed a sasquatch."

"Never heard of that guy."

That settled that, I supposed.

Björn continued, "But you know, monster children don't have to look like their mother. Just because the mother was a mermaid doesn't mean she couldn't have carried the embryos of giant elephant twins in her nasty, nasty womb. The giantess, Angrboda got impregnated by Loki and gave birth to triplets. One was a wolf, one was a snake, and one was a disfigured female zombie. This is how reproduction works with monsters. And Ariel was the worst. The worst! She was a true nightmare. You know, in the old-fashioned sense of the tales of old. She sat on me while I slept and smothered my chest with her giant, scaly flipper-tail, nearly suffocating me, while she tormented my mind with terrible visions. Did you notice all the scars on my chest during *bastu* time? They are from the evil thrashing of her tail."

I had not noticed any signs of mermaid-induced whiplash scar tissue earlier, but this was because an incredibly bushy blond tuft of hair covered his entire chest. I still nodded affirmatively anyway.

"But...was that little mermaid such a...threat?" I continued after a quick sip of my own firewater. "I mean, what was it about her that was so terrible or so evil, as opposed to, I don't know, maybe the Snow Queen or Thumbelina?"

"Thumbelina?" he scoffed with absolute derision. "What sort of threat could a girl who is smaller than a walnut realistically be? You have to be smart about these things, you know...Thumbelina has never been a threat since she is too small. But the Snow Queen, yes, you may be onto something there. That's a worthwhile thought. But she lives far away, so far, far way. So, it's a matter of distance, too...and Ariel, well, she was living much closer and behaving menacingly in her own awful way. Who else could have been responsible for tormenting me with nightly visions of underwater strangulation by the merpeople? If my visions had been of being buried alive in snow and dying during a blizzard, then okay, you know, maybe the Snow Queen would have been involved. But no, these visions had all the markings of being Ariel's work."

"Makes sense..." I lied. "So, did you take the train down again?"

"No, no, no, we sailed. Me and my friend, Patrik Crab-Killer—he's got the best deals on crab legs, by the way; if you need to buy any, I can show you where his boat is—we took my boat down there. And we sailed right up to Ariel...after a minor collision in the harbor with that boat full of women who—"

"Oh, this would be the Honvikings, right?" I cut him off. I felt rude about it because it's something that I rarely do despite being born and indoctrinated into a culture that rewards such behavior, but I was too excited about the apparent corroboration with Ingrid Törnblom's story to care. Besides, this was the same guy who had pushed me overboard without my express consent—gurgly noises don't count—so a small breach of conversational etiquette on my part felt trite in comparison.

"Oh, well, I don't know what they called themselves," Björn replied. "But they were rowing, and I remember the captain cursed at me with a snotty Stockholm accent. Usually, I would stop and help, but the mission to slay Ariel was most imperative. I was very much going insane at that point in time due to the torment she was causing on my poor, sensitive brain tissues."

"Seems fair..."

"Oh, precisely! So, we continued to Ariel's home in the Langelinie neighborhood and Patrik dropped the anchor while I jumped over-board and waded up to her...she gazed longingly at something in the distance, and it had quite an effect on me, like maybe she inflicted her torment on me because of her own sorrow, the cycle of evil or something, violence begetting violence, that sort of thing...but that did not sway my mind from the need to destroy her!

"And there were many, many tourists surrounding the beautiful young merwoman that day—because she was very beautiful. I hated her, but she was so beautiful...but as I got closer, the tourists became aware of my presence. When they saw that I had my big axe with me, they began to move away.

"And then I stepped up to the mother of all monsters and pre-pared myself for the battle-rage...because one does not simply go searching for the battle-rage, you know, the battle-rage finds you ...and only true berserkers under the blessing of the Hanged God are capable of opening themselves up to its full potential." Björn scratched his beard as he reminisced about the most significant achievement of his life. "I was so very focused, and the god of poetry once again blessed me with his arcane skills as I began to channel the battle-rage. I looked Ariel straight in the eye and said these words:

'All our times have come
Here but now they're gone
Seasons don't fear the reaper
Nor do the wind, the sun, or the rain
We can be like they are

Come on, baby, don't fear the reaper'*

"And then I let the battle-rage take me. I lifted my axe and sent Ariel down Hel-road."

"You chopped it off with just one swing?" I was impressed.

"No, not quite...my axe, Odjuretsfördärv, is a fine weapon," he answered. His axe's name basically meant "Monster's Bane," and while the term doesn't exactly roll right off the tongue, it does encapsulate the spirit of the weapon's purpose. "But bronze is a difficult material to decapitate in one swing, so I had to hack away at Ariel's neck for a while...Odjuretsfördärv is a magnificent axe with a very noble history. It has been in my family for ages, passed down from generation to generation ever since it was presented as a gift to one of my forefathers by King Thorir Hound's Foot centuries ago. That was a high honor. But, anyway, once Ariel's head had been decapitated, I knelt down and lifted it away from the sea foam and held it up high for everyone to see. Many of the tourists captured the moment on film and camera."

And this simple fact—the fact that numerous tourists of numerous nationalities had viewed this public act of self-proclaimed Neo-Norse vengeance against Denmark's most famous and allegedly spiteful tourist site—is precisely what made Björn's beheading of Ariel his most renowned feat. At the time it occurred, YouTube exploded with homemade videos of a seemingly drunken Swedish fisherman clambering up the pile of rocks upon which the landmark rests with a massive axe before going completely apeshit berserk.

The incident remains the only facet of the Modern Viking Movement that could arguably be considered to have broken through the

---

* "Don't Fear the Reaper" by Blue Öyster Cult, 1976

barrier of online obscurity and scraped the surface of the digital mainstream. While the Carlsberg Brewery is a popular tourist site in it own right, it's not nearly the tourist magnet that the *Little Mermaid* is, and so the number of onlookers there was substantially lower. Some had captured Björn's fit of vandalistic rage there as well; the incident was lauded in online comment fields at the time because of the destruction of imagery that had been notoriously and irrevocably appropriated by Nazi Germany. Conversely, only boos could be heard among the onlookers recorded in the unofficial footage of Ariel's execution, with the notable exception of a single voice that exclaimed "more cowbell!" several times over the otherwise negative grumblings.

However, that did not prevent Ariel's beheading from making a relatively notable splash online per the Modern Viking Movement's incredibly low standards. But this handful of amateur videos never went truly viral, either. The event occurred during the end of the first decade of the 21st century, so while the world was already heavily online at the time, the average person's absolute dependency on each and every social media platform under the sun hadn't fully evolved yet. Had the videos surfaced now, their potential for going viral certainly would have been greater, but I personally still doubt that they would have ever risen above the cacophony of politically-charged diarrhea, cute animal tricks, and sexual obsessions that dominate cyberspace. At any rate, YouTube has since removed all of the footage at the behest of the Copenhagen municipal government and the avaricious re-cord labels that manage the permissions of the copyrighted material that Björn had publicly performed. While the city of Copenhagen simply feared that the clips might inspire and encourage subsequent attacks on both the fairytale statue and the historic brewery, the record labels were more concerned with the time-honored tradition of sticking it to the little guy. Björn had downloaded the videos himself while they were still available and shared them with me once I was back stateside, for which I am eternally grateful.

But for now he had gone silent and stared into his half-empty *snaps* glass. He sipped the rounds now, rather than knocking them back all at once as he'd done for his first few. I continued to nurse mine.

"So, this is aquavit, right?"

"Oh, yes, top shelf stuff." Björn looked up and smiled. "Distilled by Patrik Crab-Killer himself! He sells it along with the crabs he catches; you can get a special discount if you buy both a crab and a bottle at the same time. And the crabs he doesn't sell, he uses to infuse the tasty crustacean flavor into this wondrous beverage. It is true viking firewater!"

THE BATTLE OF BILLUND

I heaved into the bowl of Björn's metallic throne, and it wasn't because of the alcohol. Rather, the crazy bastard had insisted on opening a can of *surströmming* immediately after concluding his tale about Ariel's fate. For those fortunate enough to lack familiarity with the delicacy, *surströmming* is a vile Swedish form of fermented herring that smells like putrified death. I hadn't even tasted the filth, but the day's heat exhaustion sauna experience, an uncomfortably numb brush with hypothermia, and the seafood-infused *snaps*-imbibing had knocked my internal system so off-kilter that the *surströmming*'s scent alone sent me hurtling towards the head.

I was only dry-heaving, thankfully, and it quickly subsided. I stood up and cracked open the door, which I had slammed behind me during my rapid retreat from the stink.

"Björn?" I called out.

"Yes?" he answered.

"Is the *surströmming* still out in the open?"

"No, no, no—I ate it all and have washed the can and put it in the recycling receptacle outside. The coast is clear for weak-stomached people now."

It was an indirect insult, but I didn't really care. It was far from the worst thing that'd happened to me this day, and if having a strong stomach meant enduring a lifetime of eating rotten canned fish, then I didn't mind being encumbered with a weak one.

I emerged from the head and walked back to the table where I again took my seat opposite Björn, who was still working his way through the nasty crab liqueur. At the rate he was going, he might even finish it off before this terribly botched interview/drinking session ended.

"You ready for more now, yes?" His eyes lit up at his own suggestion as he reached for my glass.

"Ah, well—do you have anything that isn't seafood flavored?" I asked, gently patting my belly. "I'm a weak-stomached person, you know."

"Mmm...I see the wisdom in your words. Let me take a look."

He went over to the bar and came back a few moments later with another glass bottle, this one formed in the elaborate shape of a troll.

"This is Trollsnot Snaps, distilled by the trolls in Trollhättan," Björn informed me.

Trollhättan is a medium-sized inland city about forty miles northeast of Gothenburg. It was once famous for being the home of Saab Automobile—made in Trollhättan by trolls, as the saying went, which clearly served as the inspiration for Björn's last comment—before the brand was purchased by General Motors, subsequently dragged through the mud, and dissolved in the wake of the 2008 financial meltdown. A Dutch company attempted to acquire Saab but failed, and a subsequent attempted purchase by a Chinese company was blocked by General Motors. Saab was then shuttered, and a different Chinese company acquired its assets and now manufactures vehicles based on Saab's technology in China under a completely different brand name while maintaining a research and development presence in Trollhättan in a shining example of globalization at its finest.

Björn removed two stoppers, one from each nostril of the Trollsnot Snaps figurine's massive nose, and pulled the troll's hat upwards, which was attached to the troll's cranium by a thin rod and apparently served as some sort of lever. He grabbed my glass, held it directly beneath the figurine's big, honking nose, and began to pump the troll's hat. A slightly hazy liqueur with a faint orangish-brown hue squirted out of the troll's sinus cavity and into my glass. Once he had filled it to the rim with the troll's nasal drippings, he handed it back to me and stoppered the nostrils once more.

"We don't want any troll bodily fluid leaking onto the table, now do we?"

I supposed we didn't as we once again went through the obligatory skåling motions and drank.

The Trollsnot had a strange taste. It wasn't great but it was surprisingly smooth. I couldn't quite place the flavor but it seemed like some sort of strange mix of cardamon and carrot with a peaty aftertaste. I was just glad that it didn't taste like ocean scum and took another sip.

"Good Trollsnot, yes?" Björn asked.

"Oh, spectacular." Truth was, it had already started to grow on me. "What is it made out of?"

"Oh, that is a secret that only the trolls know. But they make it underground in the darkness where the sunlight cannot get to them."

"Well, I suppose that makes sense," I muttered, seeing an opportunity to redirect the conversation. "Anyway, what happened after your encounter with Ariel? Were there ever any repercussions?"

"The serpent awoke, if that can be considered a repercussion," he stated.

"That isn't exactly what I had in mind. I was thinking more about the Danish authorities. The Spear-Danes, I assume, they treasured Ariel; she was something of a national treasure to them after all...even if she was also a monster. Didn't they seek you out for interrogation or even to arrest you? Either for slaying Ariel or the Carlsberg beasts?"

"No, or if they tried to, they never found me. But I think the Spear-Danes had bigger things to worry about than a slayer of monsters who was only there to help them out. Such as the monsters themselves, like the serpent."

Sometimes in the game of life you just have to know when to throw in the towel. There's always the possibility that you may embark upon the grand journey of learning from failure, which might even eventually lead to later success. But there's also the less renowned and much more common journey of trying and failing and trying again and failing again ad infinitum till you finally decide to just call it quits. I've seen and experienced enough of such dead-end, pointless situations that I now easily identify when an honest effort is heading straight up the on-ramp towards becoming a complete waste of time. Some might call it "being negative" but I prefer to call it "being realistic" and "not delusional." It's not a popular sentiment in the U.S., of course, where the dominant culture has always swayed to the symphony of phony optimism, but here, on a forlorn fishing vessel anchored in a Swedish archipelago in the dead of winter, it served me well. So, I fully gave up on my present line of inquiry about repercussions with the Danish authorities and instead embraced a topic that I'd quite honestly rather know more about anyway: the dreaded serpent of Denmark. I wondered how its behavior and habitat compared to that of the incredibly clumsy one that had been slain by Stieg Blomkvist and Åke Nordansjö.

"Tell me more about this serpent," I said as I finished off my Trollsnot.

Björn reached for my glass with one hand as he picked the troll's nose with the other and began the hat-pumping refill procedure.

"Oh! It was a terrible monster!" he declared. "It awoke and ravaged the countryside, causing terrible, terrible destruction! And the Spear-Danes, they did nothing about it. In fact, they tried to stop us!"

"Are you referring to the informal garrisons based in the unsanctioned fortresses that they'd established to protect against invasions?" I asked. It seemed like Björn was making a clear reference to the system of defenses that Jørgen, the undead Spear-Dane, had recently told me about. Or at least he had in my own mind.

"Yes, yes, yes!" Björn responded excitedly. "We were there to help them slay the monster! But what did they do? They met us on the field of battle instead because they thought we were an invading force! They had it all so wrong! They had it so, so wrong..."

His animated behavior suddenly dissipated and he slumped down in his chair, going quiet and staring into the depths, shallow as they might be, of his shellfish liqueur.

"Well, how did you know the serpent was causing trouble?" I asked. "It sounds like it was far from your home. Did you dream about it?"

"It was, uh…intuition, I think you'd say," he sighed. "Like the angry boner dream that started it all. I just knew. I could sense it. And I could sense the direction it was coming from, too. I don't know how or why. Powers from Old One-Eye, probably. But I had a period of peace and calm." He looked up and smiled meekly. "When Patrik Crab-Killer and I first got back from Copenhagen, things were good. Ariel was dead, so she could no longer torment me and treat me like a naughty, naughty horse in the middle of the night. I slept well, very, very well. But then some inkling that something wasn't quite right began to creep up under my skin. It made me so jittery. I felt a pull, like it was a gravitational force field or something, and it got stronger every day. Like I was being guided by a higher power and that my mission for Odin was not yet over. And that maybe this was the moment he'd anticipated all along, and that the other monsters were only just practice slayings. I wasn't sure, of course, but I couldn't just sit there and do nothing, you know? You don't go against Odin's wishes. That's always been a bad idea. He might trick you into slaying yourself or impregnate your daughter or something if you upset him, and no one wants Odin for a son-in-law. So, I got all my fishing friends together and we went to Denmark."

Björn then proceeded to explain how he, Patrik Crab-Killer, and four additional fishing buddies piled into a station wagon and began their journey.

"It was our treasured Vikingmobile," he explained. "You see, at this time, I was doing very well with the fishing, and so I had just bought myself a brand new Volvo V70, which was stylish but also very safe—an excellent family vehicle, and we had a family of six fishermen going to Denmark. And I had the special paint job done to it, which cost extra but was very much worth it. It was all blue with yellow trim, and on the doors we had the insignia of the Tre Hjälmar—the Three Helmets, of course."

"Oh, definitely." I supported his assertion.

The Tre Hjälmar, or Three Helmets, was clearly a Neo-Norse subversion of the Tre Kronor, or Three Crowns. The Tre Kronor is one of Sweden's most prominent national symbols and as such it rises atop a golden spire above Stockholm's City Hall against the blue backdrop of the sky. It also adorns the blue and yellow jerseys of the Swedish men's and women's national hockey teams and can be found among other various official and unofficial documents and decorations throughout the country. The symbol itself consists of three golden crowns, two side by side with a third centered below them, and is most commonly found resting on a blue background. It dates to the Late Medieval Period of Swedish history, but its specific origins remain shrouded in the mists of time, with several discordant theories claiming to hold the answer. Whatever the exact origins of the Tre Kronor may be, the Tre Hjälmar painted on Björn's Vikingmobile was clearly inspired by it. The Tre Hjälmar is essentially the same symbol, but rather than depicting a set of royal headgear, it instead depicts three horned viking helmets.

"But you say 'was.' Did something happen to the Vikingmobile?" I asked. I was intrigued by this so-called Vikingmobile. I hoped that I could see it and perhaps even go for a ride in it. Not at this moment, of course, since Björn was totally sloshed and I wasn't trailing far behind the impressive progress he'd made in that endeavor, but perhaps someday, such as possibly tomorrow.

"Oh, no, no." He shook his head despairingly. "I had to sell the Vikingmobile. My fishing business has really plummeted in the wake of the financial crisis, you know. The new owner told me he was going to redo the paint job. Can you believe that?"

He had been staring intently at his glass, but now he looked up and met my eyes with his. I thought I saw a tear slide down one cheek, but it was difficult to determine with certainty since it immediately disappeared into the bushy bristles of his puffy beard, never to be seen again.

"Shit..." I mumbled, both in regards to the unfortunate fate of the Vikingmobile and to the increasingly intoxicated sensation provided by the Trollsnot.

Silence descended over us for a moment as we mourned the loss of the beloved automobile. Then Björn stood up and walked to a stretch of wall where a handful of framed photographs hung. He plucked one off the wall and returned to the table, setting it down in front of me.

"This was the Vikingmobile," he sighed.

I lifted the frame and took a closer look. The photograph showed the aforementioned bright blue and yellow Volvo V70 from an oblique angle, parked on a coastal road, glistening in the sun with water in the background. The Tre Hjälmar insignia was clearly visible on the driver's side door, and a grotesque, oversized horned helmet that Björn had failed to mention sat atop its roof. There were no other vehicles in the image, or any people, either. It looked professionally done, as if Volvo had contemplated an advertising campaign featuring an entire line of vehicles with Vikingmobile-inspired paint job and gaudy roof-ornament upgrade options.

"It's beautiful," I said. "*Jag beklagar sorgen.*" I am sorry for your loss, in Swedish, or more literally: I complain [regarding] the sorrow. The Trollsnot was on the verge of helping me make a major break-through in terms of verbalizing numerous unnecessary and ama-teurish Swedish language soliloquies.

"*Tacka tacka,*" he thanked me for my condolences. "She was a fine lass and voyaged us to Spear-Danish country so nicely."

He explained that he had driven the Vikingmobile to the ferry in Gothenburg, where he and his fishing cohorts boarded the boat and enjoyed the three-hour voyage across the Kattegat to Frederikshavn in Denmark, where they disembarked. While the Danish authorities allowed the Vikingmobile free passage, in compliance with the Schengen Agreement that governs all of Western Europe, it could hardly have gone unnoticed.

I wondered how the Spear-Danish legions had learned that an uninvited Swedish Vikingmobile had landed on their shore. Once upon a time, mounted Spear-Danish coast guards would have met any newly arriving force and led them to the nearest mead hall for an audience with the king or one of his jarls, but in this brave new world there was no such interception. The Spear-Danes were holed up in their system of ring-forts, mostly keeping an eye on the Germans to the south, so it seemed entirely plausible that the Swedes could have arrived unnoticed, at least at first. That's essentially what Jørgen the Draugr had told me when we were hanging out inside his hobbit hole burial mound brewery, anyway.

At any rate, the Swedes left Frederikshavn and began their search for the serpent. Björn drove, without really knowing where he was going, adjusting course on the fly because his "brain possessed a super strong homing beacon for slithery serpents."

They passed through the charming Danish countryside and, after nearly three hours of driving, entered Billund in the middle of the Jutland peninsula. Dusk had settled over the Kingdom of Denmark and was spreading its cold darkness across the land as the Vikingmobile neared the center of town when from out of the dark haze rose the legendary Legoland, reaching towards Valhalla's lofty heights in a shiny, glimmering light of plastic building block glory.

The iconic Legoland amusement park, which is presently the most popular tourist attraction in Denmark outside of Copenhagen, was completed in 1968. Billund had been selected for its location because the town is also home to the global toy company's headquarters. The Billund amusement park has since been joined by additional Legolands scattered across the world as the toy empire continued its expansion in the late 20th and early 21st centuries. There are now three additional Legoland Parks in Europe beyond the Danish location, two in North America, and six in Asia, as well as countless, smaller Legoland Discovery Centers. And while I would never actively dispute Björn about the uncanny powers of his slithery serpent-seeking sixth sense, I did wonder if he subconsciously harbored some sort of deep-seated nostalgia for the memory of a popular plaything or family vacation from his own childhood and whether that had somehow directed him to this particular location despite his own lack of full self-awareness on the matter.

"And so I parked the Vikingmobile in the big Legoland parking lot," he continued, his speech becoming slightly slurred. "It wasss completely empty and...you know, we were able to park in one of the premium spaces for free." He burped. "So, that was nice."

The Swedish fishermen then emerged from the vehicle and congregated at the main entrance, which was locked since the venue was closed for the day because the men had arrived after business hours during the nighttime. But this did not dissuade them from attempting to fulfill their mission right then and there.

"So, we climbed—we climbed over the wall...and got in that waaayyyy," Björn added with a sheepish smile.

As they neared the center of Legoland, the would-be monster-slayers caught their first glimpse of the monster looming above the surrounding miniature buildings, fearsome and spectacular in its dreadful glory. Björn led his entourage directly to a massive dragon, just as he had intuited he would. The dragon happened to be an inanimate Lego dragon rollercoaster, but that was beside the point.

"The monster was bright, bright, bright green!" He slammed his *snaps* glass down and small droplets of spittle flew from his mouth. "With huge enormous wings that spread a dark, dark shadow across the whole city! And it had fierce yellow teeth! But...it didn't move at all whatso-soever. It just...sssat there, being all very wicckked and very evil...but not daring to attack the...the innocent Spear-Danes!"

We had arrived at the part of the story where I no longer simply desired but, in fact, downright needed more Trollsnot. I reached for the bottle, pumped the troll's fortified mucus into my glass, and immediately downed half the fluid in the next instant. Apparently feeling motivated by my initiative, Björn refilled his own glass with his precious crustaceous liqueur and began slurping it up.

He clumsily set his glass down, lifted his free hand with his index finger outstretched, and declared, "We had found the serpent! And the time had come for the pre-battle ssspeech!" He hiccuped. "I had brought a flask of the true viking firewater, and so I got it...got it out, and I held it up high to Odin's glorrryyyy, and I toasted the brave guys with these words..." he paused as he caught his breath, and then slurred this stolen verse:

> 'Whiskey, gin, and brandy
> With a glass I'm pretty handy
> I'm tryin' to walk a straight line
> On sour mash and cheap wine
> So join me for a drink, boys
> We gonna make a big noise
> So don't worry 'bout tomorrow
> Take it today
> Forget about the cheque
> We'll get hell to pay
> Have a drink on me.' "*

Björn paused to catch his breath once again and looked me in the eye. Then he lifted his glass and practically shouted, "Yeah! Have a drink on mmmeeeeeee!"

I raised my glass in salute and together we both drank again.

The evening really deteriorated after that. Björn continued to relate the trials and tribulations of his exploits in Billund, but the clarity of both his thoughts and his speech dwindled with remarkable rapidity. I was hardly in a sober state of mind myself, but next to Björn I looked like an acrobat pulling off stunts on the high-wire with perfect athleticism and precision.

Apparently, after his poetic oration, Björn passed his flask around to his entourage, who all shared a swig of the firewater. Then they collectively attacked the dragon. Björn had brought his axe, Odjuretsfördärv, of course, and went to work with it, hacking apart the plastic that comprised the dragon's head attached to the front car of the rollercoaster. He inflicted the most damage of any of the men, not only because he relied on his tried and true battle-rage-induced decapitation techniques, but also because his friends were each only armed with a gaff—a type of long pole equipped with sharp hooks that fishermen use to lift and maneuver heavy fish. They really made a mess of the dragon's body and tail and were attempting to "slice the

---

* "Have a Drink on Me" by AC/DC, 1980

stupid animal's ribcage apart to find its icky heart" when the Spear-Danish army arrived.

"The Spear-Danes, they did not know we were on their side!" Björn blurted out with notable coherence. "We killed their monster for them…but they acted like, oh…we weren't their friends…"

I surmised that some regiment of Jørgen's underground Spear-Danish brotherhood had somehow learned of Björn's movements and actions, probably because he had been driving the most attention-getting vehicle in the entire nation earlier that evening. However it had happened, they had tracked him to Legoland and now confronted him. While delusion clearly formed a great motivational force for both the Swedish monster-slayers and the Spear-Danish defenders of the realm, I understood that each groups' delusions were not shared ones, and I suspected that everyone involved was also experiencing a pronounced lack of sobriety. Drunk driving is rare in Scandinavia, as it should be, but Björn and his buddies had managed to get properly sloshed since parking their car, whereas the Spear-Danes, who had just arrived at the scene, may have potentially been more sober, at least at first. In all likelihood, they had brought along some of their special Spear-Danish home-brew themselves and were busy catching up to the Swedes. In any event, I never found out, because Björn drunkenly glossed over this portion of the story and instead jumped right into the fray.

"I couldn't believe…my eyes." Björn took yet another swig from his glass. "Thousands upon thousands of individual Legos appeared, all ready for battle!" He hiccuped again. "They may be short little guys, but in numbers so big they are, uhhh…a formidable opponent. Yes, a forrmmmidable opponent! And they had heavy artillery. I saw Lego soldiers behind canons and in tanks, trucks, and boats. They were all…they were all waiting for the command to attack! But we had prepared for such an encounter. We cccalled in the cavalrrryyy."

Which is when it really started to get weird. I hadn't done much talking up to this point anyway, but now I literally just sat back and listened to Björn's inner skald charge full-speed ahead, completely unencumbered by the restraints of sobriety or polite conversational etiquette. Due to the ridiculousness of the situation that supposedly unfolded at Legoland, combined with Björn's own increased incoherence and presumed flights of fantasy that entered the story, I remain rather dubious about the reality of the actual proceedings themselves, as well as the manner in which they took place.

Anyway, as the story goes, the Swedes called in their cavalry, which consisted of Dalahästar, the famous, brightly-painted wooden horse figurines. It sounded like these toys had been kept in the fishermen's' pockets and that they simply pulled them out when the Spear-Danish Lego army arrived. The Swedes placed these wooden horses squarely on the ground facing the Lego horde.

For several long moments, the two toy armies stood silently staring into the depths of one another's souls, while the Swedes and Spear-Danes reviewed their respective battle strategies. The scene, according to Björn, was terrifying. The Legos clenched their weapons tightly, sweat forming on their plastic brows, while the Dalahästar neighed impatiently, appearing to tug against reins that were not there.

Being a self-proclaimed disciple of the Father of War, Björn took this opportunity to pledge the battle to Odin. He grabbed Patrik Crab-Killer's hooked fishing gaff, and with a shout of "may Odin take you all!" tossed it in an arc through the air over the Spear-Danish and Lego forces, where it thudded ineffectively onto the asphalt pavement behind them.

And then the two forces charged. The Lego battalions unleashed earth-shattering war cries in their frenzied rush to cross the no-man's-land first and draw Dalahästian blood. From the opposite direction, the Dalahästar, discontent to idly await the coming of the slaughter-storm, galloped headlong into the approaching plastic swarm, unfaltering in their intent to trample the enemy at full speed. The forces met in an eruption of cheap plastic clashing against soft wood.

"The...sssuperiority of our horses crushed the pitiful front lines of the Lego bastards," Björn said, then drifted away, lost in thought.

I waved at him to bring his attention back to the story at hand.

"Huh? Oh, yeah." He fidgeted in his seat but picked the story up right where he had left off before his train of thought had taken a short, little detour to nowhere. "Their bodies piled high in the trenches...it was like Ragnarök...*eller något...fy fan...*"

It remains completely unclear to me whether the men on both sides were basically kneeling on the ground, playing with these toys in a make-believe sort of battle, or whether Björn was indeed intentionally conveying the notion that some mysterious life-force had come over both toy armies, possessed them, and now pitted them against one another in a strange gambit to increase the death-count and collect as many dead souls as possible, which was, actually, exactly the sort of thing that Odin would try to orchestrate.

Then, in the midst of the slaughter, a miniature bear unexpectedly materialized. Small, yet towering in comparison to the members of both armies, the bear, in a complete fit of pure battle-rage, ripped into the Lego forces, detracting even from the extreme carnage inflicted by the Dalahästar.

"I...could ssscarcely believe what I was seeing," slurred Björn. "I had been admiring our cavalry destroy the Spear-Danish forces." He hiccuped once again. "And then this small bear suddenly appears in the middle of the battle...battlefield! I couldn't believe it was real... it was too sssmmalll...*det var som fan! Men*...uuughhh...there it was, rampaging and slaughtering and killing and maiming. I was mesmerized...and then Crab-Killer tapped me on the shoulder. He asked me if I was all right. I turned to look at him and when I turned back to the battle, the b-b-bbbear *hade försvunnit*...it had just vvvaan-ished..."

But the battle raged on. The heavy Lego artillery, finally within firing range, pounded the ranks of the Swedish cavalry, mortally wounding those caught under its deadly rain. Far-flung shrapnel picked its victims indiscriminately, ruthlessly butchering both Dalahäst and Lego alike, and everywhere the dust of the battlefield stirred, impairing the vision of all. Blinded, Lego warriors wandered unwittingly beneath the ever-downward bucking hooves of maddened Dalahästar. Screams of agony filled the night air as more and more Legos fell, never to rise again.

Then came the Bionicles.

From out of the depths of the Lego ranks they emerged. Menacing, stealthy, heavily armored, and comparatively large in size, the Bionicles were everything that the ordinary Legos were not. While still requiring construction in proper Lego fashion, the Bionicles eschewed the standard rectangular building block forms for more robotic and anthropomorphic constituent units. The Bionicles had been targeted to a slightly older audience than the traditional Lego toy kits, and once assembled, essentially looked like sleeker versions of Transformer toys. While discontinued by the Lego Group in 2016, they had been a popular and highly advertised franchise within the Lego universe at the time of the Battle of Billund.

The Bionicles charged past their shorter comrades and plunged into the thick of battle. Dalahästar fell immediately, the technologically advanced weaponry of the Bionicles easily slicing through their cheaply painted hides, delivering the quickest of deaths. The Bionicles waded deeper and deeper into the slaughter, killing every Dalahäst that stood in their way.

"The Bionicles were fucking insane!" Björn exclaimed, sounding temporarily more sober in light of this apparently exciting detail. "Our cavalry was severely out-out-outnumbered. But!...We were winning the battle up till then even with the Lego artillery pounding our ranks...when they brought out the Bionicles...*det var som fan*... eevvvverything...changed."

The remaining Dalahästar quickly mobilized and turned to face this new threat. The Bionicles, previously bent over in the act of merciless slaughter, now straightened, and towering above the fresh Dalahästian corpses, beckoned their opponents closer. The Dalahästar charged.

The Bionicles met them with grim pleasure, swiftly decapitating the foremost mid-gallop in a bloody spectacle that stirred up clouds of doubt in the minds of those that followed. One line of Dalahästar faltered and broke. Then another. And another. And so it went until even the rear waves of Dalahästar had also halted and reversed direction, driven backwards by a stampede of their own retreating forces.

At this point in the story, Björn spilt firewater all over the table in an inadequate attempt to once again refill his glass.

"*Vad fan!* What did Crab-Killer make this...bot-bot-bottle out of-...holes?" He hiccuped. "*För helvetets skull...jävla hål...*"

I had been nursing my Trollsnot, really trying to stretch out the present pour, but as I sat there watching Björn mutter to himself about the dastardly magic tricks that evil giants like to play on accomplished drinkers, I decided to take another tiny sip. The motion caught his attention, and he looked up from his stupor with a mildly bewildered expression on his face.

"Uh, the cavalry..." he began again. "It was...a...a disgrace..." Some more unintelligible muttering transpired, and then: "...fight and die with honor, the dumb beasts fled. Deserve...glue factory! Cowwwards...Spear-Danes...cavalry stampe-pe-pe-peding...stampeding in retreat...*trampade ihjäl...vi var...vi...*were...we were...routed."

Essentially, the Dalahästar swarmed Björn and his men in their reckless retreat. Utterly panicked, many of the toy horses slipped and fell upon the bloodied amusement park ground. Some supposedly suffocated in the struggle to regain proper footing, their faces inescapably buried in the thick gore that now covered everything. Those that survived only did so long enough to face execution at the plastic hands of the pursuant Bionicles.

Björn and his friends meanwhile reached the main entrance and made a mad dash for the Vikingmobile. Once they were all seated and buckled up, Björn floored the gas pedal and tore out of the parking lot, speeding back to Frederikshavn for the return ferry as the screams of the dying Dalahästar slowly faded in the pale summer night sky.

FEAR AND LOATHING IN WESTERN SWEDEN

Björn lurched out of his seat and collapsed on the cold metal floor, the empty glass of viking firewater clanging hollowly beside him.

This development meant that our discussion was now concluded. It also presented me with a new and awkward dilemma: attempt to awaken a drunken and potentially ill-tempered warrior-poet or simply leave matters to fate and just walk away? Odds were he wouldn't choke to death on his own vomit while sleeping it off, so I flipped off the light and started to make my way out towards the deck.

But it just didn't feel right. He had welcomed me into his buoyant abode, generously kept my shot glass full of firewater throughout the evening, and thoroughly indulged my curiosity about the pivotal role that he had played during the Modern Viking Movement. He had, of course, also bullied me into stripping down naked and pushed me overboard earlier in the day, but I also believed that everything he did had been well-intentioned. And now I was about to show my appreciation by abandoning him on the cold, hard floor of his boat's messroom.

I turned and looked at the crumpled heap of intoxicated humanity lying motionless in the dark. After a moment's further hesitation, I walked back down and knelt beside the fallen skald.

His breathing was a steady gurgling noise, a snore almost but not quite, and the pale moonlight spilling in through the portholes cast a silvery sheen upon his gruff face. He looked eerily at peace, his stony heart clearly warmed by the faithful companionship being provided by the always-dependable friend circulating through his veins. He had never re-adjusted well to the mundanity of regular, everyday life in the post-modern viking world.

During one interlude from our earlier conversation, he had confided to me that he had started his own recreational fishing company after his inglorious retreat from Legoland. Through it he has managed to make a relatively resplendent living by harvesting herring and charging exorbitant fees to adventurous, well-to-do tourists who wish to temporarily forget the inhumanity of office life by pretending to untangle nets and gut fish for a living instead. Which is all good and well, but it's got to be difficult to return to the daily grind after having singlehandedly vanquished the Spear-Danes' monstrous afflictions at the instigation of Odin.

"I've always hated being subjected to the senseless whims of those in positions to judge me and belittle my previous accomplishments," he'd said. "And I've always harbored an extra sensitivity about my swimming abilities, but that is another story entirely, you know...."

But that was then and this was now, and I was presently reaching my battle-untested hand out to slap his furry face. I hoped he wouldn't bite it off; I had no desire to go through the rest of my life as an uncourageous, mortal mirror image of Tyr, the god who had lost a hand when he stuck it in the mouth of a monstrous wolf who then bit it off during a round of typical Norse god shenanigans. I much preferred to earn the inebriated gratitude of a morose skald. I held my breath.

"Hhhkkkththwwww!" he gurgled vehemently and I lost my balance, flinching like a maniac and toppling over backwards, slap pathetically undelivered.

I struggled back to an upright position and froze. I was really having doubts about what to do now. That gurgle had obliterated my confidence. Completely obliterated it. The last thing I wanted was a roused and angry Neo-Norseman on my hands. And even if I did slap him, he might not wake up. Maybe I should just leave him as he was and go.

Or maybe he would appreciate being covered with a blanket? Or would that just get the blanket dirty and then cause him undue irritation upon waking? Why the hell was I even worrying about this?

I got to my feet and went outside.

The illumination wasn't much better on deck. The village of Klädesholmen's street lights shimmered only dimly, with the moon's faint glow casting a desolate and uninviting aura across the buildings along the harbor's edge while the island of Tjörn spread itself out in complete darkness behind them. The whole nightscape felt foreboding, and I couldn't help but recall the troubling conversation that I had overheard during the bus ride north from Gothenburg earlier that same day.

A local father and son had been discussing Tjörn's prevailing ailments, and according to them, the island is not only full of gangsters, spies, and grizzly bears, but also pestilence, smoke, and—most shockingly of all—even Volvos. As I have always done my utmost to avoid talking to strangers unless absolutely necessary, I didn't engage them to find out more, but as soon as I heard the word "gangsters," I found myself conjuring up unsolicited visions of segregated, socioeconomically disastrous slums such as the notorious Rosengård or even the bad parts of Gothenburg's very own (and for English-speakers, ironically-named) borough of Angered. I had spent the rest of the ride silently hoping that I wasn't heading straight into a world of abject poverty, rampant unemployment, violent crime, and religious hatred.

Thus it was with great pleasure that when we finally rolled over the bridge to Tjörn I saw that it didn't possess the appearance of a slum at all—rather than a decaying concrete jungle comprised of tenement housing and burnt-out car carcasses, it's a green oasis surrounded by rocky outcroppings and the deep blue of the sea. But looks can be deceiving. Angered is reputed to contain some scenic nature reserves of its own within its boundaries, so maybe these views of Tjörn were likewise misleading. Or were my fears just the unsubstantiated byproduct of a senseless world overrun with hysterical frenzy? I wasn't sure, but I wasn't about to run the risk of getting assaulted by a Neo-Nazi dickhead, assassinated by a covert operative, or mauled by either a wild bear or a militant Islamist on my way back to the bus stop. The streets were dark and the seed of fearful doubt had dug itself way too deep. The only person I knew who could set the record straight for me was passed out drunk down below.

Shit.

I went back below decks.

The warrior-poet hadn't budged and his snoring continued unabated, intermingled with the occasional mumble. I knelt beside him once again in the shadowy darkness and resolved myself once and for all to slap him. I exhaled slowly, calling on Thor for the courage to help see me through this predicament.

It had no effect, so I slapped him again, a little harder. Again, no effect. I tried a few more times, all to no avail. I sat there shaking my head.

But then he mumbled something: "...*jävla lilla sjöjungfrun...*"

I leaned in closer to see if he had any other pearls of wisdom to impart.

"...*den där jävla lilla sjöjungfrun...betalade med livet...jagar efter mig ännu...*"

His words suggested that he was suffering from an antagonistic dream about the *Little Mermaid*. His slurred voice quivered with fear even though she posed no current threat to him, which he knew better than anyone else, since his axe had ended her life and shattered her soul. I didn't understand how her present form could be anything other than the hollow shell of a sorrowful existence. And to be totally honest, I hadn't really understood why it had been a threat in the first place.

But that didn't matter, because now I just knelt there, still staring at him in the dark because in all my own goddamned incompetence, I didn't know what the hell to do.

He wasn't waking up in response to my meager slapping efforts, but his cabin wasn't far away. Perhaps I should just drag him to his bed? Why not. I was too much of a coward to leave the boat anyway. I could try to figure out what to do with myself once I was done dealing with the grossly inebriated Neo-Norseman.

I bent down, reached under his arms, and started to drag him backwards across the room. He was a heavy guy and it almost made me feel mighty—like I was tugging a giant's boulder across a majestic fjord to a colossal mountain rising vertically straight up out of the watery depths below, or something. The illumination provided by the moonlight spilling in through the portholes only contributed to the epic atmosphere of what was, in all honesty, a ridiculous mission.

And his beard kept brushing up against my hand, which was off-putting. I admired his beard, but I didn't really want it to be touching my skin. There were traces of crustacean-infused firewater and spittle in it, and only Odin's ravens knew what else.

We had made it about halfway there when he stirred slightly and muttered something mostly unintelligible about the dead mermaid again: "...*död, död...sjöjungfruns blod har rinnat överallt...nu jagar hon i mörkret...måste bavara mig själv...*"

I just about lost my grip but continued onwards. We were almost there now. I could nearly reach out and touch the bunk and its bedding of salvation. I pressed onward, Björn dragging along the floor behind me like a useless sack of disassembled Ikea furniture.

And then we were there. Just like that, the voyage had ended and the time to scale the summit had arrived.

I propped him up against the base of the bunk, but he slid downwards against it when I let go to reposition my hold on him. I stepped over his body and turned to face him and noticed a mirror mounted on the wall above, casting our dark, absurd reflection right back at us.

I grabbed him under the arms again and heaved upwards. His head slouched forwards as I continued to push and pull his torso up the bunk's siding. It flopped backwards again once his shoulders breached the edge of the mattress and his mouth leaked out something that sounded a little more agitated than his previous outbursts: "...*var är hon?...hon måste dö...helvete tar henne för alltid!*"

I half squatted and braced my feet to nudge the rest of his torso onto the bed. With that accomplished, it was simply a matter of kneeling on the bed myself and dragging his lower half up to join his upper half. I caught another glimpse of our shadowy reflection in the mirror and nearly laughed. I was kneeling over his contorted body like a sadistic serial killer, the blankets were rumpled into total disarray, and his feet and ankles were still dangling over the edge.

I started to crawl backwards when he opened his bloodshot eyes, peered disconcertedly in the direction of a porthole beside my head, then blinked, focused, and looked straight at me. Several tears slid down his cheek to nestle among his thick, blond bristles.

My heart froze, and so did my tongue, as we stared at one another for a brief moment in the dark silence.

Then, still holding my gaze, he spoke one of his infamous skaldic verses:

> "The light in the window is a crack in the sky.
> A stairway to darkness in the blink of an eye,
> A levee of tears to learn she'll never be coming back,
> The man in the dark will bring another attack.
>
> Your mamma told you that you're not supposed to talk to
>   strangers.
> Look in the mirror, tell me—do you think your life's in danger
>   here...???
>
> No more tears."*

And then he passed out again. I hesitated, curious to see if he would say anything else worthy of the great skalds of yore, but he didn't, so I clambered back down off the bunk. Björn lay in it, disheveled and filthy from his disgraced retreat across the floor, but I was pleased with myself.

I still didn't know what I was going to do with myself, but I was pleased.

---

* "No More Tears" by Ozzy Osbourne, 1991

OUTRO

I sat on the Flygbuss as it made its way through Gothenburg's tightly-packed city center towards the Riksväg 40 motorway that led to Landvetter Airport, ten miles to the east. As with most transatlantic flights departing from Europe, mine was an early one. Dawn had not yet arrived, and the city lights were gradually overtaken by shadowy forests and the slurry heaves of snow and dirt and grime that line highways all throughout the northern hemisphere at this time of year.

I had left Björn Svensson tucked away in his bed two nights before, found a pen and paper in his galley to write a short thank you note, leaving my phone number and email address, and then started the long walk back towards the bridge that crossed over to Tjörn. It felt like a demented twist on the classic collegiate walk of shame. Only I wasn't leaving after some banal tryst as the sun rose, but instead after some bizarre, unanticipated drinking session with a surly fisherman in the dead of night at the edge of nowhere.

By then it had been too late to have any hope of catching another bus back to the city, but I had seen advertisements for a little hotel beside the bridge. To my luck, the reception at Salt Och Sill was still open at that ungodly hour, and the hotel had many vacancies since winter is not the busy season for touristy Swedish fishing villages.

I had finally returned to Gothenburg the previous day after some deliberation regarding whether I should go check on Björn or not. Eventually, I had decided to do so. After knocking on his door and hearing no answer, I had quietly crept inside and found him snoring in his bed. He hadn't pulled a Jon Bonham, thankfully. The loss of Björn wouldn't have resulted in the demise of an epic band like Led Zeppelin, but choking on his own vomit and dying in his sleep after drinking too much would have still qualified as a serious disappointment. I let him be and made my way back to Gothenburg.

The day had been spent strolling around the center of town, slurping sugary coffee beverages while admiring the canals and historic architecture. Mostly, it was a calm day of quiet contemplation about my stint in the Northlands. I was pleased that I had successfully tracked some modern vikings down and managed to convince them to tell me their stories, but I also knew that there were many more stories relating to the Modern Viking Movement that remained untold. The modern vikings who had sacked the abandoned Dutch market town of Dorestad were among the most famous in the unhallowed halls of cyberspace, yet they remained mysterious and unidentified. The same applied to the modern vikings who had reestablished an active trading center at Birka in Sweden as well as those who had attempted to re-colonize the Orkney Islands. While I felt that I had accomplished a decent job at uncovering many hidden truths about the Modern Viking Movement, I also knew that many more remained unknown.

But my current expedition was, for all intents and purposes, now completed. That reality hit home all the more heavily as the bus approached the airport, its classic 1970s-era concrete and glass structure fulfilling its utilitarian promise of bland functionality. A short while later I sat near the gate, sipping an iced latte and munching on a final cardamon bun as I waited to board the plane. Truth be told, I didn't really want to go back to Boston. Had it been feasible, I would have loved to stay in Scandinavia longer and attempt to dig up more dirt on the world's most obscure cultural phenomenon, but unemployed tourists have very real limitations, and so it was time for me to go home. I didn't know exactly what real-world horrors awaited me in the coming months, but I knew that I would at least work on compiling my recordings and notes of these modern vikings into some comprehensible format. That would help give my life some meaning.

That task is now completed, and it took a much longer time than I had initially anticipated, but I can honestly say that the sense of purpose it provided was real and substantial. It did not last forever, of course, because nothing ever does, and the struggle to contend with the banality of life continues more or less as it always has.

But even at the point in time when I boarded the plane at Landvetter, I knew that this was how it would be. In the end, we're all just who we are—some would call it fate—and the world chugs along according to its own machinations. We remain mere cogs in its various, multifaceted wheels, generally unable to change either ourselves or the lot that has been granted to us on this mortal plane of existence. But we can try, and if there's something that is worth trying for, then that isn't all bad, even if it ends in futility more often than not.

So, I took my seat on the plane, buckled up, and while the pilot maneuvered us to the runway, I thought about what the future might hold. And as we accelerated and took off, the words of the great skald David Byrne of Talking Heads fame reverberated through my mind, shedding their undeniably profound light on the trajectory of both personal and general human progress in modern society:

> "And you may find yourself living in a shotgun shack
> And you may find yourself in another part of the world
> And you may find yourself behind the wheel of a large automobile
> And you may find yourself in a beautiful house with a beautiful wife
> And you may ask yourself, well, how did I get here?
>
> Letting the days go by, let the water hold me down
> Letting the days go by, water flowing underground
> Into the blue again after the money's gone
> Once in a lifetime, water flowing underground
>
> Same as it ever was
> Same as it ever was
> Same as it ever was
> Same as it ever was
> Same as it ever was
> Same as it ever was..."*

---

* "Once in a Lifetime" by Talking Heads, 1980

Acknowledgements

Oh, where to begin? I began this blasted book in the first decade of the 2000s and it took me over ten years to complete via a highly dysfunctional, stop-and-start process that involved many derailments and detractions in that otherwise enthralling game we like to call "life."

First and foremost, thanks to my parents, sister, and the rest of the family. I didn't talk much about this project during its awfully slow gestation period but appreciate the ever-present support and encouragement for my various endeavors.

Special shout-outs to Doomsday Mike and Barbarian Lord Matt for being solid friends and always being willing to let me bounce stupid ideas off both of you.

Glasses raised to Corwin Ericson for kindly giving a very late version of my manuscript a meaty gander and to Sydney Taylor for giving it the good old-fashioned, bleeding-red-ink treatment.

Thanks also to the handful of online friends and acquaintances I've managed to make over the years via the cyberspace cesspool. Of those, there are too many to list, but I've been pleasantly surprised to make such connections and I believe you all know who you are. The same goes for all the other folks who've offered encouragement along the way in real life. Much appreciated.

Horns up to the various editors who've chosen not to reject my writing over the years, whether paid or unpaid, online or in print, factual/informative or totally made-up and nonsensical.

And, of course, I'd like to raise a solid skål to the modern vikings themselves who so willingly let me interfere with their daily lives and annoy them with my pestering interrogations about their questionable life decisions:

To the young delinquents in Geithus: thanks for the hot chocolate and I hope you all stay "inside the law" in the coming years.

Thanks to Trond Trondsen and Henrik Askildsen for showing me a grand but socially exhausting and embarrassing time in the Trøndelag. The mead hall was lovely, the hot tub wonderful, and the dogs great companions. My pair of Trondsko shoes are super comfy and snug and I cherish them.

Thanks also to Stieg Blomkvist for showing me a memorable time at Sweden's best Boston-themed restaurant chain in Peter Forsberg's hometown. I hope that your totalitarian architectural overlords aren't robbing you of the will to live and that Åke's hanging in there all right.

To the members of Varjagikaarti: thanks for the authentically depressing Finnish drinking experience. Please don't die.

Tusen tack till Helena Bringholm. Du är en underbar kvinna och jag hoppas att allt fortsätter att gå bra för dig! Ring mig, kanske?

To Ingrid Törnblom: I apologize for my dimwitted, zombie-like behavior and humbly thank you for your time.

Jørgen, my homeboy: 'sup, bro? Keep on brewin', if you're real.

And to Björn Svensson: you pushed me overboard into the freezing water, and I still have mixed feelings about that. But thank you indeed for telling me your story, sharing your vermin-of-the-sea sandwiches with me, and letting me taste the sweet, sweet mucus of Trollsnot Snaps.

I do not wish to extend any special thanks to Olafur Shitty-Pants since he is a mean old prick, or to Agneta of Geithus since she cursed me.

And finally, I'd like to thank humanity in general for its undaunting deprevations and relentless decline of integrity and common sense. Without us all, as an abominable whole, I might never have found the motivation to write this book in the first place.

ROWDY GEIRSSON is the translator of *The Impudent Edda* and editor of *Norse Mythology for Bostonians*. His writing has also appeared in *Scandinavian Review*, the Sons of Norway's *Viking Magazine*, *Medieval World: Culture and Conflict*, *Metal Sucks*, *Reactor Magazine*, *McSweeney's Internet Tendency*, and a slew of other humor sites. Visit him online at www.scandinavianaggression.com and follow him on Twitter @RGeirsson and Instagram @rowdygeirsson, or don't.

SCANDINAVIAN AGGRESSION

- Sagas of Pathetic and Banal Exploration
- Visual Arts of Norse Inspiration
- Beavis and Butt-Head Starring Odin and Thor (at metalsucks.net)
- Heroes of Norse Proliferation
- Norse History for Bostonians (at mcsweeneys.net)
- Viking Brews and Booze
- T-Shirts Decreed by the Norns (at spreadshirt.com; shown at right)
- Guide to visiting New England's Vinland monuments
- Curated list of recommended Norse-themed novels (at bookshop.org)
- Epic Defeatism